CW01019791

# Struck Off

# Struck Off

## Tom Farrell

The Pentland Press Limited
Edinburgh • Cambridge • Durham • USA

© Tom Farrell 1998

First published in 1998 by
The Pentland Press Ltd.
1 Hutton Close
South Church
Bishop Auckland
Durham

British Library Cataloguing in Publication Data.
A Catalogue record for this book is available
from the British Library.

ISBN 1 85821 601 X

Typeset by CBS, Felixstowe, Suffolk
Printed and bound in Great Britain by Bookcraft (Bath) Ltd.

To Anne

# FOREWORD

By Norman Davies, OBE, JP,
Registrar, The General Dental Council, 1981-96

*Struck Off* is an outstanding first novel by Tom Farrell.

In a thrilling story which, once begun, is difficult to put down, he covers, at breakneck-speed, a wide ranging plot which involves many of the medico-legal dilemmas which lie just below the surface in the society of the late nineteen-nineties.

His treatment of the disturbing potential for the transplantation of bought human organs stretches credibility to the limit yet at the same time is close to reality. His use of hypnosis brings an uncomfortably disturbing additional dimension to an already spine-chilling thriller.

Farrell draws heavily on his own experience over many years as a member of the General Dental Council's Professional Conduct Committee – a mirror image of that of the General Medical council – to create a nerve-jangling record of the medico-disciplinary process, which will fascinate any doctor, dentist or lay person.

*Struck Off* is action packed and a thoroughly compelling novel on which its author is to be commended.

# ACKNOWLEDGEMENTS

I would like to thank Mr Michael Brudenell and Dr Christopher Dulake for kindly reading the manuscript, and Mr Norman Davies for giving so much of his valuable time to read the manuscript and write the Foreword.

# HUMAN ORGAN TRANSPLANTS ACT, 1989

'A person is guilty of an offence if he makes or receives any payment for the supply of, or for an offer to supply, an organ which has been or is to be removed from a dead or living person and is intended to be transplanted into another person . . .'

## Chapter One

It was in the early 1980s that Sir Jeremy Fawcett, the President of the Royal College of Surgeons, sat in a small room adjoining the Council Chamber of the General Medical Council, dreading what the day had in store for him. He had been at the GMC for almost three weeks – the longest three weeks of his life – answering charges of unethical behaviour, and if the charges were proved, he would almost certainly be found guilty of serious professional misconduct and be 'struck off' the Doctors' Register. His face was ashen and wet with perspiration as his liver tried to cope with the near lethal dose of whisky he had consumed the night before. The early morning paracetamol was wearing off and his head throbbed violently. Any moment now the door of the Council Chamber would open and he would be called back to face the verdict of his peers on the Professional Conduct Committee. Two of the most powerful men in medicine would face each other across the floor of the Chamber. One would decide the future of the other. 'And I'm the other,' he thought miserably. He sat motionless and expressionless, imprisoned by his depression. The adviser from the professional insurance society who had organised his defence sat quietly with him, as he had done with dozens of doctors when they waited for the GMC to decide their fate. Some of them had been in tears. Others, like Sir Jeremy, just sat in bitter stony silence. Tears from a grown professional man always embarrassed him, but they were easier to deal with than this black emptiness. At least there was some communication. His thoughts were abruptly interrupted when Fawcett suddenly snapped out of the strait jacket of his depression.

'Christ, what a mess!' he said, 'What a bloody mess!'

'It could happen to anyone, Sir Jeremy,' his companion said. 'Even if you get "struck off", it's not the end. You'd probably get back on again in a year or two.'

'You don't bloody well understand,' retorted Fawcett, looking at him with ill-disguised contempt. 'How could you? Surgery is my life. I come alive in the operating theatre; the adrenaline races. I can't live without it.'

Great surgeons were like great musicians or great artists, he reflected. It wasn't just a question of technique – anyone could learn that. Their performances went far beyond mere technical skills and they had such supreme confidence that they appeared arrogant.

'If I'm struck off,' he said fiercely, 'I'm finished. It'll all be over. I'll never pick up a scalpel again.'

'You'll feel better in the morning,' the adviser rejoined rather foolishly, as he poured more black coffee into Fawcett's cup.

'They might just as well take me to Lincoln's Inn Fields,' he said. 'Stand me up in front of John Hunter's statue opposite the Royal College of Surgeons, and shoot me. I'd be as finished as that.'

He buried his head in his hands. 'I should have ended it all last night,' he said morosely, 'like Stephen Ward, the osteopath in the Christine Keeler case, but I didn't have the guts. He did; he took the barbiturates, and never gave the judge the opportunity of sentencing him.'

Now that his rigid control had gone, he couldn't stop talking. The words tumbled out.

'I could have finished it. It would have been so easy. Some cyanide capsules in the whisky, and that would have been that. Who wants a defrocked surgeon, no matter how famous?' The adviser sat in embarrassed silence, becoming increasingly alarmed at the talk of suicide.

'My reputation will count for nothing,' he went on. 'Colleagues will shun me. I'll have to give up teaching. What's left?' He shrugged. 'It'll all be over.' He thought of the lecture he was due to give in six weeks' time at a major international conference. 'They won't want me now,' he said to himself, 'except perhaps out of curiosity.' He knew that if he were 'struck off', that would be the end of the lecture circuit. The invitations would dry up overnight. 'If only I'd come from a long line of officers in a famous regiment, I'd have known what to do – shoot myself. But I don't; I come from a long line of doctors.'

Jeremy Fawcett was tall with fair hair, angular features, pale complexion and narrow lips, with more than a touch of cruelty about them. He looked aristocratic. His life had been mapped out since childhood. Both his parents were doctors and on his father's side there had been a Fawcett doctor in every generation right back to the early eighteenth century in the small Surrey town where his father still practised. There was no pressure on Fawcett, but there was never any doubt that he too would go into medicine. It was not only the family environment, it was in his genes. He followed his father to a Surrey public school with a tradition of sending boys into medicine, and then up to Gonville and Caius College, Cambridge.

At Cambridge he boxed, got a blue and a broken nose, played a lot of cricket, and met Melanie Clarkson, who was reading medicine at Newnham College, Caius being an all-male college at the time. She was a beautiful woman and found she could plan her life more easily with a steady male. It wasn't such a battle to keep the amorous undergraduates, and sometimes the amorous dons, at bay. She was tempted at times but remained loyal to Jeremy. They stayed at each other's homes during vacations, and both sets of parents were happy with the arrangements and expected them to marry when they qualified.

They were both bright, but medicine wasn't an easy ride and they had to work hard to keep up with their basic medical studies. Sometimes they were envious of the arts undergraduates, who seemed to have much less work to do. 'It was our choice,' Melanie said, when they had to refuse an invitation from their arts friends to join them at some exciting event, or when they did not see them in College for weeks at a time and knew they were 'living it up' somewhere else. 'We've just got to put the work in.' But Melanie, in particular, was determined to live life to the full. He remembered one particular evening, 'Let's do something wild tonight,' she had suggested.

'Such as?'

'Gatecrash Trinity May Ball?'

'Oh God,' Jeremy responded. He would have much preferred a romantic dinner on their own.

'Come on. It'll be great fun.' She put her arms round his neck and kissed him. 'Am I leading you astray?' she asked, looking up at him.

'I wish you would,' he said gently, pulling her down on to the bed. She didn't resist when he caressed her breasts. They remained together for some time until she kissed him and sat up. 'You almost undressed me,' she said, re-buttoning her blouse. She kissed him tenderly before filling two large glasses with dry sherry.

They sat quietly and then after a second sherry she stood up. 'Wow!' she said, 'that's getting to my head. And we haven't even started the evening yet.' She kissed him. 'See you back in about half an hour,' she said, showing him out.

He went back to his room to change and when he returned she was dressed in a long, white, off-the-shoulder dress with a hand-painted flower design; and she was wearing a turquoise and seed-pearl-and-gold bracelet on her wrist and antique pearl-and-amethyst pearl-drop ear-rings.

'How do I look?' she asked, standing back.' Do you like mother's jewellery?'

He took her in his arms. 'You look wonderful,' he said kissing her. She gently pulled away saying, 'Mind my lipstick.' Then she saw him staring at the spray of orchids pinned to her dress. 'An undergrad from Clare sent them. I've never even met him,' she said, and when she saw his half-raised eyebrows she remarked: 'It would be a shame not to wear them.' He became quiet and his face clouded over. She unpinned them and put them in a tiny vase. 'Who needs orchids?' she said, determined not to let anything spoil the evening. 'Come on, you bring the champagne. I'll bring the glasses.' With that they strolled down to the river. She held his hand as they walked. 'Jeremy,' she said. 'You don't need to be jealous. You'll just screw yourself up.' They continued in silence until they reached the river bank.

'That'll do,' Melanie said excitedly, pointing to an empty punt. 'We'll borrow that.' She waited for Jeremy to clamber aboard. 'Light the lantern,' she said. They drifted up river and soon approached the security guards provided by the Trinity rugby team. 'Don't look so worried,' she laughed. 'You're in your penguin suit. You can swim. They'll only throw us in the river.' She waved to the guards, gave them a broad smile and raised her glass of champagne as they floated past.

They landed on the grassy banks and quickly mingled with the happy crowds extending up to the old courtyard around which Harold Abraham had raced before the clock had finished striking twelve.

Melanie loved parties. Most of the time she was a serious student but a metamorphosis took place when she put on her party frock. She didn't even need a drink to lift her. She radiated happiness and excitement.

'You're a Jekyll and Hyde,' exclaimed Jeremy jokingly.

'Don't call me a skitzo,' she laughed.

At Trinity Jeremy tried to steer her away from the bowler-hatted porters, but she teased him by walking up to them and giving them a lovely smile.

'I can do without the hassle,' he said. She kissed him lightly. 'I'll protect you. Don't worry, just drink up.' So he drank up and relaxed.

It was late when they walked back along the narrow lane alongside Caius. Jeremy pulled her as close as possible when they stopped by the 'Gate of Honour' and kissed her passionately.

'You'll break my bones if you squeeze me so hard.'

'I just want to be as close as possible,' he said, kissing her again, 'you looked magnificent tonight.'

They walked on slowly in silence.

'What's coming up in the lift then?' she said quietly.

'Let's get married,' he said, kissing her gently. 'I can't wait until we're qualified; I'll go insane.'

Her impish sense of humour almost made her say: 'You'll probably go insane if you do.' But she didn't.

4

'I love you Jeremy,' she said, 'but I wasn't thinking of marriage before we'd qualified. We're only twenty-one years old; there's plenty of time.'

Most students had finished their undergraduate life when they left Cambridge but Melanie Clarkson and Jeremy Fawcett would be medical students for another three years or so in London before they qualified as doctors.

'You can't love me,' he said miserably.

'I do,' Melanie said, kissing him, and when he didn't reply, she said: 'I suppose I'm being selfish, but I want to be a doctor first.'

'Let's get engaged then.' He wanted to commit her; she was too wonderful to lose; he wanted to own her; he wanted his ring on her finger to warn all the other men to keep away – to be able to say: 'She's mine'.

'We don't need a ring,' protested Melanie, 'I'm yours without that.'

Jeremy Fawcett had to settle for that. Two years later they both graduated and left Cambridge for London to start their clinical medicine at St Luke's Hospital.

John Wright also arrived at St Luke's on the same day in October to start his medical training, but he had arrived there by a quite different route.

His childhood was about survival in a spiritually and materially deficient home with little food, a drunken mother and a violent father who, apart from short periods as a labourer during the Second World War, was usually unemployed and who drank most of his 'dole' money on the way back from the Labour Exchange. There were no books in the council house, but there was a constantly blaring radio and a copy of the Socialist *Daily Herald.* The only social contact was the weekly visit of the council's rent collector.

As a child he was secretive. He didn't communicate with the rest of the family. He became a loner. It was a kind of defence mechanism. Life was easier if he kept quiet and kept to himself. When it became too much for him, he would go to the shed at the bottom of the tiny garden and sit quietly with his elder brother's pigeons, gently stroking their heads. Sometimes, as he sat there, a stray bird would fly in, an exhausted racing pigeon with a metal band on its leg. He would imagine that the bird had flown hundreds of miles, perhaps even from a foreign country, and he half expected to find a message tucked underneath the ring, which would have brought some excitement to his life, but he never did. Even this peaceful haven was to end.

On his return from the pub one afternoon, his father staggered straight to the pigeon shed. He emerged with two birds still twitching, their necks hanging limply to one side, and threw them at John Wright's feet.

'Get these plucked,' he snarled. 'We'll see what they taste like.' The ten-year-old boy sat there rigidly staring at the pigeons he had been holding just a few minutes before moving at his feet.

'You don't eat until you do,' his father shouted.

The boy's silence made him even more violent. He picked up one of the birds by its feet and threw it at him.

'You'll stay there until you do,' he threatened.

John shuddered as he felt the soft warm bird hit the side of his face.

'I'll teach you, you stubborn little bugger!' shouted his father as he beat him around the head with his rolled up copy of the *Daily Herald*, 'You've got to learn to do what you're told.'

He might not have been so mad if John had cried. It was the stubborn silence that infuriated him.

'Go to bed!' he screamed. 'And stay there until you're ready to come down and pluck these birds.'

John went up to his bedroom. He never plucked the pigeons and his father wouldn't let him have any food for two days.

When the Second World War started in September 1939, John Wright was just fourteen years of age. His grammar school was evacuated to the country.

'Don't think you're skiving off with the rest of them,' his father said. 'You're old enough to work. It's about time you brought some money in.'

His mother and the rest of the children were evacuated to Wales and he never saw them again. He started work at the beginning of the war as an office-boy in a factory on the Thames, but the pride he felt at being a wage earner and receiving his first pay packet – two pounds for the week – was short-lived when his father took most of it.

During the blitz in the East End he grew up rapidly. He was only two miles away when the German bombers set the Thames factories alight in 1940. A few months later he saw London lit up like a giant fireworks party as thousands of incendiaries rained down. He was uncomfortably close to the Bank underground station when a direct hit killed a hundred civilians. One night a naval mine floated down quietly on its parachute to devastate hundreds of flimsily built council houses close to where he slept in his Anderson air raid shelter, which was half submerged in the mud of his backyard. The first thing he noticed when he walked to the tram stop the following morning – even before he saw the damaged houses – was the pungent smell of the acrid smoke from smouldering furnishing fabrics. It was eerie. A whole neighbourhood had disappeared during the night. The houses were rubble. The people had all gone, either dead or moved into temporary accommodation. The area had been cleared up by the rescue services. It was now deserted and silent. All signs of human existence had gone except for the policemen urging the inquisitive to 'Move on'. That night he went to the cinema, occasionally looking up at the flimsy roof when he heard the noise of the anti-aircraft guns overhead, but mostly he ignored them.

When he saw dead bodies he was curious, not sympathetic. He had become hardened by years of childhood introspection and loneliness, the aggression of his father, and the violence of war. His emotions were all locked in and wouldn't be liberated until he found an excuse to leave his father, which he did at the end of the war.

'I've found a better job on the other side of London,' he said.

'It's a long journey,' his father replied, spitting into the open coal fire. 'It'd better be worth it.'

'I'm going to find lodgings over there.'

'What about me?' said his father, looking alarmed. 'Who's going to look after me?'

'I'll come home at weekends.'

'You'll have to pay your full keep.'

And with that John Wright left his council house in the East End.

His search for lodgings in North London was surprisingly easy. He rang the door bell of a large house near his new factory and it was opened by an old lady. She was a spinster, kind and charming, short and stooped, with thinning hair.

'Come in,' she said, 'and tell me about yourself.'

He found himself talking quite freely to her about how his years of study at night school during the war had enabled him to become a qualified electrical engineer. His technical training had also kept him in a reserved occupation, out of the armed forces.

'And now I've been offered a better job in this area. That's why I'm here.'

She showed him around the three-storey, double-fronted Victorian house. It was, in fact, the old lady's family home. She had lived there all her life and at the beginning of the century there had been living-in servants; but now, this elderly, refined gentle woman was down on her luck, and taking in lodgers in order to keep her home.

'You may call me Birdie,' she said. 'Everyone does.' He had never called an old lady by her Christian name before, and it took him some time before he was able to use her nickname without embarrassment. She showed him to his room, and it was about the size of the entire ground floor of his council house. His clothes and few personal possessions were lost in the vast mahogany wardrobe.

At dinner he met the other lodgers. Dr McTaggart, a consultant physician at the local hospital, was a charming Ulsterman with a keen sense of humour, educated at a tough boarding school in Northern Ireland before reading medicine at Queens University, Belfast. His entire life was dedicated to medicine.

'I'm married to medicine,' he would say, when asked why he had never married. 'I couldn't cope with a wife and children as well.'

He was neither hetero- nor homosexual, but seemed perfectly content with life.

'Doctors should be like Catholic priests – celibate,' he would say.

Stanley Smythe was altogether quite different. A freelance salesman buying and selling anything he could see a profit in.

'Why have you got that Lancaster car up on blocks in the garage?' asked John, 'you never use it.' He had never been for a drive in a motor car, and he always hoped Smythe would invite him, but he never did and the car remained unused in the garage.

'Business,' Smythe said, 'supply and demand. It's almost impossible to get a new car so soon after the war. The factories are still changing over from making tanks.' He tapped the side of his nose with his index finger. 'I'm not allowed to sell it for a year, but then – I'll make a killing.'

Smythe was an ugly man with thick pebble-lens spectacles and a large red bulbous nose. He salivated and slobbered as he went through his endless sales patter. He introduced John to Soho nightlife and when he went off with a prostitute, he always tapped his pocket. 'Always use a banger,' he would say, 'don't get a dose.' But John Wright left him in London and made his way back to his lodgings.

Logan, the third lodger, who worked as a clerk in the same factory as John Wright, was a tall, lantern-jawed Southern Irishman with a great sense of fun, an incorrigible practical joker who went into uncontrolled hysterical laughter when Birdie – on her return from church one Sunday morning, activated a 'whoopee' cushion he had hidden under her favourite chair. He had a story for every occasion and enjoyed his stories better than anyone else. Logan was a very likeable character, always excellent company, who wanted to be a writer.

John Wright had never spent a night away from his East End council house before, but he was adaptable and intelligent. Imperceptibly he changed. He became more middle class. He started to pronounce words more accurately. Birdie would often correct him.

'"Draw-ing" not "draw-ring", John,' she would say. He was young enough not to mind. In later years he thought of his time in Birdie's house as a kind of middle-class finishing school.

His decision to go to Australia had been sudden. The Australian government was encouraging immigrants with an assisted scheme which was virtually a free passage.

John Wright and his father could never be close after the childhood years of violence and drunkenness, but now the gap had become so enormous that communication was impossible. His father waited for him every Friday evening when he returned from Birdie's house.

'Where's my money?' he would ask, and as soon as he got it he was off to the pub to return home shouting drunk and prepared to take on anybody.

When John told him he was going to Australia, he became alarmed.

'How am I going to manage?' he asked. 'I've looked after you all these years. Now you're going to leave me.'

John grunted in contempt.

'You're the only one I've got left,' his father whined. 'Your mother and the rest of them never came back after the war.' But, as soon as he saw that John was determined to go, he reverted to his normal aggressive style.

'You traitor!' he screamed. 'Piss off then!' He spat at him: 'D'you think I care?' He pushed him out, slamming the door violently and John could hear him screaming through the door: 'Don't ever bleeding well come back!'

His luggage was on the boat and he had left his job at the radio factory. It was at a small farewell party arranged by Dr McTaggart that he met Pauline Browne.

She was McTaggart's house physician, an attractive fair-haired Scot with the most enormous china blue eyes and a soft Scottish accent. John Wright had never met anyone like her before. She was a young, beautiful, intelligent, professional woman, privately educated and a graduate of Edinburgh University. She smiled at him, carrying on a light conversation, and seemingly oblivious to his rapt attention. When the party was over, he went back to his lodgings and tried to sleep, but couldn't get the smiling face out of his mind.

The next day he picked up and replaced the telephone receiver three times before he summoned up sufficient courage to telephone her at the hospital. His voice sounded so unnatural that he scarcely recognised it.

'No, you can't speak to Dr Browne. She's in the middle of a busy clinic.'

'I'm sorry, but it is important,' he mumbled. The operator softened. 'Is it for an appointment?'

'Well it is,' he hesitated, 'kind of.'

'If you tell me what "kind of" appointment, I can make it for you,' she

9

replied. 'You don't need to speak to Dr Browne.'

'No,' he said firmly, 'it's a personal matter, of extreme urgency. Only Dr Browne can deal with it.'

'Doctor,' the operator said, taking the easy way out and putting the call through, 'there's a young man on the telephone who sounds as if he'll die if he doesn't speak to you.'

'Can't you save him?'

'No, he won't go away. You'll have to have a quick word.'

'Sounds like a case for the trick cyclist,' said Pauline Browne.

'Dr Browne,' she said, the telephone accentuating her Scottish accent, 'how can I help you?'

'This is John Wright,' he said without any preamble. 'Will you have a drink with me tonight?'

She was astounded, very busy and slightly annoyed, but she agreed.

She knew that Wright was going to Australia soon and she felt she should be friendly to someone her chief had introduced her to. There were no other thoughts in her mind but John was persistent and saw her every day, and after about a week she realised that she was looking forward to their meetings and was spending much of her time thinking about him. She was a devout Catholic and persuaded him to go with her to Mass in the crypt of a bombed-out church in the city on the following Sunday morning.

'Did you enjoy the service?' she asked. He enjoyed being with her but he had never been to a church service in his life before.

'It was all bells and smells.'

'It's more than that,' she smiled.

Their relationship moved on and they started kissing and embracing, and within a few days were spending hours in each other's arms.

Dr McTaggart wondered why she looked so tired each morning.

'Doctor, you're looking tired,' he said in his professional way, as if talking to a patient. 'Are you working too hard?' He was surprised when she blushed deep crimson.

John Wright began to question his motives for leaving England. 'Am I right?' he asked Pauline, 'is there a pot of gold waiting for me?' Pauline remained silent in his arms. 'D'you think I should go?' he asked. She longed to say 'Please don't,' but she answered, 'I'll miss you terribly, but you must decide yourself. You'll have to make your own mind up.'

He knew in his heart that the real reason he was going was to get as far away as possible from his father, but he never told her this. Their daily meetings were becoming more emotional. At the end of the third week of knowing Pauline Browne, he knew he couldn't go. Frantic telephone calls to Australia House unscrambled the arrangements but it was some weeks later before he got back the single case containing all his luggage. Pauline was overjoyed. She was two years older than John but felt quite comfortable with him.

She introduced him to the theatre and took him to Promenade Concerts. He began to appreciate music. When they were together, they were in a world of their own, lost in their infatuation, but there was never any question of sex. As far as Pauline was concerned, that would have to wait for marriage. Not that she had thought about that very much.

'What are you going to do with your life?' she asked one evening.

'Love you,' he said, kissing her.

'You can't do that all the time.'

'Oh, yes I can,' he said, pulling her into his arms.

'What about using your talents?'

'I shall be using them continuously,' he said, 'to love you.'

He had never spoken like this to a woman before. There had been no display of love between his parents, only bitterness and aggression. His role models were from books and films, but with Pauline, he found, the words seemed to flow out naturally.

'Be serious,' she said, extricating herself from his arms.

It came as a complete surprise when he said: 'I want to be a doctor.'

'But you've only just become an engineer,' she protested. 'Why don't you build on that? Take a higher qualification.'

John was despondent when Pauline didn't immediately welcome his decision as McTaggart had. 'Medicine's the only subject worth studying,' he had said, 'and the sooner you get started the better.'

'It wouldn't be so bad if you were able to start at the same level as other medical students,' Pauline continued, 'but you've got to go back to the beginning.'

Although John Wright had a professional engineering qualification, this didn't allow entrance to a university. His science-based subjects were good enough, but he still had to satisfy the university in English and a foreign language. Once Pauline Browne had accepted that he was going to study medicine, she became his teacher. She spent many hours testing his French vocabulary and improving his English.

When he received confirmation that he had passed his Entrance Exam. for London University, Pauline was as excited as he was.

'I know just the place to celebrate,' she said, taking him to a superb little French restaurant in Soho.

'I'd never have done it without you,' he said.

'You sat the exam – not me,' she answered, 'but anyway, it's only the beginning. It'll be a year or two before you get into medical school.'

'Okay,' he said, 'but, at least I'm on my way.'

'Here's to 1st MB. Your first medical exam.' she said, raising her glass

He enjoyed dissecting the dogfish and the frog; teasing out and identifying the nerves and blood vessels. It was enthralling to cut very thin sections of plant stems and stain them so that he could see their cellular structure as he peered down the microscope. It was so different from the mathematics-based studies he had been used to. At the end of an intense, year-long course, he passed in physics, chemistry, botany and zoology. He was elated, but knew that he had to face the difficult task of finding a hospital to accept him. The medical schools were filled to capacity and were giving priority to ex-servicemen returning from the war. 'Why couldn't I have been a war hero?' he asked himself, 'instead of being in a reserved occupation.'

The interviewing committee gathered in the Dean's room. 'I often wonder why we bother to interview students,' remarked the Medical School Secretary. 'We know their "1st. MB" grades; we've got the headmaster's report – and often these days a service record as well. What do we gain from the interviews?'

'They might have two heads,' the Dean laughed, 'but seriously, they do have to deal with the public. We need to assess their personality and suitability.'

'It takes a devil of a long time,' complained the Secretary.

'The hospital is a community,' the Dean pointed out, 'everyone has to pull their weight.'

He looked around the table and nodded to the Secretary. John Wright came into the room and sat facing the Committee.

'So you want to be a doctor,' said the Dean. 'Why?' Wright squirmed.

Finally, the Dean came to his 'key' question. 'We're going to train you to be a doctor,' he said. 'You're going to get a lot out of us. What are you going to give back?'

He knew he could find lots of students with good academic records, but he wanted something more. In Wright's case he was impressed when he discovered that he had gone along to the well known Nomads Club a few years ago and learned to play rugby, and that now he was in the first fifteen. After Wright left the room, the Dean looked at the Secretary.

'How would we have found that young man without an interview?' He paused to stamp the application form 'Accepted'. He doesn't have very high grades. He left school at the beginning of the war when he was just fourteen. And what sort of headmaster's report could he have produced?' He looked at the School Secretary, expecting him to reply, but he didn't. 'What's more,' he went on, 'without an interview, I might have missed a good rugger player.'

The Committee laughed. They knew that the Dean, a former Oxford blue and an international, was the President of the hospital rugby club, and his burning ambition was to win the Hospitals' Cup.

Pauline Browne and Dr McTaggart, who had almost become a father figure, were overjoyed at the good news but sad that Wright would have to leave North London and find lodgings near to St Luke's. They both insisted that it was important that he lived close to the hospital so that he could take an active part in medical school activities, many of which took place in the evenings or at weekends.

Pauline had stamped her personality on her small apartment. It was warm, comfortable and welcoming. The curtains and fabrics were of soft colours and the furniture a mixture of modern and antique. Because she lived alone, the flat was always tidy. There was no living-in man to mess it up. As she waited for John Wright, she gave a final polish to the Davenport chest her parents had given her when she qualified. They always dined in the kitchen, but by switching off the main lights, leaving a soft light in the dining area and a single candle on the small table, they caused the kitchen apparatus to disappear into the shadows. When the meal was ready, Pauline would say: 'Come into the bistro.'

She was a good cook. She loved collecting recipes and always chose wine very carefully, and John's appreciation of good food and wine began at her table. Her favourite red gingham table cloth and napkins were on the table. The table was set with neat rows of cutlery on either side of the straw table mats.

Pauline poured a small amount of the wine into the large plain glass for him to taste.

'Good ruby colour; clear; good berry fruit on the nose.' He tasted the wine. 'Superb – a well balanced claret.'

'It's only a cru bourgeois,' she rejoined, 'but it should drink well.'

'You look after the wine,' she continued, moving the bottle towards him. He carefully half-filled the large claret glasses so as not to disturb any sediment at the bottom of the bottle.

They both felt relaxed. John had no immediate exams to pass and his programme was fixed for some years, provided he continued to defeat the examiners. Pauline shared his happiness and was pleased her protegé had not let her down. In her more serious moments that's how she regarded him. They enjoyed being together. As they sat at the kitchen dining table, they were completely oblivious to the rest of the world. John thought how incredibly lovely she looked that evening. She had let her blonde hair down and it was resting on her shoulders. He knew that during the day, when seeing patients, she would tie it up.

'It's more professional,' she said. 'I can't have my hair falling in their faces or on their bare chests, can I?'

'I wouldn't mind it falling on my chest.'

'If you were my patient,' she said, kissing him, 'you'd behave yourself – as they all do.'

'How does she cope with randy male patients?' he wondered. 'I bet some of them get an erection; I would.'

John Wright was often physically aroused when he was close to Pauline but he never tried to seduce her. Without saying anything, she seemed to have established the ground rules for their relationship.

As he enjoyed his claret, he looked across at her. The flickering candle was lighting up her English rose complexion and causing her blue eyes to sparkle.

'What an incredible woman,' he thought. 'How lucky I am to have met her. She's lovely, intelligent, good fun – almost saintly.'

'I love you,' he said gently. 'When I become a doctor, will you marry me?'

Pauline was taken by surprise. She was unprepared for this blunt proposal.

'Let's go into the sitting room,' she replied.

They snuggled up on the small sofa and kissed.

'I'll always love you,' she said, 'but we're on a high at present. We've got to be realistic.'

'I thought I was being,' he said.

'Darling, you're going across to St Luke's soon. You must enjoy your undergraduate life to the full.'

He felt shattered. 'You mean this is the end?'

'No, no – please, I don't mean that!' she answered, 'but I don't want you to feel restricted by a commitment to me. You missed out on your teen-age years; at least enjoy university.' She put her arms around him, running her fingers through his dark hair and tracing his profile with her index finger. Then she kissed him gently. 'You're very handsome, you know.'

John remained silent until finally: 'Don't you understand?' he asked disconsolately, 'I love you; I want to be with you for the rest of my life.'

He was confused. Pauline insisted that she wanted them to continue, but that she was unselfish enough to encourage him to live a separate life across the other side of London as a medical student. Perhaps she really wanted to finish with him. She would have no difficulty in finding a man; she could do much better than him.

'I should have gone to Australia,' he said miserably, 'it was crazy expecting you to marry me. Why should you? A penniless medical student from the slums of the East End.' He tried to brighten up. 'Perhaps I'd better be going.' Pauline restrained him as he tried to stand up, holding his face between her hands and kissing him full on the lips. She put her arms round him and he rested his head on her breast.

'I'd marry you because I loved you,' she said, 'nothing else would matter.'

'I suppose I was naive,' he said.

'No you weren't. I'm just not as certain as you are about the future,' she said. 'I'm not sure what I want to do with my life. I have to find out before making any personal commitments.'

They sat silently, Pauline fondling his ear and occasionally bending down to kiss his head. 'Darling,' she said hesitantly, 'I know I'm being selfish, but I want to work in Africa for a while; that's why I can't be sure.'

'Why didn't you tell me?' he protested. 'I would have understood.'

'I've only just heard,' she said. 'I've always had this feeling since I was a child, that I'm meant to do something like this.' She pressed his head against her breast almost as if she were comforting a child. 'You may wish to join me if I'm still there when you qualify.'

She drove him back to his lodgings and in the months running up to October, when he was due at St Luke's, they met most days. They even went to Scotland and stayed with her parents for a week. Their romance was still entirely platonic. John wondered whether she would ever go to bed with a man. Perhaps medicine and her Church were sufficient to satisfy her emotional needs.

He left Birdie's house and moved across to St Luke's in early October. He had found a flat close to the hospital which he shared with three other medical students. When Logan heard about the arrangement, he promptly named it Bedside Manor.

Shortly afterwards Pauline went off to Africa to work as a general medical officer in a Catholic missionary hospital.

## Chapter Two

John Wright arrived at St Luke's on a Wednesday in October, and on the following Saturday afternoon he played rugby for the hospital. In the evening a rugby 'hop' had been arranged in the sports pavilion. Nurses and medical students crammed into the small wooden clubhouse decorated with 'trophies' stolen over the years from various parts of the country. The two-piece band – a piano and bass – thumped out the waltz and the quickstep, and the dancers stumbled around on the knotted wooden floor, roughened over the years by hundreds of rugby and cricket studs. He found himself dancing with a girl called Jane Perkins. She was a shapely, attractive pleasant nurse, easy to talk to, and they spent most of the evening together. He had never danced so close to a girl before. Gallons of beer were drunk in spite of the difficulty of getting to the small hatch in the wall from which the groundsman dispensed it straight from the wood.

When the dance was over, they went down the pavilion steps on to the sports field. He immediately took her in his arms and kissed her passionately and then led her towards the side of the field away from the crowd leaving the pavilion, and kissed her again.

'Don't be in such a hurry,' she said, 'it's too muddy.'

They walked back slowly along the main road to the hospital, stopping every now and then to kiss.

'All we need now is for Matron to come by,' she said. 'She wouldn't like one of her nurses behaving like this in the street.'

'But you're off duty.'

'That wouldn't make any difference to her,' she answered.

'You're not even in uniform.'

'Nurses should always behave like ladies,' she said, mimicking the matron's mincing tones. 'You're never off duty; you may be called on at any time. Yours is a vocation.'

At the hospital they walked past ambulances delivering patients to Casualty. Jane pushed the swing doors open and beckoned. 'Come on,' she said, 'I'll show you how to get into the Medical School.'

'I've only been here four days,' he said anxiously, 'don't get me expelled.'

'Well, if you don't want to,' she shrugged, 'I'll say goodnight.' Then she started to walk on into the hospital.

He quickly followed her. 'Don't worry,' she reassured him, 'there's nobody there this time of night.' She laughed, 'I won't get you into trouble.'

'Not much,' he replied.

The front door to the medical school was locked at six o'clock every evening, so Jane Perkins led him along the main hospital corridor, passing doctors and nurses and an occasional patient on a trolley, and then through a door marked 'Pathology Dept'. They climbed two flights of stairs and went along a passageway past a series of small rooms used for testing human samples of various kinds, and then down some stairs into the Medical School, just by the Dean's office. He was so excited by this passionate woman whom he was holding close to him, that all thoughts of being found in the darkened Medical School temporarily left his mind. They walked along a narrow corridor between the library and some lecture theatres.

'No, not the Men's,' she said, as he led her towards the Men's Common Room, 'Let's go to the Women's; it's more comfortable.'

He shuddered when he thought what the Dean would say if he found out that they were not only in the locked up Medical School, but also in the Women's Common Room at one o'clock in the morning. Jane led him by the hand alongside the main Lecture Theatre and up a small flight of stairs. 'Sod!' she said, 'It's locked.' He was relieved and started to turn back. 'Don't go,' she said, 'I'll show you how to open this.' With that she rattled the door handle up and down violently. As the noise echoed through the empty Medical School, he became increasingly worried. He thought of the enormous effort he had had to make to get into Medical School. 'Four days as a medical student,' he muttered to himself, 'and I'm kicked out.' He expected a porter or the night sister to come across at any moment from the main hospital to investigate.

'Got it,' exclaimed Jane triumphantly as the door clicked open. 'Come on,' she said, leading the way, 'I'll lock it once we're inside.' The room was in darkness and when they looked out through the uncurtained windows, they could see nurses in the main hospital corridor no more than thirty yards away.

'Keep away from the windows,' said Jane. He led her to a large green leather sofa and they made love. They stayed there for many hours and made love twice more. Jane had got up from the sofa and was standing looking across to the hospital. She was proud of her figure and she knew that he was looking at her silhouette in the half light from the windows.

'What d'you think?' she asked, turning towards him.

'Come here,' he said, gently trying to coax her back on to the sofa.

'Now, now!' she said, 'you're insatiable. You're worse than I am. We'll go for a swim.'

'What?' he laughed, 'in the middle of the night?'

'Follow me,' she replied.

Naked, she led him from the Women's Common Room along the side of the lecture theatre to the shower room in the basement of the Medical School.

'Close all the doors,' she said, producing a roll of hospital sticking plaster, and began sealing round the doors and drain.

'That should do; turn on all the taps.'

The shower room gradually filled with warm water and steam.

'Leave them on,' she insisted, when he began to turn the showers off. 'We're bound to get lots of leakage.'

They floated around in the warm water with the showers streaming down on them.

Jane looked at him floating next to her. 'You're like the good ship Venus,' she said, 'is that permanent?'

He tried to get hold of her. 'No, no,' she said. 'You'll drown me!'

She put her arms round him and turned him over on his back. 'But I don't mind drowning you.'

They splashed around until the dawn light started to filter through the reinforced glass of the basement windows.

'Time to move,' said Jane, as she pulled all the sticking plaster away and the water level started to fall. When it was down to six inches, they opened the doors and it flooded through into the locker room. On Monday morning the School Secretary summoned the hospital plumber to inform him rather crossly that the shower room had flooded yet again, and would he investigate the drains once more.

'I must get back into the Nurses' Home before roll call,' said Jane as they dressed. She looked in the mirror. 'God, my hair! What a mess! How am I going to face men's surgical ward in two hours' time?' They went back through the Pathology Laboratory into the main hospital.

'What the hell?' she said, looking at her watch, 'It's too late to get any sleep; I'm hungry. Let's have some breakfast.'

John raised his eyebrows, but he had ceased to be surprised by anything Jane did or said.

'Where shall we go – into town?' he laughed, not really believing she was serious.

She led him along the front of the hospital to the Nurses' Home. It was five o'clock in the morning. The Home had been firmly locked since ten o'clock the previous evening. Nurses weren't allowed out and men weren't allowed in at any time. Jane Perkins went to the iron railings alongside the entrance. She started to clamber over.

'Give me a leg up,' she said, 'I don't want to tear my stockings.'

He climbed over himself and they moved quietly along the side of the Nurses' Home down a slope, so that they were level with the basement rooms.

'Stay here for a moment,' she whispered, 'I shan't be long.'

He waited outside the basement window, trying to make himself as inconspicuous as possible in the dawn light. The hospital lights were still on and he could see an endless procession of nurses and doctors moving along what was, in effect, the main artery of the hospital as they went about their duties. Jane was away so long that he began to wonder whether she was coming back at all, but at last she re-appeared. She held her finger to her lips. 'Shh,' she whispered. 'Climb in quietly.'

She led him from the small storeroom into the hospital kitchen, which occupied the entire basement area under the Nurses' Home. One or two of the staff said, 'Hi Jane,' as she walked across to a small table set behind a screen.

'Sit down, sir,' she invited him, with mock civility. The chef appeared and served them a superb cooked breakfast.

'Don't make a noise, Night Sister will be down shortly,' he said, grinning at John. 'If she finds you here, we'll all be for it.'

Jane Perkins looked across at John Wright with an amused expression. 'You do look frightened,' she said. He felt his stomach muscles contract and he stopped eating and scarcely dared to breathe when he realised that the two women on the other side of the screen were two hospital sisters ordering a special meal for a patient. Jane Perkins could only contain her laughter long enough for the lift doors to close behind the sisters.

'I'm sorry,' she said, 'I mustn't laugh. But you look so worried.'

They finished eating. 'Thanks Joe,' she said, kissing the chef on the cheek, 'you're a real friend. I won't forget.'

'I'll hold you to that,' he said.

As they made their way out of the kitchen towards the storeroom, John watched in horror as the lift doors opened and two nurses came into the kitchen pushing a trolley. He saw his whole career disintegrating before his eyes. They pushed the trolley towards them.

'Good party, Jane?' enquired one of them grinning.

'Great,' she said, and with that they went back through the potato store and over the iron railings to the front of the deserted hospital.

'I've got to get back into the Nurses' Home without being caught,' she explained, looking anxious for the first time.

As they entered the hospital, she clasped his hand tightly. They passed through a small side door and walked quickly along a corridor between the bedrooms of the resident house surgeons and physicians, through some swing doors, and back into the main hospital corridor, which was teeming with early morning activity.

'Christ!' she said, pulling him into a ward entrance, 'Matron's coming down the corridor. I don't think that bloody woman ever sleeps. If she sees me, I'll be suspended for six months – or expelled, if she's in a particularly bloody mood!'

They waited silently until she had passed, and then went back along the corridor for a few yards, up one flight of circular stairs, through a door marked 'Private', and then Jane Perkins disappeared through the emergency exit door of the Nurses' Home, calling out: 'Give me a ring some time.'

John walked slowly back to his flat repeating to himself over and over again: 'God, what a woman!' Never in his wildest fantasies could he have imagined such a night. It was now full daylight and thankfully it was Sunday; he didn't have to go into the hospital. He climbed into his bed but was too excited to go to sleep immediately. He thought of Jane Perkins getting ready to go on duty at seven o'clock and eventually drifted into sleep mumbling: 'So this is medical school life.'

He quickly adapted to the life. He was a chameleon, not only changing his outward appearance but also the way he thought, spoke and behaved. It was not affectation; it just happened gradually and naturally as he reacted to the environment. He seldom thought of, and certainly never spoke of, his childhood in the East End or the years of the blitz when he had lived and worked in London, and the German bombs rained down night after night. The hospital community was mainly young, mostly unmarried, the majority living away from home for the first time and enjoying their freedom. There were many hundreds of nurses, physiotherapists and radiographers, and these greatly outnumbered the male medical students, who were a mixture of young students straight from school and mature ex-servicemen – some with distinguished war records. There were relatively few female medical students. It was an opportunity to mix and get to know a large number of people. John Wright had never been in this kind of environment before, and found that he was going out with a different girl every night and rapidly getting the reputation of being one of the 'studs' of the medical school.

The early part of his medical training concentrated on the basic sciences, and he was as fascinated with the detailed anatomy of the human body as he had been with the dogfish and the rabbit. The anatomy department was on the top floor of the medical school, so that the stench of formalin didn't pervade the whole building. Anatomy was considered by many medical students as a dull chore which just had to be mugged up, but at St Luke's the anatomy lecturer, Bill Summers, had become a legend to generations of students. His coloured drawings on the blackboard were so vivid that it hardly seemed necessary to dissect out the various structures in the long dead cadaver. The male students loved him because of his humour; the females loathed him because so many of his asides were distinctly sexist. There were very few women studying medicine just after the Second World War, but he resented any. 'I suppose I'm a chauvinist – but medicine's a man's profession,' he would say to the class.

'The human brain,' he would tell them as he drew on the blackboard, 'weighs about three pounds in males.' He would pause and look around to make sure that he had everyone's attention: 'but less in females. As you would expect.' This would produce a loud roar of laughter from the men but on occasions female students would be so incensed that they walked out. At anatomy John Wright excelled, but he coasted along in other subjects. It was a reaction to the years of intense study that he had to do before he was in a position to start medicine.

He still thought of Pauline as his girlfriend, even though he had been sleeping around at the hospital. Pauline, with her strict Catholic codes, wouldn't approve, but she wanted them to be less committed. Anyway, neither he nor the nurses he had been with attached a great deal of importance to their liaisons. Sometimes one or other would get hurt, but it wasn't usually too painful and they got over it fairly quickly. There were some nurses like Jane Perkins who could never refuse an invitation to a party, however nebulous; and some of the parties at Bedside Manor might only consist of two or three couples meeting at eleven o'clock at night at the end of the second nursing shift. Jane Perkins was an institution. She became known in the medical school as 'Perks for the boys'. But even she was longing for a more meaningful relationship.

'Oh, for a steady male,' she confessed in a serious moment. 'I'm fed up with this wild life, breaking in these young medical students.'

'You'll be talking marriage next,' protested John flippantly.

'Yes, please,' she said, 'if you're serious.'

He laughed. 'I'm not the marrying sort.'

'Oh yes you are,' she said, putting her arms round his neck, 'you'll do fine.'

He filled her glass and talked about something else.

Two months before his second medical examination, he gave up all parties and kept his head in the books. He had no intention of failing his 2nd MB. Success in this would allow him to move on to clinical medicine. He would actually be let loose in the wards and clinics working with patients. It would be a kind of apprenticeship. When the examination results came from the university in the summer, he read the letter three times before he believed it.

'I've passed – I've bloody passed!' he yelled to his flatmates, and then he telephoned Pauline Browne, who had just returned on leave from Africa. He could already imagine himself in his white coat with a stethoscope carelessly dangling round his neck as he walked the hospital wards. It had taken him over four years to reach this stage.

He went across London to see Pauline the following weekend and she spent most of her leave with him. She took him to Scotland to stay with her parents. They welcomed him, never asking about his background or his intentions towards their daughter. They were both schoolteachers and were very proud of Pauline. It never occurred to them that she would ever behave other than in a sensible and Christian way.

'Will you come to Mass with me on Sunday?' she asked, 'I'd be thrilled and so would my parents.'

'You'll have to tell me what to do,' he said. 'I don't want to embarrass you.'

'You couldn't do that,' laughed Pauline. She gave him some books on the Catholic Church.

'You're trying to convert me,' he said as he flipped through the books.

'Dealing with life and death can be very harrowing without the support of a religious faith,' said Pauline seriously.

When they returned to London, he stayed in her flat. They never shared the same bed; he slept in the spare room. Their relationship remained entirely at an emotional level. They would kiss each other, sometimes passionately for long periods, but it never went beyond that. The relationship remained a-sexual and sometimes John thought it adolescent. He longed to make love to her but for the most part he accepted her code. When he was alone, he often wondered whether she would be passionate like Jane Perkins or just quietly submissive.

'D'you love me as a man?' he asked one evening after one glass of claret too many.

'Of course I do,' answered Pauline gently. 'You are a man. How else could I love you?'

'But we don't love as a man and a woman,' he said. 'I'm sure you love all sorts of people of both sexes.'

'You are the only man I've loved in my life,' she replied.

'I often dream of you,' he said, hesitating for a moment. 'I dream of being in bed with you.' He kissed her passionately. 'Cuddling up naked and making love.'

They stayed together until Pauline gently kissed him, pulling away to refill the coffee cups.

He was experienced enough to know that there came a time in most relationships when it would become sexual, and if it didn't, it usually ended, but their relationship was different. It was almost ethereal. 'At least,' he thought, 'as far as Pauline is concerned.'

At the end of the summer he went back to St Luke's and shortly after, Pauline returned to Africa. They corresponded regularly. Pauline found her work in the missionary hospital fulfilling. She ended her first letter: 'I hope you will be able to come out and visit me sometime. With all my love. God bless.'

John Wright's medical studies had become much more interesting and he was beginning to understand why he had had to slog away at the basic sciences for the past two years. He remembered the words of his anatomy teacher, Bill Summers: 'These sciences are the basis of medicine. Without them we'd be back in the fairground.' He was attached to a medical firm and followed the consultant and his entourage round the hospital wards.

On one occasion the consultant stopped at the bed of a very sick male patient. 'Now, Wright, don't try and hide,' he said, as Wright tried to shrink his large frame at the back of the group, 'What can you tell us by simply looking at the patient?'

'Well, sir, he's not a good colour,' he said, swallowing hard. 'He's cyanosed. He's having difficulty breathing. In fact, he's actually wheezing.' He paused and then went on: 'He's a large man, but he looks weak and fatigued. And he has a cough.'

'Anything else?' asked the consultant.

'I can see that the ends of his fingers are clubbed.'

The consultant looked at the patient. 'Don't mind us talking about you,' he said reassuringly, 'it's the way these young doctors learn.' Then he turned back to Wright. 'Carry on,' he said, 'what are you likely to discover on examination?'

'He's probably got pain in the chest, sir,' replied Wright. 'He may feel dizzy or faint.' He looked thoughtfully; 'I wouldn't be surprised if his blood pressure and cholesterol were high.' He hesitated and went on: 'The chances are that he is a heavy smoker.'

'So, then, Dr Wright,' the consultant asked, 'what is your diagnosis?'

'Lung disease, sir,' rejoined Wright without any hesitation, 'maybe of non-inflammatory origin.'

Even as a new medical student, Wright knew he mustn't use the word 'cancer' in front of a patient. Wright produced his diagnosis slowly and deliberately, as if it required a lot of thought, whereas he had discussed all the cases with the consultant's house surgeon at the Rugby Club bar.

'Well done, Wright.'

The consultant left the group and walked out of the ward with the senior registrar and the ward sister, followed by the house surgeon, who grinned at Wright and gave him a huge wink.

'We must watch that young man,' said the consultant, 'he's got potential.'

With his surgical firm Wright went into an operating theatre for the first time in his life to be greeted by the registrar: 'If you faint, don't fall on to the patient.' He scrubbed up and, clad in his green gown and rubber gloves, stood by the operating table holding a retractor or using suction to keep the operating field clear of blood. Operating on a body was quite different from dissecting a formalin-soaked cadaver. It seemed like a dream when a major operation was being carried out. He could see the heart and lungs moving, blood oozing from vessels until they were tied off, and all the time the anaesthetic bag filled and emptied as the patient breathed. He wrote to Pauline: 'The patient doesn't really seem to be a human being on the operating table. He has no free will, no consciousness, and no awareness of what's happening to him. He's delegated responsibility for his life to the surgical team.'

In his two weeks in Casualty he witnessed all the drama of an Accident and Emergencies Department in a busy hospital. He was allowed to splint up fractured limbs with plaster casts, and became a dab hand at suturing. After Casualty he lived in the hospital for six weeks doing his 'midder', delivering his quota of babies.

There were seven medical students in his surgical firm: six men and one woman. When John Wright first saw Melanie Clarkson, he thought, 'God, what an incredibly beautiful woman.' She had deep rich brown hair, smooth complexion, a broad smile, a warm outgoing personality, and an enormous sense of fun, and not even her loose fitting white coat could hide her superb figure. She was highly intelligent, with an instinctive feel for diagnosis, scarcely ever getting sidetracked with obscure details, just homing in on the important signs and symptoms. He invited her out. 'I'm spoken for,' she said demurely, and then grinned. 'No, I really can't,' she said when he persisted.

24

John tried to persuade her on many occasions but she wouldn't change her mind. It was always Jeremy Fawcett, whom she had met at Cambridge. 'We've been going together for three years. It's become a habit,' and then, thinking this might sound disloyal, she said, 'but a nice one.' She had been a boarder at Roedean, near Brighton, before going up to Cambridge. Her father, Sir David Clarkson, was an eminent Chancery barrister. Not only was Melanie committed to her comfortable relationship with Jeremy Fawcett, but she was fully aware from the female grapevine of John Wright's reputation in the nursing school. 'I'm not going to be another name on his list of conquests,' she said to herself.

Wright had an instinctive dislike of Fawcett. 'It can only be jealousy,' he thought. 'I've no other reason to dislike him.' They were in the same medical firm so they couldn't avoid each other. Any semblance of friendship ended when Fawcett heard Wright say, as the group walked down the ward to the next patient, 'Come on, Melanie. Come to the party tonight.' He was incensed and confronted Wright as soon as the ward round was over.

'Just leave Melanie alone,' he said threateningly. 'She doesn't welcome your approaches.' He moved towards Wright aggressively. 'And neither do I.'

'Get stuffed,' said Wright, looking him squarely in the eyes. 'I don't need your advice and neither does Melanie. She can run her own life.' Then he said quietly, 'If she tells me I'm being a nuisance, I'll stop immediately. It'll be up to her – not you.' And with that he turned away, adding: 'She might say "Yes" one day.'

Fawcett's face was white with anger. His body was so tense that both his hands were clenched into fists, and there was no disguising the look of hatred. Wright could only just see his pin-point pupils under the lowered eyebrows and was sure that if they hadn't been just outside a ward in the main hospital corridor, Fawcett would have attacked him. 'I've warned you,' he yelled at Wright, 'stay away!'

'Grow up,' said Wright, 'she's too good for a creep like you.' With that he walked calmly away. Fawcett had really thrown down the gauntlet and Wright was happy to pick it up. He'd have loved to take Melanie to the Medical School Summer Ball but doubted whether she would come. He was aware that she lived in the top-floor flat of a converted house opposite the hospital, and as he walked to the hospital on a Sunday morning he noticed that some work was being carried out to the roof. He knew that Melanie was away visiting her parents at their cottage on the Kent/Surrey border and wouldn't be back until the evening. He walked round the side of the house and came across some builders' ladders. With these fully extended, he was able to get up to the third-floor level, and climbed over a parapet on to a flat area. On tiptoe he could just see through a small bathroom window into Melanie's flat. But how to get inside? The bathroom window was too small. His eyes travelled up a drainpipe to the junction of two roofs. The roof to the right must be Melanie's flat. He shinned up the drainpipe, expecting it to pull away from the wall at any moment and send him crashing fifty feet to the ground below. It wouldn't take long to get me into Casualty, he thought wryly, as he clambered on to the roof and stood on a narrow lead-lined area looking up at the roof of Melanie's flat. About eight feet up was a roof light, but how could he get to it without a roof ladder? He was wearing rubber-soled shoes and he slowly and carefully climbed up the sloping roof until he reached the roof light.

The small window was immediately above a dining table strewn with medical books. This must be the right flat, but how could he get in? He examined the window and could see that it was closed by means of a long screw with a ring on the end operated from inside by means of a long handle. As he looked down through the window, he could see the long handle resting against the wall. Unless he was prepared to smash the glass, there was no way in. He levered the window upwards but there was no movement. As he jiggled the window, he felt the glass move, and he found that he could slide the single pane of glass sideways by about a quarter of an inch. He daren't risk breaking the glass, but he might be able to remove the entire pane and then replace it. There was only one thing for it; to return another day. So he quickly went back down the drainpipe and the ladder to the ground.

During the week he armed himself with a sharp knife and some putty from the hardware store. The following Sunday he again extended the ladder and climbed on to the roof, being thankful that this was taking place at the back of the house, not in full view of the hospital. He was surprised how easy it was to cut the old putty away and ease the glass pane out of the window frame. Some debris dropped down on to the medical text books on the dining table. From his pocket he carefully removed a box containing one red rose and an invitation card with the inscription:

Dear Melanie,
    Please come to the Medical School Ball with me.
        John Wright

He slipped a nylon fishing line under the box flap and gently lowered it to the table below, and then, carefully letting one end of the line go free, he pulled the line up, leaving the box on the table amidst the medical books.

The glass pane slid back into the window frame and he sealed it by pushing the putty round the edges with his thumb. If the police investigate, he thought, looking at his finger prints in the putty, I've left my signature for them.

On Monday morning, when he walked past the flat to go into the medical school, he was excited to notice that the builders had removed the ladders from the site. This would make the mystery even more difficult to solve.

Melanie Clarkson opened the double lock of the front door and went in to land her case on the dining table. Immediately she saw the red rose through the transparent lid of the box. Intrigued, she opened it and read the invitation. She looked around and wondered how the box had been delivered. It was too large to come through the letter box, and in any case there was no way it could have got from there on to the table some twenty feet away. No one had been in the flat since she had left on Friday evening. The flat door had special Chubb security locks. She noticed some specks of dust on her books and on the carpet and looked up to the roof light. Lifting the long handle, she fitted the hook into the ring at the end of the screw and turned, but the screw fitting didn't move; the window was tight shut.

'The enterprising villain!' she laughed. 'How did he do it?' She would have loved to have accepted the invitation because of the audacity of it, but she knew that that would be the end of her with Jeremy – and, she thought, of my reputation.

He must have delivered it through the roof light, she thought. There's no other way. She shuddered at the thought of John Wright climbing on to her roof. If he'd slipped, that would have been the end of a promising doctor. She wasn't a gossip and she didn't tell anyone – least of all Jeremy – about the invitation.

Melanie did go to the ball with Jeremy and had to admit to being slightly envious when she saw Wright with a pretty nurse from Women's Surgical. She smiled across the dance floor at him, which annoyed Jeremy. He became even more annoyed when Wright insisted on dancing close to them on a crowded floor.

'Let's go and have a drink,' he said loudly, pushing past Wright. 'It's getting very crowded in here.' He led Melanie to join a group of medical students in the Common Room bar. To his horror, Wright and his partner strolled across and started talking to them and when Wright asked Melanie to dance, he was almost speechless.

'D'you mind?' Melanie asked. He gave her a small cold smile and shrugged. 'Jeremy doesn't seem to like you very much,' she said as they walked on to the dance floor. 'Why's that?'

'I don't know. Must be our chemistry.'

'I thought that only applied to opposite sexes,' she laughed. They danced together for thirty minutes before she said, 'We'd better go back.'

'What did I do to deserve that?' The pretty nurse partner he had left with Fawcett asked angrily, 'I've never been with anybody so twitchy. He didn't even look at me. He kept looking over my shoulder all the time – scarcely said a word to me.'

'You must have made him nervous,' laughed John.

Wright had not made any contact with his father and he had no wish to see him, so he stayed at Bedside Manor during the summer vacation. He went into the hospital to watch operations, to work in Casualty, or play poker – a game he had become expert at during the war. In those days, every time the air-raid siren sounded, he used to go down to the basement air-raid shelter in the factory where he worked to join the poker school. In the Medical School he played all day in the Men's Common Room. The less successful players used to run up large debts which they were in no position to settle, so they would go 'on the books', meaning to settle their debts after qualification. Wright was owed large sums which he never expected or intended to collect.

Pauline Browne was now firmly established in Africa and her letters didn't suggest that she ever expected to return to the UK to work.

Hospital student life started to get back to normal in the autumn, and as Christmas approached, the rehearsals for the pantomime got under way. John Wright went to the pantomime rehearsals because he knew Melanie would be there. This year it was *Babes in the Wood*, but the title was irrelevant since the whole operation was to parody the consultants and the teaching staff. The students were experts at identifying the eccentricities of a teacher and grossly distorting them. Dr Alred became All Red Dragon, Dr Rooney, the orthopaedic surgeon, the Tree Surgeon Looney. Jeremy Fawcett was the musical director, leading the small orchestra and playing the piano. Melanie Clarkson was one of the babes; John Wright doubled as stage manager and one of the chorus. It was an exciting time and very little medicine was done in the weeks leading up to Christmas. It was a hospital tradition and everyone tried to attend. Each night throughout the week the pantomime played to a full house. On the last night the cast was 'on a high'. All anxiety had gone and they were enjoying being on the stage. The babes, who were all female, a mixture of nurses, physiotherapists and medical students, were singing the woodpecker song. They were dressed in green operating gowns and caps, with face masks dangling round their necks and heavy white operating boots on their feet. In their most angelic voices and without a trace of suggestion they sang:

'I put my finger in the woodpecker's hole and the woodpecker said, 'Cor bless my soul,
Take it out, take it out, re . . . move it.'
The babes rotated their index fingers at the male chorus as they sang. John Wright glanced across the stage at Melanie Clarkson, and she looked at him with a wicked grin. As well as rotating her finger, she beckoned him. Then she became aware of what she was doing and looked down, and he was sure that she was blushing beneath her stage make-up. The song, well known to generations of medical students, was a great success, with the audience joining in three noisy encores before the show was allowed to continue. The show overran by an hour, which was common on the last night. Finally, the curtain came down with

> 'Mary from the mountain glen
> Her urine's full of albumen.
> She's coming here to check her date,
> I bet you that she's six months late
> . . .
> . . .
> So they diagnosed toxaemia
> . . .'

The adrenaline was flowing as they prepared for the end of show party on the stage. There was a wide range of drinks, from the coarsest wine to reasonable Bordeaux Superieur, beers of every description, whisky, gin and cider. The popular tipple at the time was gin and strong vintage cider. The orchestra played chorus after chorus of the Woodpecker song, Mary from the Mountain Glen, Nellie 'Awkins from the Old Kent Road, and the Vegetable Compound song. They never seemed to tire of singing the songs over and over again. Jeremy Fawcett was in his element, playing the piano and conducting the singing, jumping up every now and again and waving his arms to encourage the singers to new heights.

In the early hours of the morning the music was still thundering through the Medical School, which was deserted apart from the pantomime party on the stage. With all the electric lights shining from the uncurtained windows, it was like a liner adrift in the ocean. The noise couldn't be heard in the wards; otherwise the matron would have had it stopped even if she had had to call the police, which she had actually done on other occasions.

'Raucous medical students are not going to disturb my patients,' she said to the Dean. She was a spinster whose life had been devoted to nursing and the Dean sometimes wondered whether she had known any 'raucous students' when she was a young nurse. 'I doubt it,' he thought.

Melanie Clarkson and John Wright had had too much to drink. They went off to the Women's Common Room and John put his arm round her and gently pulled her towards him. She didn't resist when he kissed her. They sat on the long green leather sofa, which he had last shared with Jane Perkins, and talked for a long time.

The music stopped. They could hear Jeremy shouting. 'Just one more time.' Melanie knew he would be standing with his baton raised.

'I first met Nellie 'Awkins down the Old Kent Road,

Her drawers were hanging down.

She'd been with Charlie Brown.

I put a filthy sixpence in her filthy . . . hand,

She was a dirty old 'ore.'

'I don't think I'll ever get used to these medical school songs,' Melanie said.

Wright got up and closed the door.

'Come on now,' she said, 'how did you get into my flat?'

'I paid a cat burglar a large sum of money.'

'Please – tell me.'

'If you come out one evening, I'll tell all.' He leant across and kissed her.

'All right,' she said finally, 'but Jeremy had better not know.'

'You sound as if you're married to him already.'

'We're sort of engaged,' Melanie shrugged. 'He's been my steady for some years. He'd be very cross if he found out.'

The Common Room door opened and Jeremy Fawcett stood there slightly unstable.

'When the cats away . . .' he said, making no effort to hide his displeasure.

Melanie stood up quickly, sensing there might be some unpleasantness, and took his arm.

'It's time to go,' she said. 'Goodnight John,' and quickly led Fawcett out of the room.

They met in Shepherds' Market in Mayfair the following evening. John felt very apprehensive. He didn't think that Melanie would turn up. They had both had too much to drink the previous night, and he was sure that in the sober light of the next day she would have second thoughts. To his joy, however, she came into the pub fifteen minutes after the arranged time.

'I'm sorry I'm late,' she said, 'I didn't want to arrive before you and have to wait.' She laughed. 'I might have been mistaken for a Mayfair version of Nellie 'Awkins and been propositioned.'

'I thought you wouldn't come.'

'Well, I'm here.'

John felt quite relaxed and talked easily to her. She told him a lot about her life, her childhood, her education at Roedean, and about her family. She even talked about Jeremy Fawcett.

'The families have become friends,' she said. 'Before we know what's happening, they will be arranging a wedding. My mother would love that.'

'You mustn't,' said John.

'I certainly won't if he finds out about this,' she answered. 'He gets insanely jealous about other men – especially you.'

'So he should,' said John gallantly.

Later that night at her flat she realised that she still knew nothing about John Wright. Apart from telling her about the delivery of the invitation through the roof light, most of the conversation centred around her. 'Perhaps I didn't give him a chance,' she thought. She had to admit that she found him attractive. There was no doubt that he was handsome, but it was the air of mystery about him which intrigued her. She knew his reputation but didn't want to believe that he was an out-and-out lecher. 'Perhaps he is just a frustrated romantic,' she said to herself laughing, 'with large gonads.' She was amazed at his determination to deliver the invitation and the danger involved – not only the physical risk, but the danger of the police catching him and charging him with burglary. He would have had great difficulty in persuading the police that he had climbed on to the roof of a tall house just to deliver a rose to a girl he fancied. She could imagine the station sergeant: 'pull the other one, mate.'

They travelled back to St Luke's on the upper deck of a red London bus. 'This is the easy way,' she said, as she opened the front door. He looked around the small flat. 'I couldn't see much from the roof light.'

It was a great luxury for a student to have a flat of her own, but Melanie's parents regarded it as an investment. Instead of paying rent, they had bought the flat, not only for Melanie's use but also for the younger brother who was already talking about becoming a doctor. When they had both finished their medical studies, they would sell it and make a handsome profit. 'That's how the rich live,' John thought.

They listened to some music for a short time whilst they drank their coffee. Then he kissed her goodbye and walked back to Bedside Manor.

Melanie knew how quickly the hospital grapevine worked and was becoming increasingly concerned that Jeremy would find out. She walked across from the hospital to her flat with him and summoned up the courage to tell him.

'There's something I must tell you,' she started hesitantly. Her mind was racing, her feelings confused. In a way she felt that she had been disloyal, done something underhand. She had been with Jeremy for so long that it was like letting a friend down. 'But he doesn't own me,' she thought. 'Why should I feel guilty?' But she did. 'Well,' he said lightly, 'come on. Tell me the dark secret.'

She took a deep breath. 'I've been out with John Wright.'

'How could you?' he shouted, staring at her in astonishment and anger, 'with that bastard – You know what he's like!'

Melanie didn't say anything.

'You'll be just one more on his list,' he snarled, and then added viciously: 'If you're not already.'

'It was only a drink.'

'Are you going to see him again?'

'I don't know.'

'Of course you bloody well know,' he screamed, standing over her shouting, his face drained of blood, his body shaking with anger and his right arm almost involuntarily raised as if to strike her.

'You're frightening me,' she said, 'do you have to shout? They'll hear you in the wards.'

'I don't bloody care if the Matron hears,' he shouted, 'or the Dean.'

Melanie was surprised how calm she remained. 'I'm sorry,' she said, 'I just wanted to be open with you.'

'I'll finish that animal,' Fawcett yelled, 'if its the last thing I do.' And with that he stormed out of the flat, kicking the door violently and shouting: 'Whore! Whore! Whore!' as he stumbled noisily down the uncarpeted stairs.

Melanie could still hear him shouting as he crossed the narrow road outside the flats to go back into the hospital.

For some time after he had gone, she sat quietly and cried. She had known that he wouldn't be pleased when she told him, but she hadn't expected him to react so violently. He seemed to be completely out of control. 'After all the years we've been together,' she thought, 'and I don't really know him at all.'

Eventually, she tidied herself up, put her white coat on and looked in the mirror. 'Oh well,' she said, when she saw her red eyes, and went off to meet John Wright in the Medical School Common Room. He could see that she had been crying and led her outside the crowded room into the quieter corridor.

'I've told Jeremy,' she said, 'it's all over between us.' John Wright put his arm round her, kissed her tenderly, and wiped the tears from her cheeks.

'He was so furious,' she said, 'I couldn't believe it. I'd never seen him in such a state. I thought he was going to hit me.'

Jeremy Fawcett tried to put Melanie Clarkson and John Wright out of his mind, but it was impossible. They met every day in the medical school, on teaching rounds standing round a patient's bed, in the lecture theatre and in hospital clinics. Melanie managed polite conversation but Fawcett and Wright sullenly ignored each other.

Jeremy Fawcett went out with one or two nurses, but he found the effort to be bright and entertaining a strain after the easy relationship he had enjoyed with Melanie. He decided that he didn't like women any more. He was consumed with hate and jealousy every time he saw Melanie and John together. About one week after he had stormed out of Melanie's flat, he met John Wright in the basement locker room under the Medical School. There was row after row of tall, free-standing green metal cabinets, in which medical students stored their outer clothes before donning their white coats to go into the hospital. He deliberately crashed into John Wright as he made his way to his locker.

'You're blocking the gangway,' he said menacingly, 'get out of the way!'

'Cool it,' replied Wright, 'this isn't exactly Piccadilly Circus. There's plenty of room.'

'You bastard! Get out of my way,' yelled Fawcett, as all the pent-up hatred erupted. 'There'll never be enough room for the two of us in medicine.'

'Just get lost,' said Wright, trying to ignore him. 'It's about time you grew up.' Fawcett stood close to Wright, crowding him. 'Melanie won't want you when I've done with you,' he said threateningly.

Wright pushed him away from his locker. 'Can't you understand Melanie's finished with you?' he said. 'It's all over between you.'

Fawcett became uncontrolled and violent. He rained blows on Wright's face and body. Wright felt the pain when his upper lip was crushed against his teeth by a vicious left jab, and a right cross to the side of his jaw made his head shudder. Fawcett only knew one way to fight – standing with his guard up as if he were in the boxing ring at Cambridge. He hit Wright with vicious left jabs to the face and right hands to the face and body, using Wright as a punch bag. His hands were so quick that Wright felt defenceless. Wright fell back against his locker and stayed down waiting for his head to clear.

'Get up and fight, you coward!' yelled Fawcett.

Wright had learned to fight in the East End. Whenever his father walked home from the pub through the council estate proclaiming that he was 'the uncrowned King of Ireland', all the local boys would run up and push him over.

'You're drunk! You're drunk!' they would yell as they pushed him. When he staggered to his feet, he would hurl his bowler hat at them.

'Here's your hat, your Majesty,' they would say, bringing it back to him. When he snatched at it, they would pull it away and he would fall over again.

They would follow him jeering all the way to his house.

'Get out and get my bowler!' he would say to Wright as soon as he got inside. 'And don't come back until you do.' John would be faced with the choice: fight the boys and get the hat, or return empty-handed and be beaten by his father.

He crouched by his locker until his eyes cleared. It was now the street fighter versus the public school boxer. He kept as low as he could and slowly advanced towards Fawcett. 'Come on then,' jeered Fawcett, his thin lips twisted in a cruel leer, 'if you want some more.' He beckoned Wright towards him and started to pick him off with straight lefts. Then as he set himself to deliver a right upper cut to force Wright to stand up straight, Wright suddenly hurled himself at him and forced him against the wall. He brought his knee up viciously into Fawcett's groin and as he gasped for breath, he head-butted him, following up with a crashing right to the nose. It was all over so suddenly. Fawcett staggered and lurched backwards on to the lockers, which fell like a pack of cards. His nose was distorted and his face gashed as he hit the sharp corner of a cabinet. Blood poured down his face and dripped on to his white coat. He slowly staggered to his feet. 'You'll live to regret this,' he snarled almost incoherently through his swollen bleeding lips, 'I'll hound you forever.' And he did at every opportunity. The only time he was not in daily contact with Wright over the next thirty years was when he was conscripted into the army just after qualifying and had to spend two years in the Royal Army Medical Corps.

Fawcett required immediate treatment. His forehead needed twelve stitches and the ENT surgeons had to reset his nose. For weeks he had the most vivid black eyes from the bruising. When Melanie politely enquired whether he had had an accident, he said he had tripped over in the locker room. She thought this unlikely but never connected the damaged face of John Wright with Jeremy Fawcett. He had said, 'It happened in a rugby match.'

John Wright started to see Melanie every day. They went to parties, pubs, to the theatre, using the free tickets given to the hospital when performances were not fully booked, and sometimes Melanie would cook supper in the flat. They had enormous fun together and Melanie wondered why she had put up with the dullness of her relationship with Jeremy Fawcett for so long. They were so happy in each other's company that they would sit together reading without feeling the need to make conversation. Melanie Clarkson wasn't one of those women who need attention all the time. John introduced her to the country areas of Kent he had known so well a few years earlier. They walked from Eynsford to the centuries-old flintstone church at Lullingstone and as Melanie was idly flipping the pages of the visitor's book, John Wright's name stared up at her between Jane O'Connor's above and Joyce Andrew's below.

'Which one were you with?' she asked. 'Perhaps they were both yours.'

John held his breath as Melanie flicked over the pages, and then, to his relief, she closed the book and put it back on the pile.

'There must be fifty years of signatures there,' she said. 'How many times does your name appear?'

'I was with Jane O'Connor,' he said, ignoring her question.

'What did she do?'

'It's a long story. Just a girl from the past,' he replied, 'before I got into medicine.' He hoped that would be the end of the conversation but Melanie wouldn't be put off.

'Come on,' she persisted. 'Tell me about her. Where did you meet? I'm interested.'

'It would only bore you,' he answered, taking her into his arms and kissing her.

But Melanie held him away. 'I want to know all about you,' she insisted gently. 'I need to know if I'm going to love you.'

He could have avoided the question; he was quite expert at changing the subject when the conversation moved to his background. He didn't want to talk about it. Sometimes he felt that the years of drunkenness and violence in the East End were just something he had had to endure before he could start his life. As a last resort he would say to persistent questioners: 'I don't want to talk about it.' It would take a very determined person to carry on after that. Melanie stood looking straight up at him, holding his hands without saying anything, and just waited. John led her to a pew and they sat down close to each other, and once he started, he found that the words flowed out. He spent the next two hours telling her about his childhood and his struggle to make something out of his life. Melanie sat there absolutely fascinated; she didn't interrupt once. She had been taken into a world that was completely alien to her upper middle-class protected upbringing, and she wondered whether she would be at St Luke's training to be a doctor if she had been in a similar situation.

'I knew you were different,' she said, kissing him tenderly, 'Now I know why.'

John ran out of words. He felt a sense of relief, as if he'd been under psychoanalysis giving up the hidden secrets stored in his mind for so many years.

'I'm so proud of you,' said Melanie, 'I'd like to tell the world. Perhaps I'll write an article in the *Medical School Journal*.'

'Please don't. I couldn't stand it. I'm comfortable with the mystery.'

'Okay, it's our secret,' she laughed.

They left the small church, where they had been undisturbed for two hours, and caught the Green Line bus back to London. Melanie held John's arm and pulled herself close to him. They were very quiet on the bus and the journey was half through before Melanie broke the silence. 'I'm jealous of Pauline Browne,' she said. 'Do you still think of her?'

'I still write to her in Africa; I shall never forget her.'

'Were you in love with her?'

'Yes, I was. But she was in love with medicine and the Catholic Church.'

'Well, I'm into medicine and Catholicism,' Melanie said quietly, 'can't I love you as well?'

In May she invited him to join her at the family's weekend cottage on the Kent-Surrey borders. Her parents were out of the country so the house was empty. It was less than 25 miles south of London but was in lovely countryside, quite remote, with farmland stretching endlessly below as far as the Ashdown Forest and beyond. Above the house was a thousand acres of National Trust woodland, mainly beech and ash. In the summer, throughout the hours of daylight, the view was completely unobstructed by a single house or building. At night the lights of houses hidden in the trees twinkled their presence. The house was very old. In fact Melanie said that a house had been recorded on the site in the Domesday Book. The present house had been converted from two old stone farm cottages and a cattle barn. The thick walls of Kentish sandstone and the small leaded windows kept the house cool in the summer and warm in the winter. The drawing room, known by the family as the cattle shed, had bare stone walls, an old polished red-brick floor and an oak-beamed ceiling. It was charmingly furnished with antique furniture. There was a Jacobean dresser with a marble-framed Italian mirror above, Persian carpets on the walls and floor, a large open stone fireplace, Georgian chests and a fruitwood bureau, large sofas into which one could sink, and paintings of Melanie's ancestors, as well as one of her as a smiling six-year-old with a missing front tooth. It was the most incredible house John Wright had ever been in, and he wouldn't have been surprised to see it written up in one of the fashionable magazines. His favourite room was the dining room, a dark cool room with just sufficient space for a long dining table which would seat ten. There was a brick fireplace, never used, but serving as a wine store. Hanging by its long handle on the window side of the fireplace was a lacquered copper warming-pan.

'My father used something like that,' he said, pointing at the warming pan, 'same principle anyway. Just before he went to bed he would put a brick in the fire, and when it was hot enough, he wrapped it in an old blanket and put it in his bed.'

'Sounds highly dangerous to me.'

'The blanket did scorch, but it never caught fire.'

'He'd have been better off using a warming-pan.'

Just behind Melanie's father's chair at the head of the table was an old polished pine cabinet let into the wall where a door had once been. The family collection of drinking glasses was housed there. They were mainly 18th and 19th century and when the cabinet lights were on, they sparkled like precious stones. A large oil painting of Melanie's grandfather looked down from the wall and John noticed that wherever he was in the room or in the garden outside, the piercing blue eyes appeared to follow him.

'Grandfather's watching you,' Melanie said laughing, 'you'd better behave yourself.'

Melanie's parents were dedicated gardeners who spent weekends weeding and grass cutting. And as if they hadn't enough plants to look after, they had a conservatory fitted to the house which could be entered through double doors from the drawing room. This was full of hibiscus, geraniums, French jasmine, ficus trees, mimosa and orange and lemon trees. It was a wonderful place to have a drink in the winter or early spring, and sometimes Melanie served supper there. Great care had been taken with the lighting. Lights had been hidden behind carved wooden screens, inside Cretan pithoi to shine upwards, and tucked behind plants. With a candle-lit small dining table it was a magic place. The garden was terraced into the hillside, with numerous lawns and flower beds. The swimming pool was hidden behind a high beech hedge.

Melanie had driven her parents to Gatwick, so she had use of a car. She collected John and they drove into the country. It was an unusually hot May. The garden was springing to life. Wisteria and lilac were in bloom, and the roses were beginning. John could see the giant magnolia as he looked up the garden from the swimming pool. Melanie's mother always had the pool cleared out and working by the first of May. John rolled back the blue plastic heat cover. The water was clear and blue. He checked the temperature. It was 72 F. The hot fortnight combined with the pool heating had done the trick.

'You don't need trunks,' said Melanie, 'unless you've got something you don't want me to see.'

John stood naked outside the pool hut.

'No – I'm normal, I think,' he said.

He looked at Melanie standing at the water's edge naked, preparing to dive in.

'God, you're magnificent,' he said. 'You'll drive me mad.'

'Is that a sign of madness?' she grinned, pointing at him as he dived in to hide his embarrassment. They spent the entire afternoon around the pool, swimming and playing the silly games lovers do, and then went off through the farmlands into the bluebell woods to the duck pond and back past a Plantaganet manor house for tea.

'You're pretty clued up on the countryside,' he said, when she told him the names of rare wild flowers or identified a bird call.

'I learnt at my mother's knee,' she said.

'I wonder what I learnt at my mother's knee?'

'Probably more than you think.'

The first night they dined in the kitchen. 'See whether you can find a suitable bottle,' she said. He descended the narrow stone steps to her father's wine cellar. His eyes opened wide in amazement when he saw the first-growth clarets of incomparable vintages which he had only read about. There were Margaux and Haut Brion, and even a 1928 Latour, covered in dust after more than twenty years in the cellar. 'We'll never be forgiven,' he thought, 'if we drink the best wines.' He selected a lesser wine and took it up to the kitchen, carefully holding the bottle upright as he did so, so as not to disturb any sediment.

'I didn't bring a first,' he said, 'this Giscours should be fine. I'll take the cork out to let it breathe.'

'You sound like a wine buff,' laughed Melanie.

'My father always kept a good cellar,' he quipped. They both enjoyed the joke. He doubted whether his father had ever tasted wine. Brown ale and bitter were his drinks, followed by a chaser of whisky if he had any money in his pocket or if he could find anyone to buy him one.

Melanie left him in the conservatory with a glass of cool Mersault whilst she put the finishing touches to supper. The old cottage kitchen was very small, and the dining table, with its yellow patterned table cloth, was pushed against one wall. Alongside the Chateau Giscours were two large claret glasses.

'Will you try the wine, please?' He quarter-filled the large glass and held it to the candlelight.

'Absolutely clear. A deep ruby colour with brown round the edges,' he said pompously. He gently swirled the wine around the glass to release the bouquet. 'Good fruit,' he said, sniffing it. 'Just a perfect mature claret.'

'I am impressed,' she said, knowing that he was play-acting. He had far more confidence with wine than Jeremy Fawcett had ever had.

After supper she sat him in the drawing room. 'Don't go away,' she said, 'this will keep you company until I come back.' She put a large brandy balloon of Armagnac beside him. He sat cupping the glass in his hands, the warmth releasing the distinctive bouquet of the brandy. He sank deep into the large sofa, thinking of Melanie, the house and his career. As he finished the brandy, he said out loud: 'Life's great.'

'Are you talking to yourself?' asked Melanie as she joined him on the sofa.

'I was just thinking how wonderful life was,' he said, 'how wonderful you are.' He kissed her tenderly. 'How lucky I am to be here.'

'You're only in a cowshed,' she laughed.

'Some cowshed!' he said. 'I've never seen such a beautiful house.'

They sat quietly for some minutes sensing that something important was going to happen. Melanie was the first to move. 'It's time for bed,' she said, kissing him. He put his arms round her as they climbed the narrow oak stairs to her bedroom. As they stood by the open windows, they could see rabbits playing in the moonlight on the lower lawns, and the fish pond beyond was covered with a silver sheen.

'Darling,' exclaimed Melanie as he kissed her passionately, 'I do love you.' John held her close and slowly undid the buttons on her blouse. 'Just a minute,' she said, undoing the last button and letting the blouse drop to the floor.

'Striptease?' she said as articles of clothing were discarded.

They stood naked in the moonlight and if anyone had been in the garden below, they would have seen them as ghostly figures. But they were alone. None of the thousands of pairs of eyes in the woods were human.

'Hold tight,' said John as he carried her across to the four-poster. They lay there for some time in each other's arms. They kissed passionately and began exploring each other's bodies gently with their hands. Melanie's hand moved slowly up John's inner thighs.

'You don't need that,' she said, as she carefully rolled the condom off. 'I've just finished the curse.' She felt him hesitate. 'Don't worry,' she said, 'it'll be all right.'

He was surprised to find her a virgin, but she didn't allow his concern to inhibit him. She suddenly lifted herself up and thrust on to him, holding her breath as she felt him go through the hymen. When they had finished, they lay quietly in each other's arms, wonderfully relaxed and happy.

'Were you surprised?' Melanie asked.

'Of course not.'

'Liar!' she said, biting his ear. 'Not even when I adopted the missionary position?'

'The what?'

'The missionary position. One of the consultants told us that the missionaries used to teach young women that the only moral way to make love was lying on their backs, with the man on top.'

'I thought you were just being submissive.' She pushed a pillow in his face. 'I'll soon change that,' she said, and climbed on top of him. They were too excited to sleep. 'I love you,' he said. 'I think you're terrific.'

'I am a medical student and I've read the books.' She wriggled closer to him and kissed him. 'And,' she added laughingly, 'I've made a special study of the male anatomy, just in case I got into this kind of situation.'

'Didn't you expect to?'

'A girl never knows.'

'Are you sure you won't get pregnant?'

'I'll use the rhythm method,' she said, 'we Catholics do.'

'I hope you're right.' He ran his fingers through her hair. 'I'm for belt and braces.'

'Don't worry,' she said, 'it adds to the excitement.'

She gently massaged his chest. He could feel her hands moving slowly down his body in gentle circles.

'There's only one way,' she said, 'to be a hundred percent sure.'

'No,' he said, 'no, not the operation! I won't have it.'

She continued caressing his thighs with her finger tips.

'Not surgery,' she laughed, as she took her hand away, 'abstinence.'

'Okay,' he joked, 'I'll take the surgery.'

Over the next five days they were obsessed with making love at any time of the day or night, even in the woods. At night they would swim in the water made incandescent by the underwater lighting and then dry each other as they ran upstairs to bed.

Melanie periodically burst into song.

'We are from Roedean.

Good girls we are,

We have lost our virginity.'

Jeremy Fawcett's name only came up once.

'All those years together,' said John, 'it must have been hell for him at times.'

'There were moments when I thought he was going to take me by storm,' she said reflectively. 'I suppose I hoped he would at the time. But I'm glad it didn't happen; if it had, we wouldn't be here now. I'm really old-fashioned, a one-man girl.'

She pulled John towards her. 'He wasn't so primitive as you,' she said, kissing him passionately. 'He didn't rouse my animal instincts.' And they made love on the sofa where they were.

After five wonderful days they returned to St Luke's and saw each other every day. John spent a lot of time in Melanie's flat opposite the hospital without actually moving in. At the beginning of August they went up to the flat after a day in the hospital, Melanie poured two glasses of dry sherry and sat down beside John.

'John, darling,' she said, without any preamble, 'I'm pregnant. I've missed two periods and I've had the test.' John recoiled as if he had been hit in the solar plexus. He felt the colour drain from his face and the breath from his body.

'I'm sorry. It's my fault. You wanted to take precautions,' said Melanie. 'You looked shocked.'

'I am,' he said.

'What d'you want to do?' she asked. 'There's no way I'm going to try to get rid of it – even if it could be done legally.'

'We'll have to get married,' he said, beginning to recover his composure.

'Just to make an honest woman of me?'

'No, because I love you,' he replied, kissing her fondly.

'Don't marry me out of any sense of duty,' she said, even though at that time, in the 1950's, she was well aware of the social disgrace a baby out of wedlock would be. It had been drummed into her since childhood.

'I do love you,' he said, holding her in his arms. 'I want to spend the rest of my life with you.' He kissed her. 'What will your parents say?'

'They won't be pleased – their darling daughter pregnant.'

Melanie's parents were even more shocked than John Wright had been. Sir David Clarkson was a tall man with almost white hair, good features and a face with myriads of smile lines around his eyes and mouth as if he were just about to grin. He was a man who smiled a lot but his face had no hint of humour as he sat thoughtfully facing John and Melanie.

'I can't say I'm happy about this,' he said, 'but what's happened has happened; we'll have to face up to it.' He was sure that Melanie wouldn't have got into this situation with a casual acquaintance.

Melanie could see the strain on John's face. She squeezed his hand reassuringly. It couldn't be easy for him to meet her parents for the first

41

time under these circumstances.

'Daddy, darling,' she said, 'we were planning to get married on qualification. This has just brought it forward a little; that's all.' Then she kissed him on the cheek.

Sir David relaxed and went out of the room returning with a bottle of Veuve Cliquot and four champagne flutes. His face smiled for the first time.

'To your happiness,' he said, raising his glass, and then he added laughing: 'And to my first grandchild.' They finished the bottle of champagne without any difficulty.

'You'll have our full support,' he said. 'In a few years time this slight hiccup in timing will be irrelevant.' With that he went to bed.

'Melanie, you'd better both sleep in your bed tonight,' her mother said. 'You're virtually married anyway.' She laughed. 'If you started in separate beds, I'd be disappointed if you didn't get together during the night.'

She felt strangely uneasy sleeping with John in her parents' house with her parents there, in spite of her mother's encouragement. Lady Clarkson kissed them goodbye as they left for St Luke's the following morning. John Wright found this embarrassing because his mother had never kissed him as a child, and he wasn't used to this form of greeting. When they had left, Melanie's parents spent hours talking about their daughter's future. They knew nothing about John except that he was a medical student.

'I suppose that's something,' remarked Sir David, 'at least he'll have a job. But it would have been so much easier if she'd married Jeremy Fawcett.'

'Maybe,' his wife rejoined, 'I haven't said this before, but I found Jeremy rather dull at times.' She laughed. 'He wasn't very exciting. I can't imagine him getting Melanie pregnant before marriage.'

John Wright moved into Melanie's flat; there was no point in paying rent for Bedside Manor.

'At least we don't have to worry about contraception for a while,' she said as she lay in John Wright's arms in bed on their first night in her flat.

The forthcoming marriage and baby had concentrated their minds. They were both determined to carve out careers in medicine. John had decided that it had to be surgery. Melanie was going for anaesthetics or obstetrics and gynaecology – obs and gobs. General practice was not for them; but their first concern was to qualify. The hard slog to become consultants would come later, and would require years of training in appointments approved by the Royal Medical Colleges, as well as passing higher examinations.

'Leave all the arrangements to Mother,' Melanie said. 'She'll love it; all we have to do is to turn up.'

Melanie's mother wasn't happy with a registry office. She had wanted a wedding in their local Catholic church where Melanie had gone to Mass every Sunday when she was at home, with a grand reception in the garden.

'At least,' she said to David Clarkson, 'we must make an occasion of it. It'll have to be an up-market registry office and then Claridges.' He raised his eyebrows at the mention of Claridges.

'It would have cost much more at home,' she said, 'what with the marquée, the caterers, hundreds of guests. There'll only be about twenty now.'

Of the twenty, ten were medical students from St Luke's. John's old friend Logan was best man, and McTaggart was there with Birdie in her special hat, which she kept for church and weddings. The rest were Melanie's family. Pauline Browne sent a telegram from Africa: 'Much happiness. All my love and God bless.' Melanie's parents did wonder where John's family were, but accepted whatever explanation Melanie had given them. The wedding was a happy, relaxed occasion, and apart from one rendering of 'Why was he born so beautiful?' the medical students were surprisingly well behaved. Melanie's father and the best man, Logan, made witty speeches, and after the last guest had gone, the couple returned to their room in the hotel. Their honeymoon was to remain at Claridges for the weekend. A bottle of champagne sat unopened in an ice bucket to be consumed later.

'You looked wonderful,' said John, taking Melanie in his arms. 'I was so proud.'

'Don't squash junior,' she laughed. 'D'you think they knew?' She smoothed the front of her dress. 'Does it show?'

Melanie was one of those women who didn't really notice until she was well into the pregnancy. Certainly the medical fraternity was not aware for some months. Jeremy Fawcett noticed first.

'Putting on weight, Melanie?' he asked, and when to his surprise she blushed, he said sneeringly, 'Any morning sickness?' The other medical students in the firm all stared at her. 'Melanie, you didn't tell us!'

'I'm going off Jeremy Fawcett,' she said at lunch, 'I can't believe I spent so many years with such a hateful man.'

They planned to stay in the flat although it was four floors up and not ideal for a baby, or for the increasingly pregnant Melanie.

'Why don't you come down and spend the last three months with us?' asked Melanie's mother. 'The country air will do you good.'

'No,' said Melanie firmly, 'I want to be a doctor and a mother. I'm determined to continue at St Luke's.'

She continued her medical studies, often working with John, testing each other's knowledge, which reminded him of the time he had studied with Pauline Browne to get into university. Ward rounds during the later stages were a little uncomfortable, but the teaching consultant and the ward sister looked after her. She was provided with a chair each time the teaching group gathered round a patient's bed. The baby boy was delivered by Caesarean section at St Luke's, and a week later Lady Clarkson drove Melanie, John and the baby down to the country.

Within a relatively short time Melanie got her life organised around her baby. When she couldn't take the baby with her, she would leave it in the maternity wing and pop in and feed it during the day. Everyone in the hospital was very helpful. They both worked hard. John Wright became obsessive and studied for twelve to fourteen hours a day. He always seemed to be on a ward round, in a clinic, at a lecture or in the medical school library, or, whenever he could, in the operating theatre.

'Aren't you burning the midnight oil too much?' asked Melanie.

'No, I'm fine,' he answered. 'Don't worry, I'm hooked on medicine; I'm an addict. I can't learn enough.' He kissed her. 'Anyway, I started late; I've got to catch up.'

His efforts were rewarded when he sat his final examinations and was awarded the University of London Gold Medal for the best medical student in the entire university.

He never left St Luke's. The hospital was anxious to keep him, partly because of his obvious potential but also because he was still playing rugby for the first fifteen. The selection committee allocating house surgeon's jobs spent hours deliberating on the relative merits of the newly qualified doctors. Suddenly the door burst open. 'I want Wright,' said the senior surgeon, a rugby fanatic and former Cambridge blue: 'Don't send me anyone else.' And as he walked out, he added, 'If you do, I'll send them straight back.'

Even though they were now doctors, the relentless study continued as they trained to be specialists. Life was busy, but they sat down every evening for an aperitif. It had become a ritual, and they usually drank dry white wine.

'What a fascinating time,' said John, savouring his Chablis.

'To be . . .?' Melanie asked.

'To be a surgeon,' he said, 'what else?'

'What's changed?'

'The first kidney transplant,' he said excitedly. 'From one twin to the other. This is only the start,' he said, not giving Melanie a chance to reply. 'Soon it'll be livers, hearts, lungs – you name it.'

'What about the spare parts?'

'No problem, patients will donate them,' he assured her. 'It'll become the norm. If you have an accident your organs will be used.'

'Maybe,' she said. 'I'm not sure that when I die I want to be cut up and farmed around.'

Substituting a diseased or damaged organ had long been the dream of surgeons. They were beginning to overcome the technical problems, but rejection was something else. The rejection of foreign cells was one of the body's most fundamental defences and it wasn't going to give this up lightly.

Many people remember what they were doing when President Kennedy was assassinated. John Wright remembered what he was doing when the first heart transplant was carried out by the South African Professor Christian Barnard in 1967. The replacement of a human heart captured not only his imagination, but that of the entire world.

In less than ten years Wright was a consultant surgeon at St Luke's. Melanie was following a similar path in anaesthetics but her second pregnancy delayed her progress. He often wondered why they had only two children. It was nothing he was doing; Melanie must be using some kind of contraception.

'Here's to number three,' he said, raising his glass after a very passionate weekend. She kissed him tenderly, 'I expect you're sterile by now,' she said smiling, 'or I'm barren.'

John Wright had a real flair for surgery. It all looked so easy when he operated. Other surgeons would say that if they were for 'the chop', they would want him to carry out the operation. He became more and more involved in transplant surgery and after a few years, did nothing else. He was innovative and carried out transplants which no other surgeon would attempt. He was always pushing out the frontiers, and was already being talked about as a surgeon with a great future. His success was not only based on his surgical skills, but on his meticulous planning of a new operation. He left nothing to chance.

Seven years after being made up to consultant, he walked into the operating theatre at St Luke's to meet his new theatre sister.

'Hello, I'm Jane Perkins – replacing Sister Joan,' she said. 'D'you remember me?'

## Chapter Three

John Wright was taken aback, and momentarily at a loss for words.

'Of course I do,' he said, moving towards her to shake hands. 'You haven't changed.'

'It's been a long time,' she said.

She was indeed as attractive and shapely as she had been when she had initiated him into the seamier side of medical school life. John Wright put this out of his mind as he scrubbed up to carry out a kidney transplant. Jane Perkins still used her maiden name at work, even though she had been married. She was cool and efficient and everything went like clockwork in the theatre. He enjoyed working with his new sister. Their relationship in the operating theatre was strictly professional. He called her 'Sister' and she called him 'Mr Wright' or 'Sir'.

They had worked together for about six months and at the end of a session they would have coffee with the other members of the transplant team. About a week before Christmas they had just finished the list when Jane Perkins produced a bottle of brandy. 'I thought we'd have an early Christmas drink,' she said, pouring out the brandy.

'That's the last thing I want', Wright thought, but he had to join in. The other staff gradually left. 'We might as well finish this,' she said, refilling his glass. 'We deserve it; it's been a long session.'

'I must be going,' he said, 'I've things to do.'

'It is Christmas,' replied Jane, 'we haven't got a list until next year.'

As she leaned over him to refill his glass, he could feel her breasts firmly against his shoulder. He finished his brandy and stood up. 'Thank you for the coffee and brandy, Jane,' he said. 'Have a good Christmas.'

'That's no way to wish me a Happy Christmas,' she protested, standing in front of him. 'Aren't you going to kiss me? You can do better than that,' she said, as he kissed her lightly on the cheek. 'Let me show you.' She pulled him close and kissed him with her mouth invitingly open, and when, after an initial resistance, he responded, she ran the tip of her tongue slowly around his lips, tracing the borders of his mouth. When he finally broke away, he

46

almost ran from the theatre. He tried not to think about her over the next few weeks, but every now and again she seemed to drift into his mind for no apparent reason. He would be reading an article in *The British Medical Journal* and would find himself thinking of his first night with her in the medical school when he was a new student. She seemed to be getting more attractive each time he met her. She had changed her hair style and whenever their eyes met above their face masks, he recognised both an invitation and a challenge. He knew she was available if he dared. She was a determined woman but he had no intention of getting involved with her – not even, he said to himself, for 'a one-night stand'. She had certainly stirred him, but most men would have been excited by a beautiful woman behaving as she did. He remembered that every time he got close to her in the old days, and they kissed, they would make love. It was a kind of conditioned reflex and it wouldn't take much for it to rise again.

'But this is fantasy,' he said sternly to himself. 'It was just a Christmas kiss.'

His relationship with Jane Perkins changed dramatically when he was called back to the hospital at 2.00 a.m. to deal with an emergency following a kidney transplant. He scrubbed and gowned and moved into the theatre. He was fairly certain that there was internal bleeding. Jane Perkins fed the instruments into his hands as he worked to stop the haemorrhage, and then the patient was taken back to the ward with a drip still feeding into a vein in the arm to maintain blood pressure. Everyone except Jane Perkins had left the theatre, either to return to duty or to their beds. John Wright had removed his gloves, gown, and operating boots, and was standing in his underpants when she came into the surgeon's room.

'You're still in good shape,' she said admiringly, as she put a cup of coffee down on a small table. 'You haven't lost much.' He started to put his shirt over his head.

'What's the hurry?' she said, moving towards him, 'you haven't got a train to catch.'

She moved closer and then quickly flicked the light switch off.

'For Christ's sake,' he shouted, 'turn the light on.' She put her arms round his waist. 'Don't make so much noise,' she laughed, 'you'll ruin my reputation.'

'Jane, I'm a married man,' he said, 'and I intend to stay that way.' She pulled him closer. 'This won't harm your marriage,' she said, 'this is just for old times' sake.' He tried to break free. He could feel her hands around his waist, moving round inch by inch, slowly slipping down his underpants.

'We must stop,' he said, making a half-hearted attempt to pull away, but she gently continued, slipping them over his hips and then on until she reached his genitalia. She paused there and he was so quiet that she knew that all his resistance had ended.

'D'you want me to stop?' she asked.

'God, no,' he said, and started kissing her passionately: her face; her neck; her breasts.

'Don't eat me,' she said, and quickly left the room to return with a pile of green operating gowns.

'All sterile,' she said laughing, as she laid them on the floor. She placed a chair back under the door handle so that it couldn't be opened. 'Just in case,' she said. They made love on the floor; she had lost none of her old skills.

Afterwards they lay together. 'Thank you,' she said, kissing him, 'I've wanted you again ever since we started working together.'

As John Wright drove home he was filled with remorse, cursing himself for his inability to control himself or the situation. It mustn't happen again; but Jane Perkins had other ideas. She found it easy to seduce him. 'You're my love machine,' she would say as he reacted spontaneously to her touch. 'One flick of the switch and you're alight.'

Before long they were meeting twice a week in her flat. They never went out.

When he arrived they had a glass of champagne and then got into bed. Afterwards she would give him supper and he would leave.

'I'm conducting some research on pancreas transplants,' he told Melanie. 'The only time I can find is in the evening.' She trusted him completely, and even when she rang his office in the hospital and got no reply, she just assumed that he didn't want to be disturbed. The affair went on for six months and Jane Perkins became more and more emotionally involved. She knew she was a bit of a nymphomaniac, 'but this is more than sex,' she told herself, 'it's filling my entire mind.' She could think of nothing else but John Wright: how loving he was, how handsome and kind, how intelligent and understanding, how empty life would be without him.

'I'm deeply in love with you,' she said, clinging to him as he tried to leave. 'I can't bear you leaving me to go back to Melanie.' She sobbed in his arms. 'You can't love her,' she cried, 'or you wouldn't come here twice a week. Why don't you leave her and come and live with me?'

John Wright was startled. 'How naive I've been,' he thought, 'in imagining that this could just go on until she became bored or found someone else.'

'I'm very fond of you,' he said, 'but I can't leave my wife and family. You wouldn't want that.'

'I must have you,' she sobbed hysterically, 'I've always wanted you from the first night we spent in the medical school.' He tried gently to move away, but she clung to him. 'If we'd met later on, near qualification,' she said, 'we'd have married – I know we would.'

John knew that there had never been any likelihood of that. Jane had always been a 'bike', always game for a good ride. She quietened, and he kissed her goodbye, determined to end the affair. Their professional training enabled them to cope with their work together. Wright made sure that he wasn't left alone in the operating theatre with her. He never saw her outside the hospital for three weeks until the private telephone rang in his office.

'I must see you,' said Jane, 'I must talk to you.' Whatever happened, he was not going to meet her outside the hospital again. She must have had plenty of men friends since she divorced her husband four years before. Some of them must have been serious but she'd got over them. 'It will all settle down in time,' he thought.

'Jane, it wouldn't help,' he said, 'affairs do end.' He could hear her crying. 'I must see you,' she said. 'If you won't come here, we can meet in London.'

'I can't,' he replied. 'We must make a clean break.'

'You must help me,' she pleaded, 'it's destroying me; I can't sleep.' She sobbed down the telephone: 'Please help me, I'm frightened I'll do something silly.'

They met in a bar in the Strand, close to the Savoy Hotel. He was shocked to see her tear-stained face. This wasn't the tough, resilient woman he had known. He put his arm round her and talked to her gently, but she was beyond reason.

'You're not going to leave me,' she shouted, bursting into renewed tears. 'I won't let you!' The whole bar stopped to listen and stare at them. John Wright got her out of the bar and drove her home.

'Jane, I'm sorry,' he said, 'I hate seeing you so upset.'

'I'll tell your wife,' she threatened. 'Then we'll see who's upset.'

He tried to kiss her on the cheek but she pulled away. He turned and left her at the open door, sobbing hysterically and shouting: 'Don't leave me. Please!'

As he drove home, he couldn't believe that she would contact Melanie. When she calmed down, she would see how pointless that would be. She was basically a mature woman of the world, who would cope sensibly with life. He met her twice a week in the theatre and was alarmed by the change in her appearance. He was as charming and friendly as he could be to her, but she became more and more sullen. Her face was pale and drawn with deep dark shadows under her eyes.

'What's happened to our serene and confident Sister?' his registrar asked.

'I think you should have a word with her; she looks ghastly.' He added lightheartedly, 'It may be just the menopause.'

John Wright stayed behind and talked quietly and supportively, trying not to sound like a doctor consoling the distressed relative of a patient.

'What can I do to help?' he asked sympathetically. She immediately burst into tears. He put his arm round her as she sobbed loudly. 'I thought you were different,' she said, 'but you've just used me.'

'That's not true,' he replied, 'it wasn't like that.'

'You just wanted sex,' she said, 'like all the other students and doctors over the years.'

'No, it was more than that,' he said, trying to calm her.

'I'm no more important to you than a piece of furniture,' she said, 'just an object to satisfy you.' She cried quietly. 'Why can't we carry on as before? I promise, I won't be a nuisance.' She was in his arms. 'Please, I won't make any demands on you. Just come and see me whenever you want to.'

'We must make a clean break,' he insisted gently.

'No, I can't,' she said, beginning to sob again. 'I'll kill myself.'

'Wouldn't it be better,' he said, 'if you moved to another theatre so that we weren't in weekly contact?'

'You don't want me as your mistress any longer,' she screamed, 'and now you don't want me in the same operating theatre.' What little reason she had left had disappeared. 'You're just a selfish bastard. You're wife is going to know what a shit you are.' He tried to quieten her down but she had really flipped.

She stayed in the theatre after he had left, sobbing incessantly. 'What's the point?' she asked herself. 'I'll show him.' She went across to the anaesthetic machine and turning on the oxygen and nitrous oxide, held the nose-piece to her face. 'I can't take any more,' she muttered as she sucked the gases deeply into her lungs, like a drowning man gasping for air. 'I must escape,' she said as she clambered on to the operating table. As the gases seeped into her system, she calmed. She leaned over to the anaesthetic machine and pushed the halothane lever across. 'Just a touch,' she mumbled, 'I must sleep; I've had enough pain.' She drifted into unconsciousness in the empty theatre.

'Christ!' said the night sister as she pushed open the swing doors to the theatre some hours later. Jane Perkins was lying alongside the operating table, her right leg bent awkwardly under her body and blood oozing from a cut on the side of her face. 'I can just about feel a pulse,' she said to the staff nurse with her, 'push the machine across.' She held a face mask in position and turned on the emergency oxygen. As she lifted the chin, it freed the airway and the breathing became easier. Whilst she waited, she stemmed the bleeding with a pressure pack. She could hear the staff nurse on the telephone: 'Casualty Officer and anaesthetist to Theatre 1,' and within minutes they were there.

Jane spent the next few weeks in a private ward. The consultant psychiatrist spent many hours talking to her. He was sure she wasn't addicted to anaesthetic gases and he didn't believe she had intended to kill herself. After all, he thought, the anaesthetic machine wasn't set to dangerously high levels, and Jane Perkins had been around operating theatres for many years. If she had wanted to end it, she would hardly have bothered with such a high percentage of oxygen or used such a small amount of halothane. 'With the settings you used,' he laughed, 'you'd still have been there if you hadn't fallen off the table.'

Jeremy Fawcett visited her in his capacity as the doctor who looked after the nurses. 'How are you, today?' he asked in his best bedside manner. Her leg had been set and splinted with a plaster cast. 'I'm fine,' she said laughing, 'you can sign my plaster, if you like.'

'Jane,' he said, 'what's it all about?' He had known her since they were students and he knew she was a pretty tough woman who had been around; not the kind of person he would have expected to attempt suicide.

'I wasn't trying to kill myself,' she said. 'I just wanted some relief from the black depression I was in.'

'D'you want to talk about it?'

'I don't mind; you're my doctor,' she said. 'It's all confidential, isn't it?' She told him the whole story of her affair with John Wright.

'With John Wright?' he said incredulously, 'What are you going to do about it?'

'I was going to write to his wife, but what's the point?'

'Don't you think he's just used you?'

'I suppose so, but I've used him,' she said. 'He was desperately important to me; I wanted him to use me.'

'But he's a hospital surgeon, with wife and children,' said Fawcett, 'he shouldn't have allowed it to happen.'

She looked at him and noticed the jagged scar running obliquely down across his forehead. 'Why didn't you get that scar fixed?' she asked. He was momentarily taken aback by her sudden change of direction.

'I couldn't be bothered,' he said. 'Anyway, it would still be underneath.'

'That sounds mysterious,' she said, beginning to talk to him as a man rather than as her doctor. 'Makes you look rugged. I don't like men who are too pretty.'

Fawcett didn't want light conversation; he certainly didn't want to flirt with her, but he wanted her on his side.

'Don't you think you should tell Wright's wife? Isn't it your duty?'

'I'll think about it,' she said unenthusiastically.

She was calm and relaxed with the anti-depressants. Soon after Fawcett left, the nurse came in with a large bouquet of flowers. She looked at the card: 'So sorry, get better soon, John.' He hadn't been to see her and she wasn't sure how she would react if he did.

Two days later Fawcett joined some colleagues and their wives for dinner, and to his horror John and Melanie Wright were also there. 'God,' he thought, 'do I have to make friendly conversation with Wright all evening? Perhaps not,' he said to himself. 'Great shame about Jane Perkins,' he said looking at Wright, 'can't think how such a stable woman got herself into such a mess.'

'Perhaps she was addicted to halothane,' suggested Melanie. 'It's happened before to theatre staff.'

'More likely depression,' Fawcett said, 'an unhappy love affair. Don't you think, John?' He enjoyed watching Wright squirm.

'Who knows? answered Wright, 'but it is very sad.'

Fawcett looked across the table at Melanie. 'Jesus,' he thought, 'you look radiant tonight.' She seemed to get more beautiful with age. 'That bastard Wright deserves all he gets, cheating on her.'

He visited Jane the next day. 'Have you decided whether you're going to write to Melanie?' he asked, 'I think you should.'

'Aren't you going to ask about my leg?' she teased, 'or is this just social?'

'I'm sorry, but I do feel strongly about this.'

'No, I can't,' she said calmly. 'He wouldn't come back to me; he'd just hate me for the rest of his life.' She shrugged her shoulders. 'What's the point? It's happened before, it'll happen again.'

That evening Fawcett sat in his room drinking whisky, his mind racing. Eventually he said to himself: 'I've waited years for this.' He typed the letter on plain white paper.

Dear Mrs Wright,

I thought you should know that I have been having an affair with John for the past six months. We've been meeting every Tuesday and Thursday in my flat. I knew John many years ago when he was a medical student and have been working with him in the theatre since January last year.

I hate to write this letter, but we are desperately in love and want to live together. We seemed thrown together by fate and couldn't help ourselves.

    I'm sorry to cause you so much unhappiness.
            Yours sincerely,
              Jane Perkins

Before signing the letter, he studied the consent form Jane Perkins had signed before the operation on her leg. He practised on a sheet of paper over and over again until he could sign her name identically. He drank another large whisky before going out and posting the letter.

Two days later, on a Saturday morning, Melanie Wright was going through her personal post. Some bills, a letter from George, her son at boarding school, the latest edition of *The British Medical Journal* and a letter in a blue envelope. She looked at it curiously. 'Hm,' she said sniffing. 'No scent; must be a man.' She slit open the envelope with an ivory handled paper knife and as she read, she trembled. She was ashen. All the blood had drained from her face. She could hear her teeth chattering inside her head. Her chest felt so tight that she could scarcely breathe. John Wright had popped into the hospital to see a patient and then they were going to Melanie's parents for the weekend. He came back into the house cheerfully and immediately saw that Melanie was upset. She didn't say anything, but handed him the letter.

'I'm terribly sorry; I've been so stupid,' he said, 'It didn't mean anything. All that talk of loving her is nonsense.'

'With that woman?' she shouted, 'She's been with nearly every doctor in the hospital!'

'I don't want to blame her,' he said abjectly, 'but she made all the running.'

'Wasn't I exciting enough for you?' Melanie screamed, 'were you just bored with me?'

'No, it wasn't like that.'

'What was it like then?' Was it love?'

'No, it wasn't love.'

'It was lust!' she shouted. 'It was available and you couldn't resist. It was there, so you took it.'

She looked at him with contempt. 'You've destroyed the family, and all you can say is that it was someone else's fault. How pathetic you are.'

'I'm sorry,' he said miserably, 'I don't know how I let it happen.'

'I'm not sharing my husband with anyone else. Marriage is sacred to me.' She paused, breathing deeply. 'I'd have trusted you with my life,' she said, breaking into tears.

'Surely our marriage can survive one meaningless affair?' he pleaded, 'at least let's talk about it.'

'There's nothing to talk about,' Melanie retorted. 'We're finished; it's over.'

'But the affair ended weeks ago. That's why she wrote to you,' he said, 'out of spite.' He moved towards her but she put her arm out to stop him. 'Don't touch me,' she said.

'I've even had her removed from Theatre 1,' he said, 'so that we don't work together.'

Melanie shook her head. 'No, I couldn't trust you any more,' she said, 'I don't want to spend the rest of my life looking over my shoulder for the next affair to surface.'

'But, I promise,' he said, 'it won't happen again. Please forgive me. Let's start again.' He could see that nothing he was saying was having any effect on her.

'I know how much I've hurt you,' he said despondently, 'I'll never forgive myself, but what are you going to gain from breaking up the marriage?'

'At least I'll retain my pride,' said Melanie.

She picked up her weekend bag. 'I'll divorce you as quickly as I can,' she said, 'and I don't want to find you here when I return tomorrow evening.'

John Wright collapsed in an armchair. Tears filled his eyes. 'How could I have destroyed the most important thing in my life?' he said to himself. He sat with tears streaming down his face for hours, something he had rarely done before even as a child. He had never been so disturbed in his entire life. He knew that he would have to move out, but he was hopeful that after a short while Melanie would relent and forgive him. He packed two suitcases and moved into a small hotel. During the next weeks he telephoned her repeatedly but she remained adamant and wouldn't even discuss a reconciliation. 'The divorce is in the hands of my solicitor and he will be making contact,' was all she would say and, true to her word, the divorce went through with maximum speed. After the divorce he saw his children George and Sara fairly often at half term and during the 'long vacs', but even though he tried to be bright and cheerful, he could see that they were deeply hurt. They felt that he had let them down. 'And I have,' he thought. 'And all I wanted was to provide them with a stable, loving environment, in complete contrast to my own childhood.'

When he met Jane Perkins in an outpatients' department, she said:

'I'm sorry about your divorce.'

'I bet you are, you bitch,' he said. 'I hope you're satisfied.' He never spoke to her again until they were thrown together by chance some years later. If he saw her in the hospital, he would walk past ignoring her, staring straight ahead as if she weren't there.

Melanie was working at St John's, another London hospital, as a consultant anaesthetist, but their paths seldom crossed. They occasionally met at the children's schools, or when the children were being shuttled from one parent to the other as the children of divorced parents are. Three years after the divorce, Melanie wrote him a letter to let him know that she was re-marrying and to congratulate him on his election to the Council of the Royal College of Surgeons.

Her friendship with Jeremy Fawcett was renewed after a chance meeting at the Royal Society of Medicine and after a short time she agreed to marry him.

She couldn't pretend that it was the passionate relationship she had enjoyed with John Wright, but she was quite fond of Jeremy and knew him quite well.

'I'm surprised you haven't married before,' Melanie said.

'I never really got over losing you to that bastard Wright,' he replied. 'I knew he'd let you down sooner or later.'

'So you were just waiting to pick up the pieces?' She smiled, and kissed him gently.

They developed what she called a comfortable relationship. But it wasn't easy to forget Wright even if she had wanted to. Whenever she picked up a medical journal, there would be an article by him on transplant surgery. His output was prolific. He must be spending his entire life on work, she thought, and she wasn't surprised to read a review of his text book on surgery, which had just been published. Not only was John Wright operating, writing and carrying on his research, but he was devoting many hours to his duties at the Royal College of Surgeons. He was already being talked about as a future President.

Sir Roy Summerfield sat in his magnificent scarlet and gold Presidential gown, with his Vice President on his right and the Secretary of the College on his left. The ornate silver College mace rested on the table in front of him. He waited for the members to quieten before announcing the next item on the agenda. As soon as he announced 'Election of President,' all conversation stopped and he could sense the immediate atmosphere of tension and excitement in the Council Chamber.

'I've finished my three-year term,' he said, looking round the room at many of the leading figures in surgery, 'so you will have to elect a new President this time. And I don't have to remind you of the importance of the Royal College in medicine and surgery.' As he went on, the surgeon next to Wright leaned towards him; 'But I'm sure he's going to.'

'We are concerned with promoting the highest possible standards in surgery,' the President continued, 'and because of our long history and prestige, we can speak with authority to Government, to universities and even to the Prime Minister. And I know you will bear all this in mind when you elect your new President.'

He sat down and nodded to the College Secretary, who sent the ballot papers round the long oak tables. The name of every eligible member was listed.

John Wright sat quietly in the oak-panelled room, looking up at the portraits of famous surgeons. Immediately facing him was the portrait of John Hunter, the eighteenth-century surgeon, the father of modern surgery. Out of the fifty eligible members, only five received any votes in the first round. The College Secretary counted the votes. 'There is no overall winner,' he announced. 'The member with the lowest number of votes will drop out.' After the third ballot the voting was 18, 18, 14. Wright and Fawcett were level at 18 votes each.

Jeremy Fawcett sat with his mouth so dry that he had difficulty speaking to his neighbour. For months Fawcett had been discreetly lobbying, entertaining members at his club, dining them at his home, having long telephone conversations with them. 'What are the floating fourteen going to do?' he muttered to himself. The final ballot papers were distributed. 'It is now between Mr Wright and Mr Fawcett,' the Secretary announced.

Wright and Fawcett watched the two separate piles as the Secretary counted the ballot papers. They looked identical.

'It's neck and neck, John,' his neighbour said. Wright and Fawcett held their breath as the Secretary stopped counting, expecting him to stand up and announce the result; but instead he started to recount. At last he was satisfied, and rose to his feet to give the result of the election.

'Mr Fawcett 26 votes, Mr Wright 24 votes.'

The President stood up: 'I declare that Mr Fawcett has been elected President and wish him every success.'

At the end of the meeting, Wright went up to Fawcett. 'Congratulations,' he said, offering his hand. He knew he could never be President now because his term on Council would be finished before the next election in three years' time. During the remainder of his time there he would have to sit and watch Fawcett conducting the affairs of the College.

Fawcett left the meeting and telephoned Melanie.

'I've done it,' he said excitedly, 'I've pipped Wright at the post.'

'Congratulations,' she said happily, although she did spare a thought for John Wright and secretly wouldn't have been too upset if he had won.

'Thank you, my lady.' Fawcett knew that a knighthood almost went with the job.

'We'll deal with that if it comes,' replied Melanie pragmatically.

In the middle of November he received an official-looking letter at his home. Melanie picked it up. It was marked 'Urgent, Personal' and 'From the Prime Minister'.

'What's the Prime Minister writing to you about?' she said, handing it to him. 'I didn't know you were so well connected.'

He opened the letter carefully and then let out a yell.

'Wow. Just read this.'

Melanie read: 'The Prime Minister has it in mind to submit your name to the Queen with a recommendation . . . she raced to the end of the sentence – 'a knight'. She was so excited that she scarcely took in the next line. 'Before doing so, will you assure the Prime Minister that this is agreeable to you.'

'Darling,' she said, throwing her arms round him, 'I'm so pleased for you.' She picked up the letter again.

'It's only November. We're going to have to keep this secret for almost two months until the Honours List is published.' All thought of continuing breakfast had gone. 'It'll be unbearable,' she said. 'Not even being able to tell my parents.' Jeremy Fawcett took the letter from her. 'It's not every day we get a letter like this.'

Just a few miles away John Wright sat alone at breakfast opening a similar letter. His enormous contribution to surgery had been recognised by the Establishment. It was a complete surprise to him. It was something he had never thought about once he had failed to become President of the Royal College of Surgeons.

'Life's a funny old game,' he said, smiling wryly. 'Who knows what's round the corner?'

Jeremy Fawcett checked the New Year's Honours List in the morning newspaper to make sure that there hadn't been some terrible mistake and it hadn't gone through. The thrill of pride when he saw his name quickly turned to anger as he went down the list.

'Wright's been knighted as well,' he shouted. 'Can't think why.'

'Be fair,' Melanie said, 'he deserves it.'

Among the many letters of congratulations John Wright received was one from Pauline Browne, who was still in the missionary hospital in Africa but expecting to return to the UK on leave within a few months. 'We must meet and celebrate in style,' she wrote. He also got a letter from Melanie.

'Why did you have to write to that bastard?' Fawcett shouted. 'You're married to me now.'

'Don't be so ungracious,' Melanie said. 'You forget, he's the father of my children.'

Jeremy Fawcett sat there sullenly.

'You must try and behave in a civilised way,' Melanie insisted. 'After all, he is a colleague of yours.'

'Colleague!' he shouted. 'He's no colleague of mine; I hate him.'

And with this emotional outburst, he stormed out of the house slamming the door. 'Why does he behave in this churlish way?' she asked herself. 'It's only because it's John. He wouldn't do it over anyone else.'

She didn't understand the antagonism between them. 'I suppose it's my fault,' she thought. 'Perhaps he hasn't got over taking me on second-hand.' She was always loyal to Jeremy but when she wrote to John, her loyalty waned a little as she remembered the time in the small country church when he had told her of his early struggles in the East End, and she felt a pang of regret that their marriage had failed.

The investiture was at Buckingham Palace in March. Fawcett arrived early and almost the first person he saw was Wright. He was forced to carry on a polite conversation, but inwardly he was seething.

'Why do I have to share everything with him?' he thought. 'My wife, my profession, and now my day at the Palace?' They were carefully rehearsed before meeting the Queen, and although a formal occasion, it all went smoothly and with such relaxed charm that it felt informal. Melanie got George and Sara out of university and they sat with all the other relatives watching the ceremony and listening to the military band. She was proud of her men as they walked towards the Queen, turned, bowed and received their honours. It was a happy occasion and when it was over, they had their photographs taken outside with the Palace as a backdrop.

'You go first,' John said, taking the initiative to avoid any embarrassment, and standing back while Melanie, Jeremy and the two children were photographed. Melanie surreptitiously wiped away a few tears as she watched him being photographed with George on one side and Sara on the other. Still in their morning suits, they all went off to the House of Lords to have lunch with one of the Health Ministers.

'What a lovely day,' exclaimed Melanie, when they got home in the early evening.

'I could have done without Wright,' growled Jeremy. 'He's been plaguing my life for years. Why doesn't he go somewhere?'

After the emotional 'high' of the investiture, John Wright came down to earth with a bang on arriving at St Luke's the following day.

# Chapter Four

His surgical firm was waiting for him at the entrance to the ward and as he walked towards the first patient, his registrar gave him the medical history. The medical students collected round the bed.

'Sir John, this is Mr Wright,' said the registrar.

John Wright looked aghast. His father was sitting up in bed with his eyes almost popping out of his head in surprise. Wright felt himself go crimson with embarrassment. His father was never at a loss for words, no matter where he found himself.

'Sir John, is it? 'Ow are yer, Johnny? I thought you was in Australia,' he chuckled. 'You're a dark horse. Why didn't yer come and see me?'

Sir John had never had such rapt attention from his students. They scarcely breathed as they watched the drama. They looked at Sir John, waiting for him to react, but he seemed speechless. His father went on:

'They've all left me – yer muvver – all the family. I dunno where any of them are. All I know is yer two bruvvers was killed in the war.' He looked at his son. 'That's why I'm ill; no one to look after me.'

Sir John Wright forced himself to speak to his registrar: 'Just carry on with the ward round; I'll catch up later.'

The firm moved further down the ward, though their attention was not on the next patient but on John Wright and his father.

'It wouldn't be right for me to treat you,' said Wright when he was alone with his father, 'I'll arrange for another surgeon to look after you.'

'I don't mind that,' replied his father. 'But you'll have to give me some money to look after myself when I come out of hospital.'

'I'll see what I can do.'

He left him and asked the ward sister to arrange for another surgeon to treat him. The story of Sir John's meeting with his father went round the hospital like a bush fire. The students were greeting each other with ''Ow are yer Johnny?' Jeremy Fawcett took over the treatment, starting with a long detailed family history. John Wright's father wanted a share of his son's success and he told Fawcett that he had starved himself to help his son get started in medicine. Fawcett rubbed his hands in glee at Wright's embarrassment and took great delight in talking about it in the Consultants' Staff Room.

'John, I saw your father today. I was very interested in your life in the East End.'

Wright grunted and left the room. Soon afterwards Fawcett left to visit a patient whose condition was giving cause for anxiety. He was a young man named James, the son of Simon Connor, an entrepreneur and property owner whose wealth was a byword. When Fawcett examined the young man, he found what he had feared, serious signs of deterioration. His uraemia had worsened. His breath was laden with the pungent smell of urine, and the protein levels had shot up. He was back on dialysis. His eye condition was causing concern and there were worrying signs of neuropathy with areas of numbness and muscle cramps in his legs. The big toe on his right foot was numb and he had wrist drop.

Simon Connor was sitting by the bedside as Fawcett examined his son and he followed him to his room. 'Sir Jeremy,' he said, 'I'm terribly worried. I don't have to be a doctor to see he's going downhill. What are you going to do about it?'

'I'm afraid his condition has worsened,' replied Fawcett. 'I think his only chance now is a kidney and a pancreas transplant. We have to deal with both the kidney failure and the diabetes.'

'What about the eye condition?'

'If we can give James one good kidney,' he said, 'and his own supply of insulin from a new pancreas, we might stop the eye condition getting worse.' He saw the look of dismay on Connor's face so he added, 'With luck there could be some improvement.'

Simon Connor paled at the thought of such major surgery but he had confidence in Sir Jeremy. 'Let's get on with it then,' he said, 'as quickly as possible.'

'It's not as easy as that, the transplant is urgent, but the best I can do is to put him on the list and as soon as suitable organs are available, I'll operate.'

'How long will that be?' asked Connor anxiously.

'I can't tell you,' replied Fawcett. 'There's a waiting list. They're all urgent. It could be weeks, could be months. That's the best information I can give you.' Connor was used to getting his own way. 'I'm a very rich man, Sir Jeremy,' he said, 'isn't there some way we can get James to the top of the list?'

Simon Connor was a billionaire who had made his fortune in the property bonanza of the 50s and 60s. Stories of his deals were legendary in the business.

One afternoon he had bought and sold a London theatre twice over, making a handsome profit on each occasion. He would drive to a Midland or Northern city and buy properties for development without even getting out of his Rolls Royce.

'It's about time they had a new city centre,' he would joke to his chauffeur as he sat in the back drinking champagne. 'I'll knock this lot down, and as soon as we get some of the big nationals – Sainsbury's or Marks and Spencers – coming in, the rest will go like hot cakes.'

He was used to dealing; it was second nature to him. He knew in this case that any financial offer would have to be substantial. It would be no good offering peanuts. 'All I want,' he thought, 'is for James to get better and lead an ordinary life – money is not important.'

'Sir Jeremy,' he said, 'I'll pay you a quarter of a million pounds if you can put James at the top of the list.'

Fawcett held his breath at the mention of such a large sum. 'I can't become involved in any commercial transactions,' he said in his best pompous professional manner, 'I can't change the waiting list. I must stick to the ethical guidelines of the profession.'

Simon Connor wasn't easily put off. He had noticed the momentary holding of breath at the mention of a quarter of a million. 'Can't you use a quarter of a million?' he asked. 'Most people can. You can have it how you like, it doesn't matter to me. Unnamed Swiss bank account – shares in my company . . .' and when Fawcett didn't reject the suggestion outright, 'you can even have it in cash – if you've got somewhere to store it. Just think of it – a quarter of a million and no tax!'

Fawcett stood up. The situation was getting out of hand and he wanted to end it. 'I've made the position clear,' he said, 'money can't change it.'

'OK, you don't want a quarter of a million for yourself,' Connor persisted. 'Why not a trust fund for research in transplant surgery?' He noticed the interest in Fawcett's eyes. 'The Sir Jeremy Fawcett Research Fund – to perpetuate your memory.'

Fawcett felt himself blush as he contemplated his name being remembered along with that of Hunter and the other famous surgeons.

'I might put up twice as much,' said Connor, 'if the trust could be named after me.' Then as an afterthought he added, 'Or my son James. "The James Connor Trust".' He repeated the words slowly to himself. 'The James Connor Trust. Yes, that appeals to me.'

Fawcett would have loved a trust at the Royal College in his own name but he couldn't accept Connor's terms. Neither, he thought ruefully, would the College. 'There's nothing more I can say,' he said. 'Let's hope suitable organs become available soon.'

Connor was crestfallen. He had thought he had Fawcett moving in his direction at one stage.

'I know you'll do your best, Sir Jeremy,' he said. 'If you do have second thoughts about my offer . . .' He trailed off and didn't finish the sentence but just held his hands out expressively, palms uppermost and then, as he left, 'I'm very flexible about any financial arrangements.'

Jeremy Fawcett knew that there was no way he could get involved in arranging the sale of organs, or of allowing patients to jump the queue. 'But,' he thought, 'if organs do become available quickly, Simon Connor might still be persuaded to donate a large sum to the College. That would be ethical. Many grateful patients make gifts.' He left his room and continued his ward round followed by his entourage of junior surgeons and his firm of eight medical students, all chaperoned by the ward sister. They stopped at the bed of John Jackson.

John Jackson's life effectively ended when he nodded off to sleep as he travelled back to London on the M1. It was late at night and he had already driven three hundred miles. The front seat of the car was comfortable, rather like sitting in an armchair. There was no traffic on the road. The automatic gearbox needed no intervention from him, which might have kept him awake. His concentration lapsed and tiredness overcame him as he sat in the overheated car. As he lost consciousness, a jerk on the power-driven steering wheel drove him off the road at ninety miles an hour, the car careering down a bank into a stone farm building. It was, in fact, the only solid structure in the field. His car had seemed drawn to it like a magnet.

He was extricated from the battered car and when he arrived at St Luke's, his condition was critical. His skull and some facial bones were fractured. The brain was severely damaged and could be seen, like a male cod's roe, glistening through the fractured area. There was massive bleeding from the head, and the rib cage was depressed on one side. Emergency surgery was carried out by Sir Jeremy Fawcett which helped to stabilise the situation and then, to everyone's surprise, John Jackson regained consciousness in intensive care about ten hours later. He kept fading in and out of consciousness and was expected to die at any time. During his conscious periods he was quite lucid, and insisted on being told the truth about his medical condition.

'Am I going to die, Sir Jeremy?' he asked. 'If I am, I want to know.'

'You are seriously ill,' Fawcett started.

'Tell me the truth,' interrupted Jackson.

'It's too early to assess the outcome,' replied Fawcett. 'We can't be sure at this stage.'

At the end of the ward he discussed the case with his group.

'The prognosis is very poor,' he said. 'I expect him to drift off into permanent unconsciousness at any time. And then it's highly likely he'll go into respiratory and then cardiac failure.' He gave a slight shrug of his shoulders. 'We may be able to maintain breathing with a ventilator – but he'll probably be brain-dead by that time.'

Two days later Fawcett found John Jackson conscious but weakening. 'I want my organs to be used,' he said, 'not turned into ashes in a crematorium.'

'I wish more people felt like you,' answered Fawcett, 'many more lives could be saved.'

'How do I go about realising my asset?' he asked. 'They're all I have to sell, to provide for my wife and young son.'

'I'm afraid we don't buy organs in this country,' said Fawcett.

'Why can't I sell them?' Jackson asked. 'I want to sell them. They're mine.'

Fawcett knew that he couldn't get involved as a broker; neither could the hospital.

'You can have the lot for one hundred thousand pounds,' suggested Jackson.

'Take what you like – eyes, kidneys, heart, liver. Just make sure the money goes to my wife.' He looked up at Fawcett pleadingly. 'Please help me. I know I'm dying,' he said. 'I'm serious about this.'

In the back of Fawcett's mind hovered the conversation he had had with Simon Connor. He was an ambitious man and the thought of his name being perpetrated at the home of surgery, with a research fund in his name and almost certainly an annual eponymous lecture – The Sir Jeremy Fawcett Lecture – to commemorate him filled him with excitement. He could picture the scene. All the important names in surgery would be there. The invitation speaker would be someone of international repute who would be led in procession by some future President of the College, along with the Council members in their academic gowns as the audience stood in respect.

John Jackson would almost certainly be dead within a few days; why not arrange for Simon Connor to meet him, and then he wouldn't be involved in the transaction himself? He felt that as long as he could be kept out of any commercial dealing between the patient and Connor, he could not be accused of acting unethically. The Trust Fund at the Royal College could be set up by a donation from Simon Connor direct to the College, with the request that it be used for a research fund in the name of Sir Jeremy Fawcett. In this way Sir Jeremy would not handle any of the money from Simon Connor.

Connor would negotiate directly with Jackson for the organs, and with the College to establish the Trust. It did pass through his mind that a big fat sum in a Swiss bank account would be welcome, but unethical and even perhaps illegal. 'Perhaps I'll get the blood and tissues checked out, just in case,' he thought. 'If the blood groups are incompatible, we can forget all about it straight away.' Somehow he hoped that they wouldn't be suitable because he knew that if they turned out to be a good match, he might find it difficult to resist Connor's offer.

He telephoned Connor the following day and invited him to his club in St James'. The club was one of the most exclusive in London and the sheer style made Connor uncomfortable. Over dinner Fawcett told him about John Jackson. 'I'll arrange for you to visit him,' Fawcett said, 'you may have to come at short notice. He drifts off into unconsciousness for long periods and he may not recover.' Connor listened carefully.

'Once you've agreed a price, make sure he signs the hospital organ donor form,' Fawcett continued. 'It'll be up to you then to pay his widow. You'll have to trust me to ensure that the organs are used for your son's treatment.'

'That's no problem,' answered Connor. 'I won't pay any money to John Jackson's widow – or contact the Royal College of Surgeons until the operation is carried out.'

'The entire arrangement will have to be one of trust,' Fawcett concluded.

He saw the ward sister the following day. 'Sister, could you arrange for John Jackson to see his solicitor – Simon Connor. He says he has some legal matters to attend to.' He wrote the telephone number on a slip of paper. 'Give him a ring. That'll be simplest.'

As soon as he received the call, Connor had himself driven to St Luke's in his Rolls Royce.

'I want a hundred thousand pounds,' said Jackson. 'The money to be paid to my wife.'

Connor agreed the asking price without demur, although he knew he could have paid less. After all, John Jackson was scarcely in a position to bargain. When he thought about it later on in the day, he realised that this business deal with John Jackson was the most bizarre he had ever been involved in, negotiating for part of a dying man's body – and even more bizarre, he thought, when Jackson insisted on a written contract. Connor regarded the contract as a private matter between him and the Jacksons; there was no need to tell Sir Jeremy. As far as the hospital was concerned, John Jackson signed the standard donor form.

'Sister, would you mind witnessing our signatures,' he said, once he had drawn up a simple contract, 'I need it to sort out some of Mr Jackson's affairs.' The Ward Sister added her signature without the slightest hesitation. John Jackson placed the contract in an envelope and addressed it to his wife.

'I can post that for you,' Connor suggested, thinking that he might take the opportunity to open it and take a copy.

'My wife will be here shortly,' replied Jackson, placing the envelope on the bedside cabinet, and settling back into bed. 'Forgive me, I'm so tired,' he said closing his eyes. By the time Janet Jackson arrived, her husband had drifted off into unconsciousness. She saw the letter addressed to her and put it unopened into her handbag. Her husband remained unconscious and she sat there quietly for fifteen minutes before gently kissing him and leaving. At home she opened the letter and read the contract signed by her husband and Simon Connor, whom she didn't know. Her eyes filled with tears and she sobbed. Although she had been told by the hospital that her husband might not pull through, and her husband had discussed the sale of his organs, she had not lost hope until she read the simple contract. The contract began: 'When I die'. There was no uncertainty about it; no longer any room for hope. The two signatures and the witness's signature seemed to make it final.

The next morning when she arrived at St Luke's, the Sister took her aside.

'I'm afraid you're husband suffered a relapse during the night,' she said. 'There was a dramatic fall in his blood pressure. We've managed to control that, but he still hasn't regained consciousness.'

Janet Jackson visited her husband every day, and on the seventh day she was sitting by his bedside when he opened his eyes. She leant across and kissed him.

'Darling, thank goodness you've woken up,' she said, 'you must have been very tired. You've been asleep for seven days.' Her husband didn't reply. His eyes were open but he was unaware of her. She smiled at him. 'Come on now, wake up properly.'

He didn't respond but looked vaguely interested. She kissed him two or three times on the lips and stroked his hand. 'Darling,' she cried, 'please say something!' He cried like a child. Janet Jackson couldn't understand what was happening. 'Darling, it's Janet,' she said, 'you know me.' John Jackson blinked intermittently. She wanted to believe that he understood but couldn't reply. The Sister took her arm, led her to the end of the ward and sat her down with a cup of tea.

'Mrs Jackson, your husband is seriously ill,' she said gently. 'Even though he can open his eyes, he's really unconscious. We hope he'll come out of this – but we've no way of predicting the outcome.'

She put her arm round Janet Jackson as she tried to control her sobbing. 'There's one consolation,' she said, 'he can't feel any pain.'

'How do you know?' she retorted, sobbing loudly. 'He can't tell us.' The Sister sat quietly with her.

'I know he can see me,' she said, 'when he looks at me his eyes are interested.' The tears streamed down her face. 'And he cried like a child. He clutched my hand. How can he be unconscious?'

The Sister could have fobbed her off with some stereotyped reply such as 'You must trust the doctors, dear', but she felt that close relatives had a right to know what was happening. 'I know it's difficult,' she said, 'but he really is unconscious. We've carried out numerous tests. They were all negative. The eye movements you've seen are controlled by the lower brain. It's his upper brain which isn't functioning.'

When Sir Jeremy Fawcett examined John Jackson later that day, he was sure that he had moved into a Persistent Vegetative State. 'PVS?' he said to his registrar. 'He hasn't responded to a single question. We've not had a single word or any other kind of response from him. What do you think?'

'He's lost to this world, I'm afraid.'

Fawcett had admired Jackson's courage and determination to do the best he could for his family when he had been at death's door, but if he remained in PVS, all his efforts to sell his organs might now come to nothing. He could survive for a long time, but was it worth it? Was existence in the vegetative state better than death? 'It's a kind of living death,' he thought as he left his bedside.

The hospital continued to care for him, feeding him through a gastrostomy tube entering his stomach through a small incision. All the auxiliary services were mobilised to try and improve the quality of what was left of his life. Janet Jackson tried to believe that she saw some improvement when her husband was propped up in bed in a sitting position. At least he seemed able to hold his head up straight. 'Darling, please talk to me,' she said, longing for a response. 'If you can hear me, try and blink. Please.' She tried to will him to reply but he looked straight ahead, and although there were slight eye movements, they were not focused, nor were they elicited in response to her questions.

She tried to induce him to respond to her questions by way of finger or toe movements, and when she saw a tiny movement of the right big toe she became excited, but it wasn't repeated. She visited the hospital daily and gradually became resigned to the situation and no longer had much hope for his recovery, although she always asked Sister about him before she left after each visit.

'John is in a fairly stable physical state,' Sister explained, 'but there's no activity in the higher brain. He could continue for months – even years, in his present condition.'

Janet Jackson had been reading articles in popular journals that before her husband's illness she wouldn't have looked at.

'You mean he's a vegetable,' she said. 'He's in this permanent vegetative state I've read about.' The Sister took hold of her arm. 'Come and have a cup of tea,' she said, and led her to her room.

'Janet,' she said, 'if John recovers, he's unlikely to lead any kind of normal life.' She looked at Janet Jackson to see whether she was composed enough to continue. 'We've got to talk about his treatment. He might go into heart failure. He might get a serious infection.' Janet Jackson looked up anxiously, wondering what was coming next. 'If he does, d'you want us to treat him?'

'You mean let him die?' Janet Jackson said, beginning to cry. 'It would only be allowing nature to take its course,' Sister said, putting her arm round her shoulders to comfort her.

'I can't bear to give up,' she said, wiping the tears from her eyes, 'a miracle might happen. I'm praying every day. Please keep him alive.'

Fawcett saw Jackson that evening and was convinced that his provisional diagnosis of PVS was correct. He also knew that the ethical guidelines of the profession discouraged doctors from confirming the diagnosis for at least a year. All thoughts of using him as an organ donor had gone from his mind. Only physical life remained but it was still life. Simon Connor was becoming increasingly frustrated.

'With all my money,' he said to Fawcett, 'I still can't get my son treated.'

'I'm afraid John Jackson's out of the picture,' Fawcett said, 'at least for the moment.'

'Can't I get quicker treatment abroad?' Connor asked irritably.

'You might get kidneys abroad, but you'd be unlikely to get a pancreas.' Fawcett stood up to go but Connor remained seated.

'You won't get your money,' said Connor, 'if you don't come up with the treatment soon; I'll find someone else.'

Fawcett had already come to the conclusion that he wasn't going to get suitable organs for James Connor quickly, and that his dream of a trust in his name at the College would never be a reality. In a way he was pleased because he knew that in getting involved with Connor, he was skating on very thin ice.

'You could try China,' he said, almost flippantly, 'you might get organs from an executed prisoner.'

'I've heard that patients are coming into Western Europe to sell a kidney,' persisted Connor, 'why can't you get one of those?'

'I know there are some countries where questions aren't asked about where organs come from, but that's not the UK. And I'm having nothing to do with it – even if I knew how to go about getting one.' As he left, Connor he said: 'Your best bet is to hope that suitable organs turn up soon from UK sources.'

He walked back along the hospital corridor to the Consultants' Staff Room to find Wright in conversation with another surgeon. In spite of the animosity between them, they were forced to behave in a civilized way in the hospital. Neither made any effort to talk if it were avoidable and when they had to, it was a stilted, forced conversation, and usually it was Fawcett who started. Wright's instincts remained as they were when he was a child, when he went to the pigeon shed in the garden to get away from his drunken father. Given a choice, he preferred not to be in the same room as Fawcett. He tried to rationalise his feelings at times. It wasn't the fight in the Medical School as students all those years ago; it wasn't that Fawcett was now married to Melanie; it wasn't that he had pipped him at the post to become President of the Royal College of Surgeons. 'It's that I just don't trust the guy,' he said to himself. 'Call it animal, instinctive, emotional or whatever. It's real.'

'What are we going to do about the shortage of organs?' Fawcett asked Wright, almost as soon as he came into the room.

'Animals,' said Wright, without hesitation. 'Chimpanzees – pigs – or some similar mammal. They would have to be genetically engineered to avoid rejection.' He quickly finished his coffee, and as he walked out of the room he heard Fawcett say: 'Have to be pigs. The populace would riot if we used chimpanzees. Too like us and more difficult to breed in large numbers.'

Two weeks later Fawcett was called to Jackson's bedside. His breathing had stopped and he was going into heart failure as the supply of oxygenated blood petered out.

'Unless we start his heart,' he said to Sister, 'he'll be dead within minutes.' He placed the electrodes from the defibrillator on Jackson's chest. The massive electric shock started the heart.

'Right,' Fawcett said, 'Intensive care and ventilator.'

If Janet Jackson hadn't wanted all efforts to be made to resuscitate him, her husband would now be dead. Fawcett carefully examined him. His heart was beating and blood was coursing through his veins, but he knew that it was only the technology. Taken off the ventilator, he would soon die. 'I'm afraid he's brain dead,' he said to Sister. He knew that he was no longer a human being but an object, with parts of his body kept going by means of technology. He would remain permanently unconscious. The Sister watched as he shone his torch into John Jackson's eyes. She could see that the pupils remained fixed and widely dilated and did not constrict with the light. He gently moved the head from side to side and the eyes remained stationary. 'Doll's eyes,' he said. He put his finger on the eyeball but the eyelid didn't move. He lifted the head to one side. 'Thank you,' he said, taking the syringe of ice-cold water from the Sister and syringing it into Jackson's ear. The Sister watched closely but the eyes remained staring straight ahead.

'No question about it,' said Fawcett, 'he's dead.'

He would have been prepared to write a death certificate right there and then, though the heart was still beating, but he knew he must follow the established guidelines. 'We'd better get the consultant neurologist and a senior registrar to check the diagnosis,' he said. They examined Jackson the next day and agreed that John Jackson was dead.

Fawcett was amazed that Jackson had survived so long when he remembered what he was like when he first saw him.

'There's one more crucial test,' he said. 'Let's disconnect the ventilator and feed oxygen into his lungs to see whether he can breathe unaided.' He watched with the Sister. 'Nothing,' he said, 'no respiratory movement; no movement of the chest at all. The respiratory centre in the brain stem is out of action.'

John Jackson was put back on the ventilator and the tests were carried out again the following day. The neurologist thought that he detected a slight movement when he moved the tube in Jackson's throat, but it wasn't repeated. He was quite satisfied with the diagnosis of brain death.

'Before brain-death,' Fawcett said, 'the priority was John Jackson. Now it must be to keep the organs in the best possible condition for use as transplants.'

The Sister knew the procedures, and all life support systems were continued. She knew that it was essential that organs weren't deprived of oxygenated blood before they were removed, or they would deteriorate significantly.

'We'll operate tomorrow,' Fawcett said to Connor on the telephone. The same day, by the second post, Fawcett received a letter from his underwriting agency.

Dear Jeremy,
    The results of the last three years of accounts have appalled all of us in this Syndicate and we are fully aware of the financial difficulties these have caused Members.
    Your position is considerably worse than average . . .

. . . the gross loss from the past year, coupled with provision for strengthened reserves, comes to a figure of just under £500,000.

The analysis shows that not all of the losses require settlement at this time . . . but the sum of £350,000 is due for settlement by the end of July.

Our past discussions have indicated that a loss at this level would cause severe financial problems following on the losses of previous years . . .

I feel that we must meet shortly to discuss the best way of dealing with this loss.

Yours sincerely,

Sir Jeremy Fawcett had been persuaded by Melanie's father and his rich friends in the country to become a Name at Lloyds. 'You're sitting on a large capital sum,' Melanie's father said, 'your houses are appreciating almost daily with inflation. You should use the capital. Lloyds is the best investment we've ever made.'

His bank manager tried to warn him off.

'If you have to think twice about changing your Bentley every year, don't become a Name,' he said. 'It's for very rich people. You don't have the financial resources. Sooner or later there will be some bad years and the Names will have to pay up.'

'That's why he's a bank manager,' Melanie's father laughed. 'Won't take any risks. I've been making a considerable profit for years.'

Fawcett's greed got the better of him and he joined what turned out to be a high-risk syndicate. He had received a good return in the early years but now his situation was so grave that he was at his wit's end. 'There's no way I can raise £350,000.' He shuddered when he thought what personal bankruptcy would do to his career.

He read and re-read the letter, his mind searching for a solution. He felt like a cornered rat having to fight for survival, and it wasn't until he had downed two large malt whiskies that he felt calmer. Halfway through the third malt he found the courage to telephone Connor.

'Simon,' he said, using his Christian name for the first time, 'I'm being pressured for £350,000 by Lloyds. Would you be prepared to pay this for me, instead of setting up the Trust Fund at the Royal College?' Connor was surprised at the proposition after the high ethical stance Sir Jeremy had previously adopted. 'They're all the same,' he thought, 'when the pressure's on.' He was a businessman and he had already told Fawcett that he didn't mind how the money was paid. His surprise turned to alarm as he listened to Fawcett's slurred speech.

'Are you all right, Sir Jeremy?' he asked, 'you sound as if you've been drinking.'

When Fawcett didn't reply, he asked directly: 'Are you drunk?'

'Of course not. I've just had a small whisky. If I sound strange, it's tiredness – that's all.'

'I offered you £500,000 to set up a Research Trust at the Royal College of Surgeons in James's name. I was prepared to do that to help the work of the College. My offer to you was for £250,000.'

'I appreciate that, but I'm desperate,' Fawcett replied. His speech had become clearer but he spoke very quickly, trying to cover up any change in his diction. 'I don't know whether I'll be able to carry on practising.'

'You must try and relax, Sir Jeremy,' said Connor, becoming increasingly alarmed by the conversation. 'There must be some way of resolving your financial dilemma.'

'I've exhausted every avenue,' Fawcett insisted, 'the banks have put the shutters up.' He paused to gulp some more whisky. 'I don't suppose you would lend me the extra £100,000?' The line went quiet for so long that Fawcett thought Connor had just left the phone and gone off. 'Simon?' he said.

'I'm still here,' Connor answered. Normally his business instincts wouldn't have allowed him even to consider an unsecured loan of this kind, but because Fawcett was going to operate on his son the next day, he felt under pressure.

'All right,' he said, 'I'll settle your debt with Lloyds.'

'That's incredibly generous of you, Simon.'

'It's not generosity; I'm thinking of James. I don't want you stressed up when you operate on him,' he said, 'and what's more, you'd better stop drinking. I don't want you drunk either.'

Normally Fawcett would have replied to such a remark in caustic tones, but for the sake of financial salvation, he had put himself in Connor's hands.

'I'll confirm it in writing,' said Connor.

'That's hardly necessary,' replied Fawcett, not anxious to have the details written down. 'I'll let you have the demand and you can pay Lloyds direct.'

'I can pay Lloyds direct, but you'll still need a letter from me to keep your agent happy, and probably the bank manager as well, until they get their money,' Connor replied. 'I certainly won't pay you anything at all until after the operation.'

Fawcett spent a restless night wondering what the General Medical Council would have to say about his transactions with Connor. But, why should they find out? 'I haven't been personally involved with the purchase of organs.

71

I haven't discussed money with Janet Jackson. Connor hasn't been in touch with the College yet,' he told himself. He argued that he hadn't behaved unethically, but he knew that if it ever came out, it would raise quite a few eyebrows in the surgical world. At very least he would have to resign from the Presidency of the Royal College.

He drove to St Luke's trying to put all thoughts of his financial problems out of his mind so that he could concentrate on the operation. Once he started, he knew that his professional training would take over and he would be focused on his work. The first person he met inside the theatre was Jane Perkins.

'I'm sorry,' she said, 'your regular Sister was taken ill this morning. Matron asked me to take over rather than cancel.'

'That's fine,' he said. He knew that she was an excellent nurse, probably more experienced than his usual Sister.

They scrubbed up and moved in to the theatre, where John Jackson was lying on the operating table still breathing through a tube down into his lungs. The anaesthetist was holding the black rubber mask on his face.

Fawcett incised beneath the ribs, extending the incision vertically to provide better access to the pancreas. The wound was held open with retractors and he quickly identified important structures as he worked towards the spleen.

'There she is,' he said, as he gently lifted the spleen to expose the pancreas. He cut through the pancreas, dividing and sealing off the main blood vessels, and lifted the pancreas and spleen out of the body into a bowl of ice-cold saline.

'Let's wash the blood out,' he said as he placed a soft plastic tube into the artery. 'We don't want coagulated blood in the pancreas.' He washed it through with an electrolyte solution until he was satisfied. 'Okay, that's clear now. Double pack it in ice.'

'That's the bit of pancreas,' he said, 'now for the kidney.' He quickly removed the left kidney, being very careful not to damage its blood supply. As he cut through the ureter, a small amount of urine was expressed. The blood vessels holding the kidney were cut through and the kidney immersed in a cold solution and kept in an ice box. He was pleased that he had removed the kidney himself. 'At least,' he thought, 'the blood vessels and ureter will be the right length.'

Two hours later Fawcett started to operate on James Connor in an adjacent theatre. He cut through the abdominal wall just below the ribs and gently retracted the tissues to enable him to displace the spleen. He worked methodically, clamping and tying blood vessels. Jane Perkins worked with him almost as a robot, or 'on automatic pilot', as she would say.

'We'll soon see,' said Fawcett as he joined the blood vessels from John Jackson's pancreas to those of James Connor.

'Tremendous!' exclaimed Jane Perkins excitedly as she watched the blood flow into the new pancreas. 'A lovely pink. I wonder whether he's already getting insulin from it.'

'Too early,' answered Fawcett as he systematically closed the wound. He made an incision down to the groin to change the malfunctioning kidney.

He had been in the operating theatre for many hours and now that it was over he was exhausted – physically and emotionally drained. James Connor was taken to intensive care with an airway tube in his mouth to recover.

When Jane Perkins had finished in the operating theatre, she went along the hospital corridor and as she passed John Wright's room, she hesitated and then stopped and knocked on the door.

'What d'you want?' asked Wright bluntly, 'we've nothing to say to each other; I've got work to do.' He looked down at his papers.

'Please,' Jane said, 'I must talk to someone.'

'Find someone else,' answered Wright rudely.

'Why do you behave like such a bastard to me?' she shouted, losing control. 'I've never done you any harm. Why are you so vicious?'

'You bloody well know. You destroyed my marriage,' he shouted.

'How did I do that?' she screamed. 'All I did was to sleep with you for six months. You came of your own free will.'

'Look, I don't want to waste any more time on it,' he said. 'It's over now.'

'I didn't come to talk about us,' she said more calmly. 'But since you've started, I think I deserve an explanation.'

'Don't let's piss around,' he said. 'You wrote to Melanie telling her about us.'

'But I didn't.'

'Who else could have done?' he asked. 'We were the only two who knew about it.'

'I swear on the holy bible I did not write to Melanie,' she said.

'I have the letter with your signature. How can you deny it?' He went across to a cabinet and removed a letter from a small drawer.

'There it is,' he said, tossing it to her. 'Just read it and clear off.'

She picked up the letter. 'I didn't write this,' she said indignantly.

'I don't type anyway. And even if I did, I wouldn't have typed a letter like this. I would have written it longhand.'

'That's your signature, isn't it?' he shouted. He laughed derisively. 'Why should anyone forge it? Especially when no one else knew about us.'

'I never told a single person,' said Jane, 'except for my doctors, and that was confidential.'

'What d'you mean your doctors?'

'Well, I had to tell the psychiatrist, didn't I?' she said, 'because he was treating me for depression.'

'Who else did you have to tell?'

'The surgeon who looked after me, Jeremy Fawcett.'

'Fawcett! You told Fawcett?' he said incredulously.

'He asked me whether I wanted to talk about it. I was a bit gaga at the time with the tranquillisers. I assumed it would be in confidence. I can't believe he could have done it.'

'Could he not?' shouted Wright, 'could he not? It was either you or him. I can't believe it was the psychiatrist.'

'I swear to you,' she said, 'it wasn't me. I told Jeremy Fawcett I wasn't going to write to Melanie.'

'What did he say to that?'

'He said it was my duty to write. You shouldn't get away with it.'

'Where would he have got your signature from?'

'I don't know,' she said. 'I signed a consent form. Perhaps he copied that.'

'D'you have any objection to me confronting him with the letter?'

'I'll come with you.'

Wright was beginning to believe her, and felt ashamed of his callous behaviour to her over the years. 'I'm sorry,' he said, 'if you didn't send the letter. There didn't seem any other explanation. Leave it with me for the moment.' He put the letter back in the small drawer. 'What was it you came in for?' he asked.

She explained her concern that John Jackson wasn't completely brain-dead when the organs were removed.

'The tests must have been checked by other doctors,' he said, 'there's little room for error.'

'I definitely saw the blood pressure rise and movement in the patient's throat when the endotracheal tube was moved,' she said, 'that must mean some activity in the brain stem, mustn't it?'

'Maybe, but these anomalies do occur. You could complain to the Hospital Authorities,' he said, 'but it's scarcely worth it.' He stood up. 'If you want my advice, I wouldn't jeopardise your own career by making an official complaint. The evidence isn't strong enough.' The last thing in his mind was any desire to protect Fawcett, but he knew that Jane Perkins would be the loser if she went ahead.

The following day he collected Jane Perkins' hospital notes from Records and studied the consent form. The signature was an exact copy of that on the letter to Melanie. It was so identical that it almost looked like a photocopy, even to the overwriting of the capital 'J' to make it clearer. He met Jane in his room.

'I'm going to invite Fawcett to tea,' he said, looking at Jane thoughtfully. 'But I'll look a proper Charlie if he didn't send it.'

'He must have,' she said.

'You're prepared to meet him?' he said, 'It might get rough.'

'I wouldn't miss it for all the tea in China.'

Wright telephoned Fawcett and asked him to join him for tea to discuss something important. Fawcett was surprised when he walked into Wright's room and found him with Jane Perkins. 'Perhaps they're at it again,' he thought.

'Have a seat,' said Wright. 'Tea?' Fawcett was becoming more mystified. Wright was behaving in an unusually friendly manner. He sat down and then, as Wright passed the letter to him, it all changed.

'Why did you send that letter to Melanie?' he asked.

'What the hell are you talking about?' said Fawcett. 'What's this got to do with me?'

'Jane didn't send it,' rejoined Wright. 'You're the only other person who knew about our affair. It must have been you.'

'I'm not going to stay here listening to this nonsense,' said Fawcett, standing up to leave, but Wright stood between him and the door.

'Not just yet. Sit down,' he said, pushing him back into the chair. 'Just take a look at this signature.' He handed Fawcett Jane Perkins' consent form.

'You've copied every little detail, haven't you? Even the corrections.'

'It looks just like Jane's signature to me,' said Fawcett, tossing it on the table. 'What's all the fuss about? You're not denying you had an affair?'

'No, I'm not saying that. That wouldn't be true. I'm saying you used information given to you in confidence by Jane when she was your patient. You then used it to forge this letter to Melanie, deliberately to break up my marriage.'

'She had a right to know,' answered Fawcett, 'whoever sent it.' Wright let him stand up. He hadn't expected Fawcett to admit it, but at least he now knew that Wright and Jane Firkins knew.

'The trouble with you, Wright,' said Fawcett, as he moved towards the door, 'you've got no breeding. You'd no business marrying Melanie in the first place. She's above your class. But I suppose you've done well for an

East End yob.'

Wright moved towards him, his fingers outstretched, wanting to take him by the throat and throttle the life out of him, but he controlled himself.

'You haven't finished your tea. Don't go without it,' he said, picking up the cup and throwing the contents over him.

Fawcett left the room with tea dripping down from his head on to his white coat, but he wasn't too dismayed because he was pleased that Wright knew. 'What can he do about it?' he asked himself. 'Apart from hate me. And I wouldn't want it any other way.'

The day after the operation Simon Connor saw his son and was amazed how well he looked following such horrendous surgery. The new pancreas was not yet operating fully, and he still needed small amounts of insulin, but hopefully only for a few more days. His new kidney was already making a dramatic improvement in his health.

James was being carefully monitored for any sign of rejection, infection or clotting in the blood vessels attached to the new organs. Any leakage of the pancreatic juices into the abdominal cavity would require urgent re-operation. About a week after the operation, James Connor no longer needed daily injections of insulin. The vast improvement was obvious to Connor and he felt confident enough to settle with Janet Jackson and Sir Jeremy. He sent a cheque for one hundred thousand pounds to Janet Jackson, thanking her and her husband, and he met Fawcett in his Club to pay the Lloyds debt, which would clear Fawcett's immediate financial problems. It was a large sum of money but it was worth it to see James so well. James Connor left the hospital days later. To Fawcett this signalled the end of what he regarded as an unsavoury episode in his life, when he had become involved in the purchase and sale of organs. But it wasn't the end because a month later he was dining at the Savoy with Simon Connor.

'Sir Jeremy, a business colleague of mine is seriously ill,' he said as they sat waiting for dinner. 'His kidneys are failing. He's on and off dialysis all the time. He's been told he needs a new kidney.' He drank his champagne slowly. 'He's an important man,' he said, 'Chairman of an International Company.'

'I'm sorry to hear that,' Fawcett replied politely, 'but I'm sure he's being well looked after. Who's the surgeon?'

'He's abroad at present. I'd rather he came back to the UK to be treated by you.'

'Either he's a close friend of yours,' Fawcett thought, 'or you've got some commercial interest.'

'I wish I could help,' he said, 'but there must be more than four thousand on the waiting list for kidneys. And, it's getting longer all the time.'

'Since you operated on James, I've been in touch with my contacts in Europe and the Middle East,' said Connor, beckoning the waiter for two more glasses of champagne. 'I've found that it's possible to buy kidneys abroad quite easily.'

'You can count me out,' replied Fawcett. 'I've finished with all that. I'm never going to get involved with the purchase of organs again. And that's final.'

'Why not – is it illegal?'

'Perhaps not at present, but it's unethical. Sufficient to get me struck off the Medical Register if the GMC heard about it.'

Connor looked thoughtfully at the myriad of small bubbles in his champagne, and then finished it before carefully removing a newspaper cutting from his wallet. He passed it to Fawcett without comment. 'The advertiser is willing to pay £10,000,' he read, 'to any person prepared to provide a kidney for a seriously ill patient.' Connor put the cutting back into his wallet.

'That's running continuously in journals all over Eastern Europe and the Far East,' he said. 'They're getting hundreds of replies.'

'We wouldn't accept kidneys from such a source in this country,' Fawcett said.

Simon Connor leaned across towards him. 'I happen to know,' he said, lowering his voice, 'that some of these kidneys are coming into the UK. And being used on private patients.' He laughed. 'Some of these surgeons must be making a fortune.'

Fawcett was getting decidedly uneasy at the direction the conversation was taking.

'I'd be surprised if that were happening on a large scale.'

'Let's continue over dinner,' said Connor, standing up and leading Fawcett to their table. As they got to the main course, Connor changed tack. 'Sir Jeremy,' he said. 'How are you going to pay me back that extra £100k I lent you?'

'I was hoping you would let me delay repayment for some months,' said Fawcett. 'You know how weak my financial position is after Lloyds.' He paused, waiting for some kind of reply, but Connor remained silent so he felt compelled to go on. 'I would prefer to repay the money over the longest possible period.'

'But I want the money now. Not in ten or twenty years' time,' said Connor. 'Anyway, there's no way you can pay me back out of income.'

Fawcett had thought about this at length and knew that the only way he could clear the debt would be from capital. But what capital? Lloyds had taken all his. If Connor would wait until he retired, the lump sum from his pension would help, but that was unlikely to be sufficient. He knew that he would have this debt hanging around his neck for the rest of his life. And no doubt some would remain to be settled from any estate he left.

'I'll pay you back as soon as I can.'

'That's no use to me,' replied Connor, 'why should I wait indefinitely?'

Fawcett had long ceased enjoying his dinner. All he wanted was to get up and go, but he knew that he daren't.

'Sir Jeremy, you're going to have to resort to drastic actions to deal with this debt,' he said as he poured more claret into their glasses and savoured it thoughtfully. 'Otherwise you're going to be hounded by me for the rest of your life. And finish up a pauper.' He looked at Fawcett: 'Let me make it easy for you. Get you off the hook.' Fawcett listened attentively, hoping Connor was about to suggest some easy solution, but he wasn't.

'You operate on this business colleague,' said Connor, 'and I'll cancel the debt. Couldn't be simpler.' He waited just long enough for the waiter to clear the table. 'I'll bring a live donor into the country. You remove one of his kidneys, and off he goes. Everybody's happy.'

'You make it sound so simple,' rejoined Fawcett, 'but the kidney will have to be compatible. Who will do the tests so that we get a good match?'

'Sir Jeremy,' he said, 'it's been done before. The patients haven't all died; the kidneys haven't been rejected; they must have been matched.'

'Just tell me what you want,' continued Connor as Fawcett remained silent. 'That's all you have to do. I'll find the medical people to do it.'

All Fawcett wanted was to be allowed to carry on treating patients and conducting his research. 'You're turning surgery into a supermarket,' he said miserably.

'There's always a commercial angle,' answered Connor. 'Treat this unfortunate man, and your financial problems will be gone. You'll be able to live again.' He laughed. 'You can be as ethical as you like afterwards.'

Fawcett had stopped eating but he continued to drink as Connor calmly continued his dinner and behaved as if this was a normal business meeting; which it was, as far as he was concerned.

'Other professional and business people use their skills without restriction provided they operate within the law,' he said, 'why can't you surgeons? If society doesn't like it, let it change the law.'

Fawcett had lost his appetite so Connor cut short his own meal and ordered two large Remy Martins. 'If you don't treat this business tycoon,' he said, 'I'll find another surgeon.' He drank his brandy as he waited for a reply. 'I must have your answer. If you won't do it, I'll want that hundred grand back immediately.'

Fawcett finished his brandy with a gulp and placed the glass down so heavily on the table that the diners on adjacent tables looked up.

'That's blackmail,' he said loudly.

'No. It's business – straight forward business,' said Connor. 'I'm just trying to make it easy for you to repay your debt. If you don't want my help, just say so.' He paused to let that sink in. 'If the answer is "No", I'll put the matter in the hands of my solicitor first thing in the morning.'

Fawcett had had too much to drink, but his mind was crystal clear. Just one operation and the huge debt would be gone forever. Connor watched him closely. He could see him wavering so he applied some more pressure.

'If it does go to court,' he said, 'I've no doubt all the circumstances of the loan will have to be disclosed.'

'I'll do it,' said Fawcett finally. 'I'm so desperate. I'll have to take a chance.' Having made the commitment, he felt the relief that a guilty man feels when he confesses. 'As you say, it's not illegal,' he said with a dry laugh, 'I shouldn't finish up in gaol.'

'Your GMC may consider it unethical,' Connor warned, brightening now that Fawcett had agreed, 'but it's the proper treatment for this man. The only question of ethics must be money allowing him to jump the queue.' He beckoned the waiter for some more champagne. Fawcett was amazed at Connor's capacity for alcohol.

'Why should organs only be given away?' Connor went on, becoming more garrulous and excited as the alcohol took effect. 'They're just a commodity like anything else. Think of the person selling the kidney; he or she must need the money for some urgent purpose. Otherwise, why should they go through the pain and suffering of the operation?'

Fawcett left Connor to arrange for the businessman to be brought to England so that he could assess him and make arrangements to admit him to a private hospital as soon as a kidney was available. Connor was amazed how quickly his new-found contacts in Europe were able to find a young man prepared to sell a kidney. A telephone call, followed by the transfer of £2,000 into the agent's bank account, secured the deal. Within a week his eight-seater twin-engined jet landed on a small airstrip in Eastern Europe. He climbed out of the plane and walked across to the terminal building – little more than a large shed – to collect the patient and settle the balance of the price with the agent. He looked around the small room. There was only one man there who stood up and introduced himself in perfect English.

'Where's the patient?' asked Connor.

'There's been a last minute hitch,' the agent explained. 'He's too frightened to have the operation in a foreign country.'

'Why didn't you find this out sooner?' Connor shouted furiously. 'Our patient is already in hospital being prepared for the transplant, and now I'll have to return empty-handed.'

'He knew he had to go to England,' he said, 'but this morning he lost his nerve.'

'You've really buggered me about, haven't you?' said Connor, advancing belligerently towards the man. 'This is the last time I'll do business with you.'

'Calm down,' the agent said, 'all is not lost.'

'What d'you mean?'

'He's desperate to get the money,' he said. 'We can remove the kidney here and you can fly it straight back to England.' He watched Connor hesitating. 'We've done it many times before,' he said.

Connor was in a dilemma. He tried to contact Fawcett on the telephone, but he couldn't even get a connection through to the UK. 'What should I do?' he asked himself.

'In England,' said the agent, 'you remove kidneys at one hospital and transplant them many miles away. It is hours before they are used.' He shrugged his shoulders. 'What's the difference? You'll be back in England within a few hours.' He looked at Connor inquiringly. 'We could have the kidney removed and packed ready for transport,' he said, 'in not much more than an hour.'

Connor nodded his head. 'All right, get on with it,' he replied.

About one and a half hours later the agent returned with the packaged organ.

'I'll pay you the balance,' said Connor looking down at the agent, 'when the kidney's used. I don't know what's in that container. You might have got it from the local butcher's shop.'

'Oh no,' the agent said, leaping forward and producing an ominous looking gun from his side pocket. 'Either I get the money or I'll take the kidney back.' He stood about a yard from Connor, pointing the gun at the centre of his body. If he had fired, there was no way he could have missed. 'And I'll keep the deposit,' he said, still keeping the gun aimed at Connor. 'It's up to you.'

'I'm sorry you've resorted to firearms,' said Connor. 'It won't help you. This is a business matter.'

'Come on, don't waste time,' said the agent, slowly moving the gun from side to side as if selecting the best target. 'Hand it over.'

Connor remained perfectly still. 'D'you think I'd come here,' he said, 'to a small isolated airfield to meet a complete stranger, without some protection?' He continued quietly, but very clearly: 'Just inside the plane, to either side of me, are my two crew members. They'll have no hesitation in killing you immediately should you be foolish enough to fire that gun.' He looked at the agent contemptuously. 'I don't know whether you are familiar with the Armalite. The bullets are quite small but they travel with such high velocity that they produce shock waves inside the body and leave a massive exit wound. And, if they should hit a bone, it shatters and sends spicules of bone all over the place. They make quite a mess. But that won't bother you because you'll probably be dead at the first impact.'

He paused to observe what effect his words were having. He saw the look of uncertainty on the agent's face.

'Put the gun away,' Connor said with quiet authority. 'You'll only get yourself killed.' He stepped back slowly and the two crew members moved across aiming their rifles at the man on the tarmac. The agent hesitantly put the gun back in his pocket.

'Let's get this straight,' said Connor. 'If we're going to do business, no more cock-ups, no more guns. You got that?'

And with that the door was closed and the plane took off. The Lestair jet left the runway at around 130 knots and climbed steadily at 4000 feet per minute through thin white cloud to its cruising height. It was such a thrill to fly this plane that Connor often took the controls himself, but he had other things on his mind. He sat drinking a large glass of malt whisky, thinking about the sale and purchase of organs. 'There's so much money to be made,' he thought, 'it can only be a question of time before organised crime gets into the act. And guns will be routine then. And probably murder as well, should there be a supply difficulty.'

Flying conditions were good. They picked up the Brussels' control at 28,000 feet and soon after contacted London. As they gradually lost height, they passed over Manston and were soon clocked on to the Biggin Hill beacon, and with the tail wind the jet landed at the old fighter 'drome three hours after take off. Within an hour Connor was in the private hospital.

'I can't have anything to do with this,' Fawcett said, alarmed at the development.

'But it's the same kidney you would have had,' Connor pointed out. 'What's the difference? It's been in this vacuum flask for four hours instead of in the patient's body.'

'Are you sure it's the right kidney?' Fawcett asked, 'And that it's only been out for four hours?'

'Yes,' Connor answered, 'I'm absolutely sure.'

'All right, we'll use it,' Fawcett said reluctantly.

He placed the kidney in the pelvic cavity and joined the blood vessels with careful sutures.

'The moment of truth,' he said to the theatre sister, 'we'll soon see.' He watched with relief as the patient's blood flowed into the new kidney, changing its colour, and when a stream of urine flowed out from the ureter splashing his gown, he knew the kidney was working. He quickly connected the ureter to the bladder. The businessman made a quick recovery. Instead of being a very sick man, his health improved every day and he left hospital within weeks.

If Fawcett could have operated alone in the theatre, he could have maintained complete secrecy, but he couldn't work without his transplant team. The story of the kidney arriving from Eastern Europe in a vacuum flask soon went round the hospital. Wright met Fawcett in the Consultant's Staff Room. They had ceased making any pretence of friendliness towards each other after the forged letter confrontation.

'Fawcett,' said Wright, 'what's this I've been hearing about you using kidneys from Eastern Europe. I hope you're behaving ethically?'

'It's got nothing to do with you,' countered Fawcett icily.

'It all seems rather shady,' said Wright. 'And I want you to know that if I find evidence that you're behaving unethically, I'll blow the whistle on you.'

'I don't need lessons on ethics from you,' retorted Fawcett.

'Perhaps you do,' said Wright. 'If you do anything to bring this hospital, or the profession, into disrepute, I'll personally write to the GMC.' He paused at the open door before leaving. 'And what's more, I'll sign it myself. I won't forge someone else's signature.'

That evening Fawcett dined with Connor at the Savoy. He did this reluctantly because now that he had resolved his financial difficulties, he wanted to get back to his normal lifestyle, although he still looked anxiously at his post every morning for any official-looking letter which might be from the GMC. 'The sooner I break with Connor the better,' he thought. He wanted to forget his dealings with him.

In spite of Fawcett's misgivings, the atmosphere between the two was much more relaxed, but he was soon to learn that it was true that there was no such thing as a free dinner. Connor was a business man. He had become rich by spotting opportunities and exploiting them. He remembered the conversation he had had with the agent on the tiny airfield in Eastern Europe.

'I'm turning them away,' he said, 'I've got so many people who want to sell a kidney, I've started a waiting list.' Connor could understand this because, as the agent said, 'The money's peanuts to us, but it's a fortune to them.'

There seemed to be no problem with the supply of kidneys, no problem with demand because Fawcett had said there was a lengthening waiting list, and the facilities to carry out the transplants were available. And there was no reason why the patients should only be British. Patients would come from Europe, the Middle East and the USA, to avail themselves of a quick, efficient service. And if the sale of organs becomes illegal in the UK, 'So what?' said Connor to himself. 'It takes time to get a law through both Houses of Parliament and by that time I'll have moved the service abroad, or even on to a boat.'

'You've transformed James,' remarked Connor. 'With his spare parts, he's a new man.' Fawcett acknowledged his thanks and looked forward to a pleasant dinner. He noted that Connor had ordered a bottle of Chateau Margaux – his favourite claret. It wasn't every day that he had the opportunity to drink a first growth. Connor tasted the claret and nodded to the wine waiter.

'Why don't we go into transplant surgery in a big way?' suggested Connor. 'You've got the skills; I've got the finance.'

'You can't be serious,' Fawcett said. 'I've told you before, that chapter of my life is closed.'

Connor gulped down half of his glass of Margaux as if it were just orange squash.

'Sir Jeremy,' he said, ignoring the rebuttal, 'let's look at the figures. Two ops a week, £25k a throw. You'd be on £2½ million a year.' He waited to see whether he could detect any response in Fawcett's face. 'You don't even have to collect the fees; I'll do all that.' Fawcett remained silent. 'You just operate and get filthy rich, that's all you have to do,' he said with a laugh.

'No,' said Fawcett, 'I'm not even prepared to talk about it.'

'Let's get this straight,' Connor said, angered by the brusque reply. 'I've been more than generous with you. Now I see a way of getting my money back, I'm going to take it.' He paused just long enough for the waiter to refill his glass. 'If you're not interested, I'll soon find another surgeon – who wants to be a millionaire.'

'You would bring surgery into disrepute,' Fawcett said. 'Most people would find the sale of parts of the body deeply offensive.'

'Maybe most would,' Connor said, his hackles beginning to rise, 'except those urgently in need of a kidney. Or those needing the money desperately.' He went on contemptuously: 'Or surgeons needing the money. I don't know how you put up with your crazy system. I read of an Indian the other day who circumvented the waiting list by marrying a woman so that he could have one of her kidneys. After the operation he paid her off and never saw her again.'

'I've made my position clear,' Fawcett said, 'I'm having no part of it.'

'You owe me,' Connor said, his petulance turning to anger, 'you've used your privileged professional position to extract large sums of money out of me.' He quaffed his Chateau Margaux, and beckoned the waiter for another bottle before continuing: 'It was emotional blackmail,' he said in a loud voice.

'That's a gross distortion of the facts,' Fawcett said, getting alarmed. 'We agreed a deal. I carried out my part of the bargain. Now I want out. Surely you can understand that.'

'What I do understand,' Connor said viciously, 'is that you've broken the rules of your GMC. And they'll call you to account if they find out. And you've no guarantee I won't tell them.'

'What will you gain by doing that?' Fawcett asked nervously, feeling his stomach muscles tightening with fear, 'even if you get me struck off, it wouldn't make any difference to you financially.'

'No, but it would ruin you financially,' Connor said spitefully, 'and professionally.'

They parted on bad terms.

A week later Fawcett's private telephone rang. 'Sir Jeremy, I've a very interesting proposal to put to you.' There was no mistaking Connor's voice. 'I can't discuss it on the telephone, let's meet for dinner.'

Fawcett politely refused. 'I've got two critically ill patients,' he said, 'and I have to be on call in case anything blows up.'

'But this is important,' Connor persisted. 'I think we should meet.'

Fawcett was determined to end all contact with Simon Connor.

'I'm afraid it's not possible.'

'Your professional reputation is at stake,' said Connor.

'What d'you mean?'

Connor wouldn't elaborate over the telephone and insisted on a meeting.

Fawcett arrived at the Savoy, and as usual, was cordially greeted by Connor and was soon drinking a very dry sherry. Over dinner, as they worked their way through the roast beef and the Burgundy, Connor began the approach work.

'Sir Jeremy,' he said, 'my contacts in the Middle East have told me about a very rich Arab.' He could see the apprehension on Fawcett's face as he continued. 'So rich that his capital is snowballing all the time. He'll only ever be able to spend a fraction of the interest.' He gulped his wine and

swilled it round his mouth like a mouth wash. 'This man's got everything –
except health,' he said. 'He's not selfishly pursuing his own pleasures. He's
doing an enormous amount for the poor – building houses, hospitals and
schools.'

Fawcett was preparing himself for the crunch.

'I'd hate to see this man die young before he's finished his work,' said
Connor.

'What's his problem?' Fawcett asked.

'He's seen numerous cardiac specialists in the Middle East and in the States.
They all say one thing: he needs a new heart – and he needs it soon.'

'Any moment now,' thought Fawcett.

'He's been told you're the best transplant surgeon in the world.' He paused
just long enough to dab the corners of his mouth with his napkin. 'He wants
you to give him a new heart.' And then he added, so dramatically that Fawcett
felt like giving him mock applause, 'Give him life so that he can carry on
with his good work. There'll be a large fee for you, of course.' He sat back
in his chair, pleased with his performance, waiting for Fawcett's reply.

'There's no way I'm getting involved,' said Fawcett firmly. 'I'll not
jeopardise my career any further.'

'D'you have a choice?' Connor asked bluntly. 'Either you treat this patient
or I go to the GMC. It's up to you.' Fawcett had gone very pale. 'I told you
your professional reputation was at stake. Why can't you treat this one
patient and bank a large fee? You'll only be doing your job. You've been
trained to treat patients. I'm not asking you to rob a bank. Just to save a
man's life.'

'No further business deals,' Fawcett said, standing up, 'with you, or anyone
else.' He turned and walked out of the restaurant.

Over the next few days he worried as to whether Connor would carry
out his threat and go to the GMC, but finally he persuaded himself: 'No, he
won't go. He's a business man. He'll find another surgeon and soon realise
that he was better off with someone out of the limelight. Anyway, if he did
go to the Council and succeeded in getting me struck off, no other surgeon
would touch him with a barge pole. No, he won't do it,' he decided.

A week after the ill-tempered meeting at the Savoy his private telephone
rang.

'Sir Jeremy, have you thought any more about my proposition?'

'I've made my position quite clear,' Fawcett said, 'there's nothing more
to say.'

'Don't hang up,' Connor said, 'if you do, I'll go straight to the GMC. I've
collected the evidence. I've spoken to various people at St Luke's to check

the facts.'

Fawcett's blood pressure shot up more than a few notches at the thought of Connor asking questions at the hospital, but he knew that he must put an end to it.

'I'll just have to face up to it,' Fawcett said. 'The GMC may accept my explanations.'

He heard Connor laugh down the telephone. 'You're living in cloud cuckoo land if you think you'll stay on the Register after the GMC have seen the evidence I'll produce.'

'We'll see,' said Fawcett, trying to bluff it out.

'Before you commit professional suicide,' Connor said, 'wouldn't it be sensible to talk to me? I'm talking of sufficient money to provide you with financial security for the rest of your life. Just for one operation! Why don't you at least listen to what I have to say?' He could almost hear Fawcett's mind racing. 'Just one more operation and your future will be secure,' he said. 'I won't bother you again, I promise.'

Whatever he said, Connor was thinking that one more unethical operation and Fawcett would be hooked. With his name and reputation discreetly used, he would be able to scoop the richest patients from the world market. Just one more twitch on the line and he would take the bait. Once hooked, he could drive down the fees and start to make money.

'We're talking about a quarter of a million pounds,' he said, 'for one operation. You can forget you ever met me after that.'

Fawcett hadn't replaced the receiver but the line remained silent for so long that Connor thought that he had just left it on his desk and gone out of the room.

'Sir Jeremy. Are you still there?'

'Yes,' he replied tersely, 'but I must go.'

'Before I go to the GMC,' Connor said, 'wouldn't it be worthwhile to have one short meeting?'

The pressure was such that eventually Fawcett agreed to meet Connor in his office in Park Lane.

'Let's waste no time,' Fawcett said, ignoring Connor's outstretched hand and his offer of a drink. 'What you're resorting to is blackmail.' He sat facing Connor. 'If you go to the GMC, he said aggressively, 'I'll go to the police. I may be struck off. But you'll go to prison. It's up to you. I'll take you down with me.' Connor had seen this kind of bluff many times before in his business career.

'How can it be blackmail?' he asked calmly, 'I'll only be doing my duty as a citizen. Protecting the public from an unethical surgeon.'

Fawcett shuddered inwardly at being referred to as 'unethical'. Probably the worst insult that could be put to a professional man. He wanted this man to disappear from the face of the earth. Before he had met him, his career had been racing ahead and he could even imagine himself in the House of Lords one day. But now Connor was dangling him on a piece of string. Pulling him in directions he had no wish to go.

'You're threatening me,' Fawcett shouted. 'Either I operate unethically, or you go to the GMC. That's blackmail.'

'You've no evidence of any threats,' Connor said dismissively.

Connor waited patiently for Fawcett to reply but he remained silent.

'I'm offering you two things,' Connor said, 'a lot of money and peace of mind.'

After half an hour of Fawcett being surly and Connor trying to sound like the most reasonable man in London, Fawcett asked, 'What guarantee do I have that after this operation you won't find another rich patient who needs urgent treatment?'

'You have my word, Sir Jeremy,' he said, knowing that he was home and dry. 'That is all I can offer.'

Fawcett had little faith in Connor's word, but he was in a corner; and there was the quarter of a million pounds. He thought grimly: 'If I'm going to be struck off, I might as well be rich first.' He just had to hope that Connor would lose interest in his new business venture. Surely he must have more than enough money. But he failed to understand that Connor was an addictive entrepreneur who couldn't resist the opportunity to make another fortune. The excitement of the early days had disappeared when he had floated his property company and gone public. Now he latched on to any new project to get the adrenaline flowing.

Finally Fawcett accepted a glass of champagne and they discussed the arrangements.

'As soon as you give me the matching information, I'll contact my agent for a heart,' Connor said, as casually as if he were going to order a replacement pump for his central heating system.

'But where's he going to get it from?' Fawcett asked anxiously. 'An impoverished peasant selling a kidney is one thing. But a heart?'

'I don't ask questions, but you know better than I do that thousands of suitable hearts are buried every day. I expect the agent does a deal with the relatives.' Connor leant across and poured more of the champagne into Fawcett's glass. 'Drink up,' he said, 'you worry too much.'

'Another thing,' Fawcett said, 'Hearts are more time-sensitive than kidneys. I like to use them within four hours of them being removed from the donor's body. If not, they may not re-start.'

'No problem,' Connor said confidently, knowing that with bad weather it could easily take six hours. 'These doctors,' he thought, 'are over-cautious. It's just like the "sell by" dates on food. They're only a guide.'

Ten days later he telephoned Fawcett. 'We've located a suitable heart,' he said. 'The patient's brain-dead and on a ventilator.' Fawcett tried not to think about the donor patient, who he might be – or how he had died. 'Or,' he thought, 'who made the diagnosis of brain-death.'

Simon Connor met Tulley on the small Eastern European airfield. This time there were no guns or unpleasantness or suspicion. The agent handed over the cool container. The balance of the price was paid and Connor's jet was soon on its way back.

Connor sat in the Lestair, drumming his fingers on the table as he drank malt whisky and cursing as he watched the weather close in. In spite of the heavy cloud over SE England, they were making good time, but as they approached Biggin Hill, they could see the blanket of fog over the airport. It didn't need Air Control to tell them they couldn't land. They were re-routed to Luton and rushed through the airport and into a waiting car.

'Put your bloody foot down,' Connor shouted. 'Can't you go any faster?' Their speed touched a hundred and ten at one point and seven hours after leaving Tulley they arrived at St Luke's.

'Take off was delayed,' Connor said. 'It can't be much more than five hours since the heart was removed.'

'Are you sure,' Fawcett asked? 'a man's life is at stake.'

'Yes,' Connor said glibly. 'Could have been less.'

Fawcett's instinct was to abandon the operation. Not only was he involved in buying organs, but he was also breaching the surgical guidelines he himself had helped to establish.

'There's a lot of money riding on this op,' Connor said as Fawcett hesitated. Fawcett knew that all the time he prevaricated the clock was ticking and the chances of the heart re-starting were getting less. He nodded to Sister.

The heart/lung machine pumped oxygenated blood round Sheikh Abdullah's unconscious body whilst Fawcett removed his diseased heart. He placed the new heart into the chest cavity and sutured it in place, hoping it would start spontaneously. The heart which had been beating strongly in a stranger's breast earlier in the day remained still. Electrical stimulation made no difference. The heart would not start. His worst fears were realised. The heart/lung machine was disconnected, and the enormous incisions in the chest closed. The patient was dead. Even the electric pacemaker couldn't start the heart beat.

Fawcett went back to his room and sat in miserable depression drinking a large whisky. 'How could this have happened?' he asked himself. 'How can I explain it away? A heart from an unknown source? God knows how long it had been out of the donor's body. And it had been purchased.' The death on the operating table had to be reported to the Coroner's office and an autopsy carried out to determine the cause of death. Fawcett hoped it would go through without any questions being asked and a death certificate issued, but the Coroner began asking questions, and the more he asked the more suspicious he became.

'Sir Jeremy Fawcett or not,' he said, 'I want an inquest.'

At the inquest the Coroner asked himself the question: 'Was this so grossly negligent that Sir Jeremy's actions brought about the death of Sheikh Abdullah? If the answer was 'yes', then it was 'unlawful killing'. After hearing the evidence, he decided that though the patient was in end-stage heart failure and likely to die at any moment, that's exactly what it was – 'unlawful killing.'

A few days later the police contacted Fawcett. He was arrested, charged and released on bail. St Luke's was shaken. Their senior surgeon arrested! They had no option but to suspend him until the case had been tried. He was not allowed in the hospital or Medical School. There was no question of maintaining any teaching contacts with students.

At the trial it became a contest between the two expert witnesses. 'Four hours was never intended to be an absolute deadline,' the defence expert argued. 'Hearts transplanted after four hours don't all fail to start. Four hours is only a guide. It might be better to say that as the time between removal of the donor heart and its use increases, the chances of a successful transplant diminishes.'

The defending barrister said: 'Sheikh Abdullah was critically ill – at death's door, and the chances of another heart becoming available at short notice were remote – almost non-existent. What would be the point of cancelling the operation and allowing the patient to die on the waiting list? At least if Sir Jeremy operated, there would be a chance.' He then painted a dramatic picture of the situation Sir Jeremy was in. 'Connor told him the heart had been removed not much more than five hours before. The patient was likely to die at any time. Surely, in these circumstances, any conscientious surgeon would carry on.'

He looked up from his notes at the jury to make his final plea. 'Many more patients will die in the future,' he said dramatically, 'if you find Sir Jeremy guilty.'

The jury were out for three hours and returned with a 'not guilty' verdict.

Fawcett shook hands with his lawyers and went back to St Luke's, his reputation tarnished but not shattered.

'You were sailing close to the wind,' remarked Wright when he met him in the hospital corridor on his first day back. 'You were lucky this time. I'd have charged you with murder. If you'd abandoned the operation, the patient might still be alive today.'

'I don't have to listen to your diatribe,' Fawcett said, trying to walk on, but Wright stood his ground.

'You're a good surgeon,' Wright said, 'but there's something missing. You've got no integrity; you're weak. You haven't got the bottle to say "No" when you should.'

'Get out of my way,' said Fawcett, pushing past him.

Back at St Luke's, Fawcett began to relax as each day passed without a letter from the GMC. Most of his colleagues were sympathetic; at least to his face. It was only 'that bastard Wright' who had been offensive. About a month after the unsuccessful heart transplant, he was called back to the hospital to see James Connor, who had been re-admitted.

'What've we got, then?' he asked his registrar.

'It's not good. The kidneys aren't functioning well. Plasma creatinine and protein levels in the urine are going up.'

'Blood pressure?'

'Diastolic's climbing.'

'Must be rejection. What about the pancreas?'

'Seems to have stopped sending insulin into the bloodstream. He's back on daily injections.'

James Connor responded well to treatment with the immune suppressive drugs for some days, but then his condition deteriorated and Fawcett knew that he must operate again.

The night before the operation his emergency bleeper woke him. When he arrived at the hospital at two o'clock in the morning, James Connor was already dead. Attempts to resuscitate him had failed.

'It's sod's law to happen in this case,' Fawcett said. 'How am I going to tell Connor? It's not going to be easy,' but he found the tough, ruthless entrepreneur completely shattered by his son's death.

'My whole life is pointless,' he said. 'Why couldn't it be me? Why did James have to die?' He was in tears. 'I have enough money to buy anything I want: cars, yachts, women. All I want is my son.' His wife had died five years before and since then he had become closer to James and they had spent much of their time together. Now it was over.

'We did all we could to save him,' Fawcett said, putting his arm round

Connor's shoulders. 'The emergency team spent most of the night trying to revive him.'

'I don't blame you, Sir Jeremy,' Connor said. 'If you couldn't save him, I don't suppose anybody could.'

Fawcett left St Luke's and drove slowly home. There was no question of going back to bed. Sleep was out of the question. He was still drinking black coffee when Melanie came into the kitchen.

'Tough night?' she said, kissing him. She had never seen him looking quite so shattered. 'Who was it?'

'James Connor,' he said. 'He died in the night.'

He showered and returned to the hospital at nine o'clock. Over the next months he gradually put the James Connor case out of his mind. At least, he thought, Simon Connor will get off my back now.

Jane Perkins had met Connor when he was visiting his son. She knew he was a widower and extremely rich, and she watched with envy when she saw him arrive at the private patient's entrance in his gleaming, chauffeur-driven Rolls Royce. He was a pleasant enough man, and she had no ulterior motive when she wrote a letter of sympathy to him on the death of his son, offering to meet him and talk about James if he felt it would be helpful. To her surprise, Connor invited her to come and see him. She went along to his London house in Park Lane and found him deeply sad, filled with remorse, and in spite of his wealth, lonely.

'I do appreciate your coming to see me,' Connor said, 'I feel guilty over James; I feel I've let him down.' His eyes filled with tears and Jane Perkins put her arm round his shoulders. 'Nobody could have done more,' she said. She stayed with him for two hours and as she left she said: 'If you'd like me to come again, I will.'

'Please, I'd like that,' Connor said. 'I'll send the Rolls for you.'

She saw him a number of times and her counselling helped to remove some of the self-recriminations. He seemed happier, and he began to talk quite freely with her.

'D'you know, I admired John Jackson,' he said one evening. 'He had such guts.'

'When did you meet him?' she asked. 'He wasn't in the same ward as James.'

'I saw him just before he became permanently unconscious,' he said. 'I was able to help his widow, a very nice woman.'

'How d'you mean, help?' she said, her curiosity aroused.

He told her of the £100,000 he had paid to Janet Jackson for her husband's organs, and with a little coaxing, Connor told her the whole story of the organs flown in from Eastern Europe for Fawcett's other patients. They started going out in the evenings to dinner; Jane Perkins had never experienced such luxury. 'You'd better come and see how the other half lives,' she said one night as she got into the Rolls to be driven home. 'Come and have supper with me.'

He arrived with two bottles of Krug and after the champagne, and wine with dinner, followed by two large brandies, he knew he wasn't fit to drive home.

'You'd better stay the night,' suggested Jane.

'I could get my chauffeur out of bed,' he said, 'or call a taxi and get the car picked up tomorrow.'

She held his face in her hands and kissed him passionately. 'What would you rather do?' she asked, kissing him again, 'it's up to you.'

They slept together and became lovers, and within six weeks Connor was talking of marriage.

'You must talk to someone about Jeremy Fawcett,' Jane said. 'What he did was unethical. He shouldn't be allowed to get away with it.'

'I'm not bothered too much about ethics,' he replied. 'It was a business deal as far as I was concerned.'

'But medicine isn't a business,' said Jane. 'We're dealing with human beings.'

'I think patients have the right to do what they like with their own bodies,' Connor said. 'If they want to sell organs, why not? Freedom of choice is a basic right. More important than medical ethics.'

'You are being very profound, darling,' said Jane, 'but it's wrong, and we must do something about it.'

'So much for freedom of choice,' he thought. He was no longer his own man. Jane Perkins was determined to get her own way. Connor was so infatuated that he couldn't refuse her anything. He was like putty in her hands. He had become completely dependent upon her for his physical and emotional needs.

She visited Wright and told him all about Simon Connor and John Jackson; about organs flown from Eastern Europe and the large sums of money Fawcett had received from Connor.

'He's a disgrace to surgery,' she said. 'We can't let him get away with it.'

Wright, as much as he hated Fawcett, didn't like the idea of whistle blowing, of telling the GMC, in spite of what he had said to Fawcett. When he first started to study medicine, he always remembered Dr McTaggart at Birdie's house saying: 'Dog doesn't eat dog. In other words doctors must look after each other,' but this was so serious that the GMC must be involved.

Fawcett's programme at the Royal College and at St Luke's was so intense that he had little time to dwell on the past until one morning the letter he had been dreading dropped through his letter box. The envelope was clearly marked 'General Medical Council' and he held it for some minutes before opening it, trying to persuade himself that it was probably just a notification of an election to the Council, but as soon as he started to read the letter he sat bolt upright.

Dear Sir Jeremy.

The following allegations have been received by the Council and the President has asked me to seek your observations on these charges before deciding whether they should be referred to the Preliminary Proceedings Committee for further consideration.

From Sister Jane Perkins

'I am a theatre sister at St Luke's hospital and was assisting Sir Jeremy Fawcett when he was removing a pancreas and a kidney from Mr John Jackson for transplantation to Mr James Connor. Mr John Jackson was a beating heart donor who had been certified as brain dead by Sir Jeremy and two other doctors.

'At the donor operation I distinctly saw the blood pressure which was being monitored jump up as Sir Jeremy removed the organs. I also saw the tube in Mr Jackson's throat move. The oesophageal reflex still seemed to be functioning. Because of these factors, I am sure that Mr Jackson was not completely brain-dead when the organs were removed. I drew Sir Jeremy's attention to these movements but he continued to operate.'

From Simon Connor

'Sir Jeremy Fawcett operated on my son James to transplant a new pancreas and a kidney from a patient named Mr John Jackson. Sir Jeremy arranged for me to see Mr Jackson in the hospital ward and I agreed to pay his widow one hundred thousand pounds for one of his kidneys and his pancreas, should Mr Jackson die.

'I also paid to Lloyds of London the sum of three hundred and fifty thousand pounds to clear Sir Jeremy Fawcett's debts. As it turned out, the operation was a failure and my son James is now dead. The payment of the Lloyd's debt was negotiated by Sir Jeremy over the telephone the evening before he was due to operate. It was only because I was under such stress worrying about my son's operation the next day that I accepted his proposals.

'Before my son died, when I still had faith in him, Sir Jeremy also agreed that I would purchase a kidney from an agent in Eastern Europe for the treatment of a business man. I flew this organ to England in my private plane, and following the operation I agreed to cancel Sir Jeremy's outstanding debt to me of £100,000.

'I also purchased a heart from an agent in Eastern Europe to enable Sir Jeremy to carry out a transplant on a rich Arab patient.

'It seems to me that Sir Jeremy's behaviour was unethical, more influenced by commercial considerations than the proper care of patients. My son would still be alive but for Sir Jeremy Fawcett's treatment.

'I look to the Council to deal with this matter in order to protect other members of the public from being treated in this unethical manner.'

Fawcett read the letter two or three times and felt that his world was falling apart. His head was pounding. Early in the morning he contacted his professional insurance society and a meeting was arranged for ten o'clock the next day. He arrived early and found the Professional Advisor from the insurance society and a solicitor from a firm specialising in handling medical affairs already there. They questioned Fawcett for two hours until they were satisfied that they had all the information they needed to answer the charges. About a week later Fawcett received a draft letter for his approval. It was addressed to the President of the General Medical Council.

Dear Sir,
We are replying on behalf of our member Sir Jeremy Fawcett, . . . with respect to the complaint by Jane Perkins . . . could her clinical assessment of John Jackson be more reliable than that of Sir Jeremy Fawcett . . .

The complaints by Simon Connor are about financial issues not professional conduct . . .

Sir Jeremy was not concerned with the sale or purchase of organs . .
.

The payment of his professional fees to Lloyds was a commercial arrangement . . .

The additional loan of £100,000 . . .

. . . no need for the matter to be considered by the Preliminary

Proceedings Committee . . .

    Yours . . .

It didn't take the President long to come to a decision when he read the reply. 'Let PPC look at it,' he said to the Registrar. 'I'm uneasy about the whole business. I don't intend it to be swept under the carpet without proper consideration.'

When the Preliminary Proceedings Committee, made up of doctors and lay members, considered the charges, they were in no doubt that they should be answered in public before the Professional Conduct Committee.

Fawcett received the official letter from the Council informing him of the date of the hearing. He knew that there would be a press release giving brief details of the case, so he expected the public and press galleries to be full, and he had no doubt that the television cameras would be outside the building.

'It'll be three weeks of hell,' he said to Melanie, 'and the thought of Wright sitting on the PCC is the end. He of all people, sitting in judgement on me!'

'I'm sure he'll be absolutely fair,' she said.

'We'll never agree about that,' he snorted. 'I'm going to object to him being on the Committee.'

'What grounds would you have?' she asked.

Fawcett couldn't tell her that it had all started with a fight in the Medical School – over her. Nor could he admit to his insane jealousy when Wright had taken her from him. He couldn't tell her about the forged letter.

'I'll leave it to my counsel,' he said. 'He'll know what to say.'

But, in fact, Wright left the Professional Conduct Committee of his own free will, because he knew that if it became known that he had had meetings with Jane Perkins and Simon Connor, the Privy Council would almost certainly quash the verdict on appeal. And then he muttered to himself, 'That would be ironic; Fawcett struck off by the GMC, and put back on by the Privy Council because of me.'

# Chapter Five

Fawcett met his advisers an hour before the start of the hearing to discuss any last minute developments. At ten-thirty the registrar rang the bell to announce the beginning of the proceedings. The President and the ten members of the Professional Conduct Committee were seated at a rectangular table. Fawcett recognised most of the doctors, but he didn't know the two lay members. On the right hand side of the President sat the legal assessor, a senior barrister to advise on points of law. Both sides were represented by Queen's Counsel supported by solicitors and clerks. Sir Jeremy also had the assistance of a senior member of his professional insurance society.

The President of the Council, a renowned academic surgeon, was sitting as chairman on this occasion. The Council Chamber was too tall and too narrow to be well proportioned. It was an air-conditioned, half-panelled room with red covered chairs. Along one side was a stained glass window with the names of previous Presidents going back to Sir Benjamin Brodie, probably the most important surgeon of the nineteenth century and the first President of the Council in 1858. Fawcett noticed the blank panes ready for future Presidents and thought: 'Whatever happens at this hearing, I shall never become the leader of the profession. I've blotted my copybook. My name will never be up there.'

The President cleared his throat. 'Miss Lesley, you represent the Council?' Helen Lesley stood up, replied, 'Yes sir,' and then sat down.

The President looked towards the defending barrister.

'Mr Evans, you represent the defence?'

'Yes Sir.'

He turned to Fawcett. 'Sir Jeremy, will you please stand whilst the charges are read.' As soon as Fawcett had stood up, the President turned to his left.

'Registrar, will you read the charges,' the President said.

'Sir Jeremy Fawcett, that being registered under the Medical Act,

(a) you removed a kidney and a pancreas from Mr John Jackson before he was brain-dead, and even after being informed of clinical signs suggesting that there was some activity in the brain stem, you continued to remove

96

the organs.

(b) You arranged for your NHS patient Mr Jackson to sell his organs for one hundred thousand pounds for use in James Connor, a private patient of yours, and therefore knowingly acquiesced in the sale of human organs.

(c) You persuaded Mr Simon Connor to pay three hundred and fifty thousand pounds to settle your debts with Lloyds and in doing so abused your professional relationship with him.

(d) You treated Mr Patrick Selby, a business man, with a kidney you knew had been purchased in Eastern Europe and therefore knowingly acquiesced in the sale of human organs.

(e) You treated Sheikh Abdullah with a heart you knew had been purchased in Eastern Europe and therefore knowingly acquiesced in the sale of human organs.

And in relation to the facts alleged, you have been guilty of serious professional misconduct.'

As the Registrar sat down, the President invited Helen Lesley to open the case for the Council.

Helen Lesley stood up. She was born in the UK, the eldest daughter of West Indian parents who came to London just after the war. She was dressed in a smart two-piece black suit and a blue and white striped blouse. The only other colour came from the large turquoise ring on the third finger of her left hand, which picked up the light when she moved her hand from her jacket pocket to emphasise a point. She was of medium height, with dark skin and a mass of short tight black curls, and with such an infectious grin and beautiful diction that she almost charmed the answers from witnesses.

Jane Perkins was the first witness. She took the oath and stood before the Committee. Helen Lesley asked her to speak up and address the answers to the Committee.

'Will you give your name, professional address and qualifications?'

'Jane Amanda Perkins, Theatre Sister, St Luke's Hospital. I'm a State Registered Nurse.'

'Were you the theatre sister when Sir Jeremy Fawcett was removing donor organs from Mr John Jackson to be used in the treatment of Mr James Connor?'

'Yes, I was.'

'When the organs were removed, did you consider that the patient was brain-dead?'

'No.'

'Why not?'

'I distinctly saw the blood pressure rise.'

'What action did you take?'

'I drew Sir Jeremy's attention to this, and asked him whether the patient was really brain dead.'

'What did he reply?'

'He said that the patient had been examined by him and two other doctors and all the tests were negative.'

'Did that satisfy you?'

'No, not really, because I'd had considerable experience of working with transplant surgeons and I've never seen this reaction before.'

As she gave evidence, she was aware that Fawcett was glaring at her with a look of scarcely concealed hatred on his face. She tried not to look at him as she replied to Helen Lesley.

Helen Lesley asked, 'Was there anything else which alarmed you?'

'Yes, when the anaesthetist moved the endotracheal tube in the patient's throat, I saw movement.'

'What did this signify to you?'

'It suggested that the oesophageal reflex was still present, which it shouldn't have been if the patient was brain-dead.'

'Did you draw Sir Jeremy's attention to this?'

'Yes I did, and he said: "Don't worry, Sister".'

'Sister, could I ask you what you understand by "brain-dead"?'

'That there should be no brain stem activity.'

'Did you think that any of the reactions you saw were evidence of brain stem activity?'

'Both the movement in blood pressure and the oesophageal reflex are influenced by the brain stem.'

'Just wait there, Sister. My learned friend and the Committee may have further questions.'

Simon Evans stood up to his full height. He was a tall Welshman, about two stones overweight, eloquent but verbose, with a Welsh lilt to his voice, who worked on the basis that if he couldn't win the legal arguments, he would wear the opposition down.

'Sister. Do you consider your clinical judgement to be superior to that of Sir Jeremy Fawcett, the President of the Royal College of Surgeons?'

'No.'

'Do you consider it to be very inferior to Sir Jeremy's?'

'Yes.'

'Why, then, do you challenge his judgement in this case?'

'I've already said that I thought the brain stem was not completely dead.'

'Weren't you prepared to accept the considered opinion of not only Sir

Jeremy, but the consultant neurologist and the other doctor, who all certified Mr Jackson as brain-dead?'

'I've given my reasons.'

'Sister, what is your relationship with Jeremy Fawcett?'

'It's purely professional. He's the consultant surgeon and I'm a theatre sister.'

'Do you normally question the actions of the surgeons you work with?'

'No, I've never done so before.'

Simon Evans repeated slowly: 'You've – never – done – so – before.' 'Why did you, in this case?' he asked.

'It was my duty.'

'Your duty. No other reason?'

'No.'

'Sister, were you friendly with Sir Jeremy? Did you like him as a person?'

'No, not since I found that he had forged my signature on a letter to Sir John Wright's wife some years ago, which brought about their divorce.'

It tumbled out so quickly that Simon Evans couldn't stop her. He wished he'd never asked the question. 'The barrister's golden rule,' he thought: 'Don't ask a question unless you know the answer.' He certainly didn't wish to pursue the matter.

'Suffice to say,' he blustered, 'You didn't like Sir Jeremy. Would that be right?'

'Yes.'

As he sat down, he glanced at Helen Lesley, who was grinning at him.

'Sister, what was in the forged letter?' she asked as she stood up to re-examine.

'I don't see the point in continuing this line of questioning,' said Simon Evans jumping to his feet, 'It's not relevant to the charge.'

The President looked across at Helen Lesley.

'Well, sir, if my learned friend is going to argue later that Sister Perkins made her complaint because she didn't like Sir Jeremy, the Committee might like to know the background.'

'I shan't be arguing that. I shall restrict my defence to her lack of clinical knowledge,' said Simon Evans.

'In that case, I'll withdraw the question,' said Helen Lesley, smiling.

The President reminded the Committee that they must ignore any reference to forged letters when they considered the evidence.

Jane Perkins left the Council Chamber and made her way up to the Public Gallery.

'I'm glad you got that one in about the forged letter,' said Wright. 'I watched Fawcett at the time; he was quite apoplectic.'

Helen Lesley then went on to adduce the evidence for the other charges. Her first witness was Janet Jackson. She came in, a pale attractive woman dressed in a dark suit, rather nervously clutching her handbag.

'Thank you for coming, Mrs Jackson,' she said, smiling at her reassuringly. 'Mrs Jackson, did your husband have a serious car accident on the M1?'

'Yes,' Janet Jackson mumbled almost inaudibly.

'Did he discuss the sale of his organs should he not recover?'

'Yes, he was worried that he hadn't been able to provide sufficient money for me and our baby son.'

'Did he tell you that he had discussed this with Jeremy Fawcett?'

'He wanted Sir Jeremy to help him arrange the sale.'

'Did Sir Jeremy help?'

'He arranged for Mr Connor to visit my husband in hospital.'

'How do you know that?'

'Mr Connor told me.'

'We shall have to ask Mr Connor about that. After your husband died were his organs used?'

'Yes, to treat Mr Connor's son, James.'

'Did you receive any money for the organs?'

'Yes. One hundred thousand pounds from Mr Connor.'

'Were you surprised?'

'No.'

'Why not?'

'Because when Mr Connor visited my husband to discuss the sale of his organs, they signed a contract setting out the details.'

Helen Lesley turned to face the Committee.

'Mr President, I would like copies of that contract circulated. I also have the original for your inspection.'

She remained standing whilst a copy of the contract was given to each member of the Committee and to Simon Evans.

Fawcett went pale. He knew nothing of the contract. As far as he was aware, John Jackson had only signed the normal hospital donor form. His solicitor and the Professional Adviser held an urgent whispered conversation with him. Helen Lesley quietly waited for them to finish, drawing attention to their concern. She then asked Simon Evans whether he wanted more time to confer with his client.

Simon Evans stood up to address the Committee. 'Mr President, we've not had the opportunity of considering this document before and I think that is most irregular. Nevertheless we are prepared to continue.'

Helen Lesley passed the original contract to Mrs Jackson. 'Is this the contract your husband and Mr Connor signed?'

'Yes.'

'How did it come into your possession?'

'When I visited my husband later in the day, when Mr Connor had been to see him, I found it in an envelope addressed to me.'

'Did you ask your husband what it was about?'

Tears streamed down Janet Jackson's face. After a short break she composed herself and refused an adjournment.

'My husband was unconscious and he never regained consciousness.'

Simon Evans did not cross-examine and there were no further questions.

Simon Connor walked slowly across the Council Chamber. He had lost weight since Fawcett saw him last; much of his old bounce and confidence had gone. He still held himself partly responsible for his son's death.

'Mr Connor,' said Helen Lesley, 'when your son James was at St Luke's, did you discuss his treatment with Jeremy Fawcett?'

'Yes.'

'What did he tell you about James's treatment?'

'He said James's condition was getting worse. His severe diabetes was causing eye problems and his kidneys were failing.'

'What treatment did he recommend?'

'He said that he felt that a transplant of a kidney and part of a pancreas was necessary.'

'Did you accept this?'

'Yes. I'd gone to Sir Jeremy Fawcett because he had the reputation of being one of the best transplant surgeons in Europe. I'd confidence in him.'

Helen Lesley paused and then, taking a step towards Simon Connor, looked up at him.

'Did you discuss buying organs so that James could get his treatment quickly?'

'Yes I did, when I discovered there was a waiting list.'

'Can you tell us about the conversation?'

'At first Sir Jeremy refused to discuss the purchase of organs. He said that it would be unethical for him to be involved. I then suggested that the money could go to the Royal College of Surgeons to set up a research trust in his name.'

'What did he reply?'

'He insisted that he couldn't be involved in any financial transactions. I thought that was the end of the matter and that I'd just have to be patient and hope that suitable organs would soon be available.'

'Then what happened?'

'Some days later Sir Jeremy telephoned and invited me to meet him in his club in St James.'

'What form did the conversation take?'

'He said there was a car accident patient in the hospital who might be a suitable donor for James, but he didn't want to be involved himself. I'd have to arrange the sale with the patient – Mr Jackson – myself, and also the transactions with the Royal College to make the donation for the research trust.'

'Did you see Mr Jackson?'

'Yes, Sir Jeremy telephoned me and told me that he'd asked the ward sister to contact me. He said he'd told her that I was Mr Jackson's solicitor.'

'Did you discuss the purchase of the organs with Mr Jackson?'

'Yes, I agreed to pay his widow one hundred thousand pounds.'

'Was that a verbal agreement?'

'Sir Jeremy had wanted it to be, but Mr Jackson insisted on a written contract.'

Helen Lesley passed the contract to Simon Connor.

'Is that the contract?'

'Yes.'

Helen Lesley passed the contract to the President and said,

'It is the one which I have already circulated, sir, when Mrs Jackson was giving evidence.'

She turned to continue questioning Simon Connor.

'When did you next hear from Sir Jeremy?'

'He telephoned me about two weeks later to say that Mr Jackson was brain-dead and he planned to operate on James the next day.'

'When did he next contact you?'

'That evening.'

'Was he his normal calm, assured self?'

'No, he was hesitant – agitated. He'd just received a demand for three hundred and fifty thousand pounds from Lloyds' and asked me to settle this for him instead of giving the money to the Royal College.'

'What was your reply?'

'I told him that my offer to him was for two hundred and fifty thousand pounds. I'd agreed the higher sum to set up the research trust at the Royal College.'

'And what did he say to that?'

'He pleaded with me to lend him an additional one hundred thousand on top of the two hundred and fifty thousand so that he could settle his

Lloyds' debt.'

'Did you agree?'

'Yes – eventually.'

'Were you happy to do this?'

'No, I wasn't. It was contrary to all my business instincts.'

'Then why did you agree?'

'I was being put under intolerable pressure by him.'

'Could you explain that?'

'Well, Sir Jeremy was going to operate on my son the following day. I was very worried about the operation. To have the surgeon who was going to carry out the treatment on the telephone the evening before in a distressed condition, pleading with me to lend him money, gave me considerable concern.'

'Mr Connor, would you have lent Sir Jeremy the hundred thousand pounds if he hadn't been operating on your son?'

'Certainly not. It was emotional blackmail. He was using his position as surgeon to my son to borrow money from me.'

'What were the repayment conditions?'

'I said we'd talk about that after the operation.'

'Why did you do that?'

'I was more concerned with my son's treatment at the time. I'd have agreed to almost anything. I wanted to calm him down.'

'You said earlier that he sounded hesitant and agitated. Did you notice anything else about his speech?'

'Yes, it was slurred. He'd been drinking.'

'Did you say anything about this to him?'

'I told him that it would be better if he didn't drink any more that evening.'

'How did he react?'

'He didn't reply.'

'Was that the end of the telephone conversation?'

'Except that I told him I'd confirm the arrangement in writing.'

Helen Lesley showed him a letter.

'Is this the letter confirming the financial arrangement?'

'Yes.'

She gave the letter to the President and circulated copies to the Committee members. She paused to allow the members to read the letter and then continued her examination of Mr Connor.

'Mr Connor, can we now move on to the treatment of Mr Patrick Selby. Did you ask Sir Jeremy to treat him?'

'Yes I did.' He swallowed hard and felt for his handkerchief to dry his eyes. 'My son James was alive then, and I'd complete confidence in him.'

'What was the arrangement with Sir Jeremy?'

'I was to bring a patient in from Europe who would donate a kidney for a sum of money. Sir Jeremy would remove the kidney and use it to treat Mr Selby.'

'Is that what happened?'

'No, the patient refused to come to England at the last moment, so the kidney was removed abroad and I brought it back in a vacuum flask.'

'Did Sir Jeremy know that you were buying the kidney?'

'Yes.'

'Did he know how much you were paying for it?'

'Yes, I showed him this newspaper cutting.' He felt in his wallet and produced the advertisement and passed it to Helen Lesley. 'The price of £10,000 is included in the advert.'

'What financial benefit was Sir Jeremy getting from this operation?'

'I agreed to cancel his debt to me of £100,000.'

'Did you do that?'

'Yes.'

Helen Lesley checked her notes and sat down.

The President nodded to Simon Evans, who started his cross examination.

'Mr Connor, I understand your extreme sorrow at the death of your son James, but do you have any criticism of the way Sir Jeremy treated him?'

'I sometimes wonder whether the financial pressures he was under allowed him to concentrate properly when he operated.'

'But neither you nor anyone else has complained about James's treatment?'

'No.'

Simon Evans lowered his voice, which had the effect of bringing out the Welshness.

'Mr Connor,' he asked, gently, 'if all had gone well, and James was now alive, fit and well, leading a normal life, would you still have made this complaint to the General Medical Council?'

Simon Connor swallowed hard, blinked to clear his eyes, and looked across at Fawcett and then up to Jane Perkins in the public gallery.

'Probably not.'

Simon Evans persisted.

'You said probably not. Could that be certainly not?'

Simon Connor shrugged.

'I can't believe that I'd have complained if all had gone well.'

Simon Evans hesitated but continued.

'Is your sorrow now turning to anger at the large sums of money you have paid out?'

'Nothing can alter my sorrow, but I am angry over the money. A small fortune and my son is dead.'

'Mr Connor, didn't you approach Sir Jeremy offering large sums of money to obtain quicker treatment for your son?'

'Yes.'

'Before you approached Sir Jeremy, had he discussed money with you at all?'

'No.'

'He never led you to believe that he could expedite your son's treatment if you paid him handsomely?'

'No.'

'To be absolutely clear about this. You initiated the financial discussions. Before that, in no way did Sir Jeremy lead you to believe that you would get quicker treatment if you paid extra. Is that correct?'

'Yes, that is so.'

'Now, Mr Connor, if I can ask you one or two questions about Patrick Selby's treatment. Was it satisfactory?'

'Yes.'

'Is he fit and well?'

'As far as I know.'

'So, again there was no complaint about the treatment?'

'No.'

'You've told us that you went to Eastern Europe and returned with a kidney. Did Sir Jeremy go with you?'

'No.'

'So he couldn't have seen you passing money across for the kidney?'

'No, he wasn't there.'

'So, what it comes down to, Mr Connor, is that you might or you might not have paid money for the kidney.'

'I have copies of the banker's draft showing the amount.' Connor passed these to Simon Evans, who scrutinised it carefully.

'These show a sum of money. There's nothing about a kidney on them. This money could have been transferred for some other purpose.'

'Why should I invent such a story? No one in Europe's going to give me a kidney for nothing.'

'Be that as it may, there is no documentary evidence that you purchased the kidney, is there?'

Simon Connor didn't answer.

Simon Evans continued: 'Now, could we turn to Sheikh Abdullah's treatment. Was Sir Jeremy present when you paid for the heart?'

'No.'

'He wasn't involved in handling any money?'

'No.'

'Did he even know how much you paid for the heart?'

'No.'

Simon Evans turned to look at the President and the Committee and then sat down, rather pleased with his cross examination.

The President looked around the Professional Conduct Committee.

'Are there any questions?' he asked.

There were none.

'Thank you for giving evidence, Mr Connor,' he said. 'We understand your enormous sadness at the loss of your son. You do have our sympathy.'

Fawcett looked up to the public gallery and saw Simon Connor enter and sit next to Jane Perkins. She smiled at him and squeezed his arm reassuringly.

The President nodded at Helen Lesley. She stood up.

'I have one more witness, sir.' She called Dr Tulley.

Simon Evans didn't know who Dr Tulley was. He had a hurried discussion with his solicitor and Fawcett, but they had no information about this surprise witness. Simon Evans sprang to his feet.

'Mr President, this is the second time evidence has been introduced during the hearing. This puts the defence at a great disadvantage. If we'd had proper disclosure, we'd have been better prepared. I reserve the right to ask for an adjournment after the witness has given evidence.' With that he sat down.

Helen Lesley faced the President.

'Sir, I understand my learned friend's concern, but it wasn't until this morning that we knew that Dr Tulley would be in the country available to give evidence.'

Dr Tulley came into the Council Chamber and took the oath by affirmation. His appearance signalled a complete disrespect for the Committee. He was of medium height, with wiry red hair and either designer stubble or he hadn't bothered to shave for two days. He looked tired and dissipated as if he had spent the night in a Soho brothel. His open-neck shirt showed an expanse of greying hair and he looked as if he had slept in his casual suit.

Helen Lesley smiled at him; she wanted him on her side.

'Dr Tulley, are you a medical doctor?'

'Yes, but I've been off the Register for some years.'

'What work are you doing now?'

'I run an agency buying and selling organs. Mainly in Europe.'

'Did you sell a kidney to Mr Connor?'

'Yes.'

'How much did he pay you?'

'A deposit of £2,000, and then the balance of £8,000, making a total of £10,000.'

'Did you know who the kidney was for?'

'Yes, Mr Patrick Selby.'

'How did you know that?'

'I'm very meticulous with my ledger entries. The kidneys all have to be matched and the correct kidney has to go to the correct patient.'

Helen Lesley looked at her notes and went on:

'Dr Tulley did you sell any other organs to Simon Connor?'

'Yes, I obtained a heart for a patient named Sheikh Abdullah.'

'How much did he pay you?'

'Fifteen thousand pounds.'

'Do you have any documentary proof of these sales?'

'Yes, I have papers covering the sales. They include the patient's names, the matching details and the price.'

He passed them to Helen Lesley, who handed them to the President.

The President studied them, and thought that they were exactly the same as any other sales documents. The fact that the sale involved human organs seemed irrelevant to Tulley. He might as well have been selling motor cars.

Helen Lesley felt she had done enough.

Simon Evans looked at Dr Tulley with ill-concealed contempt as he began his cross examination.

'Dr Tulley, you said you had been off the Medical Register for some years. Why is that?'

'I was struck off.'

'If you've been erased, why do you still refer to yourself as Dr Tulley?'

'I'm still a qualified doctor even though I'm no longer permitted to practise in the UK. I don't treat patients so there's no question of misunderstanding.'

'How long have you been off the Register?'

'About ten years.'

'And have you been dealing in organs ever since then?'

'For most of the time.'

'What organs do you deal with?'

'Mainly kidneys, but I can usually find other organs at a price.'

'Where would you get a heart from?'

'I'm not prepared to discuss my sources.'

Simon Evans turned and looked at the Committee, and then went on.

'Dr Tulley, why have you come across to England to give evidence? You must know that any commercial transactions with human organs would be considered unethical over here.'

'You can call it what you like. It's a valuable service. There are many patients living normal healthy lives because of my agency.'

He paused to scratch his beard and run his hand through his red hair.

'They'd be dead by now – but for me. I don't suppose they're too worried about medical ethics. I'm not. Never was.'

Simon Evans tried to stop him but Tulley ignored him.

'I'm a businessman. Doctors shouldn't set themselves up as gods. At the end of the day – they provide services which pay their wages.'

He looked at the President and said with a sneer on his face,

'Let them not forget that.'

He was enjoying himself, saying what he thought to the General Medical Council. It had been so different ten years ago when he was in the dock. Simon Evans seemed at a momentary loss for words.

'It's a question of supply and demand,' Tulley continued, 'my agency is redressing the balance.'

Simon Evans tried to discredit him and sow seeds of doubt in the minds of the Committee, but the more he persisted, the more convinced they became that this man would only sell a kidney or a heart. There was no way he would have donated them to help patients, least of all ones he had never met. The thought of Simon Connor landing on the small airfield in Eastern Europe to be met by Tulley with a matched kidney or heart without an exchange of money was beyond belief. This man was no longer concerned with medical ethics, even if he ever had been. His motivation was entirely commercial.

Helen Lesley turned for a brief conversation with her instructing solicitor and said:

'Mr President, that is the case for the Council.'

Without waiting to be called, Simon Evans stood up, brushed imaginary specks of dust from the lapels of his jacket, looked briefly at his notes on the lectern, and began his defence of Sir Jeremy Fawcett.

He called Sir Jeremy, who took the oath and remained standing.

'Sir Jeremy, are the diagnostic criteria for brain death well established?'

'Yes, they've been in use for some years, and tested in thousands of cases.'

'Did you follow the recommended tests exactly?'

'Yes.'

'Was there any doubt in your mind that Mr Jackson was dead when you certified him as such?'

'No.'

'And when you removed the organs?'

'No.'

'Why was it necessary to use brain-death as the criteria for the end of life, rather than the cessation of the circulation?'

'The new definition came in with transplant surgery. It's more accurate. When the brain stem is dead, the patient is dead – even though some organs can be kept alive by mechanical means.'

Simon Evans looked at the Committee, wondering whether they all understood the answer.

'Sir Jeremy, could you explain that further?'

'Because some organs are still working is irrelevant. Human life with all its uniqueness ends when the brain stem stops functioning.'

'You've heard the evidence of Sister Perkins and others suggesting that there was still brain stem activity. What do you say to that?'

'The brain stem tests carried out by two doctors apart from myself on two separate occasions were all negative.'

'Is it possible that there was some minor activity in the brain stem?'

'That's a possibility, but in view of the precise tests carried out there was no doubt in my mind that all life had ended. There was no possibility of recovery. Mr Jackson was dead.'

Simon Evans went on to refute the second charge.

'Sir Jeremy, if we can move on to deal with the use of Mr Jackson's organs to treat James Connor.'

He paused to drink some water.

'Did you have any commercial interest in the sale of Mr Jackson's organs? To put it crudely, were you on a percentage?'

'No, I only suggested that he might like to talk to Mr Connor. It was for them to come to an arrangement if that's what they wanted.'

'When did you first learn of the details of the arrangement they did come to?'

'It was when Mrs Jackson produced the contract in her evidence.'

'Could I ask you about the proposal to set up a research trust at the Royal College of Surgeons. How was this related to James Connor's treatment?'

'Not at all. Mr Connor was considering making a large donation to the work of the Royal College. It was a charitable gesture. He wanted to help transplant research.'

Simon Evans checked his notes.

'Did you believe that it was unethical to ask Mr Connor to settle your Lloyds' debt?'

'No. How could it be? He'd offered me £250,000 to treat his son and I asked him whether he could lend me an additional £100,000. There was nothing unethical about it.'

'Do you regret telephoning Mr Connor the evening before you were going to operate on his son?'

Fawcett hesitated for a moment before replying.

'In retrospect, it would have been better if I'd left it for a few days.'

Simon Evans didn't want to prolong the questioning. In fact he had seriously considered whether he should put his client up at all. He feared that Helen Lesley would have a field day. On the other hand, he thought that the Committee might draw their own conclusions if a professional man of Sir Jeremy's standing didn't give evidence. He dealt with Patrick Selby and Sheikh Abdullah as briefly as possible.

'Did you have any detailed knowledge of the purchase of a kidney for Patrick Selby or the purchase of a heart for Sheikh Abdullah by Simon Connor?'

'No.'

'Where did you think the organs came from?'

'Simon Connor told me he'd obtain them.'

'Did you ask him where they would come from?'

'He said somewhere in Europe.'

'Did you discuss the price with him?'

'No.'

'When was the first time you knew that the organs had been purchased?'

'In this Council Chamber, today.'

Simon Evans checked his notes, and said, 'Thank you, Sir Jeremy, will you please remain standing?'

Helen Lesley stood up unhurried, adjusted her spectacles and stood close to Fawcett, alert and intelligent, quite relaxed, with her left hand thrust deep into her jacket pocket. She looked slowly at each member of the Committee to make sure that she had their undivided attention before beginning her cross examination.

'Sir Jeremy, you've heard the evidence of Sister Perkins. Do you still say that you haven't any doubt in your mind that Mr Jackson was brain-dead when you removed his pancreas and one kidney?'

'No, none whatsoever.'

'Sister Perkins did draw your attention to the increase in blood pressure.'

'Yes, she did.'

'Why didn't you stop?'

'Because all the tests which had been carried out confirmed that the patient was brain-dead.'

'Isn't the blood pressure controlled by the brain stem?'

'Yes, mainly.'

'Well, if it is mainly controlled by the brain stem and it rose when you started to remove the organs, doesn't that mean there was some activity in the brain stem?'

'There are sometimes minor reactions which are not easily explained, but these do not alter the overall fact that the patient could not breathe without the aid of a ventilator. The respiratory centre was dead. Mr Jackson's circulation was being maintained by technology, and without that his heart and breathing would soon stop.'

'So, the patient's heart was beating and blood was being pumped around his body – yet he was dead?'

'Yes, the brain was dead. The ventilator kept the circulation going but there was no way the ventilator could keep the higher centres of the brain functioning.'

'When you say the brain is dead, do you mean that the entire brain is completely dead?'

'Not necessarily, but once brain-death is established, the patient is no longer a human being.'

'Are you saying that when you removed Mr Jackson's organs, he was no longer a human being?'

'Yes, that's what I am saying.'

'You mean that even though the heart was beating and blood circulating, Mr Jackson was really a corpse?'

'It is very difficult for non-medical people to accept this, but the answer to your question must be – yes, he was dead.'

'Sir Jeremy, are you certain that Mr Jackson would have gone into cardiac arrest when the ventilator and the life support systems were discontinued?'

'Yes.'

'Are you familiar with the Quinlan case?'

'I've read an account of the case.'

'Didn't Karen Quinlan continue breathing spontaneously for many years after the ventilator was turned off?'

'Yes, but that was a case of irreversible unconsciousness caused by the persistent vegetative state. She wasn't brain-dead.'

'I accept that, Sir Jeremy, but wasn't she expected to die when the ventilator was disconnected?'

'Yes, she was.'

'So are you sure that Mr Jackson wouldn't continue breathing after you switched the ventilator off?'

'There was no way Mr Jackson could breathe spontaneously without a functioning respiratory centre in the brain stem.'

'Isn't it your duty as a doctor to prolong life?'

'I have no ethical or moral duty to force oxygen into a dead body. Mr Jackson was clinically dead when I removed his organs.'

'When you say the brain is dead, are you saying that both the conscious and the unconscious mind are dead?'

'Certainly the conscious mind is dead because the patient is unconscious. I can't answer for the sub-conscious. But without oxygenated blood, neither the brain nor any other tissue can survive.'

'Could I put it another way? When you diagnosed brain-death, was there already complete destruction of the brain?'

'I can't say that, but I was satisfied beyond any shadow of doubt that further resuscitation wouldn't have helped the patient in any way. Mr Jackson had ceased to exist as a person,' and then he added, 'Without a functioning brain stem the body is just a collection of cells.'

Helen Lesley leant down to pick up a new set of notes.

'Can we move on to the sale of Mr Jackson's organs. You've said that you had no commercial interest in the sale. Is that true?'

'Yes.'

'I accept that you didn't receive a percentage of the £100,000, but weren't you after bigger fish?'

'I don't understand the question.'

'Come now, Sir Jeremy, don't let's play games. Unless Mr Jackson sold his organs to Mr Connor, Mr Connor wouldn't have been prepared to pay a large sum of money to the Royal College of Surgeons and you would have had no chance of your trust fund. Is that not true?'

'I can't say what Mr Connor would have done if I'd been unable to treat his son.'

'Let me put it another way. You had very strong commercial reasons for wanting Mr Jackson to sell his organs. Not personal financial reasons at that time, but putting it simply – if he didn't sell, you wouldn't have your trust fund. Wasn't that so?'

'Possibly.'

'Do you normally introduce potential organ purchasers to dying patients in your hospital?'

'No.'

'Have you ever done this before?'

'No.'

'Why not? Why shouldn't all patients have the opportunity?'

'I'd be unhappy if this became the norm.'

'Why shouldn't patients be able to sell parts of their body if they wish to? Why can't they have freedom of choice?'

'It could lead to pressures on patients from unscrupulous people.'

'What about pressures from unscrupulous doctors?'

Fawcett was being boxed in.

'There could be pressures on doctors as well.'

'Isn't it the position in the UK, accepted by the profession, that it's unethical to have any involvement in the sale of organs?'

Fawcett didn't reply immediately. Helen Lesley stood looking at him, and then at the Committee.

'Take your time, Sir Jeremy,' she said, 'there's no hurry.'

Fawcett knew he had to answer.

'As I've said, it could cause problems and could never be routine.'

Helen Lesley pressed on.

'So, tell us,' she said, 'What was special about this case except the large sum of money involved?'

'I was just trying to help Mr and Mrs Jackson.'

'Wasn't it your ambition, your ego, your desire for the honour and glory associated with the possible perpetuation of your name at the Royal College of Surgeons for all time that drove you to act as you did?'

'No.'

Helen Lesley repeated: 'No, Sir Jeremy?' Then she went on, 'If we can move on to the telephone call to Mr Connor the evening before you were going to operate on his son James. We've heard that you had had this demand from Lloyds for £350,000 during the day. No doubt this was an enormous shock to you, although you must have had some prior knowledge of it. Why couldn't you wait until after the operation before contacting him?'

'I wish I had, but I was very concerned about the Lloyds debt. It seemed likely to destroy my life. I just wanted to do something about it as soon as possible.'

'Did you feel that you would be able to exert more pressure on Mr Connor if you telephoned him just before the operation?'

'No, I object to that kind of suggestion.'

'But Sir Jeremy, if you'd carried out the operation, wouldn't it have been more difficult to arrange a financial deal with Mr Connor?'

'I don't know.'

'But you heard Mr Connor say that he was so worried about your state of mind and his son's operation the next day that he would have agreed to almost anything. Weren't you more likely to do a better deal when he was in this stressful condition?'

'I never thought like that.'

'Are you saying that you never considered Mr Connor's position as a worried parent the night before his only son was going to have a most serious operation?'

'I didn't realise Mr Connor would be so distressed.'

'Were you so wrapped up with your own financial worries that you never gave a thought to Mr Connor – except as a source of funds?'

Fawcett didn't answer, and Helen Lesley didn't press him.

'You've said to my learned friend that you regarded asking Mr Connor to settle your Lloyds debts – instead of funding a research trust at the Royal College – as a purely commercial transaction. Do you really mean that?'

'Yes.'

'Yes,' repeated Helen Lesley, 'simply a commercial transaction. Just like borrowing from a bank or an insurance company?'

'It was a business arrangement.'

'Do you not think that there is, or there should be, a special relationship between a doctor and a patient – rather different from that of bank manager and customer?'

'Yes, there is under normal circumstances.'

'Do you think that the way you carried out your financial negotiation with Mr Connor abused your privileged position as a doctor?'

'No.'

'Do you not accept that you improperly exerted influence on him to lend you money?'

'No.'

'Were you drunk when you telephoned Mr Connor?'

'No.'

'Sir Jeremy, can I ask you about the treatment of the businessman, Mr Patrick Selby. In effect you agreed to treat him for the £100,000 you owed Simon Connor. Is that correct?'

'Yes.'

'Where were you going to get the kidney from since there was such a long waiting list in the UK?'

'Mr Connor was going to provide it.'

'Did you ask where it was to come from?'

'Mr Connor said he could get a suitable one from somewhere in Europe.'

'So when the kidney turned up in your operating theatre in a vacuum flask, you had no idea where it came from?'

'I knew it came from a living donor in Europe.'
'Didn't you ask whether it had been purchased?'
'No.'
'Shouldn't you have done?'
'There didn't seem much point. The kidney was in the operating theatre. The patient was being made ready for the transplant. I couldn't delay the operation.'
'You heard Simon Connor and Dr Tulley, in their evidence, say that the kidney was purchased. Have you not?'
'Yes.'
'Are they both lying?'
The members of the Committee looked intently at Sir Jeremy Fawcett, waiting for his answer. He remained silent.
Helen Lesley said:
'Come now, Sir Jeremy, it's perfectly straightforward. Either they are lying or you are. Which is it?'
'Whether the kidney was purchased or not, I had no option but to use it.'
'Be that as it may, it doesn't answer my question. Did you know that the kidney you used to treat Patrick Selby was purchased? It is a simple question, yes or no?'
'Simon Connor may have talked about buying kidneys at some time.'
'Let me try and make it easy for you. You were in a vulnerable situation. You had already broken the ethical guidelines when you treated Simon Connor's son. You still owed Simon Connor £100,000 and you had no clear way of repaying the debt. He dangled the bait in front of you. One more unethical operation and you would be free of debt. Isn't that what really happened?'
'No, I've explained the position as best I can.'
Helen Lesley leant down for a hurried consultation with her solicitor and then continued.
'Sir Jeremy, can we now turn to the treatment of Sheikh Abdullah. Was he introduced to you by Simon Connor?'
'Yes.'
'Did Simon Connor tell you that he would find a suitable heart?'
'Yes.'
'Where did you suppose it would come from?'
'From Eastern Europe.'
'Would it be purchased?'
'I don't know.'
'Sir Jeremy, if it weren't purchased, are you asking the Committee to

believe that Dr Tulley found a suitably matched heart and gave it to Simon Connor for the treatment of a patient unknown to him?'

'I had no knowledge of any commercial transaction.'

'Who was going to pay your fee, Sir Jeremy?'

'Simon Connor.'

'He would actually be giving you the money?'

'Yes.'

Fawcett felt relieved that she hadn't mentioned the unnamed Swiss bank account. At least not yet, he thought.

'How much was the fee to be, Sir Jeremy?'

'A quarter of a million pounds.'

Helen Lesley repeated the answer to make sure that the Committee had heard.

'A quarter of a million pounds. That's what you said, wasn't it?'

'Yes.'

The President looked up when he heard a muttered 'Good God' in the public gallery. In the Press gallery the journalists were scribbling madly, thinking of tomorrow's headlines.

She paused and looked straight at Sir Jeremy, forcing him to look away, and then continued relentlessly;

'You're saying that you didn't know whether the heart was purchased or not. That's correct isn't it?'

'Yes.'

'In fact, you didn't really know where the heart came from – or anything about it – did you?'

There was no answer.

'Well, it's a perfectly straightforward question. Did you know where the heart came from?'

All Fawcett could say was:

'Somewhere in Eastern Europe.'

'Could it have come from someone who'd been murdered?'

Fawcett looked startled.

'Of course not. What a preposterous suggestion.'

'How do you know?'

'The heart had been matched. This couldn't have been done if it had come from a murdered patient.'

'Well, let me put this scenario to you. Suppose that a matched patient had agreed to sell a kidney to Simon Connor's agent and once in the operating theatre, the heart was removed instead. Wouldn't that be a possibility?'

'That would be murder. You're letting your imagination run away with

116

you.'

'Don't patients sometimes die on the operating table, Sir Jeremy?'

'Yes, they do unfortunately – but they're not murdered. There would have to be an inquest and the cause of death certified.'

'Whether it was a road traffic accident or murder, you didn't know, did you?'

Fawcett stood silently with his hands gripping the lectern so tightly that his knuckles stood out white against his dark grey suit.

'Perhaps, I could sum up the position for you. You carried out a transplant operation on a patient introduced to you by Simon Connor. He also supplied the new heart – the origins of which didn't seem to concern you. He paid your fee of £250,000 – which must have been exceptionally high even for someone of your eminence – and you want the Committee to believe that you didn't insist on precise information about whether the heart was purchased?'

'Yes.'

'Yes, Sir Jeremy?'

'I didn't. Perhaps I should have done.'

'Didn't Simon Connor have to pay you such a high fee because he wanted you to behave unethically? He wanted you to operate on this patient from abroad, using a heart he would purchase? Isn't that the strength of the matter?'

Fawcett remained silent. Helen Lesley didn't press him.

She turned the page of her notes and looked up at Fawcett:

'Did Sheikh Abdullah die on the operating table?' she said quietly.

'Yes.'

'Why was that?'

'We couldn't get the donor heart to start.'

'Has this ever happened to you before?'

'No.'

'Why should it have happened this time? What was different about the circumstances?'

'Nothing. It was a routine heart transplant operation.'

'Routine, Sir Jeremy? That's what you said, wasn't it? Routine?'

'Yes.'

'Do you routinely receive organs delivered by a businessman?'

Fawcett clenched and unclenched his hands, and looked across at his barrister for help but none was forthcoming. Momentarily he glanced up at the Committee and then immediately looked away rather than face their collective gaze. Helen Lesley stood facing him, completely relaxed, patiently waiting for his reply. He knew he had to answer, and there was only one

117

answer.

'No,' he said weakly.

'Do you routinely receive organs from Eastern Europe?'

'No.'

'Do you routinely use a heart that has been out of the donor's body for more than four hours?'

'No, not routinely, but there were special circumstances.'

Sir Jeremy went on to explain the situation which persuaded him to operate. Helen Lesley stood patiently looking at him and then continued: 'Was it routine to receive a quarter of a million pounds for one operation?'

'No.'

'So, what was routine about this operation?'

Fawcett wished the ground would open up and swallow him, but there was no escape.

'I meant the actual surgery was routine.'

'Do you not accept that for transplant surgery to be successful, you have to do more than carry out the surgery?'

'I don't understand the question.'

'Well let me make it clear for you. Shouldn't you have known precisely where the heart came from?'

'I would normally.'

'Shouldn't you have known precisely when the heart was removed and how it had been looked after?'

'I would have done normally.'

'In fact, Sir Jeremy, you removed the heart from a very sick patient and replaced it with one about which you knew nothing. It just turned up in the theatre. It could have come from anyone or anywhere. Isn't that what happened?'

Fawcett stood at the lectern in the Council Chamber. There wasn't a sound; everyone was waiting for his answer. He remained silent, staring straight ahead.

Helen Lesley waited, holding her notes in her left hand and rhythmically tapping them with the fingers of her other hand. The noise wasn't very loud but it beat like a metronome inside his brain.

'Can I re-phrase the question?' she said. 'Will that help you?'

Fawcett remained silent. Helen Lesley looked at the President.

'Sir Jeremy, you must answer the question.'

'Well sir, I suppose I should have had better information.'

Helen Lesley pressed on.

'Why didn't you have better information?'

'I don't think I can add anything more.'

'There is one obvious reason why you didn't worry too much about the information, wasn't there?'

'I don't understand.'

'The £250,000 fee, Sir Jeremy. That was the reason wasn't it? The fee.'

'No.'

'No, Sir Jeremy?' Helen Lesley repeated his answer.

She stood there for some seconds looking up at Fawcett, and then at the President, who thought that he noted an almost imperceptible raising of her eyebrows before she slowly sat down.

The President looked across at Simon Evans.

'Any re-examination Mr Evans?'

Simon Evans stood up and said

'Just one matter, sir.' He turned to Fawcett.

'Sir Jeremy, were you arrested and charged with respect to Sheikh Abdullah's treatment?'

'Yes.'

'What was the charge?'

'Manslaughter.'

'What was the verdict?'

'Not guilty.'

And with that he sat down.

Fawcett thought that the questioning was over and also sat down, to be brought back to his feet by the President.

'Sir Jeremy, please remain standing, members of the Committee may have some questions.'

Sir Rodney Inchape, a distinguished scientist and lay member of the Committee raised his hand. The President repeated his name to ensure that the transcript writer knew which member was asking the question.

'Sir Rodney Inchape.'

'Sir Jeremy, when you said that the brain was dead, did this mean that all electrical activity had ceased?'

After the battering he had received from Helen Lesley, Fawcett was relieved to have a question he could answer without incriminating himself.

'Not necessarily. Electrical activity often persists after the diagnosis of brain death. The major part of the electrical activity probably comes from the cerebral cortex so that it has little relevance to brain stem death.'

'Are you saying that you didn't take an EEG to measure electrical activity?'

'The neurologist may have. It's not usually very helpful. Some brain stem dead patients have electrical activity, some have not. It doesn't alter the outcome. Lack of electrical activity is not a reliable indicator of brain death.'

'Does the persistence of electrical activity mean that the patient may still feel pain?'

'No, because the dead brain stem wouldn't be able to transmit pain impulses to the higher brain.'

'Thank you, Sir Jeremy.'

The President acknowledged the raised hand of the other lay member. 'Mrs Latham.'

'Sir Jeremy, does brain-death occur at a precise moment? I mean is the patient alive one moment, and dead the next?'

'No, it's not like that. Death is a gradual process which happens as different parts of the body fail.'

'If life doesn't end at a precise moment, when does the soul leave the body?'

'I can't answer that. That's hardly a question for a surgeon.' He didn't hear Mrs Latham mutter to the colleague on her left: 'I don't see why not.' Fawcett went on, 'I suppose that the theologians might be prepared to accept that it leaves the body about the time of death, but I really don't have a view on it.'

There were no further questions. Fawcett noted that none of the medical members of the committee had asked questions. Perhaps they were satisfied with his answers.

There were no more witnesses waiting outside, so the President had the Council Chamber cleared before the Committee started to consider whether the facts in the charges had been proved.

'Let us start with the first charge. Was Mr Jackson brain-dead when Sir Jeremy removed the kidney and pancreas?

'Was there any reason why he should have stopped in his removal of the organs when Sister Perkins drew his attention to the rise in blood pressure and the possible presence of the oesophageal reflex? Presumably, if he had decided to stop, Mr Jackson would have been kept on life support for a further period. And then what?'

He stopped and looked around the Committee, inviting them to pick up the discussion. Professor Tomlinson, a well known surgeon, raised his hand.

'Professor Tomlinson.'

'President, before the vast improvement in medical technology, both doctors and the public were quite clear when a patient was dead. When the heart stopped that was death. There was no argument. Now we have to establish brain-death simply because we are able to keep the circulation going with machines.

'I have great difficulty in understanding why this charge has been brought to this Committee. On the evidence we've heard, there is no doubt that Mr Jackson was dead, and had been dead for some time, when Fawcett removed the organs.'

Mrs Latham raised her hand.

'Mrs Latham.'

'President. Am I right in thinking that the only part of the brain which needs to be dead to establish the diagnosis is the brain stem? In other words some of the brain could still be alive?'

'You're quite right, Mrs Latham, some of the other cells in the higher brain could still be alive, but with brain stem death the vital centres, particularly the respiratory centre, would be out of action.'

The President looked around the table.

'Anything else – before we vote?'

He waited. The members were silent. Some were shaking their heads. He nodded to the Registrar, who stood up.

'Are the facts alleged in the charge proved beyond reasonable doubt?'

The Registrar looked around the Committee.

'None, sir. That is unanimous.'

As soon as they had decided that there was no case to answer on the first charge, they went on to consider the remaining four charges. The President opened the discussion and reminded the Committee that at this stage of the procedure they were only considering whether or not the facts as alleged were proved to their satisfaction. At a later stage they would have to decide whether any of the facts found proved amounted to serious professional misconduct.

'Clearly Sir Jeremy facilitated the meeting between Mr Connor and Mr Jackson. We have the evidence of the ward sister, and Fawcett hasn't denied it. We've seen the contract note, and we know that Mrs Jackson did receive £100,000.'

He looked around and saw Sir Rodney Inchape's raised hand.

'Sir Rodney?'

'President. There has been a clear involvement in the purchase of the organs. I'd go further to say that Sir Jeremy acted as a broker. He discussed the sale with both Mr Connor and Mr Jackson. He arranged for them to meet at Mr Jackson's bedside. And for reasons which are not obvious to me, he felt he had to use a deception to bring this about. He told the ward sister that Mr Connor was Mr Jackson's solicitor.' He paused whilst he checked his copious notes, and then continued.

'He also told Mr Connor that he didn't want to be involved, and the only form which needed to be completed was the official organ donor form. For me, his defence fell apart when the contract note – which he clearly didn't know existed – was produced. I've no doubt that the facts are established.'

The Committee were alarmed at Fawcett's use of organs supplied by Dr Tulley. The transaction could only have been carried out for commercial reasons. They had considerable unease about the origin of the heart used to treat Sheikh Abdullah, and also as to whether the treatment should have been carried out at all.

The President went round the table inviting each member's comments. There was little doubt as to the Committee's view, but the President still had to follow the rules.

'Registrar, let us proceed to vote.'

The vote was a formality and the decision unanimous.

After a short discussion, the Committee found the facts in all the other charges were also proven. The public and the parties were allowed back into the Council Chamber and the President announced that the facts in the first charge had not been established. The facts in the remaining four had.

Helen Lesley stood up to make her final submission and to argue that the facts proved amounted to serious professional misconduct.

'In the first place, Sir Jeremy Fawcett was driven by his desire for fame and honour to abuse his privileged position when he brought together Mr Jackson – one of his patients who was dying – with Mr Connor, for the express purpose of arranging the sale of Mr Jackson's organs.' She paused momentarily to tick her notes. 'There could be no other reason to introduce Mr Connor to Mr Jackson. He certainly wasn't Mr Jackson's solicitor.' She turned the page of her foolscap notebook to deal with the next charge.

'With respect to the third charge. When Sir Jeremy Fawcett telephoned Simon Connor on the night before James Connor's major operation to plead with him to settle his debts at Lloyds, this amounted to a serious breach of the code of behaviour expected of a professional man. His intention was to exert maximum pressure on Mr Connor when he was in a distressed state. It was, as has been said, emotional blackmail.' As she put her case, step by step, Simon Evans sat watching her, leaning forward with his left hand under his chin, occasionally making notes or turning to talk to his solicitor.

'I invite the Committee to consider the charge relating to the treatment of Patrick Selby to be more premeditated. Sir Jeremy Fawcett sat down with Simon Connor in the Savoy Hotel and over dinner they planned how they would buy a kidney for this business man. There can be no doubt whatsoever that he knew the kidney was purchased.' As she went through the evidence, Fawcett became increasingly despondent. It all sounded so damning – so conclusive and irrefutable. He glanced up to the public gallery to see Wright sitting with Jane Perkins and Connor. 'Vultures,' he thought, 'waiting to pick my bones.' Further back, almost obscured by Wright's large frame, he could just see Melanie. 'At least,' he thought, 'she's not having to make polite conversation with him.'

'Turning to Sheikh Abdullah,' Helen Lesley went on, 'Sir Jeremy Fawcett had already carried out two unethical operations. He was becoming ensnared. He couldn't refuse Connor.' She looked at Fawcett. 'Perhaps he had become complacent. Perhaps he had dared to think that the GMC wouldn't take action against the President of the Royal College of Surgeons. Perhaps the lure of such a large sum of money was too much.' She gave a slight shrug of her shoulders. 'Whatever the reasons, I have no hesitation in saying that in my opinion, the facts proved in the charges amount to serious professional misconduct.' She paused again to check her notes and leant down to ask her solicitor whether she had covered everything.

Simon Evans stood up slowly, stretching to his full height, to make his final plea. As he pleaded Fawcett's case, the sound of the Welsh valleys in his voice became more pronounced and he talked at great length, as he usually did when his arguments were weak. He argued that the facts really were concerned with business transactions. They didn't affect the treatment of patients. Mr Jackson had wanted to sell his organs to provide financial security for his wife and young son. All Sir Jeremy had done was to bring them together. What they decided when they met was a matter for them.

With respect to the treatment of Patrick Selby, there was considerable doubt as to whether Sir Jeremy knew that the kidney had been purchased. We have heard evidence that money passed between Dr Tulley and Simon Connor, but no evidence has been adduced that linked the kidney with that money. At the end of the day it was a question of whether the Committee accepted the word of Dr Tulley – a disgraced doctor erased ten years ago for drug trafficking – and Simon Connor, a self-made property billionaire, rather than that of an eminent surgeon, Sir Jeremy Fawcett.

He went on to say that Sir Jeremy does accept now that it would have been better to have discussed the financial matters after James Connor had had his operation, and not to have burdened Mr Connor with them on the night before. He sincerely apologises to Mr Connor for this lapse of consideration. But the timing of the discussion does not make it unethical. With regard to Sheikh Abdullah's treatment – again Sir Jeremy had relied on Simon Connor to find the new heart. Perhaps he shouldn't have done so. Perhaps he was naive to think that this could be done without money changing hands. But that does not make him guilty of serious professional misconduct. He went on repeating his arguments in different ways, hoping that he would eventually hit upon a formula of words to sway the Committee.

'It was,' he said, 'for the prosecution to make the case.' The burden of proof was on them. The standards of proof must be those of 'beyond reasonable doubt'. They must be sure. If they had any doubt, they must find in Sir Jeremy's favour. Finally he sat down.

As soon as the Council Chamber had been cleared, and the doors closed and guarded by members of the Corps of Commissionaires, all with sergeants' stripes and epaulettes, the President led the Committee to consider whether the facts as proved amounted to serious professional misconduct.

'There can be no question of serious professional misconduct with the first charge since the facts were not established.

'With respect to the second charge, the crux of the issue is whether it is in the interests of patients that their doctors become involved in the sale or purchase of organs. Does this kind of behaviour harm the trust which must exist between patients and doctors? Is it unethical, and if so, does it amount to serious professional misconduct?

'Before we start. Legal Assessor, what is serious professional misconduct?'

'President, for a hundred years the Council used "infamous or disgraceful conduct in a professional respect". It's only since 1969 that you've used "serious professional misconduct".' He shuffled his papers around nervously. 'What you – his peers – have to decide is whether the doctor has broken the written and unwritten rules governing the profession. You not only have to consider the effect the conduct had on individual patients, but also on patients generally, when the profession is brought into disrepute.'

'Thank you, Legal Assessor.'

The President started at one end of the Committee and expected everyone to make a contribution.

'Professor Brownjohn.'

'President, here we have an eminent surgeon – the President of the Royal College of Surgeons – being influenced in the first instance by the thought of his name being perpetuated at the Royal College by the setting up of a trust fund, and then later, when other pressures came to bear on him, being influenced by financial considerations.

'I have grave anxiety for our profession when the leading surgeon in the country behaves in this way. I don't hesitate to find this serious professional misconduct.'

The President listened intently, making notes, as the Committee sitting as judge and jury continued their discussion.

'Sir Rodney.'

'President. We've heard of the courage of Mr Jackson. His determination to do the best he could for his family. And I suppose it has turned out to be fairly satisfactory for Mrs Jackson from a financial point of view.

'But if we consider the situation which Sir Jeremy had brought about. He'd arranged for a distraught father, terribly worried about his son's treatment, to meet a dying man, who shortly after the meeting was to lapse into unconsciousness from which he never recovered. Anything could have happened at that meeting. Fortunately Mr Connor behaved honourably. If he hadn't, he might have persuaded Mr Jackson to settle for a very small sum. Or nothing at all.' He looked up from his notes and continued. 'President, if we accepted the sale of organs and it became widespread, we'd have our hospitals full of dying patients negotiating the best deal for parts of their bodies when they died. Ultimately, organs would go to the highest bidder and patients without the financial resources wouldn't get treated. I've no hesitation in saying that Sir John was guilty of serious professional misconduct.'

The discussions continued; there was little dissent, and the President finally came to the last member.

'Dr Milner.'

'As a general medical practitioner, I'd be outraged if I found that surgeons were approaching my patients when they were in hospital to arrange the sale of their organs should they die. If this became commonplace, it would cause a public outcry. I find the entire situation over the sale of organs unsatisfactory and I hope that after this case, the Council will consider approaching Government so that all commercial dealing in human organs becomes illegal.'

They then went on to consider the other charges. The President addressed Dr Milner.

'Dr Milner, you'd better be first this time.'

'President, it's beyond belief that Sir Jeremy Fawcett accepted Patrick Selby or Sheikh Abdullah for transplant surgery without having a clear knowledge of where the organs were coming from, and whether any money was to change hands to obtain them.'

Each member was invited to give their opinion. There was little disagreement. The President summed up.

'Whereas we might have some sympathy with Sir Jeremy Fawcett over the treatment of James Connor, a patient he'd known for some time and where there would have been a well developed doctor/patient bond, we can have little sympathy with his involvement in the treatment of Patrick Selby or Sheikh Abdullah. Both these patients were unknown to him and I am inclined to agree with Helen Lesley when she said "the treatment could only have been carried out for money, or the fear of being caught out, if Connor carried out his threat and exposed him".' He looked around the table. There was no dissent, just a few nodding heads. He turned to the Registrar.

'Registrar will you take us through the voting procedures?'

Outside Fawcett sat in a small waiting area with the Adviser from his professional insurance society. He had been waiting for the verdict for three hours. The alcohol had almost worn off. He looked grey and depressed, with deep black bags under his eyes and pronounced grooves running down from the sides of his nose to the corners of his mouth, suggesting that he hadn't smiled for months. He seemed lifeless. His sorrow was enormous. How could he have behaved so foolishly? Even if he were not erased, he wasn't sure that he wanted to practise again. There could be no question of continuing to teach medical students or remain associated with the Royal College of Surgeons – or St Luke's. It had been difficult enough after the manslaughter charge. Whatever happened, he knew that his high-profile life was over. He shuddered at the thought of returning to St Luke's and facing Wright and his colleagues. That bastard would have a field day! He could imagine Wright's comments: 'What are you in the market for today, Jeremy? What's the going rate for a kidney? Any discount for quantity?' Deep down he knew that even if he weren't 'struck off', and got away with a warning, he would never be able to return to St Luke's.

Behind the closed door of the Council Chamber, the members concentrated as the Registrar, an ex-army colonel, took the Committee through the various stages of the voting procedure, starting with taking no action. As each option was eliminated they were finally left with erasure as the only alternative. At the end the decision was unanimous and in their hearts they knew that this was the only outcome, but it had taken them three hours to face up to it.

It had been a hot three weeks and the members had removed their jackets. The Registrar, a stickler for the correct procedures, asked the members to replace them before allowing the public and Fawcett back into the Chamber. He felt that they should all be properly dressed before the President announced their decision.

The Registrar rang the bell, the red 'in camera' light was switched off, and the Council Chamber filled again.

Fawcett stood facing the Committee. The President looked directly at him, most of the Committee members looked down at their papers.

'Sir Jeremy Fawcett, I have to announce that after careful consideration of the facts proved against you, you have been found guilty of serious professional misconduct. Your conduct has brought about this personal and professional tragedy and brought disrepute to the profession, and the Registrar has been directed to erase your name from the Register. That concludes the matter.'

There was a commotion in the public gallery and Fawcett looked up and saw John Wright, Simon Connor, and Jane Perkins in animated conversation, all shaking hands with each other. They were rejoicing in his downfall.

The Registrar approached his solicitor and suggested that he might prefer to go out through the back of the building into the mews to avoid the press and the television cameras parked outside the front entrance. He was led out through the basement garages into the deserted mews. He hurried on to the main road and became inconspicuous on the crowded pavement. As he slowed to the pace of the crowd, he held his breath when he realised that the three people walking just a few yards ahead were Wright and, arm in arm, Jane Perkins and Simon Connor. To his surprise, Simon Connor stopped and kissed Jane Perkins full on the mouth and seemed quite unconcerned as pedestrians passed on either side. She pulled herself close and thrust her hips forward. It was clear that this was no casual relationship and it was likely that all three had collaborated over the charges brought against him. He followed them for another hundred yards before turning off. They all seemed very happy, laughing and joking. As he drew level with his turning, he could hear some of he conversation.

'Sir Jeremy, are you telling the truth?'

As Jane Perkins mimicked Helen Lesley's voice and mannerisms, the trio roared with laughter. Wright suddenly noticed Fawcett behind them.

'Look who's here,' he said, 'Sir Jeremy Fawcett – the famous ex-surgeon.'

'You bastard!' yelled Fawcett, 'I'll finish you one of these days.'

'You've done a pretty good job on yourself,' retorted Wright sarcastically. Fawcett lunged towards him and Wright defended himself by pushing him in the chest, causing him to trip and fall backwards on to the pavement.

'You'll be back in the East End soon,' Fawcett yelled from the pavement, 'where you came from.'

'You've already reached your natural home,' said Wright, 'the gutter.'

The three of them left him on the pavement and quickly crossed the road. As Fawcett sat on the pavement, he seemed to lack the energy to climb back on to his feet and pedestrians walked past on either side quite unconcerned with his plight. Melanie came across him suddenly as the crowds opened up in front of her, to avoid him.

'Darling,' she said, alarmed, 'What's happened?' Her first thoughts were 'stroke' or 'cardiac arrest'.

'Those bastards attacked me,' he said, 'Wright, Perkins and Connor.'

'Why didn't you wait for me?' she asked, helping him to his feet, 'I've been in the public gallery all day.'

'I was so depressed, I couldn't face you,' he said. 'I couldn't face anyone. I left by the back door.'

'Come on now,' she said gently, taking his arm, 'Let's get you home.'

Fawcett went straight to the whisky bottle and drank a large tumbler full almost without pausing.

'After all I've done for surgery,' he said bitterly, pouring more whisky into his glass.

'Let's talk about it in the morning,' she said. Within an hour Fawcett was unconscious.

After putting him to bed, Melanie sat down and quietly cried. 'It'll be the end of him,' she said tearfully, 'What will he do? How can he live without surgery?'

## Chapter Six

He drank heavily for a month and then Melanie gradually weaned him off spirits and got him back to drinking only wine with his dinner.

'Let's go down to the cottage,' she suggested, 'You need to get away from London.'

Her parents were away in the Far East so they had the house to themselves. They walked a lot, swam a lot, and visited most of the village pubs. After a few weeks in the country Fawcett began to talk more freely about the GMC hearing. He still blamed Wright – the East End yobbo – for all his troubles, but the charge which disturbed him most was the one brought by Jane Perkins, that he had removed organs from a living body.

'How could she? I can't believe she really thought that I would do that.'

'Well, if she didn't, she must have had some other reason.'

'Can't think what, unless Wright put her up to it.'

She almost told him not to be so paranoid about Wright, but she didn't in case he accused her of being disloyal.

'Perhaps it was to do with the forged letter incident.'

'I don't know what that was about.'

Melanie didn't press on, but she knew that she had only ever received one letter from Jane Perkins.

'When are you going to think about surgery again?' she asked.

'I'm not,' Fawcett said to her surprise. 'I've finished with it.'

'How d'you mean?'

'I've made up my mind,' he said, 'No more bodies for me.'

'Don't keep me in suspense,' she said.

'I'm going to practise as a hypnotherapist,' he replied, and sat back waiting for her reactions.

'Are you sure? Surgery's been your life. You could find work abroad.'

'D'you remember,' he asked, 'when they asked me about the subconscious at the GMC?'

Melanie nodded.

'I was a bit vague then. I still am, but I know it is a most important and powerful part of the brain.'

'Any problem with the GMC?'

'No. Anyone can practise hypnosis.'

'I hope you're not going to hypnotise me,' laughed Melanie, 'I don't want to be taken over and become a zombie.'

'I'm getting excited about it,' he said, 'Even a simple mind has greater mysteries then the most complicated body.'

'Oh, very profound.'

He leant across and kissed her. 'Don't tease. I'm serious.'

Fawcett read extensively to prepare himself for his new career. 'Did you know that some psychologists have said that hypnosis is similar to the state of love?' he said, looking up from a text book, 'being completely absorbed by one person and oblivious to the environment?'

Melanie laughed.

'Do be careful, then. I don't want a string of neurotic women on the doorstep waiting for their code word so that they can have their daily emotional high.'

'An erotic relationship develops between the hypnotist and the subject,' he read out, 'which seems to be accompanied by a desire for unconditional subjection.'

'Tell me more.'

'Do you remember that Freud gave up using hypnosis when one of his female patients came out of a trance and threw her arms around his neck?'

The technique of inducing a hypnotic trance was very simple. Anyone could be taught within minutes, but what mattered was understanding the nature of the trance and the access it gave to the buried mind. Jeremy Fawcett read about the use of hypnosis in psychoanalysis. It must be much more effective, he thought, to take the patient back under hypnosis to identify the painful or humiliating experiences causing the unhappiness, than to go through the long-drawn-out process of conscious analysis, with the mind doing its best not to divulge its secrets.

His former colleagues, and sometimes Melanie, nicknamed him 'Mesmer', after the famous Austrian doctor who used hypnosis in Paris around the time of the French Revolution.

'What sort of day has Mesmer had?' Melanie asked, when he returned in the evening.

'I saw my first patient this morning,' he said excitedly. 'Warts on a child's hand.'

'You should have given him a coin to bury in the garden.'

'Why not? That's a pretty powerful way of focusing suggestion. I'm sure it works, but if I gave a child a coin,' he said laughing, 'it would have to be a special magic hypnotic coin. To justify my fee.'

'It wasn't much of a case, but it was a start. And, I did manage to hypnotise the young girl.'

In his early cases he used direct suggestion under hypnosis to help kick some habit or phobia, smoking, over-eating, drinking or bed-wetting. Apart from the children, most of his patients were women.

'My breasts are too large and a funny shape,' one attractive woman said. 'Every time I pass a shop window, I look at my reflection.' She looked down at them as if to confirm it. 'The men in the office are staring at me all day long,' she added. 'Whenever I look up suddenly, I catch them.'

'I'm not surprised,' Fawcett thought, 'You've got a fine pair.'

However, her obsession was making her unhappy. She carried two or three bras with her and changed them frequently during the day.

'What did you tell her her breasts were like?' asked Melanie when he told her about the case – 'marbles?'

'No. She was a good subject. I hypnotised her and told her that they were perfectly normal.'

'Now, it's "throw away your bra time", is it?' Melanie laughed.

'You're not showing a proper respect for my new career,' he said.

He hypnotised a lot of smokers. 'From the time I wake you up,' he would intone, 'you will stop smoking. You will not miss cigarettes. Your health will be better. Your spouse wants you to stop. You will save large amounts of money over time . . .'

'So much for the message,' he said to himself, 'Now for the ego boost.'

'You have the strength of character to stop. You will be proud of yourself . . .'

He helped pregnant women to have pain-free births and found that the deep trance subjects could even eliminate the acute pain when the baby's head was crowned and the vagina was at full stretch.

His marriage was going well. They had much more time together and when he left his consulting room at six o'clock, it was the end of the day's work. They went to theatre, concerts and restaurants. Time had been kind to them and they both looked younger than their years. Fawcett still had a full head of hair and his skin was so smooth that there was scarcely a wrinkle, apart from the scar on his forehead. And when he looked at Melanie, he thought: 'she hasn't really changed very much from the first time we met at Cambridge.'

'How do you manage to look so young?' he asked her one evening.

'HRT,' she laughed.

Melanie was afraid that after his high-level surgical career, he would become bored with his new role as a hypnotherapist, but he seemed content as he went off to his room every morning.

'I must be off,' he would say, kissing her tenderly, 'I've got a busy day.'

One morning a new patient came into his consulting room. She was strikingly attractive – a young Sophia Loren – tall, dark and curvaceous, with large violet coloured eyes. She sat down in the chair facing him and he was momentarily taken aback by her beauty. He pulled himself together and asked: 'How can I help you?'

## Chapter Seven

Carla Narcissi had been born in Italy and emigrated to England when she was seven years old. Her father had developed a successful business importing Italian wines, mainly Chianti Classico, from Tuscany. Carla was twenty-two years of age, and a really lovely young woman and Fawcett wondered how a girl like this could have any problems. The dim lights helped Carla to relax.

'I'm too embarrassed to tell you,' she said, looking down.

'It'll be easier than you think,' Fawcett said reassuringly. 'Once you start, you'll be all right.' He smiled. 'The more you tell me, the more I'll be able to help.'

Carla summoned up her courage, lifted her long eyelashes, and looked disconcertingly straight at him, almost challenging him not to look away.

'I'm having difficulty in having a normal relationship with my fiancé, Peter,' she said shyly. 'I love him so much.' She hesitated. 'But we can't make love.'

She paused, expecting Fawcett to say something, but he remained silent.

'He gets so excited,' she said. 'I want him so much – but I can't.'

'You mean,' Fawcett said bluntly, 'he can't penetrate you.'

'I'm too tense, too small,' she said. 'I know it will hurt me. I'm frightened.'

'What about Peter – how's he taking it?'

'He's getting more and more frustrated. We're supposed to be getting married in three months' time,' she said, her eyes filling with tears. 'He's talking of postponing it.'

'What does your doctor say?'

'He says I'm perfectly normal. It must be in my head.'

'Was your doctor able to examine you?'

'Yes.'

Fawcett thought it highly likely that Carla had shown the same reaction to the doctor as she did to her fiancé, but he doubted whether there was any physical reason for the difficulty. It must be psychological.

'Have you had sexual intercourse with anyone?'

133

'No.'

'Well, maybe a simple surgical procedure of dilation would be helpful.'

'My doctor said that surgery wouldn't help.'

Fawcett agreed to treat Carla Narcissi under hypnosis. He was sure that there was some deep underlying conflict which prevented her from relaxing and caused the vaginismus. He had read once that the vaginal muscles were so powerful that a determined woman could even prevent rape. But not, he thought, with a knife at her throat or a gun at her head. He found most patients apprehensive about hypnosis. It still smacked of the fairground. Patients were afraid to pass over the control of their minds to another person, so he spent time explaining what would happen so that Carla wouldn't be frightened and would co-operate.

'Hypnosis is very simple,' he said, 'nothing to be afraid of.' He spoke quietly to relax her. 'Even when I use the words "sleep" or "deeply asleep", you won't be asleep. It's not like having an anaesthetic.' He noticed that she was already having difficulty keeping her eyes open. 'You won't be unconscious; you'll hear me talking to you and you'll be able to reply. You'll just feel wonderfully relaxed.'

She lay back on his couch and he progressively relaxed her. He intoned his instructions in a monotonous voice.

'I want you to relax your body. Make yourself as heavy as you can on the couch. Now breathe more deeply than you normally do, and each time you breath out I want you to relax a little more. Make yourself a little heavier each time you breathe out.' As he continued, he instructed her to relax each part of her body in turn.

'Let your feet go loose; and limp; and heavy. Now let your legs go loose and limp and heavy. Now your chest; and your tummy.'

He went on monotonously until the whole body was relaxed. He then took a small penlight from his pocket and held it just above her head so that she had to strain her eyes upwards to focus on it.

'I want you to concentrate on this light. And as you do so, you will find that your eyes are getting tireder and tireder. As you stare at it, your eyes will become more tired. The more you concentrate, the more tired they will become. As you stare at the light, your eyelids will become heavier and heavier, your eyes more and more tired.'

His voice droned on insistently, in a low monotone.

By this time Carla had to force herself to keep her eyes open, but she was obeying the instructions to concentrate on the light.

'I'm now going to count from one to ten, and when I reach ten, your eyes will close and you will go deeply asleep. I am going to start counting. One, two – getting tired, three, four – tireder and tireder, five, six – more and more tired, seven, eight – tireder and tireder, nine, ten – close your eyes. Deeply asleep, deeply asleep.'

As he reached ten, Carla's eyelids fluttered, her eyeballs turned upwards and she closed her eyes.

Fawcett continued so monotonously that he felt his own eyelids beginning to close.

'Deeply asleep. Deeply asleep. You will only hear my voice. All other noises will fade into the background. I want you to stay deeply asleep. There is nothing to worry about.'

He made the suggestion that all noises apart from his voice would not be heard to avoid disruption from any telephone, doorbell or passing lorry.

Carla Narcissi was already in a trance, but he set about deepening it.

'Carla, I'm going to count from one to five and when I reach five your right arm will be as heavy as a stone. I am going to start counting. One – getting heavy, two – heavier and heavier, three – more and more heavy, four – five – as heavy as lead, as heavy as a stone. Your right arm is now so heavy that you will not be able to lift it up no matter how hard you try. Just try and lift it.'

She tried hard to lift her right arm, but it remained fixed and immovable.

'Now I am going to count back from five to one, and when I reach one, all the heaviness will go from your right arm. Five, four, three, two, one. All the heaviness has gone from your right arm. Your arm is now perfectly normal.'

Carla lifted her arm freely.

Fawcett then set about producing arm levitation.

'Carla, I want you to think about your right arm once again. Instead of being heavy, it will now gradually become light. You'll feel the lightness travel from your fingertips, up your arm, to your knuckles, your wrist, your elbow, your shoulder, until the whole arm is as light as a feather. Just as if you had a balloon filled with a light gas tied to the end of your fingertips, pulling your arm up in the air. As your arm becomes lighter and lighter, it will float up towards your face.'

At each suggestion of lightness, the arm floated higher and he fed this back to deepen the trance.

'As your arm floats higher and higher, you will go deeper and deeper asleep. As it touches your face, you will go very deeply asleep.'

He watched the arm floating upwards with each suggestion and as it touched Carla's face, he continued abruptly: 'Deeply asleep. I want you to go very deeply asleep.'

He left Carla with her hand still resting against her face for a few moments, and then said:

'I'm now going to count from one to three, and when I reach three, all the lightness will go from your right arm. You arm will drop like a stone into your lap and as it does, you will go even more deeply asleep.' He counted slowly, 'One-two-three' and as Carla's hand smacked into her lap, he said, 'Very deeply asleep.'

As the arm dropped, all the muscles in Carla's body seemed to relax even more and she slumped on the couch with her head fallen sideways towards her shoulder. Fawcett knew that she was in a deep trance. She was probably a somnambule, able to open her eyes but still remain in a deep trance. He was sure that he could have penetrated her skin with a hypodermic or scalpel and she wouldn't have felt any pain.

Since it would have been his first attempt, he felt apprehensive at the thought of carrying out an analysis under hypnosis, so he decided to start with straight suggestion. 'After all,' he thought, 'if I can get her to relax sufficiently for her fiancé to get started, they'll be up and away.' Carla was reclining on the couch with her eyes closed, oblivious to the world, completely controlled by Fawcett's voice.

'Carla, I want you to stay deeply asleep. In future when you want to make love to Peter, you will relax. You will not be tense. You will not freeze up. You know that there is no physical reason why you cannot make love. It is only a question of tension. You are constricting your muscles and preventing him from entering. In future you will relax. It will not be difficult for you. The more you relax, the easier it will be.'

He decided to end the session by establishing a code word. He didn't want to go through the whole procedure of trance induction each time he saw her.

'Carla,' he said, 'The next time I ask you to go to sleep I will say the Greek word "Alpha" and when I do, you will close your eyes and go very deeply asleep immediately.'

And finally, to offset the tired heavy feeling she might have after being in a trance for a quarter of an hour, he said, 'I'm going to wake you up by counting from ten back to one. When I reach one, you will open your eyes. Feel wide awake. Perfectly normal in every way. As if you'd just woken up from a deep refreshing sleep.' He started counting. 'Ten – getting lighter, nine, eight – lighter and lighter, seven, six – lighter and lighter, five, four – lighter and lighter, three, two, one – open your eyes, wide awake.'

On one, Carla fluttered her eyelids and opened her eyes, looking calm, relaxed and smiling.

'How do you feel?' Fawcett asked.

'I feel fine. Very happy – as if I've just woken up from a refreshing sleep.'

'That's not surprising,' Fawcett thought, 'I've just suggested it to you.'

'Do you remember anything I told you when you were asleep?'

'I remember staring at a light and you saying I'd go to sleep, but I don't remember anything else.'

Fawcett knew that the suggestions he had planted deep in her subconscious would cause some reaction when she next went to bed with her fiancé. Whether they would be sufficient, he would have to wait and see. Carla returned one week later.

Fawcett smiled at her. 'How've you got on?' he asked.

'I was much more relaxed to start with. Much less frightened,' she said. 'I thought we were going to succeed.' Tears streamed down her face. 'I was so desperate to. But my muscles went tight and we had to give up.'

Carla dried her eyes and mumbled into her handkerchief. 'So I had to help him in some other way.'

Fawcett thought, 'Thank goodness she didn't leave the poor man up in the air.' He always found these vaginismus cases difficult to understand. After all, a baby's head came through the vagina. Surely an erect penis could go in. But he knew it was a real and distressing problem, and since there was no physical cause, the reason must be psychological, associated with some painful memories.

'Don't worry, we'll win,' he reassured her. 'There must have been some hurtful emotional experience in your life. Something which upset you at the time, most likely in your childhood. We'll just have to find out what it was and deal with it.'

Carla looked apprehensive and confused. Fawcett thought it likely that the powerful unpleasant memories causing her problem and the damaging emotions attached to them would have been driven out of her conscious mind and now lurked deep in the subconscious. Carla probably found the experiences so damaging that she had forgotten they had ever happened. He moved her on to the couch and encouraged her to relax.

'Alpha,' he said.

Carla immediately fluttered her eyelids and slumped into a deep trance.

'Carla, you will remain deeply asleep until I awaken you.' Fawcett sat by her side and spoke quietly and deliberately. 'There's nothing to worry about. I'm going to count from your present age backwards and when I stop, you will be that age. I'm going to start counting. As I count backwards, you will feel yourself getting smaller and smaller. And younger and younger. Your arms and legs will get smaller and smaller as I count so that when I stop, you will have the same mental age and be the same size.'

'Twenty-two, twenty-one, twenty,' he started to count. 'Nineteen, eighteen, seventeen, sixteen— As I count you are getting smaller and smaller and younger and younger.'

He continued 'ten, nine, eight.'

He stopped at the count of eight and asked, 'How old are you?'

'Otto,' Carla replied in a slow childish voice.

Fawcett realised that at eight Carla had only been in the country a short time and probably felt more comfortable speaking Italian.

'Carla, I want you to speak to me in English,' he said. 'How old are you?'

'Eight.'

He was sure that Carla was a somnambule.

'I want you to stay deeply asleep,' he instructed, 'and open your eyes.'

She opened her eyes but remained in a deep trance. Fawcett gave her a mirror, which he tilted away from her so that all she saw was the reflection of the blank wall.

'I want you to look into the mirror. You will see events which occurred when you were eight years old. I want you to tell me what you see.'

She started to hallucinate events from her childhood, and became more and more distressed.

'What do you see?'

'I'm on my bed. My papa, he is hurting me. He is pushing into me. He is holding me tight. I can't move. Please Papa, no you're hurting me. I must not tell anyone. It's our secret.'

Carla was emotionally disturbed. She shook and shuddered and pushed away with her arms. Tears streamed down her face. It was clear that she had been abused by her father when she was a child. Recovery of these buried memories and the release of the intense emotional reactions might well be sufficient for the psychological damage caused by them to disappear. Now that they had been brought up to consciousness, they could be dealt with.

He regressed her back to seven and six and the emotional distress was still present. At five she was quite different, a happy normal child describing pleasant scenes. There would have been little point in regressing her back further, because she wouldn't remember much before four years of age. Obviously the sexual abuse had started at six when she was still in Italy, and then continued for some years. Fawcett hoped that now she had hallucinated the disturbing buried memories, the emotion attached to them would disperse, and if these submerged inner tensions were the cause of her psychological difficulties, these too would clear.

Carla was still in a deep trance. Fawcett brought her back from her childhood to her present age by counting from six to twenty-two.

'Stay deeply asleep,' he told her. 'Carla, now that you have told me about the difficulties during your childhood, these buried memories will no longer disturb you. These events happened many years ago and need not bother you today. You'll find that you can now have a normal sexual relationship with Peter. You'll be loving and warm to each other. You'll not be tense; you'll relax. You'll be happy and make him happy.'

Before bringing her out of the trance, he said, 'After I wake you, you'll not remember anything that has occurred whilst you were asleep. The less you remember, the more effective the treatment will be.'

Fawcett brought her out of the trance and wondered whether she would notice that her eye make-up had been disturbed by her 'childhood' tears. Carla was quite composed and couldn't remember what had happened.

The following week he was disappointed when Carla said that she closed up at the last moment. He decided to carry on with the regression. With a quick 'Alpha', Carla became a somnambule.

'Carla, I'm going to take you back to a younger age again.' He counted back to eleven. 'You're now eleven years of age and I want you to tell me what you see in the mirror.'

He gave her the mirror, again reflecting on the blank wall of the consulting room. It was easier for patients to hallucinate staring into a blank mirror because it seemed to them like a scene from a play they were describing. It didn't concern them; it was someone else.

'What do you see, Carla?'

'I'm with Papa. We're on my bed. Mama is out.'

'Carla, tell me what is happening,' Fawcett asked.

'Papa says he loves me. It's our secret. I mustn't tell anyone. I mustn't make love with anyone else.'

She started to get agitated.

'Stop, you're hurting me,' she screamed. 'It's too painful. Stop, I'll tell Mama!'

'Get off me. You mustn't do this!' she screamed more loudly. 'It's wrong. You're hurting me. I don't want any presents.'

Fawcett calmed her down by suggestion. It was clear that her father had abused her over a long period. Whether he had actually penetrated, he couldn't know without a gynaecological examination, but whatever had happened, the fear of pain during intercourse had been firmly planted in her mind. On the other hand, he thought, her father had told her not to love anyone else, and he was sure that this was still in her subconscious. Perhaps it wasn't the subconscious fear of pain which caused her problems; perhaps it was the buried suggestion that she mustn't love anyone else that was still being acted upon many years later. He decided to remove the suggestion.

'Carla, your father told you that you mustn't make love to anyone else. That was many years ago. He only meant when you were younger. That will not apply any longer. You'll be able to make love with anyone you want to in future, and you'll find that when you make love with Peter, you'll be relaxed and happy and have no difficulties.'

Again he told her that she would not remember what had happened when she was asleep. There was no need for her to be distressed by knowing what she had disclosed. He felt very sorry for Carla. All these dreadful memories and the powerful emotions draped around them were still lurking in the recess of her mind, waiting to force their way up into her consciousness and cause her sexual problems. They were now out in the open as far as the mind was concerned. The emotional release, as she described her childhood terrors, should remove some of the inner turmoil. With such dreadful experiences over such a long period, he was amazed what a charming, extrovert young woman she was. 'Such is the resilience of the human spirit,' he thought.

During the next month he saw her weekly, and carefully taught her to hypnotise herself, and after the second session she was able to relax and say 'Beta' to herself and go into a deep trance. She would then tell herself, 'I'll relax completely when I make love to Peter. There'll be no problems. I'll not be tense or frigid. And I'll feel no pain.'

She would then bring herself out of the trance by counting from three back to one. Fawcett was aware that an emotional bond was developing between them and he looked forward to her appointments. She had complete trust and confidence in him and became quite affectionate, kissing him on the mouth each time she came into or left the consulting room. On the command of 'alpha', she would enter the trance world and Fawcett would tell her to open her eyes and feel bright and lively. As he sat opposite her, looking at this beautiful girl with sparkling eyes, it was difficult to believe that she was not fully conscious.

Even using auto-hypnosis, Carla had still not been successful. Fawcett sat in a chair alongside her as she lay on the couch, and said: 'Alpha.'

As she slumped into a deep trance, her skirt had pulled up above her knees and Fawcett found himself admiring her legs.

'Carla, it's late at night. You're in bed with Peter. You're going to make love. He's climbing on top of you. Can you feel him?'

'Yes.'

'Put your arms around him and stay relaxed.'

Carla put her arms out as if holding someone, and started to make stroking movements with her hands.

'Can you feel him on top of you?'

'Yes.'

'Now I want you to relax completely and make love to him.'

He watched her hips moving up and down. Her breasts seemed to get larger as she breathed in and out deeply.

'Stop it; Stop it!' she cried. 'It's going to hurt me. I can't! I'll be too painful! I'm too small! I can't!'

Fawcett watched Carla as her arms moved to push away her imaginary lover.

'No, No – don't!' she shouted, closing her knees tightly together.

Fawcett looked at her and wondered what to do next. He could understand how frustrating this kind of behaviour must be to her fiancé. All he could do was to make general suggestions that her love-making would be successful in future, and that there was no physical reason to prevent this. He said she would be relaxed and happy. When Carla came out of the trance, she promptly threw her arms around him, pulled him close and kissed him passionately. 'This never happened to me when I was a surgeon,' he thought.

'I expect to hear some good news at your next appointment,' he said as optimistically as he could, although he was beginning to lose hope. She kissed him goodbye and when she had left, he sat wondering what he could do if Carla still failed to have sexual intercourse with Peter. 'Whether she likes it or not,' he said to himself, 'It'll have to be the gynaecologist. Let him try with his glass cones or plastic cylinders to convince her she's normal.' He had been told by colleagues that these often persuaded a patient that they weren't small and that intercourse wouldn't be painful.

Ten days later he had seen his last patient and was writing up his notes. It was just before six o'clock and his secretary had already left when the telephone rang. He thought it was bound to be Melanie, 'Yes,' he said, flippantly, expecting Melanie to reply. 'Is that you?' but the lightheartedness left him instantly when he heard Carla.

'I'm so unhappy. Peter's going to leave me,' she sobbed. 'He's not going to marry me. We couldn't have a normal life. We couldn't have babies.' She gulped and sobbed more loudly. 'I'm going to kill myself.'

Fawcett was on full alert. 'Carla, where are you now?'

She didn't seem to know exactly where she was. It was somewhere near Oxford Street in a telephone box. He told her to get a taxi and come to his rooms.

'What's the point? What can you do?' She was sobbing incessantly. 'You've tried everything. I might as well kill myself straight away.'

He was worried that Carla in her distressed state would harm herself. 'And that will be the end of my career as a hypnotherapist,' he thought.

'Carla,' he said, with as much authority as he could muster over the telephone, 'Alpha. Deeply asleep.'

He knew that Carla would now be in a deep trance in a telephone box somewhere near Oxford Street but he didn't know where, and if she walked out into the street she might walk straight under a bus.

'Carla, stay in the telephone box until I've finished speaking to you. I want you to compose yourself. Dry your tears and then leave the telephone box and get a taxi to my rooms. Do you understand that?'

'Yes,' she mumbled.

Fawcett brought her out of the trance and sat in his room waiting anxiously for her. He watched the clock, getting more and more apprehensive as he waited for the doorbell to ring. Perhaps she hadn't gone into a trance when he had said 'Alpha'. Perhaps she was so distraught that the post-hypnotic suggestion hadn't worked. Perhaps she was even now heading for a bottle of sleeping pills or paracetamol. Or one of the London bridges. He wondered how he had ever got into this hypnoanalysis business. To his relief the doorbell rang about thirty minutes later.

He had never seen Carla in such a dishevelled state. Her beautiful face was red and puffy and stained with tears. Her hair was a mess. All her sparkle and vivacity had gone. She looked utterly dejected. Fawcett sat her down and asked her to tell him what had happened. She immediately burst into tears again, with huge uncontrollable sobs shaking her body. He put his arm round her.

'Tell me what's happened,' he said gently.

She put her arms around him and quietly sobbed for a few more minutes. Then she gradually stopped, dried her face, and even tried to smile.

'Every day we've tried,' she said, taking a deep breath, 'But I couldn't. Peter was so angry. He knew it wasn't his fault.' She paused and held her breath before blurting out: 'We tried this afternoon. Peter suddenly lost his temper. He called me a freak. Said I was useless.' She started sobbing again. Fawcett waited.

'I'm sure he loves me,' she said, trying to wipe the tears from her face with her hand, 'but I know he'll leave me.'

'Did you hypnotise yourself before starting?' Fawcett asked.

'Yes,' she said. 'I was lying on the bed wonderfully relaxed waiting for him.' She burst into tears again and Fawcett put his arm around her to comfort her. She suddenly stopped crying and lifted her face towards him.

She pulled his face towards her and started to kiss him passionately. He tried to escape but was surprised how strong she was. He stumbled to his feet, alarmed that the situation was getting out of control. Carla stood up, putting both arms round him and pulled him tightly to her. He tried to break free but she held on. She pushed her hips towards him. 'You're going to have to show me how to make love,' she said. 'It's the only way I'm going to get over this.'

'I'm your doctor,' Fawcett said, becoming increasingly alarmed. 'I can't do that. It would be wrong.'

'You've complete control of my mind and body,' Carla said, 'I know it'll be all right with you.'

'You'll get me into trouble with the authorities,' he said.

'I won't tell anyone. No-one knows I'm here. Don't be afraid.'

Fawcett was afraid. He had already been struck off the Medical Register and if this got out, he would never get back on again. And he was happily married. 'Carla, let me take you home,' he said. 'I'll telephone your father. He can stay with you.'

'If you do,' she said, calmly and deliberately, 'I'll kill myself.'

'Don't talk like that,' said Fawcett. 'We'll get over this problem. It's only a question of time.'

Carla stood in front of him and slowly undressed. He seemed mesmerised, unable to move. She discarded the last garment and stood facing him almost as if he were a judge at a beauty contest.

'Come on,' she said, 'I know you like me.' He looked at her perfect figure as she moved closer. He made a half-hearted attempt to hold her away with his outstretched arms, but she put her arms round him and kissed him passionately on the mouth. 'You're getting quite excited,' she said, as she gently moved her body backwards and forwards. 'I can feel. You do like me, don't you?'

Fawcett wanted to say: 'God, yes,' but instead he said: 'This is crazy,' trying to push her away. 'We must stop.' He stooped and picked up her clothes from the floor where she had dropped them. 'Come on, get dressed.'

'No,' she said, taking the clothes from him and throwing them to the side of the consulting room. 'I know what I'm going to do.' She took his hand and led him to the couch. 'And I know what you're going to do.' She pulled him close and kissed him again and then climbed on the couch.

She turned on her side towards him. 'Come closer,' she said as she removed his tie and started to undo his shirt buttons. 'Come on,' she insisted, gently pulling him towards her. He didn't have the will power to control the situation. She ran her hands inside his shirt, and he started responding to her kisses. There was no going back. He kissed her shoulders and breasts as she gently and then passionately caressed him. He had never been so aroused in his entire life. He explored the perfect shape of her body with his hands. In his excitement, he forgot all about her sexual problem until he found her muscles contracted, and then he didn't hesitate for a second. He had to make love to her.

'Alpha. Deeply asleep,' he said.

Carla immediately went into a deep trance.

'You're tense,' he said, 'Relax! It won't hurt. Relax!'

He felt her body relax all over, and they made love. She came out of the trance spontaneously, and he felt the enormous emotional release as she finished, and then she lay quietly in his arms.

'That was wonderful,' she said, kissing him. 'I'll be all right now. Thank you.' She rubbed her finger across the scar on his forehead as if trying to rub it away. 'I don't know what I'd have done,' she said, 'if you'd been short, fat and bald. I think I like older men.'

'Come on,' he said, getting worried about the time, 'let's get you home. You need a good night's sleep.'

'D'you think I'll sleep?' she said kissing him, 'after all this excitement?'

'I'll fix that,' he said in a matter-of-fact way. 'Alpha. Deeply asleep.'

Carla immediately went into a deep trance.

'Carla, when you go to bed tonight,' he said, in his hypnotic monotone, 'you will say to yourself: "Head on pillow. Sleep." and you will go to sleep straight away.'

He brought her out of the trance and put her in a taxi.

Melanie greeted him with: 'You're late.'

'I had a harrowing session with Carla Narcissi,' he said. 'She threatened suicide.'

'How did you treat her?' Melanie asked. 'Did you stare into her eyes and say the magic words?' And then she laughed; 'You're blushing.'

'It took some time to calm her down,' he said, looking away.

'Aren't you getting out of your depth?' she asked. 'Shouldn't you refer her on to a psychiatrist?'

'Perhaps you're right,' he said. 'I was startled when I saw her this evening. God knows what I'd have done if she'd harmed herself.'

Melanie snuggled up to him in bed that night and thought that his surprising lack of interest was because he was emotionally exhausted after dealing with Carla. Perhaps he would get over it by morning.

Fawcett would always remember the next time he saw Carla. It was Derby Day and he had backed the winner, but he would remember it because at six o'clock the outside doorbell rang. He tried to ignore it but it continued until eventually he opened the front door. She stood there, beautifully dressed, looking gorgeous.

'Can I come in?' she said, pushing past him into the hallway and then into the consulting room.

'Carla, I'm just leaving,' he said, 'I've an urgent appointment. I'll be late. I can see you first thing in the morning.'

He remained standing, but Carla sat down.

'Why don't you sit down?' she said smiling. She stretched up and took both his hands and gently pulled him down on the chair facing her.

'I must go,' he protested.

'Aren't you going to ask me how I've been?' Carla said.

'Yes, of course.'

'Well,' she said, still holding both his hands, 'We haven't managed yet.' She smiled at him gently. 'I need some more treatment.'

'Carla, I really think it would be better if I referred you on to a colleague,' he said, trying to give the impression that he didn't understand what she meant. 'There's nothing more I can do for you.'

'Oh yes there is,' she said, her hands moving up the back of his arms and with slight pressure pulling him towards her. She kissed him on the lips. 'I need some more treatment from you to overcome my problem.' And then when he didn't answer immediately, 'Don't you like treating me?'

Carla stood up close to Fawcett. She held his face in her hands and kissed him passionately. 'I think I'm in love with you,' she said.

He knew he should get up but he couldn't move. 'I'm old enough to be your father,' he said. 'This emotional bond has developed because of the hypnosis. You love Peter, not me.'

'I don't know how it's happened, I don't care. I'm in love with you; I need to be with you. I'm not sure I love Peter any more.'

Fawcett knew he must try and resist, but he only put up token resistance. Her hands and the closeness of her body were driving him mad.

'It's more comfortable in here,' he said, as he led her from the consulting room to the small flat at the rear of the premises. 'It's not as narrow as the psychiatrist's couch.'

He took her in his arms, all thoughts of his professional relationship gone from his mind. To his surprise she closed up at the last minute, but with 'Alpha, deeply asleep,' she went into a trance and relaxed and they made love.

The next morning his secretary came into his room. 'One of your admirers sent you these,' she said, holding up a large bunch of red roses.

He looked mystified.

'They're from Carla,' she said, and read out the card. 'To Jeremy darling, with love, Carla.'

'They're very demonstrative – these Italians,' he said, turning his face away so that she wouldn't see him blushing.

'She must be very grateful to you,' she replied, as she arranged them in a vase. Even though he had turned his head, she could see that he had gone deep red, but she didn't comment.

Fawcett thought: 'I mustn't become ensnared.' Until Carla had seduced him, he had had no thoughts of a sexual relationship with her, or anyone else for that matter, apart from Melanie. She was just a beautiful young woman who was a patient; that was all there was to it. But now that had all changed. He couldn't forget how alive and excited he had been. He wanted to make love to her again. 'Why not?' he said to himself, picking the telephone up to ring her, but then he thought, 'Don't be so bloody stupid,' and he put the phone down. 'I must find the will power to stop. I mustn't allow this to develop further. I will not see her again.'

'Miss Narcissi wants to speak to you,' his secretary said later in the afternoon.

'Tell her I'll ring back when I'm free.'

Carla rang again but Fawcett didn't speak to her. At six o'clock he closed the outside door behind him and went down the short flight of steps to the street. A car door opened and Carla stood in front of him on the pavement.

'I've been waiting for you,' she said, throwing her arms around him and kissing him passionately on the lips. 'Why didn't you return my call?'

Fawcett mumbled something about seeing patients all the afternoon.

'You're not trying to avoid me?' she chided, putting her arm through his.

'Come on,' she said, 'Let's go round to Elios for an aperitif.'

He tried to hold back but she urged him on, and he wasn't anxious to have a scene on the pavement outside his rooms. She led him two blocks further on to an Italian Bar Restaurant.

'Vino bianco,' Carla ordered from a smiling waiter, who brought a bottle of chilled Soave and two glasses which he half filled, leaving the bottle on the table.

'Ciao,' she said, lifting her glass.

'Good health,' replied Fawcett pompously.

'Did you like the flowers?' Carla was effervescent. She bubbled with happiness. 'Did you mind me sending them to your rooms? I didn't know your home address.'

Fawcett shuddered inwardly at the thought of Melanie's reaction if the large bunch of red roses had turned up at the flat.

'Come on, drink up,' said Carla, lifting the bottle of Soave and filling his glass, 'Be happy.'

'We can't go on like this,' said Fawcett, 'I'm married.'

'Don't worry,' replied Carla, putting her hand on top of his. 'Why don't we just see what happens? Let's live for the moment.' She leant across the small table and kissed him. 'Let's have some supper. I'll order.' She beckoned to the Italian waiter before he could stop her. 'I know Italian food.' She ordered some pasta and a veal dish with a herby tomato sauce and a bottle of Chianti Classico. The wine and the food, and the vivacious beautiful Carla, were getting to Fawcett. He held her hand on the table and behaved like an amorous young man.

'He must be rich to pull a gorgeous young girl like that,' joked the Italian waiters in Italian. 'Did he leave his Rolls Royce outside?'

'D'you love me a little?' Carla said, sensing the softening, and squeezing his hand.

'Of course I do.'

'How much?' She made it easy for him. 'Molto or quasi per niente?'

'Molto,' he answered, 'I love you very much.'

He forgot all about time until they had finished their meal.

'God,' he said, when he looked at his watch. 'Melanie will be frantic.'

'Telephone from here,' suggested Carla.

'It's scarcely worth it now; I'll be home in twenty minutes.'

In spite of his concern, they only ambled slowly back to Carla's car, holding each other closely.

'Aren't you going to invite me in for a quick coffee?' asked Carla, kissing him.

He only hesitated for a second before leading her up the steps to his flat.

'I'll make the coffee,' she said as soon as she got into the hallway.

They sat very close as they drank their coffee, their minds elsewhere.

'You've had enough,' said Carla, gently taking his cup from him. 'Kiss me,' she said, looking up at him with her mouth half open and her eyes seeming larger than ever.

'You're so beautiful,' he said, kissing her passionately. 'I love you,' and entwined they went into the bedroom and made love.

As she lay in his arms afterwards she startled him by suddenly sitting up. 'I'm cured,' she said excitedly. 'You didn't use any hypnosis.'

'Are you going to leave me now?' he asked.

'No,' she said, kissing him. 'I still need my hypnotist and his treatment.'

Fawcett knew there was no turning back. He was enraptured, infatuated

147

by Carla. She was so different from any other women he had known. When he walked into a restaurant or a bar with her, he was aware of the eyes of all the young men appraising her. His ego grew enormously. He felt young again and began to dress young, spending most of his free time in jeans and casual clothes. He had to be with her, no matter how devious he became.

'I'm planning a lecture programme,' he told Melanie. 'I'm going to talk to professional groups. It'll get my name known and they'll send me patients. It'll be good for business.'

'You seem to have forgotten about surgery,' she said. 'I'm surprised there's enough in hypnotism to keep you interested.'

It wasn't difficult to arrange a programme. Hypnosis was very popular; it was theatre. It was really an excuse to take Carla with him.

'What are you going to do to me tonight?' Carla would ask, 'Make me look silly?'

When hypnotised, she would see an imaginary tiger, enjoy a non-existent meal, or water would become wine.

He never regressed her in front of an audience, since he had no wish to take her back to her childhood and bring out the painful hidden memories which were almost certainly still in her subconscious.

'I shall have to stay overnight,' he would say to Melanie when the venue was too far. 'I'll ring you this evening.' And to his secretary, 'Book two rooms in a hotel'. But they only ever used one of them.

If Melanie went away for a few days to attend an anaesthetics conference or to see her aged parents, they spent the whole time in Carla's flat. Melanie did become suspicious. Not only was Jeremy giving a lecture at least once a week, but he seemed to have lost interest in her. They hadn't made love for months.

'Have you gone off me?' she asked. 'Am I too boring for you?'

'Darling, of course not,' he said. 'I've just got a lot on my plate at the moment.'

She had met Carla on a number of occasions but it never occurred to her that Jeremy could be having an affair with such a young woman; or having an affair at all for that matter. He wasn't that type. Carla was quite happy with the arrangements for a few months. The bond which had started in the consulting room under a hypnotic trance had developed into a real love affair.

'I love being with you,' Carla said. 'You give me confidence. I feel protected.' She had become a sexually active, passionate woman without the need of hypnosis.

'Are you sure you didn't tell me to love you when I was in a trance?' she asked when they were in Harrogate for a lecture. 'Perhaps you fancied me when I lay defenceless on your couch.' They both laughed. 'Seriously, could you have done?'

'Perhaps. But I didn't. My suggestions to you were quite proper.'

'How do I know?' Carla asked flippantly, 'And do I care? No.'

'My behaviour was quite professional,' insisted Fawcett, 'but yours was quite improper.'

'I was only asking for treatment,' she said, smiling innocently. 'I thought that's what you were there for.' And then she became very serious. 'Will I always be in your power? Will you just say "Alpha" and have complete control of me? Supposing I fell out of love with you, would you just pick up the telephone and tell me to come to you?' She drank some red wine. 'It's frightening when I think about it.'

'It's the other way round,' said Fawcett, squeezing her hand. 'I'm completely in your power. I deceive my wife. I've no real incentive to get back on the Medical Register and start surgery again. I just want to be with you all the time.'

'Why don't you, then? Come and live with me,' suggested Carla. 'Be with me all the time. I can't live like this much longer, only seeing you once a week.' She kissed him passionately. 'If you love me, how can you still live with Melanie? In the same flat, in the same bed.' She drained her glass. 'D'you still make love to her?' she asked, and when he remained silent, 'Come on, tell me. I want to know.'

'No,' he said eventually. 'Not for some months.'

'She must know something's going on. She must feel it – smell it. I know I would. Isn't it time to tell her? I want to marry you and have babies.'

Fawcett wasn't ready to end his marriage, but he didn't want to lose Carla either. But now she was putting the pressure on.

'Carla, I'm only thinking of you,' he said, 'You need time to be sure. I'm much older than you.'

'You're not old,' she said. 'I love you, but I can't wait forever. Peter wants to see me again. He telephones every day.'

'Please, Carla, give me more time to work it out. It's not easy to end a marriage.'

When they returned to London, Fawcett went straight to his consulting rooms.

'I'm emigrating to South Africa with my family,' his secretary announced as soon as he arrived. 'I'll have to leave in a fortnight's time.'

'Sod!' he said. 'Now all the trouble of finding a replacement.'

'Why not let me do it?' said Carla, when he told her about it the next evening. 'I've got secretarial skills; I'm good with people. I'll attract thousands of patients to your practice.'

'Mostly men,' he laughed. 'The telephone will never stop ringing.'

He realised he had got himself into a difficult situation. If he didn't appoint Carla, she would say he didn't love her. If he did, Melanie might get suspicious. 'God,' he thought, 'Why did I ever mention it?' Once she had the idea in her head, she wouldn't give up.

'You must appoint the best person,' Melanie said, when he casually mentioned it. 'You need a good front to the practice.' She laughed. 'Carla's certainly got that.' It never entered her head that there was anything going on between Jeremy and the 'young bimbo', as she called Carla.

Carla overlapped with the existing secretary for two weeks before she went off to South Africa. Fawcett was soon impressed with her competence and her professional manner on the telephone. With the two of them together in the practice, their lives changed. He saw much more of her than he did of his wife. They had lunch together every day and at least an aperitif in the evening before he returned home. Their lovemaking inevitably became more frequent.

'What are you doing?' Carla asked in mock surprise as Fawcett followed the last patient of the morning session to the front door and turned the key. 'D'you have something on your mind?'

'Come here,' he said, taking her in his arms. 'I've been thinking about making love to you all morning.' He kissed her. 'I almost told you to cancel the patients.'

'I hope the patients don't know what's going on inside your head,' said Carla, 'when you are putting suggestions into theirs.' They went to the bedroom and made love. 'You're so uninhibited and passionate,' he said. 'I can't believe you came to me all those months ago with a sexual problem.'

'It was fate,' said Carla, kissing him. 'After all, I could have gone to someone else in Harley Street for my treatment.'

He pulled her closer to him. 'My life would be empty without you.' Each evening they found it harder to go their separate ways.

'Darling, please don't leave me,' Carla pleaded. 'I can't stand this much longer.'

She clung to him. 'How can you love me? You keep going back to Melanie.'

It wasn't a premeditated decision to leave Melanie. She really forced him into it.

'Jeremy, what's happening to us?' she asked quietly. 'You're late or away most evenings. I hardly ever see you.'

'I've just been busy, that's all,' he said, trying to end the conversation.

'But, that's not all,' she insisted. 'You've changed so much. Your appearance, your behaviour, I hardly know you.' She stood waiting for a reply. 'I might as well not be here.'

'I'm sorry,' he said, moving towards her, but she rejected his attempt to kiss her.

'There's another woman, isn't there?' she said, challenging him.

He remained quiet for a few moments, which seemed like ages to Melanie. 'Well?' she said. And then it all came out.

'I've fallen in love with Carla Narcissi,' he said, 'and I'm going to live with her.'

She looked at him in amazement. She just couldn't believe it. She was speechless until the anger welled up inside her and burst out. He had never seen her so angry and uncontrolled.

'How could you?' she screamed, 'She's just a child.'

'I can't live without her,' he said forlornly.

'In ten years' time you'll be an arthritic old man,' she shouted. 'She'll still be a young woman. You'll be no use to her then. She'll soon ditch you.'

She wanted to hit him, she felt so furious. It was the deceitfulness of it all. Month after month of lies. She shuddered when she thought of him leaving Carla's bed and then returning to hers.

'I can't expect you to forgive me,' he said.

'I'll never do that,' she said, scathingly. 'You're on an ego trip; you'll become the laughing stock of Harley Street as you parade her around.'

'If I stayed, I could never forget her,' he said. 'I wouldn't be with you.'

'There's no way you're staying, you pathetic idiot,' she said. 'Just get out of my life and don't ever try to come back.'

After he had left, Melanie sat down and burst into tears, her emotions shredded. This was the second man who'd left her. They had both gone looking for excitement. 'What's wrong with me?' she cried.

Fawcett moved into Carla's flat. Not many of his friends wanted to meet them socially out of respect for Melanie. Carla's friends thought that he was too old for her, and he found it difficult to carry on a conversation at the flippant level of these young people. His students had been about their age and he had been used to controlling the dialogue, not taking part in a free-for-all.

'You must meet my parents,' said Carla. 'We'll take them out to dinner.'

On the surface they were happy, friendly Italians, speaking English with a pronounced accent and obviously rich.

'He's much too old,' Carla's mother said to her husband when he had gone. 'You should talk to him.'

'Don't worry. It can't go on,' he said. 'It'll finish soon enough. If we try to end it, it'll only make Carla more determined. You know how perverse she can be.'

But the affair didn't end. Carla wanted to marry him.

'When are you going to divorce Melanie?' she asked. 'I want a family before you're too old.' She laughed. 'I think I'll have four. We Italians like big families.'

'There's no hurry,' said Fawcett defensively.

'I may not wait until we're married,' she said, 'I'll soon get myself pregnant.'

Fawcett had no thought of starting a family. In reality he hadn't thought of the future at all in any practical way. It was a wildly passionate love affair with a beautiful young woman. He had never thought of the inevitable consequences.

'I'll be so proud when we take our first baby for a walk in Regent's Park in its pram,' said Carla, hugging him, 'Won't you?'

The thought of bumping into Melanie whilst pushing a pram made him shudder, but he knew that whatever he wanted, Carla would insist on starting a family.

'Jeremy's going through with his divorce and we're going to have four children,' she said to her alarmed parents.

'You must speak to him,' Carla's mother said to her husband. It was something he wasn't looking forward to. Fawcett always made him feel uncomfortable with his posh public school accent.

'I wish he'd still been a famous surgeon,' he said. 'Their paths would never have crossed then.' It was fear of the unknown which made him frightened of hypnosis, and whenever Fawcett looked into his eyes, he looked away. He said to his wife: 'I can feel the power in his eyes.'

'I despair of you sometimes,' she said, 'You talk to him. Get on the phone straight away.' She picked up the telephone and thrust it at him, and he had to arrange to see Fawcett.

'We're very unhappy about you and Carla,' he said to Fawcett. 'You're much too old; it's never going to work out.'

'I love her. I can't leave her,' he said. 'We're both very happy together.'

'But you're older than we are. And we're her parents.'

'I think she prefers older men,' answered Fawcett, with a misplaced attempt at humour. He looked at this man who had sexually abused Carla for many years during her childhood. 'Perhaps it's the way you brought her up,' he said acidly, 'especially when she was a child.'

Carla's parents had to accept the situation but never invited Fawcett to their home again.

'You'll get no help from us,' they told him.

They lived together happily for some months and were inseparable. Carla continued to work at the practice and sometimes, as they walked along Harley Street in the morning to his consulting rooms, she would hold his hand. To his intense embarrassment, she was doing just this one day when John Wright emerged from his rooms and all but collided with them.

'I'm terribly sorry,' he began, and then recognized Fawcett.

'Aren't you going to introduce me?' he asked, holding out his hand.

'I'm Carla,' she replied, shaking his hand warmly before Fawcett could say a word, 'are you one of Jeremy's friends?'

As Carla took Fawcett's hand again, Wright watched in amusement. He looked so sheepish!

'We've known one another for a long time,' he explained, 'we were students together.'

'Darling,' said Carla, 'why don't we meet for a drink one evening? I'm sure you'd both like to talk about old times.' She looked at him; so far he hadn't uttered a word.

'I'll arrange something,' he muttered eventually.

'Do that,' rejoined Wright, knowing that he had not the slightest intention of doing any such thing. He certainly wasn't going to drink with him. He watched them walk down Harley Street hand in hand.

'Well, well,' he said to himself, 'she's certainly a good looker! I didn't think he had it in him.'

In the evening they would go to a small Italian restaurant, a cinema, or one of those interminable parties which Fawcett found increasingly boring.

'Darling,' said Carla one day, 'you must get some young gear. I'll take you to the best shops – I like shopping. Melanie let you get old-fashioned.' She did indeed like shopping; she was more than happy to spend a whole morning at it. He had to suffer parading himself in front of her for hours until she was satisfied. 'Now for your hair,' she said. 'It needs to be longer – and we'll have those grey streaks touched up.'

Hitherto he had never bothered much about his appearance, but now he found himself spending more time in front of mirrors, adjusting his hair and reassuring himself. After his meeting with Wright, he had tried to avoid Harley Street if he could, by using the parallel Wimpole Street so as not to run the risk of further embarrassment. But on one occasion he was even more embarrassed. It was when he met Melanie coming out of a medical practice in Wimpole Street.

'You silly, pathetic old man!' she exclaimed loudly. She stared at him in his trainers, casual shirt and jeans, with his long, dyed hair, and roared with laughter, disturbing the professional calm of the street. 'You do look ridiculous!' she went on, still laughing and shaking her head in disbelief as she walked away.

Fawcett began to tire of the endless round of parties with Carla's young Italian friends. He tried in vain to persuade her to stay at home with him. She insisted on going out and went increasingly on her own. After she had left, he would find himself wishing he had gone with her. He always waited up for her, constantly looking at his watch and usually drinking too much. Eventually he would hear a car stop outside and peer furtively through a chink in the curtains to see Carla embracing and kissing her current escort on the mouth. It would be no half-hearted peck on the cheek.

'Darling!' she would exclaim all excited, 'you shouldn't wait up!'

'That was a long goodbye,' he would mutter jealously, and then immediately regret having said it.

'You weren't watching, were you?' she would retort with a glint of anger in her eye, 'you should know by now how demonstrative we Italians are. We like to hug one another; it doesn't mean anything.'

'I love you,' he would say, taking her in his arms. His whole life centred round her. The hypnosis practice was incidental.

'You're getting fed up with hypnosis, aren't you?' said Carla. 'Why don't you try to get back into surgery?'

'It is becoming a bore,' he admitted, 'all the patients need is a video or sound recording. They could treat themselves; all they'd have to do would be to listen.'

'Treatment wouldn't be such fun,' she said, kissing him, 'a video wouldn't have helped me very much.' She laughed. 'I preferred the personal touch.'

It was three months after they had started living together that they spent their first night apart.

'My parents want me to go to a party,' she said one Friday evening, 'some old friends are going. You don't mind, do you?' He knew that he wasn't invited. Carla's parents had made that quite clear.

At eleven o'clock the telephone rang. 'Darling, I have to stay overnight,' she said, 'The party looks as if it is going on for some time.'

Fawcett couldn't sleep; he kept looking at his watch throughout the night.

'That was some party!' exclaimed Carla, when she finally returned about midday, 'It went on to two-thirty.' She kissed him. 'Did you miss me?'

He wanted her with him all the time. His busy professional life and all the social events associated with being a leading surgeon and President of the Royal College of Surgeons had gone. As far as they were concerned, he was 'Yesterday's Man'. He seldom went out on his own and depended on Carla to provide not only love, but company in the flat as well as a social life. But Carla wasn't ready for isolation. She was gregarious and needed social contact.

From then on, every few weeks, Carla stayed overnight at her parents' house. Fawcett tried not to be inquisitive or sound possessive, but he became increasingly jealous.

'I'm sure you tell me about all these young men you meet just to make me jealous.'

'Don't be silly,' she answered.

'Are you falling out of love with me? Am I too old for you?'

'You're the only man in my life,' she assured him, throwing her arms around his neck and kissing him, 'But I can't be with you all the time. I do need space to see my friends.'

She could always find some excuse to leave him: her parents, her girlfriend just in from Tuscany; a hen party.

'How do I look?' she would say as she emerged from the bedroom beautifully made up and in a new party dress. 'Will I do?'

For some hours before she left, he would be morose and find it impossible to raise a smile when she kissed him goodbye. Sometimes, to avoid the sullen atmosphere, she would not tell him in advance.

'I'm just popping off to meet a friend,' she would say, 'I won't be long.'

He became more and more jealous and suspicious, and went with her whenever he could. He would stay close to her side at parties, whereas she wanted to move around freely and talk to her friends.

'Let's go and talk to so-and-so,' she would say, introducing him and quietly moving away. His eyes followed her all the time and when she left the room, he would suffer anguish. His mind was obsessed with Carla; he never stopped to think what was happening to his own life. He was beyond rational thinking; his emotions had taken over. It was impossible for him to contemplate leaving Carla and re-building his career in surgery.

'I shall always be grateful to you for treating me,' she said, kissing him.

She still loved him in spite of his moodiness and possessiveness. Also she felt sorry for him. 'He would be lost without me,' she thought, 'he needs me.'

She met Peter, her ex-fiancé, about a year after their bitter parting and her distressed telephone call to Fawcett.

'Peter,' she said excitedly, ignoring the beautiful red-haired Scottish woman he was with, 'It's been so long! I've missed you.' She threw her arms around him and kissed him passionately on the mouth. They spent most of the evening together and left to go to Peter's flat. They kissed in the hallway as soon as the front door closed, and went into the bedroom. 'Come on,' Carla said. She needed to show him she was normal – a real woman. Life was such fun now, she was no longer fraught with the terror that if she got into bed with a man, disaster would inevitably follow.

'I love you,' he said, 'Let's start again. Let's get married. We were always meant to be together.'

She lay in his arms for a long time afterwards. 'This is such bliss,' she said, 'but I must go.'

'Why don't you leave the old man?' said Peter. 'Come and live with me. You don't need him.'

'He needs me, and I still love him.'

'Stay here,' he said, holding her tightly as she tried to get out of bed. 'Don't go yet.'

'Let me go,' she said, kissing him, 'We'll have to see what happens.'

She was confident and outgoing but Fawcett's jealousy began to alarm her.

'Don't try and keep me caged up like a pet,' she screamed when he stood in the doorway and physically prevented her from leaving, 'Or I'll leave you for good.'

Then she calmed down and moved closer to him. 'I won't be late,' she said, kissing him lovingly, 'I promise.' Then she squeezed past him and was off.

But their life together was still mainly happy. It was only when she was out that Fawcett became morose and depressed, taking to the bottle and often being drunk when she returned home.

'D'you have to drink so much?' she asked irritably, 'You'll kill yourself.'

'What else is there to do when I'm alone in the evenings?' he replied, shrugging his shoulders.

The following morning after such altercations they would walk to the consulting rooms and work together amicably. Fawcett felt he had more control over his life during the daytime. Carla behaved quite professionally when patients were there. At lunch time it was different, and they sometimes made love in the small bedroom behind the consulting room.

'Darling, we must get dressed,' she would say, 'otherwise the first patient will find us.'

As soon as she put on her white uniform, the relationship changed and he became 'Sir Jeremy'.

'Is "Sir" looking forward to celebrating his birthday this evening?' she asked. She had just shown the last patient out, a businessman who wanted to stop blushing at business meetings.

'Why do grown men worry about such things?' Carla said. 'Okay, he blushes. So what? I think it's attractive.'

'You're tough. It's a real problem to him,' he replied, 'We've all got worries which don't seem important to other people.'

'What are yours?' asked Carla.

'An old man – and a young woman.'

'You're not old,' she said, embracing him fondly, 'You're young at heart.' She laughed. 'And in body! Now let me take you to dinner.'

They were going to their favourite Italian restaurant and Fawcett was looking forward to the bottle of the rare Sassicaia which they had managed to find for him.

'It's the best Italian red I've ever tasted,' he told Carla. 'I couldn't believe the Italians could make such fine wine.'

They were both dressed and drinking champagne when the telephone rang. Carla took the call. She was on the phone for a long time, sometimes speaking English, but then breaking into Italian. Fawcett was getting impatient and refilled his glass. He heard the receiver go down.

'You won't like this,' she said as she came back into the room, 'but I can't come with you. I'm terribly sorry.'

'Why on earth not?' Fawcett asked angrily.

'That was Jacky, my best girlfriend. You met her at a party. Her marriage is breaking up; her husband's left her.'

'Surely you can see her tomorrow.'

'She's so upset, I'm worried. She sounds desperate.'

'She must have other friends,' argued Fawcett.

'She wants to see me. She says I'm the only one she can talk to.'

Fawcett tried to re-fill her champagne glass, but she put her hand on top of it.

'I'm afraid for her; she sounded quite hysterical.'

'Why don't we take her with us to the restaurant?' he suggested in a last desperate effort to save the evening. 'You can talk there. A few glasses of wine will cheer her up.'

'I must go, I promised. I'm sorry.'

'We'll celebrate your birthday tomorrow evening,' she said, putting on her coat.

Fawcett was depressed and angry.

'You're not going to leave me on my own tonight,' he said, 'I don't care about any one else.' He stared into her eyes and said fiercely: 'Alpha – deeply asleep.'

157

Carla stopped immediately and went into a trance.

'When I wake you,' intoned Fawcett, 'you'll go straight to the telephone and tell your friend you can't see her tonight because you're celebrating my birthday.'

'I must make a telephone call,' she said immediately she came out of the trance. She picked up the receiver and dialled. 'I'm sorry, I can't see you tonight. I'm going out with Jeremy to celebrate his birthday.' She repeated his instructions word for word. After what seemed a long and difficult conversation, Carla finally put the receiver down with 'I'm sorry'.

They finished their aperitifs and were just leaving when the telephone rang again.

'I'll get it,' said Fawcett, picking up the phone before Carla could get there.

'May I speak to Carla?' He didn't recognise the man's voice.

'No. We're just off out,' Fawcett said sharply.

'Just a quick word,' the man insisted.

'No, she's already outside waiting for me. I'll take a message.'

The caller hesitated. 'Tell her Peter phoned,' he said, 'and I'm terribly upset that she can't come out tonight.'

'All right, I'll tell her.'

'Tell her the party'll be going on all night; she can come along later.'

'Who was it?' Carla asked.

'Just an old medical friend who remembered my birthday.'

Sitting in the little Italian restaurant, they should have been happy, but they were both rather subdued. Carla was not her usual effervescent self and Fawcett was angry because he knew that she was going to cancel their date to go with Peter. His birthday wasn't important. She was prepared to tell lies and stand him up. He felt annoyed and insecure; desperate to hold on to her at any cost. As they drank the red Sassicaia, they became less quiet and more relaxed.

'D'you love me?' he asked.

'Of course I do.'

They clinked their glasses together, the red wine sparkling in the candlelight.

'Why don't we get married?'

'There's no hurry,' she said, hesitating and lowering her gaze. 'We're OK as we are for the moment.'

How she had changed! A few months ago she had wanted marriage and babies, and now she wasn't sure. She was drifting away from him. He must keep her. Having seen how easy it was to control her, he began to hypnotise

158

her more and more. Carla never knew. She would go into a deep trance and receive her 'orders' by way of a post-hypnotic suggestion. He had stopped her party-going. She seemed happy to stay at home with him. Her friends couldn't understand what was happening to her. Carla virtually became a prisoner. Sometimes when she did something unusual, she would ask:

'Have you hypnotised me?'

If he suggested that they should make love, it would take place when she came out of the trance.

'That was a surprise,' she would say, when they had finished, 'I'd no idea that was going to happen.'

Fawcett felt happy again. He was with Carla for almost twenty-four hours each day. It was as it had been at the beginning of their affair. On one occasion they had just returned from the theatre and he was feeling happy and confident.

'We're so happy, why don't we get married?'

'Don't rush me,' she replied, putting her champagne down and kissing him gently. She laughed. 'I'm only just getting to know you.'

He wanted to own her, so he quickly said, 'Alpha,' and then, 'Carla, when I wake you up, I'll propose to you and you'll accept.'

He brought her out of the trance. They sipped their champagne and he put his arm round her shoulders and pulled her close.

'Carla, darling, will you marry me?'

'Yes, I will,' she replied immediately.

Fawcett knew that he might have to use hypnosis, but he was determined to keep control of her. He bought her a ring and Carla was not sure how she had become engaged, but she proudly showed the large emerald to her friends.

She was staying at her parents home overnight on a Saturday and she returned at lunchtime on Sunday. Fawcett was at the open door when the open-top Alfa Romeo Spider stopped outside. Carla bounded out of the car and kissed him.

'Darling, you must meet Peter; he gave me a lift back.'

A good looking young man of about twenty-six climbed out of the car.

'I'm pleased to meet you, sir,' he said, shaking hands.

When he called him 'sir', Fawcett thought that as far as he was concerned, 'I'm an old man.' The Spider drove off and he and Carla went into the flat. Carla said that she had stayed for lunch with her parents, which annoyed Fawcett because he had prepared lunch and was waiting for her to join him.

'I've missed you,' he said, putting his arm round her, 'I've been very lonely. I do love you.'

He tried to kiss her passionately and lead her into the bedroom, but she resisted saying, 'I'm too tired.' The atmosphere became strained. Fawcett was silent and moody but Carla tried to make light conversation. She wasn't the one to allow long periods of silence. When she was there, she had to communicate, no matter how tired she was.

'Darling, you are gloomy today,' she exclaimed, 'What's the matter?'

Fawcett mumbled something about the weekend being especially important when they had more free time, and he wanted her to spend it all with him.

'Are your parents trying to get you back together again with Peter?' he asked.

Carla was a volatile character, whose temper was always on a very short fuse.

'Don't be so jealous! I've told you before: you don't own me,' she shouted. 'We're not married yet, you know. If you're not happy, why don't you leave? Here, take your ring back.'

She started to remove the emerald from her finger. 'Please don't,' he said.

He looked so old and dejected that she went to him and embraced him.

'I'm sorry, I didn't mean that.' She stretched up and kissed him, reassuring him. 'I love you, don't be angry with me.'

'I don't know how I could live without you,' he said quietly, and then he kissed her. 'You've become my whole life.'

Carla led him into the bedroom.

'Does that make you happy again?' she asked.

About a fortnight later she went off to her parents for the weekend to celebrate their wedding anniversary. Fawcett knew that he wouldn't be welcome, so he tried to be gracious and wished Carla 'a happy time' as she went off in a taxi.

He settled down for a quiet lonely weekend, planning to have a good bottle of claret – a Ch. Palmer – with his dinner. The cork was off to allow the wine to breathe for an hour or so. He sat finishing his second glass of 'the Widow', his favourite champagne, thinking about Carla and wondering what the future had in store for them. How frequently would he have to hypnotise her to keep her? He could imagine what a stir that would cause if it ever got out into the public domain. 'But what can I do?' he thought miserably, filling his glass for the third time, 'I can't let her go.' He put his champagne flute down carefully and picked up the telephone to call Carla's parents, thinking that it was time that he tried to develop a better relationship with them, even though he detested her father. After all, it was their wedding anniversary. Carla's mother answered.

'Happy anniversary,' said Fawcett, and then, before she could reply, 'We haven't met for some time. Let's meet soon.'

'What anniversary?' she asked.

'I thought it was your wedding anniversary,' said Fawcett.

'We stopped celebrating those years ago. Anyway, it was some months ago.'

Fawcett's heart almost stopped.

'I'm sorry, I must have got it wrong. Could I just speak to Carla for a moment?'

'She's not here. We haven't seen her for months. I'm surprised that she's not with you.'

'Thank you very much,' replied Fawcett, and dropped the telephone down. And then he finished the third glass of Veuve Cliquot and the bottle of Chateau Palmer and became unconscious. He finally surfaced the following day at noon with the worst hangover he had experienced since the GMC hearing. Carla didn't return until almost four o'clock. He heard the deep throb of the Spider engine sounding more powerful than it was. Carla bounced in all sparkling and kissed him. 'Have you missed me? My parents had a good time. It was a lovely party. Lots of Italian friends. And . . .' She tailed off as she saw his face, a picture of distrust and anger. 'You look terrifying!' she said. 'You're frightening me. What's wrong?'

'Why d'you have to lie to me?' Fawcett snarled, advancing towards her aggressively. 'You haven't been anywhere near your parents. It's not even their anniversary. Where've you been?'

He looked so fierce that Carla cringed away from him.

'I'm sorry, I didn't want to hurt your feelings.'

'Where've you been?' shouted Fawcett, 'I want to know.'

'It's better you know the truth,' she said after some hesitation. 'I've been at a weekend party with Peter at a hotel in Hampshire. We met again recently and he wants to marry me. I don't know what to do. I still love him, but I love you too.'

'You've been carrying on this brazen affair for some time,' he screamed. 'Your parents haven't seen you for months. How can you say you still love me? Love requires trust and honesty – not deceit and lies.' He paused and almost said 'Alpha', but instead he said, 'You're engaged to me. You're not going to marry anyone else. I won't have you seeing Peter again.'

Carla exploded. 'I feel trapped here,' she shouted, 'You've become completely dependent on me. You don't like my friends, yours have left you. I'm not going to live like a hermit. I need people and a gay social life. Don't forget, I am still a young woman.'

'You're just a silly young slut,' Fawcett said menacingly, 'That's what you are. You just live for the moment's excitement. You've destroyed my life.'

'You destroyed your own life before you met me,' she said contemptuously. 'I didn't get you struck off; you did that all by yourself.'

She spoke the last three words slowly, and then repeated them to taunt him.

'All ... by ... yourself. All by yourself.'

Fawcett picked up a magazine and hurled it at her, and as she retreated he threw some more.

'You're a jealous old man,' she screamed as the magazine hit her chest, 'Get out. It's my flat, just go. I don't want you any more.'

Fawcett pleaded with her to let him stay. She was the most important person in his life. Life wouldn't be worth living without her. What had happened between them?

'It's too late now,' she said, calming down, 'I've made my mind up. I'm going to marry Peter. I'm not going to spend the rest of my life with an old man like you.'

The row raged for another thirty minutes, with Fawcett alternating between aggressive shouting and almost childlike pleading to let him stay. Eventually he packed his bags and left to go back to his rooms near Harley Street. For the next two weeks he drank heavily alone in his flat. To his surprise, Carla still came into the practice and tried to behave in as civilized a manner as possible. In a way this upset him more than if she had made a clean break. She seemed to be even more charming and beautiful than ever. He longed to take her in his arms and lead her through to the bedroom, and the thought of having lost her became even more painful. At lunchtime she went out, and left promptly in the evening as soon as the last patient had gone. He thought of hypnotising her at the end of the day, but he knew that Peter was waiting outside in the Spider to whisk her away.

Fawcett felt miserable and depressed. He couldn't sleep well and if he did, he woke up early in the morning thinking about her. His features seemed permanently fixed, with no animation. He couldn't bring himself to smile even when greeting patients. His obsession with Carla occupied his thoughts for most of the hours he was awake. 'And,' he thought, 'probably when I'm asleep as well.' He forced himself to go to a local pub for lunch on Saturday and after a simple lunch and two glasses of red wine (which was the usual pub standard – awful), he returned to his rooms and tried to settle with the newspapers, but his mind kept leading him back to thoughts of Carla. Her beauty, her vivacity, her sexiness and, he thought, her knack of making everyone in her presence happy. He would never hold her in his arms again.

He would never make love to her again. Melanie was right, it couldn't last. He was a 'silly, pathetic old man'.

He drank a glass of champagne and picked up the telephone to ring Carla, and as usual the answerphone was on. He was just about to replace the phone when Carla answered.

'Hello, Carla Narcissi speaking. Can you hold on – otherwise I'll have a disaster in the kitchen.'

When she returned, he said:

'It's Jeremy. Is the answerphone turned off?'

'Yes, it's all right, what d'you want?' she asked.

'Carla, are you doing anything tonight? Could we meet for a drink or a meal – for old times' sake?'

'I am sorry, Jeremy, but I'm with Peter tonight,' she said kindly. 'He'll be coming round soon.' And then she added, 'We can't meet away from the surgery any more. I'm engaged to Peter now and we're to marry in two months' time.' She tried to end the conversation. 'Thank you for calling.'

Fawcett pleaded with her to meet him for a short while.

'No, I can't. I must go,' she said.

'Carla: Alpha, Deeply asleep,' said Fawcett abruptly, before she could put the receiver down. Afterwards, he told himself that he hadn't planned to hypnotise her. It was something which had just happened spontaneously out of his despair.

Her eyelids flickered and her head lolled as she went into a deep trance.

'Carla, I want you to listen to me. After I wake you up you will leave your flat and get a taxi to my rooms. You'll not remember that I've told you to do this, but you'll come and see me immediately.'

He then brought her out of the trance. She blinked and opening her eyes, said out loud: 'I must get a taxi and go and see Jeremy.'

She went outside and hailed a taxi, arriving at the flat off Harley Street fifteen minutes later. She rang the doorbell and Fawcett opened the door. Carla looked puzzled.

'I don't know what I'm doing here.'

Fawcett forced a smile. 'Well, since you are, you'd better come in for a while.'

Carla went into the flat and he poured out two glasses of champagne. They drank in silence.

'I shouldn't be here,' said Carla. 'Peter will be angry. I must go.'

Finishing the champagne, she stood up and moved to kiss him goodbye on the cheek, but he kissed her on the mouth.

'Now, now,' she said, raising her finger.

He tried to kiss her again, but she took evasive action.

'I'm going.'

'Carla, Alpha, Deeply asleep,' said Fawcett quickly as she started to leave. He sat her down on the consulting room couch.

'Carla, when I wake you up, you'll remove all your clothes and make love to me. It'll be the same as it was when we lived together. You'll not remember me telling you to do this whilst you were asleep. But you'll carry out my instructions when you wake up.'

He counted from three back to one and opening her eyes, she immediately started to take her clothes off and put them on a chair. Fawcett looked at her magnificent figure.

'What are you doing?' he asked.

'I'm going to make love to you.'

They went into the bedroom. She started to undress him and pulled him on to the bed. He put his arms round her and started to make love. Suddenly she tried to push him away.

'What are you doing? Stop – you're raping me!'

'No, I'm not,' he said, trying to quieten her. 'You took your clothes off and said you were going to make love to me. I didn't start anything.'

'You're raping me!' screamed Carla, 'you mustn't. Stop! Get off!'

She pushed him and tried to get off the bed, but he was too heavy. She was screaming: 'Get off! Get off!'

She managed to wriggle free and stood up looking for her clothes, sobbing loudly. Fawcett tried to calm her.

'I'm sorry, I didn't start it. I'll make you some coffee.'

'Don't speak to me,' sobbed Carla, 'Don't come near me. I never want to see you again. I'm going straight to the police.'

'But I haven't done anything,' he said, trying to sound calm but feeling worried sick underneath.

'You raped me! You raped me! You bastard!' she screamed hysterically.

Fawcett was in a state of panic. He thought of his neighbours in the basement flat hearing Carla's screams, or passers by standing on the pavement outside listening.

'Carla, Alpha, Deeply asleep,' he shouted.

She continued screaming.

'Carla, Alpha. Deeply asleep,' he shouted again.

She began to quieten and he thought she was going into a trance when the doorbell rang continuously.

'God, who can that be?' He left her and opened the front door.

'Where's Carla?' shouted Peter, 'Where is she?' Pushing Fawcett out of the way he ran into the consulting room and then followed Carla's screams into the bedroom.

'He's raped me! He's raped me!' she screamed out over and over again. 'He's raped me!'

'Bastard! Bastard!' Peter yelled, lunging viciously at Fawcett, 'I'll kill you!' Fawcett was still a big strong man and he managed to hold him off.

'Stop!' screamed Carla, as he advanced towards Fawcett again. 'Get me out of here! Take me home!'

'You won't get away with this,' shouted Peter as they left. 'You're finished.'

After they had gone, there was absolute silence. Fawcett sat down and talked out loud:

'What can they do? It's her word against mine.' His mind raced on trying to excuse his actions. 'Why did she behave like that? I've hypnotised her hundreds of times, I've made love to her hundreds of times. At the beginning she begged me to have sex with her, and now she's crying rape. I thought I had complete control of her mind; perhaps I did, providing I suggested what she wanted. Now she's engaged, she's changed. All I wanted was her love back. If we'd had sex, she might have come back.'

He rambled on: 'Perhaps the text books are right. Patients won't act in a way contrary to their normal moral values in a trance. Give the bank manager a pen and a blank cheque, and he will either drop the pen or provide an illegible scribble. Maybe. But it all depends how the suggestions are put.' He shook his head. 'I should have suggested that she was with Peter. Told her to get undressed and get into bed with him and make love. But she'd probably have come out of the trance halfway through. And then what? Screaming ab-dabs.'

There was no more time for rhetoric. He could see the two policemen through the half glass door.

The police were extremely polite and courteous as usual.

'Sir, we've had a complaint from a Miss Narcissi. She's accused you of raping her. Can we come inside?'

Fawcett led them into his consulting room.

'I don't know what this is about. There was no question of rape.'

'Why did Miss Narcissi come to see you today, sir? Did you invite her?'

'No, she just turned up. It was a complete surprise to me. She rang the front doorbell and there she was.'

'You didn't telephone her?'

'No. We used to live together, but now we've parted and she is engaged to be married. So I wouldn't invite her out.'

'You're sure about that, sir?'

'Yes, quite sure.'

The policeman asking the questions looked at his colleague and turned to Fawcett, addressing him as 'Mr' even though he had noticed the 'Sir Jeremy Fawcett' on the brass plate on the outside door. 'Mr Fawcett, on the evidence presented to us, we are going to arrest you for the alleged rape of Miss Narcissi, and must ask you to accompany us to the police station to make a statement.'

'Is that really necessary?' Fawcett asked, swallowing hard, 'You seem to be taking drastic action over what was a misunderstanding. There was no question of physical pressure or violence.'

But the policeman insisted.

'As you know, sir, rape is a very serious charge.'

Fawcett was driven to the nearest police station, and then became part of police routine. He was booked in by the custody officer, and, to his horror, taken to a cell. Once in the police station, and more so when put in a cell with the iron door locked behind him, his confidence began to diminish. He was asked whether he wanted a solicitor present when he was questioned.

'Why on earth should I need a solicitor?' he said, trying to bluff it out, 'I'm sure we can soon clear this matter up.'

He was taken from the cell to the interview room. They questioned him step by step.

'You say that Miss Narcissi just turned up at your flat?'

'Yes, that's right.'

'Did you telephone her to invite her?'

'No, I have already told you I didn't. She just rang the bell. It was completely unexpected.'

'Are you quite sure about that?'

'How many times do I have to tell you? She just turned up.'

'Mr Fawcett, we've listened to the answerphone at Miss Narcissi's flat and there's a record of a conversation you had with her. D'you still say that you didn't telephone her and invite her to come round to your flat?'

Fawcett sat there in silence, his mind racing to find an answer. He knew he was being trapped.

'Since you don't accept my explanation of what happened, I must change my mind and ask for my solicitor to be present before I answer any more questions.'

'Very well, sir.'

He was put back into the cell again to await the arrival of his family solicitor – or rather Melanie's family's solicitor. Even though Melanie's father was an eminent QC, the family still went to a local firm of solicitors for legal advice. The lawyer was in his sixties, white haired, wearing a dark grey suit, white shirt and Oxford University tie. Fawcett had always thought of him as one of the old school and would have been surprised if he hadn't turned up in a lounge suit, even though it was a Saturday afternoon. The lawyer had read English at Brazenose and had then taken his articles in a family law practice in the country. His knowledge of criminal law was negligible and after discussing the case with Fawcett, he advised him that if the case proceeded, he would need a criminal lawyer. 'Until you do,' he said, "No comment" is your best answer.'

They both went into the interview room and apart from giving his name and address, Fawcett replied: 'No comment' to every question. After the interview he was locked in his cell again.

'An hour or two ago he was going to clear the matter up,' one of the policemen, exasperated by the 'No comment' routine, said to his colleague. 'Didn't need a solicitor. He's as guilty as hell, the evil bastard.'

The following day he was taken to the magistrate's court and charged. It was a short hearing.

Nine months later, Fawcett stood in the dock at the Old Bailey, pleading not guilty. The prosecuting barrister, a QC in wig and silk gown, put his questions in a quiet, detached, almost apologetic manner.

'Let me put it to you, Sir Jeremy, you did telephone Miss Narcissi and invite her to join you, didn't you?'

'No, I did not.'

'But we have a recording of your telephone conversation. Don't you accept this?'

'I don't know when the recording was made. It might have been months before.'

'But we've heard that it was the only message on the answerphone tape and it referred to Saturday. Could this have been recorded months before?'

And so the relentless wearing down of Fawcett's defence went on.

'Sir Jeremy, can we consider the message on the tape. Can you tell us what "Alpha – deeply asleep" means?'

'I think that some of the conversation on the tape must have been wiped. It doesn't make any sense at present.'

'Isn't "Alpha" the code word you use when inducing a hypnotic trance in Miss Narcissi?'

'Yes, it is.'

'Is it not the code word you used when you were treating her?'

'Yes.'

'So, were you not deliberately hypnotising her over the telephone?'

'No. We sometimes used the word "Alpha" in a joking sense.'

'Sir Jeremy, what would have happened if you said "Alpha – deeply asleep" to Miss Narcissi?'

'She would probably have gone into a trance.'

'So wouldn't it have been dangerous to use the phrase in a joking sense?'

Fawcett didn't answer. The prosecuting counsel continued with his cross examination.

'When you said: "Alpha – deeply asleep" to Miss Narcissi on the telephone, weren't you hypnotising her?'

'No – the tape recording doesn't seem to be complete.'

The prosecuting counsel turned to the judge. 'My lord, it might help Sir Jeremy to tell us where he thinks the tape is deficient if we have it played at this stage.'

The red-robed judge nodded his assent.

The Clerk switched on the answerphone tape and adjusted the volume. The journalists in the press gallery took down every word. As he listened to the recording, the barrister moved his gaze from Fawcett to Carla Narcissi. He saw her eyelids flutter and close and her head tilt sideways. There was a commotion in the court as Carla went into a deep trance. The judge ordered the recording to be switched off. He wasn't quite sure how to handle the situation. It had never happened before in his court. He addressed Carla:

'Miss Narcissi, are you all right?'

Carla remained with her eyes closed in a deep hypnotic trance. The prosecuting barrister came to his aid.

'My lord, if you will allow the recording to continue, I think we can bring Miss Narcissi out of her trance.'

The clerk switched the recording on again, and when Fawcett counted from three back to one, Carla fluttered her eyelids and opened her eyes. The judge was relieved and asked Carla:

'Are you all right, Miss Narcissi?'

'I have to get a taxi and visit Jeremy Fawcett.'

There was an audible gasp from the members of the public as they realised what was happening. It was getting late and the judge had had enough for one day. He thought that it was bad enough having members of the jury nodding off, but even worse with key witnesses going into a hypnotic trance. He adjourned the court for the day.

The following day the court was crowded. The media had seen to that when the story of Carla going into a trance was splashed across the front pages. One tabloid had two staring eyes and 'ALPHA – DEEPLY ASLEEP' spread over the entire front page.

Fawcett was reminded that he was still on oath.

'Sir Jeremy, yesterday you saw Miss Narcissi go into a hypnotic trance when she heard a recording of your telephone conversation. Was that your intention?'

'No.'

'But you knew that she would immediately go into a trance when you used the code word, did you not?'

'Yes.'

'So why else would you use the code word?'

Fawcett was running out of reasons and resorted to 'I don't know'.

'If I used the code word, would Miss Narcissi go into a hypnotic trance?'

'Probably not.'

'If anyone in the courtroom used the code word, would Miss Narcissi go into a trance?'

'It would be unlikely.'

'Would it be correct to say that you trained Miss Narcissi to go into a trance whenever you used the code word?'

'Yes, it saved time.'

'So, she was so conditioned by you. It was almost an automatic reflex?'

Fawcett hesitated before saying 'yes.'

'How many times have you used the code word on Miss Narcissi?'

'Quite a number.'

'Hundreds of times?'

'Probably.'

'Was Miss Narcissi a good hypnotic subject?'

'Yes.'

'Was she exceptionally good?'

'Yes, she was a somnambule. She could remain in a deep trance with her eyes open.'

'Would you say that she was the deepest trance subject you have ever known?'

'She was a deep trance subject.'

'Sir Jeremy, can you tell the court what is meant by post-hypnotic suggestion.'

'Well, if a patient is hypnotised, it can be suggested that they will behave in a particular way when they come out of the trance.'

'And that suggestion is planted in the subconscious mind whilst they are in a trance. Have I got it right?'

'Yes.'

'So that the court can fully understand, may I suggest this scenario. If you hypnotised Miss Narcissi and told her that when she came out of the trance

169

she would go up to the bench and sit in my lord's chair, which was empty, what would she do?'

'She would go up to the judge's chair and try and sit on it, believing that it was empty.'

'In fact, she would sit on my lord's lap.'

'Yes.'

The court roared with laughter. The judge rather testily addressed the barrister: 'Perhaps you could use other examples when you want to demonstrate the power of suggestion under hypnosis.'

Fawcett was examined and cross-examined for two whole days. Each evening he felt mentally and physically exhausted when he was taken back to his cell. He knew that there was no one in the court room who was likely to believe he hadn't telephoned Carla and made her come to his flat. His only hope of being acquitted, or at least of being dealt with leniently, was to persuade the court that even though he had hypnotised her to get her to visit him, once she got to the flat it was she who had seduced him.

'Sir Jeremy, when the doorbell rang on that Saturday afternoon and you opened the door and found Miss Narcissi there, what were your reactions?'

'I was surprised.'

'Even though you had deliberately hypnotised her and planted your instructions to visit you in her subconscious mind?'

'I didn't deliberately hypnotise her.'

'We'll leave that for the jury to decide. You invited Miss Narcissi in and offered her a drink. Is that correct?'

'Yes.'

'Can you tell the court what happened next?'

'To my surprise, she started to undress and stood naked in front of me.'

'Why should she do that?'

'She said she wanted to make love to me.'

'Hadn't she left you? Wasn't she engaged to another man?'

'We were very close at one time, and she's a very passionate woman.'

'When she was in your flat, could you have used the code word "Alpha" to hypnotise Miss Narcissi?'

'Yes, but I didn't.'

'If you had hypnotised her, could you have instructed her to remove her clothes and make love to you when you brought her out of the trance?'

'I could have hypnotised her, but I doubt whether she would have complied with such a suggestion unless she wanted to.'

'Well, Sir Jeremy, if it wasn't a question of post-hypnotic suggestion and she was making love to you of her own free will, why did she become so distressed and accuse you of rape?'

'I don't know. She probably felt guilty, remembering she was engaged. I can't explain why she acted as she did.'

'Let me put this to you: isn't it likely that you hypnotised her and planted a post-hypnotic suggestion in her mind that she would make love to you?'

'That's not what happened.'

When Carla gave her evidence she was so distressed that the judge had to allow a short recess during the day when her sobbing had become uncontrollable. She was in an emotional dilemma. This man who was accused of raping her had cured her psycho-sexual problem, and then she had fallen in love with him. During their long hypnotic sessions, a special bond had developed between them, almost that of child and parent. She wished that she had never pursued the charge, and at times she almost wished that Jeremy Fawcett would shout 'Alpha' across the courtroom and remove her conscious mind from this agony. She knew that she was really continuing because of Peter. He had been so furious when he had heard the recording on her answerphone and rushed round to Jeremy Fawcett's flat to find her naked in his bedroom. She also knew that he was suspicious and confused when he discovered that she had taken her clothes off herself. They weren't torn or damaged in any way. In fact, as she took them off she had folded them in a neat pile on a chair, and they had still been there when Peter had stormed into the bedroom. She had had to suffer the indignation of the probing questions and the emotional turmoil to clear her name, and more importantly to reassure her fiancé.

The prosecuting barrister was even more gentle with her than he had been with Fawcett.

'Miss Narcissi, why did you visit Sir Jeremy Fawcett on that Saturday?'

'I had a telephone call from him inviting me to see him. I'd said "No" to the invitation but after putting the telephone down, I put on my coat and caught a taxi to his flat. I don't know why I did this.'

'Do you think that he hypnotised you?'

'He must have done. And anyway, you've heard the tape.'

'Do you remember him hypnotising you?'

'No, I don't normally remember anything that happens when I'm hypnotised.'

He went through the evidence carefully, bringing out the fact that Carla was not acting of her free will. It was not a voluntary act to visit Fawcett; she had no control over her actions. She had been totally controlled by him.

'When you arrived at Sir Jeremy's flat, how did you feel?'

'I couldn't understand what I was doing there.'

A crucial point in the case was whether Carla removed her clothes of her own free will and then invited Fawcett to make love to her.

'Why did you remove all your clothes in Sir Jeremy's consulting room?'

'I don't know.'

'Did you feel sexually aroused by him and want to make love?'

'No, I didn't know what I was doing. I seemed to be acting out a play. It didn't seem real. It was almost as if someone else was inside my head directing my actions.'

'Did you go into the bedroom with Sir Jeremy of your own free will?'

'I went into the bedroom with him. He didn't force me to go in, but I can't explain why I did.'

'Can you tell us what happened in the bedroom?' he asked quietly.

Carla burst into tears, but the barrister continued, knowing that the tears would probably influence some members of the jury.

'Take your time, Miss Narcissi.'

'We got into bed and started to make love. My mind seemed to clear. I realised what was happening. I tried to push him off and I started to scream. He lay on top of me so that I couldn't move. I screamed and screamed and eventually I wriggled free.'

But Carla Narcissi's anguish was not over. Fawcett's counsel stood up to cross-examine. He knew that he had to discredit her. He must leave enough uncertainty in the minds of the jury, so that even though they were bound to believe that Fawcett had hypnotised Carla to get her there, they couldn't be sure that once there, she hadn't agreed to sexual intercourse, and then, at the last moment, changed her mind.

'Miss Narcissi, where did you first meet Jeremy Fawcett?'

'In his rooms. I went to him for treatment.'

'During your treatment, did you become friends?'

'Yes.'

'Lovers?' She lowered her eyes and said faintly, 'Yes.'

'How did that come about?'

'We just fell in love.'

'Where did you first have sexual intercourse with him?'

'In his rooms.'

The barrister turned towards the jury and repeated her answer.

'In his rooms.'

'Miss Narcissi, I want you to think carefully before you answer the next question.

He looked up at the jury, and then turned to Carla:

'Would I be right in believing that you seduced Jeremy Fawcett on this first occasion? It was your behaviour which brought this about?'

The tears streamed down Carla's face. As she rubbed her eyes, her precisely applied make-up smudged almost as if an artist was mixing colours on her face. She looked a sad figure as the court waited for her reply.

The defence counsel waited patiently for her to compose herself. He didn't want the jury to think him a bully. Eventually he gently repeated his question.

'Was it you who seduced Jeremy Fawcett on the first occasion you had sexual intercourse with him in his rooms?'

Carla mumbled an almost inaudible 'Yes'.

The press scribbled away as the barrister pressed on:

'Was this the only time you had sexual intercourse in his rooms?'

'No, there were other occasions.'

'Would I be right in believing that on the first two or three occasions you made all the running? You approached Fawcett, not the other way round? It was your wish to have sexual intercourse with him?'

Carla was in a dilemma. She didn't want to explain the reason she went to see Fawcett in the first place. Even though her identity was not being disclosed in court, she knew that details of the hearing would circulate round her social circle. She stood in the witness box, a forlorn figure, not answering until the judge prompted her.

'Miss Narcissi.'

She mumbled 'Yes.'

'So, let's be quite clear about this. It was not unusual for you to go to Jeremy Fawcett's rooms and have sexual intercourse with him. At your instigation?'

Again the judge had to intervene to ask Carla to reply. 'Miss Narcissi, you must answer.'

'No.'

The barrister repeated: 'No, it wasn't unusual. That was your answer. Wasn't it?'

'Yes.

'Miss Narcissi, wasn't this what happened on this occasion?'

'No.'

'Didn't you feel that you wanted to make love to him?'

'No.'

'It wasn't his idea at all, was it?'

'Yes, it was.'

'Why should the jury believe that this occasion was any different from the other times where you had intercourse with him in his rooms?'

'It was,' replied Carla sullenly.

The questioning went on and on, probing away, trying to portray Carla as a woman of easy virtue. The barrister asked her about her life when she lived with Jeremy Fawcett. It was as if he were completing a giant jigsaw, gradually building up a picture in the jury's mind of a sexually active young woman who had seduced Fawcett in his rooms and then gone to live with him, but because she craved constant excitement went off to late parties on her own and finally left him. And later, when she had found herself alone with him in his rooms, she had decided that she might as well have sex with him. When he finally finished his cross examination, Carla stood with her head bowed and her hands hiding her face, almost as if she couldn't bear anyone to see her shame. She felt so guilty.

The case continued for seven days before the judge began his summing up. He started by instructing the jury that the case revolved around whether Sir Jeremy Fawcett knew that Miss Narcissi was not consenting to sexual intercourse. If he had consent, it was not rape. If he knew that she was not consenting, he was guilty.

'We have the evidence of the answerphone tape which was inadvertently left on by Miss Narcissi, in spite of being asked to switch it off by Sir Jeremy. You may consider that this is crucial evidence which demonstrated that he did telephone Miss Narcissi, and did hypnotise her over the telephone and instruct her to come to his flat. And you've seen the dramatic effect of that telephone call on Miss Narcissi when the recording of it was played in court. Clearly Miss Narcissi did not willingly agree to visit him that Saturday afternoon. She was coerced into going, but hypnotising her and getting her to go to the flat does not constitute rape.

'Now what happened when she got to the flat? Sir Jeremy has told us that Miss Narcissi arrived out of the blue, and shortly afterwards removed all her clothes, folded them neatly and put them on a chair and then invited him to make love to her. On the other hand, Miss Narcissi has said that she didn't know why she visited him, and she did not know why she removed all her clothes and went into the bedroom with him. It has been suggested by the prosecuting barrister that Sir Jeremy hypnotised Miss Narcissi in his rooms and instructed her to behave in this way. You have heard no evidence to support this. You have heard Miss Narcissi say during cross-examination that it wasn't unusual for her to visit Sir Jeremy and have sexual intercourse in his rooms. Also, she admitted in evidence that she often "made the running". You have heard evidence from Sir Jeremy that Miss Narcissi is a very deep trance-hypnotic subject – a somnambule – who would go into an immediate trance whenever he used the code word "Alpha". It would have been very simple for him to have hypnotised Miss Narcissi in his consulting rooms. On his own admission he had already done this during the treatment of Miss Narcissi many hundreds of times. So when he coerced Miss Narcissi to visit him, was it for the express purpose of having sexual intercourse with her, with or without her consent? If you consider that she didn't give consent, because her critical faculties were unable to operate freely because of the hypnosis and the effects of the post-hypnotic suggestion to make love planted in her subconscious mind, then Sir Jeremy Fawcett is as guilty of rape as he would be if he had tied her to the bed.'

The jury was out for five hours, going backwards and forwards over the arguments. One forceful personality – and there always seems to be one when a group of strangers sit together in a jury room – put the case simply:

'Did Fawcett get into Miss Narcissi's mind and cause her to remove all her clothes and offer sex, or did she do this of her own free will?' He continued: 'She admitted in the witness box that she often started the love-making in his rooms. And it must have happened before when they were living together. A young passionate woman taking the lead. Perhaps she always behaved like that. It turned her on.'

At the end of five hours they reached a decision, more through exhaustion than logical argument. With some of them the final decision was emotional. They had seen Carla's distress. They had listened to the answerphone recording which made it clear that Jeremy Fawcett could manipulate Carla's mind as he wished. They just felt that he must be guilty.

Fawcett watched the jury file back in and take their seats. None of them looked at him. They seemed to be deliberately avoiding eye contact. The foreman stood up to give the verdict.

'Guilty of rape as charged, my lord.'

Fawcett buried his face in his hands. Until that moment he had still had some hope, but now he felt genuine fear. The thought of spending many years locked up in prison made him shake.

The judge sentenced him to five years. Fawcett's counsel tried to comfort him by saying that it could have been twice as long, and with good behaviour he should be out in less than three.

As Carla, her parents and fiancé were leaving the court, they passed close to Fawcett. Carla was crying, but her father was angry and not pleased with the sentence. He stared across at Fawcett.

'You're a dangerous old fool,' he shouted, 'You should be locked up for the rest of your life. You're much too dangerous to be free.'

Fawcett looked up. All his self control and years of professional conditioning to protect patient's confidentiality deserted him. He stood up. 'At least I made love to her when she was a grown-up woman,' he shouted back, 'not when she was a child.'

The blood drained from Carla's father's face, and he quickly led her towards the exit, staring straight ahead so that she couldn't see his face.

'Thank goodness that's over,' he said when they were seated in the car. 'You can get back to a normal life again.'

Carla looked at him, her face stained with tears.

'Will I ever be able to lead a normal life?'

'Of course you will. You'll have Peter to look after you – and our support.'

Carla dried her tears and gazed directly at her father.

'You did sexually abuse me as a child, didn't you? Isn't that what Jeremy meant? Weren't you the cause of all my problems?'

'What a dreadful thing to say. His mind had become deranged. He didn't know what he was saying.'

But Carla knew, and she looked at him with contempt.

The silence of the car journey back to the Narcissi's home was only interrupted by Carla's sobbing. She got out of the car and went straight upstairs to her bedroom, returning half an hour later with two large suitcases. Her fiancé took them from her and they left the house.

'You won't ever see me again,' she said, and looking at her father, she shouted: 'You fill me with disgust and hatred, you pervert.'

They left, slamming the front door behind them. As Carla's mother watched her only child leave, her mind exploded.

'How could you?' she shouted. 'An innocent child who trusted you!'

Her husband approached her to comfort her.

'You are distressed because of this court case. I don't know why you should believe a convicted rapist. This is absolute nonsense. I would never have touched Carla. I loved her too much.'

'Don't touch me!' she said, pushing him away violently as he tried to put his arm round her.

She had seen the expression on her husband's face when Carla had accused him, and her mind went back many years to occasions when she would awake to hear Carla screaming out in the night. When her husband returned to the bedroom, he would say:

'Carla's having one of those nightmares again.'

When her husband approached her again she quickly picked up a long-bladed kitchen knife.

'If you come near me, I'll kill you!' she said, pointing it at him.

'Be reasonable, this is madness. Put the knife down before we have a serious accident.'

He tried to wrestle the knife away from her. As he struggled, he felt a sharp pain on the back of his hand. He pulled away and saw a three-inch long deep cut with blood pouring on to the kitchen floor. Even the sight of the deep gash and the pool of blood didn't calm Mrs Narcissi.

'I hope you bleed to death,' she shouted, 'you monster!'

Then she went upstairs to her bedroom and left her husband to fend for himself.

It wasn't a fatal injury. The Narcissis stayed together, but there were many times when Carla's father wished that he had bled to death. He never saw Carla again and for most of the time his wife ignored him. Every night she would lock herself in her bedroom and if he tried to approach her, she would challenge him to go to the divorce courts, where she would make sure that all the details of his lurid past would come out. She never let him forget his guilt; his life became a living hell.

Melanie Clarkson had followed the case in the newspapers and on television, as had the entire medical profession. Even the quality press gave it a whole page nearly every day of the trial. As for the tabloids, it kept them in copy for two weeks. The headline writers had a field day:

'FAMOUS SURGEON RAPES ZOMBIE'

The tabloids soon found out where Carla lived and waited outside her flat for any snippet of news. Some of them offered her a large sum of money to write the story of her relationship with Fawcett, but she refused.

Melanie was saddened by the mess Jeremy Fawcett had made of his life. One of our great surgeons, capable of leading the profession to new standards of excellence, didn't seem to have the moral fibre to control his personal life. Secretly, she was pleased that she had always used her maiden name professionally. She had remained Dr Clarkson even when she had been married to John Wright, and she hadn't changed it when she married Fawcett.

Shortly after the trial Melanie Clarkson met John Wright at the Royal Society of Medicine in Wimpole Street. She still felt a 'buzz' when she met him. Her personality seemed to go up a notch or two; she felt more alive. She had a drink with him and agreed to join him for dinner. They dined in the quiet dignity of the RSM restaurant.

'You can't have enjoyed the trial,' remarked Wright. 'Must have been hell.'

'The whole business was difficult to understand,' she said. 'How could such a staid establishment figure as Jeremy get himself infatuated with such a young woman in the first place?' She paused briefly to pick up her sherry glass. 'And, for that matter, how did he manage to get himself struck off the Register before that?'

'I expect we'd be shocked if we knew what went on in other people's minds – even those of our closest associates.'

'Obviously I didn't know,' Melanie said sadly, 'or I might have done something about it. I feel sorry for the young woman. She'll never know for sure whether she took her clothes off because of a post-hypnotic suggestion, or because she wanted to make love to him and felt guilty at the last moment. And then cried "rape".'

'He'll never practise again – that's for sure,' said Wright. 'He'll stay struck off.' He beckoned the waiter for more sherry. 'Come on, drink up,' he said to Melanie, 'You look sad. It's not your fault.'

'Perhaps it is,' she mused, 'Both my husbands left me for more exciting women.'

'I didn't,' he laughed, 'You were exciting enough for me. I just got led astray. But I don't blame Jane Perkins for that.'

'What was all that business about Jeremy forging her signature?'

'That was a long time ago,' he said, 'Let sleeping dogs lie.'

'No,' she insisted, 'Come on – tell me. I can only remember one letter from Jane Perkins .'

'I'm afraid it was that one,' he replied. 'Jane didn't send it. In fact she'd told Jeremy that she wasn't going to at a time when she was still his patient.'

'So, not only forgery,' she said, 'but breach of patient confidentiality as well.'

'That's about it,' said Wright, 'I only found out many years later.'

'We'd still be married,' said Melanie, 'but for the forgery.'

'Yes,' he laughed, 'And I would have kept my infidelity a secret.'

They stayed in the restaurant for hours reminiscing and were the last to leave, encouraged by the waiter hovering around them. Two weeks later they met for dinner again.

'You've acquired expensive tastes,' said Melanie, as they sat in the Gavroche, 'I haven't been here before.'

'I'm trying to make an impression,' he laughed.

'You did that many years ago.'

He took her home in a taxi.

'Coffee,' she said.

She sat him down and returned with some filter coffee and two large brandy balloons.

'Armagnac?'

'You still drink it?'

'It's my favourite.'

'I remember drinking it with you,' he said, holding the brandy in his cupped hands to warm it. 'It was at your parents' home, before we were married.'

'I was never the same again,' she laughed, 'after that night.'

He finished his brandy and stood up.

'I've had too much to drink,' said Melanie, putting her glass down, 'I've got out of practice.'

He put his arm round her and pulling her close, kissed her.

She responded passionately. They stood for some minutes kissing and holding each other close and then they slowly walked out of the room and up a short flight of stairs to Melanie's bedroom. There they made love.

'D'you think I'm a hussy?' Melanie asked, 'At my age! Shouldn't we have waited for a few weeks?'

'Yes,' he replied, kissing her. 'You are a dreadful hussy.'

'Get out of my bed,' she protested, pushing him playfully. But he stayed all night.

About a month later Wright suggested: 'Let's go to Crete. We haven't been there since our honeymoon.'

They stayed in the foothills of the White Mountains for three weeks in Adonis' farmhouse in the quiet hamlet of Provarma. The simple accommodation was arranged around a central courtyard, ablaze with blue convolvulus and bougainvillaea. The garden was full of hibiscus and broom, huge bushes of geraniums and fading roses, oleander, orange, lemon, medlar and the ubiquitous olive trees. Mulberry trees were in fruit and their sickly produce stained the stone paths black.

The small hamlet started early and at six a farmer clattered down the track alongside the farmhouse to collect his mule, which had spent the night under a mulberry tree close by. The noise always stirred Wright and he put his arm round Melanie and kissed her neck.

'Darling,' he said, stroking her neck gently until she turned and kissed him. 'I'm sure you pay that farmer,' she said. Afterwards, they drifted off to sleep until breakfast.

As they ate breakfast in the courtyard, they watched the shepherd drive his sheep across the land in front of the farmhouse, their bells tinkling in a waterfall of sound, some always escaping into the courtyard itself.

'Swimming first?' asked Wright, 'and then lunch in Vrises?'

They floated in the sea off the Blue Beach at Kalami with the snow-capped mountains towering thousands of feet above them. The beach was deserted. It was too early for the Cretans, who only swam 'when the water melon pips were in the streets'; and anyway, there were no tourists in this remote part of Crete at that time.

At Vrises a whole sheep was roasting on a spit, along with ten sheeps' heads slowly turning, their opaque, unseeing eyes staring out at them. Their neighbour consumed an entire head down to the bone, carving it so effectively that it looked as if a carrion crow had been at work and left it to bleach in the Cretan sun. He skilfully dissected the muscles from the facial bones, and stripped the maxilla down to the incisor teeth. He ate the brain, the tongue, and then to their horror, the opaque eyes.

'He's missed his vocation,' said Melanie laughing, 'He should have been a surgeon.'

'It's one way of learning anatomy,' agreed Wright, 'He probably knows the insertion of every muscle in the sheep's head.'

Eating out was so cheap and such fun that it was scarcely worth cooking at the farmhouse. Anna's cafenion was only two kilometres away. She was famous for her souvlaki laced with mountain herbs and cooked on the barbecue, accompanied by a peasant's salad of tomatoes, cucumber and onions, a few black olives, and with a large slice of goat's cheese on top; chipped potatoes were served on a separate plate. The potatoes were cooked in a large saucepan of olive oil heated on an open olive-log fire next to two magnificent white goats nonchalantly munching whole oranges. With a litre of village wine, it cost the princely sum of five pounds for the two of them.

'Aspro pardo,' said Melanie, clinking the bottom of her glass of colourless raki with his in the approved Cretan way.

'White bottoms,' riposted Wright, downing the fiery liquid in one gulp.

'That's too literal!' Melanie laughed. 'Bottoms up!'

On their last night in Crete they drove through Stilos and up through the hills to Malaxa. They ate at a tiny taverna aptly named Panorama. It was cantilevered from the side of the hills, with startling views over Souda Bay and Chania, the old Venetian capital.

'It's like being on a magic carpet,' said Melanie. The clear purple night and star-filled sky seemed to envelop them like a velvet cloak. They stayed there alone on the small terrace, drinking village wine.

'Let's get married again,' suggested Wright, holding her hand, 'If you'll have me back, after all the pain and anguish I caused you last time. It won't happen again.'

'You mean you're too old for temptation,' Melanie said. She refilled their tiny glasses with village wine. 'You know I love you,' she went on, 'but I'm not sure about marriage – at our age.'

'I'd like to be committed,' said Wright.

'We can be committed without marriage,' she replied, 'Why don't we just live together? That's real commitment.'

'I never thought I'd hear you make such a suggestion,' said Wright with mock disapproval.

'I've changed,' she said, shrugging her shoulders, 'Society's changed. We're past more children.' She laughed. 'At least I am.'

Back at the farmhouse they sat in the courtyard drinking raki, listening to the chirping of the crickets, the melancholy piping of the skop owl, and the occasional movement of the tethered mule just the other side of the short stone wall.

'I'm sorry I didn't forgive you all those years ago,' said Melanie.

'I let you down,' he said, finishing his raki, 'but I never thought you would go through with the divorce.'

'I should have been more Christian and forgiven you,' she said, kissing him.

Wright hadn't been so happy for a long time. He was back with Melanie and their lives quickly got back into the same groove as before they were divorced. They went everywhere together.

'You're not only my love,' remarked Wright, 'but my best friend as well.'

They lived together in Melanie's London home, and often spent the weekend in the country with her parents, who had retired and were now very old. They could meet the two children together again, and when all four met in London, it was quite an event.

'I never liked that creep Fawcett,' said his son George, 'I never trusted him.'

'It must be difficult,' replied Wright, 'to be a step father.'

'He hated you,' said George. 'He was always talking disparagingly about your East End background – saying you weren't the right type to do medicine and that he couldn't understand how St Luke's ever accepted you.'

'Neither could I,' Wright laughed, 'it was only my rugby. I had nothing else.'

# Chapter Eight

Fawcett had been locked up in prison for three weeks before he met Jack Crayson. His instincts were to retreat within himself and avoid social contact, but he couldn't avoid Crayson. Crayson was a tiny man, not much more than five feet tall, and as bright as a button. A mathematics genius gone wrong.

'I can get into any computer system in the world,' he told Fawcett. 'If you want to get information, change information, I'm your man.'

He never seemed to stand still when he was talking. He bounced up and down on his heels as if exercising or trying to make himself taller.

'They can protect their databases with the most sophisticated systems, but with my intelligence – and nerve – I can always get in.'

'If you're so bloody clever,' retorted Fawcett, 'What are you doing in here?'

'Just bad luck. That's outside intelligence. I hacked into the bank computer and transferred the funds, but Lady Luck played a dirty one on me.'

Crayson was an old Etonian, an Oxford graduate in mathematics and a Doctor of Philosophy from Massachusetts' famous Institute of Technology. Fawcett wasn't particularly interested at first, but as he spent more time in prison, and his depression turned to bitterness, he began to enjoy Crayson's company. He reckoned fate had dealt him a duff hand. A few years ago he had been Sir Jeremy Fawcett, the President of the Royal College of Surgeons. Now he was Prisoner Fawcett. Society and the establishment had been so hard on him that he no longer felt any debt to them. His talents were in spare-part surgery. There were waiting lists around the world. Patients were dying waiting for organs. It didn't matter whether they were paupers or billionaires, without suitable organs they died. With suitable organs they lived, and they lived normal lives. He had treated young soldiers who had returned to army duties.

'You're okay. You can use your skills when you get out. I can't,' he said to Crayson. 'I haven't got the slightest chance of getting back on to the UK Medical Register – not the slightest. The GMC would say I was too much of a risk to patients, and an embarrassment to the profession.'

He talked to Crayson about transplant surgery and the difficulty of getting organs. Once he got his teeth into a problem, Crayson was like a dog with a bone – he wouldn't let go.

'What happens to all the organs in the country?' he asked.

Fawcett told him about the organ transplant service at Bristol, which kept all the matching details of patients waiting for an organ. When one became available – usually following a motor car accident and severe brain injury – the details of the potential donor would be sent to Bristol and they would run them against their database to find the best match. Crayson asked numerous questions; he wanted to know precise details; he listened attentively.

'What you would have to do is to duplicate the Bristol computer,' he said.

Fawcett used computers, but he certainly wouldn't call himself a buff.

'How would that help? I would need to get at the organs before Bristol allocated them.'

'With your duplicate system you'd have information about the patients who needed organs. And the info about the new organs.'

Fawcett looked puzzled. 'Yes, but how would I get the organs first?'

'My boy, you could do one of two things – or rather I would for you.' He was talking to Fawcett like the schoolmaster he had been for a short time. 'You could either erase the details of the new organs from the database so that they didn't know they had them, or – you could erase the matching details of the patients ahead of your patients.' He paused to make sure Fawcett was still with him. 'Then, when they checked the organs for match, your patient would come out best – and be allocated the organ.'

'Brilliant!'

'Yes I am, Jeremy,' he said with a grin, 'But unless I've missed something, I don't see how this would help to obtain a regular supply of organs.'

Fawcett got to like this criminal genius. He was friendly and he regarded Crayson as similar to himself. Both had risen to the top of their professions; both were brilliant but basically weak characters, who broke the rules when they were up against it. Neither felt that they had any obligation to society, or any duty to help anyone other than themselves. Fawcett's ambition to go down in surgical history had vanished from his mind – all he wanted was revenge and a fortune. Crayson had been younger than Fawcett when he reached the point of no return. He might have made a fortune designing new computer systems, but he hadn't got the business skills. If he'd found an entrepreneur like Simon Connor, his life could have been quite different. Connor would have set up a company with Crayson as Research Director, and Crayson would now have been a wealthy, respectable member of society, pushing the frontiers of computer science ever outwards. Neither Crayson nor Fawcett felt they should be in prison. Crayson had helped himself to someone else's money.

'I'd have paid it back when they found out,' he said, 'Now they'll never get it; it's tucked away out of reach.'

'I bet you've spent most of it by now,' said Fawcett.

'I'd break into another financial system to pay them back.'

They both laughed. Fawcett was beginning to enjoy his association with criminals. It was exciting, and the stakes were high. If criminals failed, they finished up in prison for years. The challenge was to be too clever for the police.

'My problems started with medical ethics – not the law,' remarked Fawcett. 'I didn't break the law, I upset the medical establishment.' He continued thoughtfully: 'That led me into hypnosis – and the beautiful Carla. When she left me, I tried to get her back by raping her.'

'Prisoners don't like rapists,' said Crayson. 'You've been lucky so far. You'd certainly have been beaten up if you'd raped a child.'

'I didn't regard it as rape. We'd been living together as man and wife and I didn't use any violence – I didn't tie her to the bed.'

'You tied up her mind instead.'

'Anyway – what's the use of thinking about it?'

'You got caught because you were emotionally involved,' Crayson pointed out. 'If you're going to be a successful criminal, you've got to cut out emotions – use your intellect. And whatever you do, don't look backwards,' he went on. 'Life's like the Stock Exchange. You'll never succeed if you're continually regretting not buying or selling shares when you should have.'

Crayson looked up at Fawcett and put a friendly hand on his shoulder.

'Let's think about the future. You've identified one source of organs, but it would be insufficient and spasmodic. You'd never be sure of getting them when you wanted them, and you'd have a major problem getting your hands on them.' He looked thoughtfully at Fawcett. 'You could fix the computer so that the organs were allocated to your patients, but how would you get your hands on them? And where would you operate?'

'It wouldn't be easy,' replied Fawcett.

'I've been thinking about your problem,' said Crayson, when he met Fawcett in the prison yard a few days later, 'Is there a computer network which records patients' matching details?'

'Apart from Bristol for the patients needing organ transplants, I don't believe there is.'

'What about all those patients giving blood? Aren't they tested?'

'Only for blood groups. It could be fatal to give the wrong group,' answered Fawcett, 'They're checked for HIV status, hepatitis, syphilis. Matching tests might be carried out occasionally.'

'Why couldn't the Blood Transfusion Service provide the matching tests for all patients?' asked Crayson. 'You'd then have a large group of patients with the correct matching.' He paused and went on in a matter-of-fact way. 'All you'd have to do then would be to get the organs.'

'There'd be no reason for all blood to be tested for matching,' replied Fawcett. 'And anyway, what patient is going to give a kidney – on request?'

Crayson ignored this. 'Let's see how we can get the matching tests done routinely.' His mind worked logically, step by step. 'How's the blood collected?'

'At various centres – work places, for example, or anywhere convenient for donors. The mobile units can go anywhere. It's stored at centres around the country,' he went on, 'About fifteen, I believe.'

'How many patients give blood?'

'Must be millions.'

'Healthy people?'

'Yes. The medical history is always checked. They're very strict – won't take any chances. They won't even take blood from some groups for fear of AIDS.'

'So, what've we got so far? Millions of healthy people giving blood – what, two or three times a year?'

'That's about it.'

'Is it possible to identify patients?'

'They're all bar coded.'

Crayson's mind raced on. Fawcett had ceased to be a human being; he was just an information source. 'How do we get the matching tests carried out?' asked Crayson. 'Does the Blood Transfusion Service have the skills?'

'They do the tests on a few patients already.'

'All right then – how do we get them carried out?'

'That would be impossible – there'd be no reason to do so on every patient.'

'Nothing's impossible,' Crayson said, 'Supposing they were ordered to do them – as part of a research project?'

'It would have to come from up high.'

'Well, okay. A top civil servant, or even better, the Secretary of State, sends them a letter. Wouldn't they just get on with it?'

'They'd be bound to ask questions, at least about funding.'

'All right. They get a letter from the Department of Health saying that the Secretary of State would expect the research to be paid for out of efficiency savings. No additional funds would be made available. What then?'

'You'd have to find an area where there was an ambitious manager who wanted to impress the Department,' replied Fawcett. 'Anyway – there'd have to be a contact at the Department.'

'That's a pity,' remarked Crayson. 'The fewer people involved the better. Perhaps they'd settle for contact by letter, or better still, by phone.'

Fawcett was listening to Crayson as his mind ran through the options, until he found the solution, almost like the computers he worshipped, but he wasn't sure where Crayson's mind was taking him.

'This is fascinating, but where's it getting us?'

'Don't you see?' he said, 'You've identified thousands of fit people with the matched organs you would need for your transplant service.'

Fawcett roared with laughter.

'Dear Sir. You've the correct matching details for my rich patient. Please let me have your kidneys. Or your heart.'

Crayson was quite serious.

'You're going to have to take them as you need them.'

'Mass murder – is that it?' He looked incredulous. 'I can't believe you're serious. I couldn't be involved in that.'

'If you haven't got the bottle,' retorted Crayson angrily, 'Remain a pauper. Get yourself a job as a filing clerk when you get out – if you're lucky.'

He calmed down.

'Just imagine if you were filthy rich. What a life you could lead! Grand homes in exotic places, perhaps on your own island. Beautiful women, yachts, your own executive jet – you could really live!' he said, his eyes shining with excitement, 'And what's more, you could carry out more surgery than you'd ever done in your life.'

He looked across at Fawcett.

'Jeremy – you won't have many working years left when they let you out. You're a criminal now – why not accept it?'

Over the next months they talked about Crayson's 'master plan', as Fawcett called it.

'It's almost foolproof,' Crayson agreed. 'You've got a large source of organs. All you've got to do is get them picked up and brought to your operating unit, wherever that is.'

'And then I kill them – just like that?'

'You're using emotive language. Let's say they donate their organs. If they die, someone else will live. You haven't altered the balance.'

'You're a callous bastard even to talk like that and, furthermore, you haven't even got your mathematics right. The organs from one body could be used for as many as eight patients.'

'There you go. One dies and eight live. What's wrong with that?'

Fawcett shook his head in amazement. He couldn't really believe he was having this conversation.

'Jesus, if you can't see the potential, I give up,' exclaimed Crayson. 'I could tap into the blood transfusion service of any major country and identify suitable patients in the UK, America, Germany – anywhere.'

Fawcett shook his head in disbelief.

'Just think about it – that's all I ask,' said Crayson, 'Who could possibly link you with a few hundred missing people? And in different countries. The only thing they would have in common would be that they'd given blood during the previous year.' He laughed. 'And so what? Millions do. It would take a computer genius like me to make the link, and I'm unique.'

Fawcett looked at him and saw that although he was laughing, he was deadly serious. As far as he was concerned, it was an intellectual exercise to create a scheme to defeat the establishment and make a fortune.

'I almost believe you mean it,' Fawcett said.

Crayson took him by the arm. 'Come and meet Muller.' They strolled across the yard to a man standing alone.

'Jake – this is Sir Jeremy Fawcett, the famous surgeon,' he said, emphasizing the 'Sir'.

'Just plain Mr now. They stripped me of the 'K' after the rape case.'

Jake Muller was a tall powerful man with cropped iron grey hair, a square jaw with a pronounced cleft running down the centre of his chin, an unusually small nose with wide nostrils, and very pale ice-blue eyes. There was not a hint of friendliness about him but he had an enormous presence. It was frightening to be near him. Fawcett was surprised at Crayson's flippant introduction. He soon discovered that they had worked together and had a mutual respect for each other's talents. Crayson had the brains, Muller the ruthless physical strength.

'Did you have something in mind, Dwarf?' asked Muller in a quiet voice with a Geordie accent.

'Jake,' he said, 'Tell Jeremy how you'd pick up some stranger and take him to a secret location.'

Muller focused his pale blue eyes on Fawcett and suddenly thrust his open hand into his ribs. Fawcett felt his muscles contract.

'As soon as I do this with a gun or a knife,' said Muller, 'Fear petrifies them. They become paralysed.'

He pulled at his cigarette and then threw the butt on the ground. 'Moving them is more difficult. I use a helicopter if I can. I can land it anywhere.' He looked at Crayson. 'Got a job for me?'

'Give us more time. We'll be back.'

Crayson walked away with Fawcett. 'It is simple. I'll give Jake the names from the computer, and he'll bring them to you. No need to be squeamish,' he said, looking at Fawcett who had gone very pale, 'They'll all be heavily drugged, practically dead when you get them – they'll have to be with Jake flying the helicopter himself.'

Fawcett was silent.

'Think of the money,' Crayson went on, '150K an op. Two a day, ten a week. You're already up to seventy-five million a year. We're talking big money.' Fawcett remained speechless. 'You'd need to find other surgeons to help you so as to compound your income. With three of you working, and lower overheads, you'd be well over two hundred million.' He laughed. 'You could retire after a year – unless you were greedy. For Christ's sake, show some enthusiasm,' he said, looking at Fawcett with irritation, 'You're destroying my creativity. Don't just stand there like a mummy.'

Shaking himself out of his introspection, and feeling he had to say something, Fawcett protested, 'It'd never work. To start with, who's going to bankroll it?'

'Don't worry about the money. There are lots of rich criminals around looking for investments. I might even break into one of those home banking businesses myself to raise the ante. They seem a doddle.'

'Simon Connor might even put the money up front,' he said, forcing himself to sound more interested.

'Good!' Crayson replied. 'You're beginning to use your grey cells.'

Fawcett and Crayson spent months talking about their scheme.

'Security would be vital,' Crayson pointed out, 'The fewer people in the know the better.'

'I'd have to find a "tame" anaesthetist,' said Fawcett, 'to deal with the patients when Muller delivers them. No one else needs to know.'

'Okay, Jeremy,' said Crayson, 'The drugged patient is at your operating complex. What next?'

'We'd have to keep the incoming donor patients separate from the rest of the hospital. The organs would be removed and passed through a secure hatch to the operating theatres.'

He'd almost forgotten that he was talking about live patients. The discussion had almost become a game to pass the time away. He'd started using Crayson's nickname.

'Dwarf,' he said, 'The main part of the operating complex would be the operating theatres. No one in this area would know where the organs came from. As far as they were concerned, they would be from brain-dead patients from around the world.'

Crayson was concentrating on every word. 'You would, of course, need a lot of staff.'

'Yes, nurses, physiotherapists and so on. It would be like a small specialised hospital.'

'Where would you get the extra surgeons from?' Crayson asked.

Fawcett thought for a moment and then said slowly: 'They'd all be surgeons "struck off" the Register. I doubt whether I could find them in the UK. They'd have to come from Europe or the States.'

'Brilliant,' said Crayson. 'All banned from operating in their own countries. They wouldn't be asking too many questions; they'd keep quiet.'

'That's the structure, but the detail would need a lot of work, and God knows how we would get rid of the bodies!'

'They must disappear completely,' answered Crayson without any emotion.

Fawcett shuddered. 'You're evil. These are human beings you're talking about.'

'Millions get killed in wars. Life's a lottery.' Crayson shrugged. 'I'm only protecting us. The police are at a great disadvantage without a body, should they ever catch up with us.' He went on: 'Where would the best place be for your surgical complex? I suppose it couldn't be in the centre of London or New York – though that'd be damned convenient. All the night life!'

'When Connor talked about this some time ago,' replied Fawcett, interrupting him, 'he talked about going offshore – on a boat somewhere.'

'You've cracked it!' exclaimed Crayson, throwing his arms in the air. 'Mobile but still near enough to land for Muller to get to us. And what better place for patients to recuperate than the deck of a luxury liner?' he added laughing.

Fawcett didn't really believe that Crayson would get involved in mass murder – no matter how serious he appeared. But he underestimated Crayson's determination to finish his life as a multi-millionaire. He would rather be dead than live as a pauper. He would certainly rather be in prison with his friends than starve outside.

Towards the end of his sentence, Fawcett received a letter from Simon Connor. Gone was any pretence of friendliness. The letter ran:-

Dear Fawcett,
    You owe me a large sum of money. I don't see why I should pay you

£250K for killing my son. I want the money back plus interest. You had better contact me as soon as they let you out.

Yours sincerely,
Simon Connor.

Simon Connor had been driven by his wife, Jane Perkins, to write the letter.

'You mustn't let him get away with it,' she said. 'He's evil.' And then she added viciously: 'I want him to suffer more. I hate him.'

'I don't know why you hate him so much; he hasn't harmed you.'

'He's a disgrace to the profession.'

'So what? That's not our problem.'

She couldn't tell him that it was because he had brought about the end of John Wright's marriage – not that she would have minded that under normal circumstances; she might have picked him up on the rebound. But when Fawcett sent the forged letter to Melanie, it brought about not only Wright's divorce, but years of hatred towards her.

Connor was a realist and he knew that Fawcett would be in dire financial straits when he came out of prison, and in no position to repay the £250K. To him £250K was peanuts, but to Fawcett an impossible financial peak to climb. Fawcett thought that he had heard the last of Connor and was startled to receive the letter.

'What would you do?' he asked Crayson.

'Tell him if he wants his money back, he must finance our scheme,' he said laughing, 'Or put Muller on to him. He'll be out soon.'

Fawcett didn't reply to Connor's letter.

As he ticked off the days to his release, he tried to forget about Connor's letter and Crayson's scheme.

'I'm going to leave this miserable country as soon as I can when I get out,' he said, 'I've had enough.'

'What about our scheme?' Crayson asked angrily.

'You weren't serious about that.'

''Course I was. You can't let me down now.'

'I'm not really a criminal,' protested Fawcett, 'I couldn't have done it.'

'You've been wasting my bloody time,' Crayson shouted furiously, 'Pissing me about for almost a year.' He was standing close to Fawcett and glaring up at him shaking his fist. 'You've not only pissed me about, you've involved Muller; he won't like that. You'd better be careful; you're not out yet.'

Crayson was depressed. The tremendous 'buzz' he had got when working out 'the scheme' had gone. He would have to start all over again.

'You'll change your mind,' he said to Fawcett, 'Just think about all the pretty faces you can buy when you're rich. And the shapely bodies. You could have ten Carlas.'

'I'll be out in a month,' Crayson shouted out to him as he watched him leave the prison, 'I'll find you. You'll soon change your mind when you find out how difficult it is to get a job when you're an ex-con.'

Fawcett had no intention of seeing Crayson again.

## Chapter Nine

As the prison gates closed behind him, he looked nervously about. It was difficult not to see Simon Connor's Rolls. He started to cross the road to avoid it, but a man came quickly out of the front passenger seat and closed on him. He firmly clasped his upper arm and steered him towards the car with the words: 'Mr Connor wants a word with you.' Fawcett could have struggled free, even though the man had a grip of steel, but he had no wish to be involved in a fight outside the prison gates, so he allowed himself to be guided to the car. The man opened the rear door and pushed him in, saying, 'Mr Fawcett, sir.'

Connor looked as relaxed and immaculate as ever. He poured out two glasses of champagne and held his glass up. 'Here's to freedom.'

Fawcett hadn't tasted champagne – let alone Krug – for many years. It tasted wonderful.

'What are you going to do about my money?' inquired Connor refilling his glass.

'I don't owe you any.'

'Oh yes you do. I'm not paying you £250K to kill my son. I want it back. Plus interest.'

'I don't have any money,' Fawcett protested.

'You'll have to find some,' replied Connor. 'Let me make it crystal clear. Either you find the money' – he paused to finish his Krug – 'or you could disappear from the face of the earth. And who'd care?'

'You're threatening me,' said Fawcett. 'I'll go to the police.'

'You're not dealing with amateurs now.'

'Even if I owed you money, there's no way I can pay it back. I can't practise any more, so I'll have to find other work.'

'Work – what work can you get? Chauffeur, clerk, labourer? Who wants a defrocked surgeon and a rapist?'

'I've no choice,' Fawcett replied. 'There's nothing else I can do.'

'You're going to have to use your brains.'

'What d'you mean. Crime?'

Connor emptied his champagne glass for the second time.

'That's up to you.'

He nodded to the guard in the front seat, who opened the back door to let Fawcett out.

'You've got two weeks,' Connor warned, as Fawcett got out of the car. 'Don't try and run.'

Fawcett found a small flat just south of the Thames in Victoria. The first night he left the flat he noticed Simon Connor's guard on the pavement opposite. He made no attempt to hide; he just waved across to Fawcett. For the next week, whenever he looked out of the flat windows, the guard was there. If he travelled on a bus or the underground, the man was close by. On day thirteen the guard was waiting for Fawcett as he left his flat. He gave him a letter from Connor and waited while he read it.

Dear Fawcett

I've not heard from you. My man tells me you have been moving around London. I hope you have made progress. I will send my car for you tomorrow morning at 10.30.

Yours

Simon Connor

Fawcett was desperate. 'I must go to the police,' he thought, but he could imagine Connor saying: 'This man's trying to avoid repaying me the money he owes me. That's why he's making these absurd accusations that I'm threatening him.'

'Even if they believe me,' he thought, 'what can they do? They're unlikely to provide me with protection. They'll just listen and let me go. And then what?' After his years in prison he knew that a man of Connor's wealth would have no difficulty in finding someone like Muller to finish him.

The following morning Fawcett climbed into the Rolls and went across London to Connor's penthouse office in Park Lane, overlooking the Park and a large area of London. Connor boasted that his view was better than that of the Hilton at the end of Park Lane. Connor greeted him in a friendly way and gave him a glass of whisky.

'Soda, water, ice?'

He prided himself on being a good host whatever the circumstances; at least he always made sure his guests had a drink. This was his office suite and his wife seldom came there. He looked at Fawcett and thought of the first time he'd met him – Sir Jeremy Fawcett, the President of the Royal College of Surgeons, consultant at a major teaching hospital, world authority on transplant surgery – and now ex-prisoner, with no prospect of ever practising surgery again. Right at the bottom of the heap! He savoured his whisky.

'Have you got the money?'

'No.'

Connor looked at Fawcett without any sympathy. He seemed much harder than Fawcett remembered. He was a rich man, corrupted by the power of money. Rich men and aristocrats seem to be a law unto themselves, and Connor was no exception. He felt so powerful with his wealth that he regarded himself as above the law. His money could enable him to achieve anything he wanted. He thought he could buy anyone. He looked at Fawcett, this once great surgeon.

'I've spelt out the consequences,' he said viciously, 'you're living on borrowed time, and not much of that.'

Fawcett was shattered. Two weeks of freedom and they might be his last. He had to play for time if he was ever going to get out of this country.

'Well, maybe there is a way,' he said, gulping down the last of the whisky, 'I've been working on it in prison. But it does need substantial financing.'

Connor sat back. 'Tell me about it.'

Fawcett explained the organ transplant scheme he had developed with Crayson in as much detail as he thought necessary, and ended with 'It should make millions.'

Simon Connor refilled their glasses and sat thoughtfully for a while. Then he said: 'Drink up, we'll go to lunch.'

He rang the bell and the guard appeared. 'Get the Rolls.' Within thirty minutes they were in the Savoy Grill.

'This is just like old times.' Connor raised his glass. 'I'm so pleased you're back in circulation again.'

Fawcett thought: 'About an hour ago you were going to have me disappear, and now you're pleased to see me.' He set about enjoying his lunch. He'd almost forgotten about good clarets; the Ch. Latour was magnificent. 'Let's talk business,' said Connor. 'I always knew the organ transplant business was a winner.'

'Jeremy,' he said, reverting to his Christian name, 'Let me tell you what my role will be. Apart from providing the finance, that is.' He stopped to tap the ash from his cigar and beckon the waiter for two brandies. 'The liner will be no problem, since I own a shipping line. Apart from that, I'll organise the patients and collect the fees.' He waited for any response and when none was forthcoming, went on: 'That'll be the extent of my involvement. For that I'll take 50% of the profits.'

'That's steep,' protested Fawcett. 'Crayson won't stand for that.'

'That's the deal. Take it or leave it,' Connor said dismissively. 'I'm taking all the financial risks.'

Fawcett went back to his flat hoping that he would be able to steal away quietly but his guard was with him constantly. Connor wasn't going to spend large sums of money setting up this scheme and have his key player 'doing a runner'.

Two weeks later Crayson met Fawcett in London. He was elated. 'Jeremy, I knew you'd come round to it.'

Connor took the luxury liner *Oleander* out of commission and had it made available. My people think it's going to become a medical conference centre,' he told Fawcett, 'you'd better stick to that; it'll provide good cover.'

Fawcett arranged for a surgical equipment company to install six of the most modern operating theatres. The reception area for the donor patients and the organ removal section were isolated from the rest of the ship. Without special passes, no one would be able to move between these areas. Luxury accommodation was provided for the patients. Fawcett set about finding two more surgeons. He found Al Ryan from a famous transplant hospital in the States, and Klaus Bauer from Berlin – both, as they put it, temporarily unable to practise. He had to persuade both these surgeons to come to London to clinch the deal because Connor had said, 'You're not leaving the country.'

As he ploughed more money into the scheme, he increased the security on Fawcett. He had him watched around the clock.

The anaesthetist Fawcett found was Annette Marshall, who had been struck off the British Medical Register for repeated drug offences. Fawcett was more than a little concerned about her. She would be the only one on the *Oleander* who would know that the patients supplying the organs were not brain-dead. He didn't want her blown out of her mind. If she flipped, they would all be in trouble. He would have to have the video cameras on her constantly.

Fawcett and Crayson met frequently and when Crayson first saw Fawcett's flat he said: 'What a dump – It's a slum! Why don't you move in with me?'

'No – it suits me. It's better than a prison cell.'

'Only just.'

All Fawcett wanted to do was to get on a flight and out of the country, but he was aware of the surveillance – at least he knew the usual one who accompanied him everywhere, but he suspected that there were others not known to him. Connor wouldn't hesitate to have him killed if he tried to contact the police or leave the country. He knew he had to do something soon or he'd never get away.

Crayson had written a letter to the Regional Blood Transfusion Service on Department of Health notepaper, instructing them to start testing for tissue match as well as the usual blood group on every patient who gave blood. The information was required for important research and must be kept confidential to protect the validity of the research. He signed the letter 'David Blenkinsop, Under Secretary' – and gave Fawcett's telephone number.

'Jeremy,' Crayson said, 'You'll be Blenkinsop if they call.'

'Thanks, Dwarf,' he said sarcastically. 'Supposing they insist on a meeting?'

'No problem, you'll go in disguise. I'll help you. You'll look great in a beard.'

Fawcett was alarmed at this development. He was getting in so deep that he couldn't go to the police, even if he could shake off his guards.

'You'd better give me a copy of your letter,' he said to Crayson, 'and some Department of Health notepaper in case I have to write to them.'

Later that day Fawcett left his flat in Victoria determined to lose his 'tail' and get an air ticket. He was quite prepared to go to Heathrow and get on any plane. He was getting sucked in to Crayson's insane scheme. If he didn't make a move now, he would find himself on the boat and in the operating theatre. He'd tried to slow up the work on the liner, but Connor and Crayson were leaning on him all the time. He walked slowly towards Victoria Station. His usual guard was close behind but there were taxis and buses everywhere. He waited in the taxi queue but didn't take the first taxi; he stood aside and waved the next passenger on. All the time he was looking past the taxis at the buses parked opposite the rank. He climbed into the third taxi as the bus opposite began to move away. Behind him his guard had got into a taxi and said: 'Follow that cab – as close as you can. There's fifty in it for you.' Fawcett's taxi started away and almost immediately he shouted, 'Stop the cab, I feel ill.'

As the cab stopped, he pushed a twenty pound note into the driver's hand. 'Let me out, I feel awful,' he shouted. 'Quick, I'm going to be sick.'

The taxi driver had no wish to have his cab filled with vomit. He unlocked the door, and was astonished when Fawcett ran at full speed after a moving bus and jumped aboard. He got off the bus at the next stop and looked back, and was relieved that the guard was nowhere to be seen. He hailed a taxi and went to a travel agent in Piccadilly. There was a plane to Berlin later that evening. He was so desperate to get away that he would have bought a ticket to almost any destination.

Fawcett felt lifted. At last he'd taken some positive action to break away. All he had to do now was to get to Heathrow on time. As the shop door of the travel agents closed behind him, he had only taken a few steps when he felt the strong grip of two men pinning his arms to his sides.

'You going somewhere, Mr Fawcett?'

Even in broad daylight in Piccadilly he felt helpless. If he cried out for help, no one would take any notice.

'Just keep walking.' He was urged on by the sharp pressure in his side.

They led him down to St James' where Connor's Rolls Royce was parked with the driver ready to go. It was a short journey to Park Lane.

'You must have a death wish,' Connor said, standing over him full of hate.

Fawcett's entire body was trembling with fear.

'That can soon be arranged, if that's what you want.'

'Jake,' he called out and Muller came out of an adjacent room. 'Get rid of him.'

He dismissed him with a wave of his arm. Muller got hold of Fawcett but encountered no resistance. All his strength had deserted him; he had great difficulty in standing up. His throat was so dry with terror that he couldn't speak. Muller almost carried him towards the door. The door closed behind them while Muller went down the hallway and pushed him into a small, windowless room.

'Just stay there,' he growled. 'I'll be back later for you.' Fawcett was sure he was going to die.

Connor was pacing up and down. Crayson had never seen him with such hate and fury on his face.

'You can't dispose of him now,' said Crayson.

'Why not?'

'We'll never get started without him.'

'So what? I'll cut my losses.'

'Why don't we just keep him prisoner until the off?' Crayson said calmly. 'Once on board, he'll have to co-operate.'

'I've had enough,' said Connor. 'He always buckles under pressure. I've seen it before.' He was thinking of the state of panic he was in over the Lloyd's demand, the night before he was due to operate on his son James. Crayson wasn't going to give up his dream so easily. Connor was a billionaire, but he – Crayson – needed the money. He also needed the adrenaline kick of making the scheme work.

'Once he's in the operating theatre,' Crayson argued, not prepared to give up without a fight, 'and the organs start coming through the hatch, he'll have to use them.'

Connor sat there without saying anything.

'Why give up millions and millions of tax-free money?' said Crayson. 'All he has to do is one op and he's hooked.'

Connor still sat there in a foul temper, drinking whisky.

'I'll tell you what,' Crayson said. 'Let's move Muller in with him. There's no way he could escape then.'

Connor didn't say anything, he just nodded. Crayson left the flat with Fawcett and Muller. 'I've saved your bloody life,' he said. 'If you try to pull another trick like that, I'll shoot you myself.'

Muller moved into Fawcett's flat. He watched him like a hawk. Every night he locked Fawcett in his room and pulled his own bed into the hallway so that it blocked the front door of the flat. Crayson came in daily. He wanted to know whether the blood transfusion service had tried to contact David Blenkinsop.

'We're almost ready,' he said to Fawcett. 'Anything they've got in their database I can get on my screen. My contacts in France and the States are also into their computer networks.'

He looked at Fawcett. 'Jeremy, aren't you excited?' Fawcett was far from excited. He knew that any day now Crayson would start to take lists of patients' names from the blood transfusion services computer, complete with blood groups and matching details. And then Muller would pick them up and land them on the helicopter pad on the *Oleander,* all heavily drugged, ready to be murdered, and their organs passed through into the operating theatres. Once on board the *Oleander,* he would be lost.

Muller never relaxed; he watched him every moment of the day. The only time he was alone was in the loo. Muller answered all telephone calls. 'Just a moment,' he said one day, and passed the phone to Fawcett. 'It's for Blenkinsop.'

'Blenkinsop. How can I help?'

'Charles Reed – Chief Executive of the Regional Blood Service. I thought you'd like an update on that research project.' Fawcett wanted to shout: 'For Christ's sake, stop collecting the matching information. Your computer's been hacked into,' but Muller stood beside him threateningly. The voice on the phone asked: 'Are you there?'

'Yes, I am. What's the problem?'

'We've been carrying out matching tests as a routine on all patients for three months now. How long do you want us to continue?'

Fawcett told him to carry on for a further three-month period, and then the Department would review the programme. Muller told Crayson about the call next day.

'Well done, Jeremy, you handled that call well. It won't be long now. Connor is getting an amazing response from his discreet advertising.'

Fawcett just grunted.

'There's no shortage of rich patients wanting new organs,' said Crayson. 'You're going to be busy.'

When Crayson left, Fawcett sat at the kitchen table reading the newspaper. Muller was in another room. Quickly opening the door of the wall cupboard, Fawcett removed the copy of the letter to the Regional Blood Transfusion Service and slipped it, along with a sheet of the Department of Health's notepaper, inside his newspaper.

'I'm going to the loo,' he said.

'What do you want the newspaper for?' Muller guffawed. 'There's plenty of loo paper.'

'I'm doing the crossword.'

Muller wouldn't let him lock the door, but he closed it and rapidly got out the headed notepaper. Then he wrote to the Chief Executive of the Regional Blood Transfusion Service as follows:

Dear Mr Reed,
Research Project – Matching Information
There has been a change of plan. Please stop carrying out any more routine matching tests and remove all matching information from the blood donors' records in your database.

This is a matter of extreme urgency. Please act without delay.

  Yours sincerely

  David Blenkinsop

He addressed an envelope and sealed the letter inside. The problem was how to post it.

'I'm sick of being locked up in this flat,' he said to Muller, 'let's go for a stroll.

Muller looked uncertain, but Fawcett said: 'You can get some more of those nude magazines by the station.'

They left the flat, with Fawcett still carrying his folded newspaper, and strolled round to Victoria Station.

'I might as well get rid of this,' he said, and before Muller could stop him, he slipped the folded newspaper into a post box. He looked at Muller and laughed nervously, 'Perhaps the postman can finish the crossword.'

Fawcett prayed that his letter inside the folded newspaper would drop out into the box and be delivered without a stamp.

Four days later the Chief Executive of the Blood Transfusion Service called his Deputy into his office.

'Shirley, look at this.'

'God. What are they playing at?'

'They must be economising. Handwritten letter and no stamp.'

'That's three months' work down the drain,' the Deputy said.

'Ours is not to reason why,' sighed the Chief Executive, 'You'd better do it straight away,' and then he added, 'Perhaps they'll tell us one day what it was all about.'

'I thought Blenkinsop told us, only a few days ago, to carry on for another three months,' the Deputy said. The Chief Executive shrugged his shoulders. 'God save us from civil servants.'

Five days later Crayson met Fawcett at the flat. 'We're going aboard the *Oleander* tomorrow morning,' he said. 'Muller will fly in the first patients the next day.'

'I can't go through with this,' said Fawcett. 'I wish Muller had killed me.'

'You can't mean that,' Crayson said, shaking his head. 'You haven't seen Jake at work. Once you get started, you'll be okay.' He put a reassuring hand on Fawcett's shoulder. 'You're only treating sick patients, that's all.'

Fawcett felt sick and desperate. He didn't seem able to halt the disintegration of his life. It had all started with Connor. How he wished he'd never met him. He'd gone downhill ever since, and now if his letter didn't get to the Blood Transfusion Service, he was heading for mass murder. Crayson interrupted his brooding. 'I'm running names off the blood transfusion computer tonight for a final check,' he said, 'I'll pick you up in the morning.'

At nine o'clock in the morning Crayson arrived back at the flat. Fawcett thought that he was unusually subdued. Perhaps the enormity of the crimes he was about to commit had finally got through to him. Connor's car picked them up and they got out of the lift and into the penthouse. No sooner was Crayson inside, than he tossed a computer printout on the table. 'We've got a grass,' he shouted. 'Look at these.' Connor looked alarmed. 'What d'you mean?' he asked. Crayson explained that his long list of names from the Blood Transfusion Service computer contained only blood groups – no matching.

'When I set it up some weeks ago, all the information was there. Now it's not,' he screamed and looked at Fawcett. 'Someone's grassed.' They all looked towards Fawcett.

'It can't be me,' protested Fawcett, Muller's been practically sleeping with me.'

'We'll soon bloody well find out,' yelled Crayson as he picked up the telephone and dialled the Regional Transfusion Centre.

'Mr Reed, please.' He waited, and then, 'Mr Reed, this is Roland Mason,

Permanent Secretary at the Department. Can you tell me what the position is with respect to the research trial you were helping us with?'

'Yes, that's the one,' said Crayson, 'with the matching information.'

Fawcett watched as Crayson's face went black with anger. He heard him say, 'A handwritten letter. From Blenkinsop,' and then, 'Thank you very much,' as he slammed the phone down and turned on Fawcett.

'You bastard. You've spiked the whole bloody scheme at the last moment.'

'It was your bloody stupid idea to let him live,' shouted Connor. 'Why did I ever listen to a dwarf like you?'

Connor, Crayson and Muller all advanced on Fawcett. Muller pinned his arms behind his back as Connor and Crayson punched, kicked and kneed him. He prayed for unconsciousness. Connor looked at the battered, bleeding body lying immobile on the floor and said to Muller sarcastically: 'Throw "Sir Jeremy" into the small room. And finish him this time.'

Muller locked him in the scullery. Connor and Crayson sat cursing their bad luck, drinking neat whisky.

'He hadn't the guts to be a good criminal,' Connor said loudly, 'you should have known that. He was bound to cave in.'

'I was going to fit him into the system so tightly that he wouldn't be able to get out,' Crayson replied. 'But he got lucky. It was his last throw of the dice.'

'Perhaps it wasn't such good luck,' Connor said. 'If he hadn't been so lucky he'd be working on the *Oleander* instead of buried in concrete.' He took a huge gulp of his whisky. 'It's cost me a million,' he shouted. 'No one takes me for that amount and lives.'

In the small room Fawcett regained consciousness two hours later, feeling as if he'd been tied by a long rope to the back of a car and pulled through the streets of London. He felt his body for fractures. His arms and legs weren't broken. Some ribs might be cracked; they were excruciatingly painful. He felt his face. His nose was bent and he could feel a depression on the side of his face. He looked in the mirror. His head was covered with congealed blood. He moved around unsteadily on his feet and examined the room. It was a small kitchen, sparsely equipped with a table and two stools, a tiny sink, a small fridge and a full-size electric cooker. Fawcett knew that Muller would be back soon to collect him and that there was no way they would let him live. They were probably waiting for darkness. When he thought of Muller returning, he shuddered. It was unthinkable for him to take Muller on, even if he'd been fit. He searched for some kind of weapon. All he managed was to break a leg from a stool. That, he thought, will just bounce on his head, even if I manage to hit him with it. He went over to the cooker and switched it on. It was still connected. He pulled the plug out to find about four feet of electric cable going into the back of the cooker. He put his foot on the cable and tried to break it free. As he struggled to tear it away, the pain in his ribs became intense. There were no knives or forks in the room. He searched his pockets and all he could find was a bunch of keys. He rubbed frantically at the cable insulation with a key to try and weaken it, but it remained firmly attached to the cooker. In desperation he placed the end of the largest key at the join of a wall tile and hit it with the stool leg. The tile shattered, exposing the rough surface of the wall behind. He expected Muller to burst in at any moment to find out what the noise was. He sawed frantically at the cable with the sharp edge of a piece of broken tile until with a desperate pull it came away from the back of the cooker. With his key he was able to strip about six inches of insulation from the wires. Driven by his terror, he quickly tied the live wire to the metal door handle as tightly as possible so as to make a good contact. He prayed to God that there was a metal handle on the outside of the door. 'If it's plastic,' he thought, 'I'm as good as dead.' There were no cups or vessels in the room, so with cupped hands he threw water underneath the bottom of the door until the carpet was quite soggy. 'We might as well make the best possible electrical contact,' he thought. He had to wait for Muller to unlock the door before he tried to electrocute him, otherwise Fawcett would remain locked in the scullery with Muller on the other side of the door.

About an hour later he heard Muller coming along the corridor. As he fumbled with the key he could hear him squelching on the soggy carpet. 'Christ, he's pissed himself,' he guffawed. He called through the door: 'It won't be long now, Jeremy.' Fawcett waited, standing on the low stool, shaking so much that he was scared that he would be unable to flick the switch down at the right moment. Muller put the key in the lock. Fawcett waited for him to turn it fully, and the door to start opening, before he quickly pushed the switch down. Muller screamed and howled in pain as he tried to let go of the metal door handle, but the muscles in his right hand contracted so viciously as the electricity passed through his body that he couldn't. Fawcett remained perched on his stool, terrified that Muller would fall on him as he shook and cried out. Finally Muller collapsed on the floor.

Connor and Crayson were in noisy conversation when they heard the unrecognisable screams. 'Serves the bastard right,' said Connor.

'I'll drink to that,' replied Crayson, raising his glass.

Fawcett flicked the switch up, pulled Muller into the room and closed the door. He was amazed that the main fuse hadn't blown and put all the lights out. He quickly removed Muller's gun and knife, and also what Muller called his 'dream solution'. When Muller was living in Fawcett's flat, he had boasted about his equipment and his expertise, and had shown him the drugs and syringes he used when he wanted to keep someone quiet for twelve hours.

'Let's see how effective it is,' Fawcett said out loud.

He opened the thin metal case, removed a syringe and fitted a cartridge of 'dream solution' into it. Then he quickly injected the contents into Muller's unconscious body. Fawcett hadn't bothered to examine Muller, not even to check his pulse. The shock might have killed him, but he didn't care. As he injected the drug, he said 'Sweet dreams.' He put the knife in his pocket and held the gun.

Connor and Crayson were talking as he burst in.

'What the hell,' shouted Connor, 'Where's Muller?'

'Don't move an inch,' Fawcett shouted. 'Or I'll kill both of you. Muller's already finished.'

'Come on now, Jeremy,' Crayson pleaded, 'we can work something out.'

'Shut up,' yelled Fawcett removing the syringe from his pocket and pushing it towards Crayson. 'Inject that into Connor.'

'I can't do that.'

'Inject him or I'll shoot both of you,' he said, pointing the gun at Connor. 'The drug will only put him to sleep for twelve hours. If I shoot him, he'll be asleep forever.'

'Get on with it,' Fawcett said as Crayson hesitated.

Connor sat quietly as Crayson injected the drug into his arm. He slumped into unconsciousness before the cartridge was finished. 'Put it all in,' Fawcett said. He watched Crayson push the plunger down until the syringe was empty.

'Now. Inject yourself.'

'No. No, Jeremy. I can't,' he said. 'You'll have to do it.'

'Don't piss me about,' Fawcett shouted, waving the gun at him, 'put your right arm out. Clasp your right arm just above the elbow with your left hand.'

'Come on. Clench it,' Fawcett said, pointing the gun at his face.

'Now open and close your right hand. Keep clenching with the left.'

He watched the veins in Crayson's arm coming up, and was deciding whether to put the gun down or inject him with one hand when Crayson slowly lowered his left arm.

'Clench it,' he screamed, pushing the gun into the side of Crayson's head, but he ignored him and sat with both hands resting in his lap.

'You don't need to do this,' he said, quietly, 'just let me go. I'm not going to the police. How could I?'

He watched Fawcett's face closely and saw the almost imperceptible hesitation in his eyes and the slight lowering of the gun.

'You're not thinking straight,' Crayson continued, 'we're friends. We've been friends through all those years in prison. I kept you sane. You can't kill me.'

'Balls to all that,' Fawcett shouted, 'it's your choice.'

'But what are you doing it for?' Crayson asked, 'You're not a killer and you don't have to kill me. Be logical.'

All the time he was expecting Muller to come crashing through the door. He couldn't believe Fawcett had killed him. Muller was indestructible.

'You need me to help you,' he said. 'What are you going to do with Connor? Are you going to shoot him? Put the muzzle of that gun against his head and blast his brains out?'

Fawcett looked down at the tiny man standing in his way. With Crayson unconscious, he would have been away by now. The longer he delayed the more difficult it became. 'Don't move,' he shouted as Crayson slowly walked across the room.

'I was only getting my whisky,' he said, picking up his drink and emptying it. 'Even the condemned man gets a dying wish.' Crayson knew now that Fawcett wouldn't use the gun on him. He poured more whisky into Connor's glass. 'He won't need it,' he said, handing the glass to Fawcett. Fawcett slowly put the gun down.

'Let's talk it through,' suggested Crayson, pouring out more whisky. 'Let's use our intellects to sort this out.'

In a sense Fawcett was relieved. He could have injected Crayson with the 'Happy Dreams' solution even though he didn't know what it was, but he couldn't have pulled the trigger.

'Let's see what's happened to Muller,' Crayson said, standing up, 'we need to know before deciding on the best plan.' They walked along the corridor to the scullery.

'Jesus!' Crayson said. 'Some party! You've done it well. Electrocuted him and drugged him.'

Fawcett shuddered when he heard Muller groan.

'He's still alive though,' Crayson said, 'give me a hand. Pull him away from the door.' Fawcett went into the room and pulled Muller towards the back of the room.

'Hold this,' he said, passing the stool across to Fawcett, 'I'd better check the lock. He'll be like a raging bull when he comes round.' He tried the key in the lock from the inside. 'That seems okay,' he said, removing the key. And in a flash Crayson was out of the room and Fawcett heard the key click in the lock and Crayson laughing. 'I'll leave you there,' he shouted, 'until Muller comes round. He'll enjoy your company.'

Crayson went back to the drawing room and picking up the gun Fawcett had left alongside the whisky, aimed a playful shot at Connor, still unconscious on the floor. 'It might be ten hours or more before you wake up,' he said, thinking out loud, 'I might as well leave Fawcett with Muller for a few hours. That'll terrify him. It certainly would me. He'll do anything then.' And with that he put his head back and relaxed. While he waited, he nodded off every now and again into sleep. He knew that Fawcett wouldn't live long once Muller regained consciousness, so every few hours he went along and listened at the scullery door.

But it was Connor who stirred first. After ten hours his eyes opened and he blinked. He looked at Crayson, not understanding where he was. The dazed look in his eyes gradually went, and an hour later he was sitting up and talking. Crayson took the gun and unlocked the scullery door. He didn't expect any trouble from Fawcett. 'He'll be like jelly by now.' Muller's eyes were open and he was trying to lift his head.

'You'd better come out,' Crayson said, 'before he wakes up properly.' He took him into a bedroom. 'Get some sleep,' he said, pushing him on to the bed and locking the bedroom door.

Connor had managed to get himself into an armchair. As he gradually became fully conscious, he looked around. He saw the gun on the table alongside Crayson.

'Where is he?' he asked.

'I've got him locked in a bedroom,' Crayson answered, 'he needs sleep.'

'A long sleep,' Connor growled. 'Where's Muller?'

'He's coming round,' he said – 'I hope.'

It was another three hours before Muller surfaced. His first utterance was, 'I'll kill him.'

'You can do that later,' Crayson said sharply, 'Let's make use of him first.'

He was now in the driving seat. Even Connor listened to him.

'We've still got sufficient names,' he said, 'they've wiped all the matching info from the computer, but I've got the print-outs of patients from my trial runs.'

Within a week the *Oleander* was ready and Muller landed the helicopter on the bow pad with the first four patients; two kidneys, a heart and a liver. They were already undergoing all the routine blood tests for transplant patients, and as soon as he had the information, Crayson ran it against his computer lists for best match. He had got all the information he needed from Fawcett when they were in prison together. He knew that providing the blood groups were compatible – he needed no more than four, Human Leucocyte Antigen mismatches for kidneys, but this was not so critical for hearts and livers.

It never occurred to Crayson that he wouldn't get Fawcett aboard the *Oleander* and operating.

'You worry too much,' he said, 'it's only a job.'

'You're not killing them,' Fawcett said bitterly, 'You're just taking the money.' He found Crayson's excitement unbearable. 'You'll be in the dock with us,' he shouted, 'I'll make sure of that.'

Muller watched him continuously. 'I'm looking for an opportunity to kill you,' he said threateningly, 'so don't give me an excuse. I may not be able to control myself.'

Crayson soon found a match; and if he had continued he would have found many more. It was Tom Ballard's misfortune that his name came up first. It was also his misfortune that he was a male. His wife's name had come up in front of his, but Fawcett had said 'No women. Their organs seem to survive less well.' Muller picked him up as he left the underground station to walk the short distance to his home in the suburbs. He followed him discreetly until the street was empty.

'Keep quiet. Do what I tell you,' he said, ramming the revolver into his ribs, 'and you won't get hurt.' Ballard was shaking with fear. His mouth was so dry that he couldn't have screamed even if he had wanted to.

'Just keep walking,' Muller said gruffly, 'take the next turning on the left.' He prodded him on with his gun, 'Get in,' he said when they reached his van, which was parked alongside a tall dense evergreen hedge in a cul de sac, 'and don't make any noise.' He didn't have to say anything else. The malice in his eyes was sufficient. Ballard couldn't see where he was going and he remained quietly shaking in the dark. Muller drove to an isolated farm and parked the van in a large barn.

'Get out,' he said, indicating with his gun. As Tom Ballard clambered out of the van, Muller's gun crashed on the back of his head. He slumped unconscious at Muller's feet.

'Sweet dreams,' he muttered, as he emptied the syringe into a vein on the back of his hand.

Ballard was deeply unconscious and his breathing very shallow when Muller got him into the helicopter, and twenty minutes later he landed on the stern pad of the *Oleander*. Once on the pad, the helicopter was completely hidden from the rest of the ship. A door opened and Annette Marshall appeared in operating green. She helped Muller to bring Ballard into the small reception surgery, and even though he was still breathing spontaneously, she connected him to a ventilator.

'All the patients are terminally ill,' Fawcett had told her, 'but as far as the mortuary technician is concerned, they're all brain-dead.'

Fawcett made sure that she remained isolated from the rest of the ship. The computer locks from the theatres could only be operated by him. He didn't want the anaesthetist or the technician wandering about the ship. As soon as Annette Marshall had gone inside, Muller climbed on board and flew the helicopter back to the farm, picked up his van, and went to supper.

Inside the operating theatre complex the three surgeons were scrubbed up and the patients anaesthetized. 'Jeremy looks tense today,' remarked Al Ryan to Klaus Bauer, 'can't think why. This is bread and butter to him.'

'Women trouble,' Bauer laughed as they made light conversation whilst waiting to operate. Fawcett was to carry out a heart transplant, Ryan and Bauer kidneys. On the other side of the wall, the specially trained, highly paid, mortuary technician was systematically removing Tom Ballard's organs.

'It's routine to him,' Fawcett had said to Annette Marshall, 'he's used to removing organs for post mortem examinations.'

As the organs were removed, they were washed through with an isotonic solution, placed in large metal dishes, and passed through what were, in effect, serving hatches to the theatres.

Fawcett tried not to think what was happening just a few yards away, but it was impossible. Two or three times he almost found the courage to blurt out to Ryan and Bauer, 'Patients are being murdered on the other side of that wall,' but he didn't. His mind hovered between the fear of Connor, the monstrous crime he was involved in, and the large amount of money he expected to get. He was abruptly jolted out of his introspection when the hatch opened, 'Heart coming through,' the technician called out as if he was delivering a plate of fish and chips at a roadside café. The team moved into immediate action and Fawcett carried out the operation.

'It's the establishment's fault,' he said to himself when he was back in his cabin. 'The GMC shouldn't have struck me off. They could have just censured me.'

In the organ removal room the remains of Tom Ballard had gone through the incinerator.

'May you rest in peace,' Annette Marshall said as she stood watching the technician tip the ashes overboard. He then stood with her with his head bowed and self-consciously crossed himself. He had seen the damaged head from Muller's blow and the patient was already on a ventilator when he saw him. It never entered his head that Ballard was anything other than brain-dead on arrival. He had disappeared from the face of the earth. He had really ceased to exist when Muller had rendered him unconscious and removed all identification from him before taking him to the *Oleander*.

His wife reported him missing to the police, but since they had been having marital difficulties, she felt in her heart that he had gone off with another woman. She never thought he was dead – certainly not murdered. The police didn't search very hard. It wasn't all that uncommon for a husband to call it a day and move off to new pastures without telling his wife.

But when the number of missing young male adults started to build up, Scotland Yard became involved.

'Let's see what we've got,' Superintendent Jackman said to his team. 'Fifty-five young male adults,' he paused to let that sink in – 'at least we know of fifty-five. There may be more. All from the South of England. All disappeared without trace. Mostly married with children.' He looked at his audience for inspiration, but none was forthcoming. 'There's little evidence they decided to walk, just the odd marriage difficulty, but very little else.' He stopped to light another cigarette before continuing. 'What's it all about?' he asked. 'What's happened to them?'

'Couldn't they just have left? It's not unheard of these days,' a keen young sergeant suggested.

'Don't be so bloody silly,' the Superintendent retorted. 'The faces of the missing people have been plastered all over the media for weeks. If they'd walked, someone would have seen at least one of them by now.' This outburst of temper dissuaded any further questions.

'We've interviewed all the relatives, friends, work colleagues, and all the usual contacts,' he said. 'They've been meticulously questioned. We're trying to build up a picture of the life-style of the missing persons. But I have to say our analysis of the information doesn't amount to much.' He ended the meeting with the instruction: 'Go back and re-question all the contacts. Extend your inquiries. Keep knocking on doors until we find someone who has seen one of them. Let's find the common link. There must be one.'

'The Home Secretary's tearing me to bits over this,' the Chief Constable told him later in the day, 'he's on the phone at least once a day. Both Houses of Parliament have had heated debates.

'I suppose the Opposition's blaming the Government for not providing more policemen,' the Superintendent sighed, 'and the Government's accusing the Opposition of making political capital out of it.'

'That's about the strength of it,' the Chief Constable agreed.

'We've alerted all the ports and airports,' continued the Superintendent. 'The coast-guards have been asked to report any unusual movement of ships or helicopters.' He pulled at his cigarette. 'Interpol have been informed – absolutely nothing so far.'

'Superintendent, let's face it. A large number of normal people missing. Some for weeks. They must be dead, mustn't they? What else could have happened to them?'

'I hope you're wrong, sir.'

It was scarcely necessary for the Home Secretary to go on television to warn the public to keep off the streets. By the time there were a hundred young adults missing, there was alarm in the country, especially in London and the South. The public were advised to make sure they were accompanied by another adult. Wives peeped anxiously from behind curtains at the time they expected their husbands to come home and they couldn't relax until the front doors closed behind them. The cinemas and pubs were empty. There were scare stories of flying saucers landing; of religious sects carrying out large-scale kidnappings. At night the streets were as deserted as they were during the Second World War, but still Muller continued to find his victims.

On board the *Oleander* the operating tables were in constant use.

As the pressure mounted, the technician could see the increasing deterioration of Annette Marshall.

'Are you okay, Annette?' he asked her when she looked particularly shot up.

'Yes, I'm fine,' she said, 'I'll just go and take something.' She went off to take some cocaine and returned much calmer. The technician knew she took drugs. Sometimes when she went off to 'take something', she didn't come back for some time. He would find her unconscious in her cabin.

'Come on, wake up!' he would say, shaking her, 'we've got work to do.'

'You don't need me,' she would mumble almost incoherently, 'get on with it yourself.'

He didn't enjoy working with Annette Marshall. She was an ugly woman with a receding chin, who had had an unsuccessful love life and now in middle age only found solace in drugs. 'Thank the Lord,' he said to himself, 'I'm on leave tomorrow.'

The operating theatre worked continuously for a fortnight and then the surgeons flew off for a week. The tragic Annette Marshall remained on the ship. She had nowhere better to go, and she could be sure of her drug supply from Fawcett.

'What the hell's going on?' Superintendent Jackman asked himself. 'A missing person every day for a fortnight! And then no more for a week. Then they start again.' He lit yet another cigarette. 'Am I looking for some nutter who only works at a certain time of the month? When the moon's full or something?'

He was desperate for a break. Almost the entire police force from London and the South were involved, but they had no idea what they were looking for.

'Not a single body, no sign of a fight or break in,' he muttered, 'I don't even know whether they're alive or dead.'

Crayson used to fly to the *Oleander* quite frequently and spend a few days there. He dined with the surgeons at the Captain's table. He had made sure that they had a top-flight chef aboard and a good wine cellar. After dinner they drank brandy in Fawcett's luxurious cabin.

'It's getting more and more difficult for Muller,' said Crayson, 'the whole of the South of England is alive with police. Bogies everywhere.'

'We're already millionaires,' Fawcett pointed out. 'Let's call it a day. We've treated three or four hundred patients with the donors Muller's brought in.'

He held the brandy balloon in the palm of his hand, gently swirling the golden brown liquid before putting it to his nose. 'I want out,' he said, looking at the diminutive Crayson, 'let's pack up. Disappear for good.'

'Jeremy, we are rich,' he said, pushing the buttons on his pocket calculator, 'but after all the expenses and Connor's fifty percent it won't be that much.' He looked at the calculator screen thoughtfully. 'We don't want to have to worry about money ever again. I think we must go on for a few months yet.'

'You greedy bastard,' Fawcett exclaimed, finishing his Remy Martin, 'you won't be satisfied until you're the richest man in the world.' He refilled his glass. 'I really think you want to be caught so that everyone will know how bloody clever you are. You'd enjoy the notoriety,' he said, noticing the gleam in Crayson's eyes. 'Wouldn't you? The cleverest murderer of them all.' Crayson remained strangely silent. 'They'll probably have you in Madame Tussaud's, write books about you, make films.' He saw the glazed look on Crayson's face. 'My God,' he said, 'that's about the truth of it, isn't it?'

'Are the surgeons complaining?' Crayson asked, snapping out of his daydream. 'They get one week off in three.'

'Not yet,' Fawcett said.

'Why should they?' Crayson said. 'They're "struck off" and can't practise in their own countries. We've given them the opportunity to carry out major surgery – and for high fees.' Then he added wryly, 'On a luxury liner as well. They live the life of Reilly.'

'We're tempting fate by continuing,' Fawcett insisted.

'We're mobile. We'll cross the Channel said Crayson. 'Operate in France for a while. That's the answer.' He raced on, not giving Fawcett the opportunity to interrupt. 'It's all set up. By the time the French police begin to make progress, we'll move on.'

Crayson returned to the mainland to disconnect his computer linkage with the Transfusion Service. He looked around the office. 'They'll never know I've been using their data base for the past months.'

Inside the centre one of the staff responsible for recalling patients when more blood was needed commented to her colleague: 'That's the second wife who's written in to say that her husband has disappeared and won't be able to give blood. Quite a coincidence.' But she never connected it with the hundred missing people in Southern England. If only she had told Superintendent Jackman! It might have been the piece of luck he was looking for and saved many lives.

Simon Connor never went to the stern of the ship where the organs were 'harvested', a dreadful word Fawcett used. He remained firmly on the other side of the steel partition. 'I'm a businessman. What goes on with you surgeons at the back end doesn't concern me,' he said to Fawcett. 'I find the patients, collect the fees, and make sure it's tucked away safely in unnamed accounts abroad.'

He was getting a massive return from his investment, so he was content. When he saw the rich patients on the sun deck of the *Oleander* recovering from their surgery, he thought 'Most of them would be dead but for me.' All of the patients were grateful to the brilliant surgeons who had treated them; even though it had cost them a fortune.

'Everything has its price,' said one rich patient to another, 'it's supply and demand. The greater the shortage, the higher the price. It's no different from any other business.'

'You're right there. But God knows where the spare parts come from.'

'Who cares? Pigs perhaps.' They both laughed.

The *Oleander* sailed across a tranquil English Channel and the spate of missing persons stopped in England as rapidly as it had started. The Prime Minister was relieved. The Home Secretary was relieved. Superintendent Jackman had some respite but he still had to solve the mystery; and that seemed a long way off.

'I've sent Muller ahead,' said Crayson, 'the computer links are in place with the French Blood Transfusion Service.' He passed some sheets of paper to Fawcett. 'Here we are, the first computer printouts.' Within days the *Oleander* was receiving the first French adults.

'Jesus – the garlic!' exclaimed Annette Marshall as she sat watching the technician remove the organs from the first patient. But she didn't care. All she wanted was the periodic oblivion provided by her cocaine or the halothane and nitrous oxide from the anaesthetic machine.

It took some weeks before the French police realised they had a missing person problem. 'UK first. France second. Where next?' Superintendent Jackman read on the front page of his morning newspaper. 'Christ!' he said as he read the story. 'It's starting all over again. All young men, vanishing into thin air. Identical pattern. One a day for a fortnight and then nothing for a week.'

President Mitterand spoke to Prime Minister Margaret Thatcher on the telephone and they agreed to step up co-operation. The vicious cycle went on. Muller picked up adults from the French mainland and landed them on the stern of the *Oleander* to provide organs for three or four, or more, patients.

'It's like getting spare parts from a service department in a garage,' thought Fawcett as the organs came through the hatches. But he shrugged his shoulders and used them. He had become hardened to the whole business. He had distanced himself from the harvesting of organs. He made sure he never saw the patients brought in by Muller or the technician removing the organs. The organs just turned up in the theatre and he used them. When he had become President of the Royal College of Surgeons, Melanie had said to him, 'Your name will go down in the annals of the College.'

'Now, if I'm caught,' he muttered to himself, 'my place in surgical and criminal history will be assured.' He no longer felt guilt or remorse. 'Society and medicine have turned their backs on me,' he thought bitterly. 'They didn't waste much time ripping the fame and glory from me.'

His appearance before the GMC and his years in prison were etched permanently in his mind. As time went on, he tried to rationalise and excuse his behaviour. 'I did little wrong,' he thought, 'they've driven me to this.' All he wanted now was to be fabulously rich. It had replaced his desire for fame and professional recognition.

'To hell with fame,' he thought, 'I'll stick to fortune.' But he didn't want to be caught and he was alarmed when Crayson told him about an incident in the suburbs of Paris. Muller had followed his victim carefully. 'Keep quiet and I won't hurt you,' he had said in his best French, sticking his gun in his ribs. At that moment a French police car screeched to a halt.

'What happened to Muller?' he asked.

'He got lost pretty rapidly, and within minutes he was miles away.'

'What do we do now?' asked Fawcett.

'They'll already have a photofit,' Crayson replied, 'it'll be all over the media tomorrow.'

'Let's fold,' said Fawcett, 'before someone recognises Muller.'

'You're right,' Crayson agreed, to Fawcett's relief, 'if they recognise Jake it won't take them long to find out that he was banged up with us in prison. And then even a dumb copper could start putting the pieces together.'

The young happily married French businessman who so nearly became spare parts on the *Oleander* was questioned by the police, who reported it to the senior policeman handling the missing persons enquiry, but he didn't draw the connection.

'Just another mugging,' he concluded, 'to add to the dozens we get every night on the streets of Paris.'

He read out the description. 'Tall, powerful, foreign accent, possibly German or English. No one saw his face.'

'File it,' he said, pushing it away and going back to study the reams of paper London had sent him.

'We'll go to the States,' said Crayson, bouncing up and down on his heels, 'they have so many murders over there. We'll be in and out before they realise anything unusual's happening.'

'You're too bloody greedy,' replied Fawcett. 'You've already got more money than you can ever spend; let's call it a day.'

'You can never have too much money,' Crayson laughed. He had no intention of giving up. He also knew that Fawcett would have little use for money. Connor and Muller wouldn't let him live long once the operation had finished.

The *Oleander* had a leisurely passage across the Atlantic. It was late September and the weather was good. Fawcett almost forgot the terrible business he was in as he reclined by the swimming pool and joined in the interminable parties as the medics let their hair down.

In France the police were anxiously waiting for the next missing person, but days passed without incident. At first they thought it was the usual seven days respite, but it continued and when there were no strange disappearances for two whole weeks, they breathed a sigh of relief. It was the end of the French episode. Almost a hundred young French adults had disappeared without trace.

The American public had already had intense media coverage from England and France and now it was happening in their country. There was panic bordering on hysteria. Two hundred young adults had been spirited away, and now it was their turn. They would have been less frightened if just one body had been found; it was the fear of the unknown that terrified them.

How could two hundred normal people just disappear?

'We're not going to stand by and let this happen in this country,' the President said to his Secretary of State. 'Pull all the stops out. Use the army, the FBI, the CIA. Use whatever it takes. Get it sorted!'

Police and soldiers patrolled the near-deserted streets in major cities. The public stayed in their homes behind locked doors, refusing to open them until they were sure that it was a friend or neighbour.

'What are we going to do about this?' the American President asked Margaret Thatcher and Francois Mitterand on a telephone link-up. 'Can it be some Middle East Terrorist group?' They set up a tripartite committee under the chairmanship of Commander Blake from Scotland Yard.

At the end of its first meeting in London, Blake summarised their conclusions.

'Sorry,' he said, apologetically as he went across to the overhead projector, 'if this sounds a bit like a lecture.' He slid the sheet of masking paper down on the acetate to expose the first line.

'BRAINS,' he read out, 'I've put all these in capitals to emphasise them. The brains behind this is likely to be in the UK, because that's where it all started.'

'SELECTION. There must be some kind of selection process. These young men aren't chosen by chance.' He slid the masking sheet down.

'COMPUTER. If we accept that,' he placed his pencil alongside the third line, 'if we accept that,' he repeated, 'the information almost certainly comes from some data base, most probably a computer. They aren't picked from a telephone directory.'

'LINK,' he read out, 'there must be a link between all these people. Some common factor, which we haven't hit on yet.'

He paused to move the masking sheet down to show the next line.

'So why haven't we found this common factor?' he asked, and then he read out, 'BECAUSE WE HAVEN'T ASKED THE RIGHT QUESTIONS.' He read it out again. 'Are you still with me?' he asked. There was a grunt of approval from the Committee.

'REASONS. What are possible reasons for two hundred citizens to disappear? Leaving aside personal reasons, marital problems, avoiding the police for some reason, joining a religious sect, and,' he said with a laugh, 'let's forget about flying saucers for the moment.' He placed a fresh transparency on the overhead projector. 'Assuming they were abducted forcibly,' he said, 'there are only three possibly reasons.' He placed his pencil opposite the first word.

'TERRORISM. There doesn't seem much point,' he said, 'if the group doesn't identify itself.

'MONEY. We've had no ransom notes.

'MEDICAL REASONS,' he read out. 'This is rather fanciful, I admit. It is difficult to imagine that two hundred people have been spirited away for medical reasons, but I suppose it's just possible.'

Finally, he put a third acetate on the projector screen. 'So, why are we still floundering in the dark?' he asked, and then he read out the information on the acetate.

'BECAUSE WE HAVEN'T ASKED THE RIGHT QUESTIONS.' Finally, before he sat down, he said: 'The motive must be in the common link between all these people.'

'Christ!' said Bernie Goldfine, the senior FBI agent on the Committee, 'we've asked the contacts hundreds of questions; I expect you have too. We still haven't made a connection.'

'We need more expertise,' Blake said. 'These people have been selected for some reason, from some list. There must be something they are doing or taking part in which puts them on that list.' He continued: 'Some of the contacts must know what that activity is. We just haven't asked them. It's probably something that seems so routine and unimportant that no one has bothered to mention it.'

'Well, how do we move forward?' asked Goldfine.

'An epidemiologist.'

'A what?' Goldfine exclaimed loudly, 'you'll have to spell that!'

'A questions expert,' Blake said, 'someone who questions large numbers of the public, then analyses the answers.'

'Oh, you mean a statistician,' replied Goldfine, 'why didn't you say so?'

'Kind of,' said Blake, 'but with expertise in handling health questions. The link between smoking and lung cancer was established by epidemiologists.'

'Where do we get one of these rare birds?'

'Our Civil Service will find one,' Blake assured him, 'from the universities or the Royal Colleges.'

'Sooner the better then,' growled Goldfine, 'let's hope he gives us a lead, or we'll all get our arses kicked even harder.'

'Sir John Wright's your man,' said the Permanent Secretary from the Home Office. 'He's an expert on medical questionnaires. He loves surveys and analysing the results.'

'If that's what turns him on,' answered Blake, 'let's get him.'

Wright spent some hours with senior policemen, familiarising himself with police methods. It was clear that the questions which were being asked by the police were not detailed enough; within a day his own questionnaire was ready.

'Hell, Sir John,' exclaimed Blake as he looked at the four pages of detailed questions, 'it's going to take ages getting all the contacts to complete these.'

'It's the only way, Tim,' Wright assured him, 'we can't analyse information with half of it missing.'

'Okay,' he agreed, shrugging his shoulders, 'you're the expert.'

'I'll need to spend a day with one of your men,' said Wright, 'to check the questions. We might need even more details.'

Blake thought that half the questions were irrelevant, but he called a young police inspector into his office.

'Johnson, take Sir John and revisit all the contacts associated with the last six missing persons. He'll tell you what questions he wants asked.'

'And,' he said, 'get your skates on. People are still dying in the States.'

Wright and Johnson worked their way through the hundreds of contacts. By the end of the first day, Johnson almost knew the questions by heart. Wright wanted to know everything: family history, medical history, sexuality – heterosexual, homosexual, bisexual, celibate. There were questions on finance, drugs, politics, names of clubs and associations, visits to hospitals, special treatment centres. The questions seemed endless and many of the contacts couldn't answer them all. At the end of the first day Wright went to Scotland Yard.

'Progress?' asked Blake, 'how many have you interviewed?'

'About sixteen. And that was hard going.'

'Christ!' said Blake, 'it's going to take weeks. And this is only the pilot.'

'It's a slow business,' replied Wright.

'I can't wait,' Blake decided brusquely, 'I want these pilot questionnaires completed by tomorrow. I'll give you fifty men; just get the answers.'

To Wright's surprise, Johnson turned up at St Luke's at six o'clock the next evening with two hundred completed questionnaires.

'That's tremendous,' he said.

'When Sexy's on the warpath, we move,' said Johnson.

'So that's what you call him,' grinned Wright.

'Sexy or Sexton,' Johnson replied, 'when he's not around.'

Wright fed the information into his computer.

'What've you got?' asked Blake expectantly when Wright brought the analysis into his room.

'Not much so far. All male; all fit; no health problems; no known major financial difficulties; mainly heterosexual; some thought to be homosexual; none known to be involved in major drugs; fair mix of sports, business, and social clubs; varied jobs; even spread politically; and two of them were thought to have given blood in the past six months. That's about the strength of it.'

'Bloody disappointing,' concluded Blake. 'Is it worth carrying on? It's going to take all my manpower.'

'We must go on,' insisted Wright, 'the missing link is there somewhere.'

He went back to St Luke's. All his medical duties had been cancelled so that he could concentrate on the questionnaire. 'Either I'm not getting the information to establish the link,' he said to himself, 'or, if I am, I don't understand the significance of it.'

He considered every item of information and asked additional questions. As he worked through the list of questions methodically, he came to the two contacts who thought that the missing person had given blood in the past six months.

'So what?' he said to his research assistant, 'millions do, on a regular basis.' His scientific training wouldn't let him move on to the next questions. He added a specific question: 'Do you know whether the missing person gave blood to the National Blood Transfusion Service during the past year?'

His taxi deposited him at Scotland Yard. He rushed to Blake's office. 'Is Sexton in?' he asked with a grin. The duty sergeant nodded. 'We're ready to go now,' he said, putting the six-page questionnaire on Blake's desk.

'Christ!' he said, 'it's like Topsy; it's grown!'

'But it's user-friendly. Just a tick in a box.'

'All right,' said Blake, doing some mental arithmetic to estimate how long it would take to complete, 'I'll put a hundred officers at your disposal.'

He didn't expect much from it, but since it was his idea to get an expert, he had to go along with it. Three days later he was driven to St Luke's with a pile of 5,000 completed questionnaires. 'My men have sweated blood getting these,' he said, 'they got contacts out of factories and offices during the day – no question of waiting until the end of the day. They searched everywhere; they even got one out of a public swimming pool!'

'Thank God we've got an optical character reader,' remarked Wright, looking at the huge quantity of paper in large boxes strewn over his office floor.

'Put those through the computer and see what we get. The optical reader should pick up the ticks without difficulty.' The research assistant started to move the boxes of questionnaires to the computer room.

'Dry sherry?' he said, looking at Blake.

'I'd rather have a whisky,' said Blake, 'a large one. Four fingers.'

'You'd better say your prayers,' said Wright standing up, 'I'll ring as soon as we've got something.'

'Take this,' said Blake, handing him a card, 'you can get me any hour of the day or night.'

When he got back to Scotland Yard, he took calls from Bernie Goldfine and the French police asking about the epidemiologist. They both had trouble pronouncing the word. 'How's your stats man doing?' Goldfine asked.

'The info's going through the computer at the moment,' replied Blake.

Wright's research assistant worked all night. Wright knew there was nothing more he could do except get in the way, so he went off to dine with Melanie at the Royal Society of Medicine.

'I've not seen you so enthusiastic since you first got the surgery bug as a student,' she said.

'It's fascinating being involved with Scotland Yard. This man Blake's got a super brain.'

'It's not only doctors,' Melanie laughed, 'who've got brains.'

Wright was in his office at St Luke's by seven o'clock the following morning.

'You've cracked it?' he said to his tired but excited assistant, 'I can see it on your face.'

'There's only one significant factor,' he said, turning over the pages of his analysis as Wright waited impatiently. 'There it is,' he said, jabbing his finger at a table, 'eighty of the hundred missing persons were said to have given blood during the previous twelve months.'

'Jesus!' Wright whistled, 'that can't be coincidence.'

'I'm sure it's significant, even though only one contact knew about it in some cases, in most cases it was four or five.'

'Tremendous,' he shouted, shaking the research assistant's hand warmly. 'Take the rest of the week off.'

As soon as he rushed into Tim Blake's office, Blake could see he had good news.

'We've got it,' he said excitedly, 'the missing link!'

'It's like a bank statement,' he explained, when he saw the dismay on Blake's face at the sight of the computer printout, 'just look at the bottom line!'

Blake pushed the intercom button on his desk and an inspector rushed in.

'Get this off to the FBI and the French police,' he said, handing the last page of the computer printout to the Inspector. 'Tell them to check all missing persons for a recent visit to a blood transfusion centre.'

'Why should all these people have given blood?' he said, turning to Wright, 'and then gone missing,' he added. He didn't wait for a reply. 'What would anybody need blood donors for?'

'It's a source of blood tested for blood groups,' replied Wright, 'and for the absence of serious . . .' Tim Blake didn't wait for the end of Wright's answer before pushing the buzzer again. 'Find out whether the eighty who gave blood did so at one centre.' The Inspector almost ran out of the office. 'Sexton's on high octane,' he said to his sergeant as he hastened past.

'Is there a central organisation which deals with blood?' he asked Wright.

Within seconds he was speaking to the Director of the National Blood Transfusion Centre. 'Don't waste time,' he said, when the Director started on about the confidentiality of the information on his database. 'I want the information now. I'll send my sergeant down with a list of names. I want to know whether the persons on the list gave blood at the same centre. It's a matter of life and death.' He thought he had probably said enough but he added, 'The Prime Minister is personally concerned with this. So don't hang about or she'll be on the blower.' With that he slapped the phone down. The sergeant switched his blue light on and with his siren wailing drove to the headquarters of the Transfusion Service.

'How can I help you?' asked the Chief Executive. He thought he'd better deal with the matter himself after Blake's sharp words. The Police Sergeant gave him the list of names. 'Most of them seem to live in the South London area,' he said, scanning the list. He picked up the telephone and pushed a pre-select button. 'Trevor I've got the police here, it's an emergency. I'm going to fax a list of names down to you. Can you let me know whether they've given blood in the past year?' He called his secretary. 'Get that down to Trevor at South London Region. Label it extremely urgent.'

Within an hour the fax machine clattered and issued a long sheet of computer paper. The sergeant looked at the simple cryptic message at the end: 'ALL HUNDRED PATIENTS GAVE BLOOD IN THIS AREA DURING THE YEAR.' He grabbed the paper and within twenty minutes was in Blake's room. 'So what've we got on our hands?' Blake asked, tossing the paper across to Wright, 'some maniac picking up people who've given blood?' He looked at Wright fiercely. 'Why blood donors, John?' They must be put to some use, however macabre. What could it be?'

Wright had been in Blake's office all day and for most of the time he had been listening to Blake. 'The only information that's unique to these people is that the blood groups are known.'

Blake interrupted him by shouting through the open door: 'Get the info about them all giving blood in the previous year off to Paris and Washington.' He turned back to Wright. 'Sorry John, I'm listening.'

'Blood is mainly used by doctors. So we must assume that doctors are involved,' he went on, thinking out loud, 'wait a minute,' he said incredulously as he contemplated it, 'not just blood – the organs could be used.'

'Are you saying that people have been picked up,' said Blake, staring wide-eyed at Wright, 'because they have the right blood group? Then they are being butchered for their organs?' Wright looked at Blake and saw the tough policeman go pale at the thought of it. 'My God!' Blake exclaimed, 'who could do this? Wouldn't they have to be highly skilled surgeons?'

'And a hospital with a medical support team,' answered Wright, 'with the number we're talking about – a large organisation.'

'If it's that large, where could it be? In this country? In France? The States? How do we find it?'

'It might be easier to find the surgeons,' suggested Wright thoughtfully. 'There aren't that many transplant surgeons in the world.' And then he dried up, not prepared to believe that any surgeon could be involved in what could only be mass murder.

'Wait a minute,' he said, with a flash of inspiration, 'they could be disgraced surgeons – unable to practice in their own countries.'

'You mean?' said Blake, 'struck off surgeons?'

'That's right, there can't be many of those.'

'How do I find them?'

'In the UK, go to the GMC.'

'GMC?'

'The General Medical Council. All doctors have to be registered. They would know the names of all "struck off" surgeons.'

Blake was beginning to see some framework to his long investigation. At last he could see a chink of light at the end of the tunnel. 'Thank God,' he thought, 'we've got an epidemiologist on board. Now that he had mastered the pronunciation, he enjoyed rolling it off his tongue – 'epi-demi-ologist'.

'Are we looking for a British or foreign surgeon?'

'There aren't that many UK surgeons struck off,' Wright said, 'they're more likely to be foreign.'

'Right,' said Blake, 'let's get on to your GMC first, and eliminate any possible UK surgeon.'

They sat in the Registrar's office at the GMC in Hallam Street just behind the BBC Centre in London.

'What we want to know, Registrar,' explained Blake, 'is the names of transplant surgeons struck off in the last ten years.'

'I don't need to check that,' answered the Registrar, 'there's only been one: Sir Jeremy Fawcett. At least he was Sir Jeremy at the time. Sir John will remember the sad case.'

'Fawcett!' exclaimed Wright, 'No! It couldn't be! I refuse to believe it.'

'As far as I'm concerned, he's in until he's excluded,' said Blake.

As they drove back to Scotland Yard, Blake said: 'Let's see where we are. The missing persons have been picked up off the streets to provide organs for transplant patients. That's what we believe isn't it?' Wright nodded. 'They've all given blood, mainly in the South London area. Right?'

'Yep.'

'How were they selected?'

'Either someone at the centre provided the information,' replied Wright, 'or they hacked into the computer database.'

'You're thinking like a policeman now,' said Blake. He called out to his driver: 'Instead of the Yard, take us to the South London Regional Blood Transfusion Centre. And don't piss about.'

'Information from this centre has been used to identify organ donor patients for transplants,' said Blake without any preamble.

'None of my staff would have done that,' replied the Chief Executive.

'Someone has,' retorted Blake, 'how secure is your system?' Before he had time to reply, Wright asked: 'What information are you storing? Just blood groups?'

'Routinely yes,' he said, 'apart from the research we were carrying out for the Department of Health.'

'Research?' asked Wright.

'It's confidential,' replied the Chief Executive.

'Come on, get on with it,' said Blake. 'We haven't got time to get special clearance. People are dying.'

The whole story of the routine collection of matching information set up via correspondence with Blenkinsop of the Department of Health came out. Wright looked at Blake and raised his eyebrows in astonishment. 'We'll walk back,' said Blake when his driver had dropped them off at Richmond House, the Department of Health building in Whitehall.

'Mr Blenkinsop. At once,' said Blake at Reception. He drummed his fingers impatiently on the desk as he waited for the receptionist to run his finger laboriously down the list of civil servants working there.

'No,' the receptionist said, almost triumphantly. 'We don't have a Blenkinsop.'

'Take us to the Permanent Secretary,' said Blake impatiently, 'tell him that Sir John Wright and Commander Blake of Scotland Yard want to see him urgently.'

They were escorted up to the top civil servant's well appointed office. 'What's this all about, gentlemen?' he asked, annoyed by the intrusion into

221

his ordered life. Blake asked him about the research programme. 'We don't have a Blenkinsop. We don't have a research programme. Whatever the Blood Transfusion Service have been doing is nothing to do with this Department. That's all I can say,' he said, 'except that I'm surprised they went ahead without contacting us. If we ask anyone to do anything these days, the kneejerk response is – more money or we can't.'

They walked back up Whitehall to Scotland Yard. Blake had his finger on his intercom. buzzer even before he sat down. 'Find Fawcett,' he said to the Inspector, who had rushed in, 'Start at the prison he was in.' He scribbled some details of Fawcett's background on a sheet of paper; 'Jeremy Fawcett. Struck-off surgeon. In prison for raping Carla Narcissi under hypnosis.' He gave it to the Inspector. 'You'd better get me a list of the prisoners inside with Fawcett as well.' He looked at Wright. 'Whisky?' He pushed a tumblerfull across to Wright. 'Fawcett is unlikely to have come across serious criminals before he went to prison. If he is involved, he must have had professional help.'

'You're barking up the wrong tree,' said Wright. 'It can't be Fawcett.'

'I still have to find him and eliminate him.'

An attractive female sergeant came in. 'The list of prisoners you wanted, sir,' she said, 'and a fax from Bernie Goldfine in Washington.'

'Did you get that John?' grinned Blake, sniffing the air as she left, 'Givenchy, I'm sure.'

'She's got good taste,' laughed Wright.

'Crayson, the bloody dwarf!' shouted his companion as he went down the list, 'He was there at the same time as Fawcett.' He gulped his whisky. 'The best computer crook in the business. It'd be like falling off a log for him to get into that Blood Transfusion computer.' He rammed his thumb on the intercom. button and kept it there. His staff were so programmed that they could tell the urgency by the length of the sound. To anything more than a short buzz they reacted instantly.

'Find out where Crayson is,' he said, 'he was in prison with Fawcett.'

He picked up the fax from Goldfine and read it out loud: 'We are tailing one transplant surgeon – Al Ryan. He may fit the bill. He is not allowed to practise, yet he goes away for weeks at a time. He has a very rich life-style, large house, four motorcars including a Ferrari, a thirty-foot ocean racer and an expensive mistress. As yet we have not been able to follow him to a hospital.'

'Sounds about right,' said Blake, 'd'you know him?'

'He's quite famous in the States,' answered Wright, 'I didn't know he'd lost his licence.'

Blake tried to find Crayson and Fawcett. 'Not a smell,' he said, 'let's hope Bernie's luckier with Ryan.' Bernie Goldfine's agents were following all the surgeons who had been stopped from practising in the States for one reason or another, but he felt that Ryan must be the prime suspect. According to the neighbours, Ryan seemed to be around for about a week at a time. He only spent two days of this with his wife, the remainder with his mistress.

Blake had got the telephone number of Fawcett's flat in Victoria from the Blood Transfusion Service, and this led to the flat. 'Take it to pieces,' said Blake to his men, 'don't come back until you've found something.'

The flat was so empty that it felt as if no one had ever lived there. All the bins and paper baskets were empty. There were no letters, newspapers, journals, telephone numbers – nothing. They collected samples of hair from the bedroom carpet and to their surprise, from the carpet just inside the front door.

'There's been a bed by the front door,' the Inspector said, 'why d'you think that was?'

'All the other rooms occupied?' suggested the Sergeant.

'No, it couldn't have been that. We know from the woman downstairs there were only two of them. Let's talk to her again.'

The Inspector asked all the questions.

'One was tall and quite good looking,' she said, 'I quite fancied him. At least I would have done if he'd had a decent haircut. Well spoken too. He had a scar on his forehead.'

'What didn't you like about his hair?'

'I suppose some women like it; they must do. It's fashionable. But I don't like short cropped hair.'

'What about the other man?'

'He terrified me. He was big and strong like a heavyweight boxer,' she said. 'He didn't say much – usually grunted. Wouldn't want to meet him on a dark night.' She giggled.

'Did they have any visitors?'

'I only saw one, a tiny man,' she replied. 'He was always bouncing up and down on his heels, trying to make himself taller.' She was enjoying her moment of importance. 'He talked quite posh.'

'Crayson, the bouncing dwarf!' said the Inspector. 'The old Etonian, couldn't lose his accent after all those years with criminals.'

At the Yard Blake was closeted with Wright when the Inspector returned.

'Crayson and Fawcett were definitely at the flat,' he said. 'We got good descriptions of both of them from the woman downstairs, even to the scar on Fawcett's forehead.'

223

'That's him all right,' said Wright, 'I remember that scar very well.'

Blake looked at him, sensing innuendo, but didn't comment. 'Who else was there?' he asked.

'A tall powerful man,' he laughed, 'who frightened the woman downstairs.' And then he added thoughtfully: 'Someone slept behind the front door.'

'So what?'

'There were only two men living in the flat,' said the Sergeant, 'Fawcett and the big man, and there were two bedrooms.'

'So, was he stopping someone getting out?' asked Blake, 'or someone getting in?'

'I don't know, sir. But he was definitely there, because we found samples of hair on the carpet which were different from those in the bedroom.'

'Who's the heavy, then?' Blake inquired, pushing the intercom. button. 'Get me that list of prisoners again,' he said. He grinned at Wright and touched his nose when the Sergeant with the 'Givenchy' brought it in.

'Muller! Jake Muller,' he exclaimed as he ran his finger down the list. 'Why didn't I think of it before? That's who it was. He even frightens me.'

He looked across at Wright, 'You were wrong about Fawcett. He's the one we're after.' He tapped his pen on the table. 'What a trio! A busted surgeon, a computer genius and the best heavy in the business.' He didn't dwell on it for long.

'Wire their pictures across to Washington and Paris,' he shouted to the Sergeant through the open door.

'All we need now,' said Blake, 'is the hospital. Where can it be? It can't be in space. It must be on land, sea, or in the air.'

'It can only be a ship,' they both shouted simultaneously.

'How would it be equipped?' asked Blake.

'By specialist companies,' answered Wright, 'they can't have put many operating theatres on ships.' Blake's finger was already moving towards the buzzer. 'Inspector,' he said, 'Sir John will give you a list of surgical equipment companies. Find out whether any of them have put an operating theatre on a ship within the last year.'

Whilst Wright compiled a list, Blake picked up the telephone and spoke to Goldfine. 'Bernie, we think three men are involved,' he said, 'and we're pretty sure the operating theatres must be on a ship. We should have the name of the ship soon.'

'Tim, I think you'd better get over here. And bring that "stats" man with you. Can you do that?'

'We'll come across on the next flight.'

On the *Oleander* Fawcett was pressing Crayson to end the operation. He was very rich and very tired, and increasingly worried as he watched the television pictures of the police and troops on the streets. 'I'm surprised,' he said to Crayson, 'that no one aboard has connected the missing people with the activities on this ship.'

'Why should they?' retorted Crayson. 'They're all brainwashed into believing doctors always act in the patient's interest; it's their professional training.'

They had all been sworn to secrecy to avoid publicity and unwanted attention from the media. 'We all want to be allowed to get on quietly treating our patients,' the matron had said to them.

'A few more months,' said Crayson, but Connor wanted to end it. He didn't communicate with anyone except Crayson.

'Wind it up,' he said, 'and don't leave any evidence behind.'

'You mean the *Oleander* will have to go?' Crayson asked.

'Yes. Make a good job of it.' He laughed, 'I might even claim the insurance from Lloyds.'

'Personnel as well?' asked Crayson.

'No evidence,' Connor replied. 'Leave Muller and Fawcett on board. I haven't paid their share into the Swiss bank yet.'

After dinner that night Crayson sat drinking Remy Martin with Fawcett. 'Just two more days, and it'll be all over.'

'I never want to pick up a scalpel again,' said Fawcett, swallowing his brandy.

'You won't have to,' Crayson answered, re-filling the glasses. 'I've made you a rich man. He laughed. 'Aren't you glad you met me in prison?'

'No, I'm not,' said Fawcett bitterly. 'All I ever wanted was to be a surgeon and be able to carry on my research.'

'Drink up,' said Crayson, 'you'll get over it when you start spending the money.'

'I've been too weak. You bastards have corrupted me.' He put the brandy to his nose and inhaled deeply. 'It all happened so gradually. First of all shady commercial dealings in organs; now mass murder!'

'Don't get emotional,' replied Crayson, pouring more brandy into his glass. 'I've warned you about that.'

Blake and Wright sat in Bernie Goldfine's office. 'They've been picking people up for almost two weeks,' Goldfine said, 'it'll soon be time for them to stop. And if they do, we might never catch them.' He was interrupted by the clatter of the fax machine. He swung round to pick up the sheet and passed it to Blake. 'We believe that the name of the hospital ship is *Oleander*,' he read out, 'owned by multi-millionaire SIMON CONNOR. Fawcett carried out a transplant operation on Connor's son some years ago. Connor complained to the GMC and was mainly responsible for Fawcett being struck off.'

'Now,' said Blake, 'we know it all. Except where the ship is.'

Goldfine had been on American television asking members of the public to notify the police of unusual helicopter flights or excessive motor launch activity.

'If the hospital is on a ship,' he said, 'they must be using a chopper or a small boat to take missing persons there.'

'If Muller's involved, it's bound to be a helicopter,' said Blake. 'What about the *Oleander*? Have you picked it up on a satellite yet?'

'There are so many flights and ships off the coast,' Goldfine replied, 'it could be anywhere.'

'The chopper's got a range of two hundred miles,' Blake pointed out, 'but I don't suppose the ship's still labelled *Oleander*.'

'How large is the *Oleander*?'

'A full-size luxury liner,' replied Blake.

'We'll have to check all ships of that size,' said Goldfine, 'until we find it.'

The door of the office burst open and an agent came in. 'You'd better have good news,' said Goldfine, 'coming into my office like that.'

'Bernie. We've tracked Al Ryan to a house on the coast close to Atlantic City.' Everyone stared at him as he said triumphantly, 'And there's a helicopter in a field outside.'

'Why haven't coastal radar picked it up?' snarled Goldfine, 'they've been asked to watch out.'

'I watched it come in,' he said, 'I only saw it at the last moment as it came round the side of a hill. It would have been hidden by the hill if it kept below five hundred feet; it's probably been wave hopping.'

'Right. Let's get the birds in the air,' said Goldfine, 'and find this ship.'

Once they knew the general direction, it was remarkably easy. A pilot radioed in: 'Located *Oleander* Medical Conference Centre. Please advise.'

'So bloody cocksure,' growled Goldfine, 'they didn't even change the name.'

He returned to the radio telephone. 'Give us its position and get out of the way. We don't want them moving off.' He picked up the telephone and whilst he was waiting to be connected, he said to Blake: 'This is a job for the Marines.'

After a long telephone conversation he replaced the receiver and turned to Blake. 'We move in at first light. A party of Marines will board the ship at 7 a.m. We'll land on the bow helicopter pads at the same time. Another chopper will land on the stern pad.'

Crayson felt strangely uneasy. Muller had just brought the last victim aboard. Everything had worked so well in England and France, and now they could deal with the last patients and call it a day. 'It's scarcely worth treating the patients,' he thought. The *Oleander* was due to explode and sink deep in the Atlantic Ocean. The evidence was to remain on the sea bed, lost for evermore. At least he hoped it would.

He had become friendly with an attractive nurse he had met at a party on board. She was about six inches taller than Crayson and he slept with her in his luxury cabin.

'You're getting emotional over her,' Fawcett jeered, 'what next?'

'No, no. You know me better than that,' Crayson protested, 'she's only a diversion.' But he wished he had met her ashore. 'I must be rational,' he thought, 'she'll have to go along with Fawcett and Muller.'

Fawcett had a passionate affair with a blonde physiotherapist called Mary. He had almost forgotten what sex was like. She was a gorgeous woman, about twenty years younger than Fawcett. He was the senior surgeon on the ship and she felt flattered.

'You're like a wild animal,' she said when they first made love. 'Anyone would think you haven't done it for years.'

He couldn't very well tell her that the last time he had attempted to have sex was when he tried to rape Carla Narcissi. And that had been years ago. There was no question of rape with Mary. She never said 'No', she was always available. The sea and the sun had given Fawcett a deep tan and his hair had recovered from the prison barber. In spite of the monstrous acts he was involved in, he found he could smile when he was with her.

'Does this mean anything?' Mary asked, when they were lying together, 'or is it just an on-board romance? I'm convenient for you.'

'You're very important to me,' replied Fawcett, 'you keep me sane. You calm me down.'

'Is that all I am, therapy?' she said, pulling away from him, 'sex instead of valium?'

'It's certainly better than pills,' he laughed, pulling her back towards him.

'What's this hospital ship going to do?' she asked, 'sail round the world for ever more. What's going to happen when we go ashore for good? Are we going to see each other again?'

He wanted to see her again but he knew it would be too risky. He could almost hear Crayson's voice in his head: 'Don't get emotional.' 'No,' he said to himself. I must disappear when I leave the *Oleander*.' But he began to question his actions as he always did. 'Perhaps I'd be safer with her. She might have picked up some information on the *Oleander*. She wouldn't talk if we stayed together.'

They spent their last night on the *Oleander* together. In the morning as Fawcett showered and got ready to go to the operating theatre for the last time, he kissed her. 'I can't wait to see you ashore.'

'Promise?' she said.

It was all hypothetical because Connor and Crayson had other plans.

At 6 a.m. the high speed launches were made ready. Goldfine, Blake and Wright were waiting to board their helicopter. Another chopper stood by literally stuffed with FBI agents to follow the lead plane.

'We don't know what we're going to find once we get aboard,' Goldfine said to his men. If they're doing what we think they are, they could throw anything at us.' He looked around, 'No random shooting. There are nurses and patients on board who probably think they're working on a normal hospital ship. I don't suppose they know what's going on.' He moved across to John Wright. 'This is Sir John Wright,' he said. 'He's a surgeon. Let him deal with the operating theatres. I don't want you killing patients with your horrible germs.'

He watched the launches going off. 'We'll give them thirty minutes,' he said. 'We want to get everyone there at the same time.' He looked at his watch impatiently as he waited, 'Right,' he said, 'let's go.' At precisely 7 a.m. they landed on the bow pad. A few minutes later the other chopper landed at the stern, and within minutes the Marine launches appeared. There was pandemonium on the ship as the Marines took up positions with their weapons cocked.

'What on earth do you think you're doing?' the matron bellowed as she advanced towards the senior Marine officer. 'This is a hospital ship treating very sick patients.'

'Sorry, ma'am,' he said politely, 'we've got orders to assist in the searching of this vessel. I must insist you give us every help.'

'Can't you see these patients recovering on deck? Can't you see all the medical personnel in their uniforms?' she said imperiously. 'We're a healing profession; we don't want soldiers clattering over our ship.'

Wright walked towards her with Blake and Goldfine at his side. 'Matron,' he said, 'my name's Wright; I'm a surgeon from England. This is Commander Blake from Scotland Yard. And the third gentleman is Captain Goldfine of the FBI, who is in charge of the operation. We'll be as careful as possible.'

'This is an outrage,' she said angrily, 'I shall personally stand guard over the operating theatres,' and then she stormed off to the stern of the ship. The FBI agents started questioning the auxiliary medical staff and the crew.

'Let's find these surgeons,' growled Goldfine, 'see what they've got to say for themselves.' He led the way along the deck to the stern, passing patients reading in comfortable chairs, looking more curious than alarmed.

'You can't come in here,' said Matron, standing guard at the door to the operating complex, 'this is a sterile area.' Goldfine thought, 'I bet you are as well, you old battleaxe.' He stood to one side. 'John,' he said, 'this is your territory.'

'Matron,' said Wright. 'We believe illegal transplants are taking place on this ship.'

'Absurd!' she said, 'ridiculous! I shall report you to the GMC when I return to England.'

'You do that, ma'am,' Goldfine said sarcastically.

'There are three operations going on in there,' she said, 'you can't go in until they're finished. It would put the patients at risk.'

Wright looked at Goldfine and shrugged his shoulders. 'We'll have to wait.'

Goldfine fumbled for his cigarettes.

'D'you have to?' Matron said, glowering at him as he lit up.

'I'm afraid I do,' Goldfine replied, blowing smoke into her face, and turning to his second-in-command. 'Jesse, what's happening at the other end?' he asked.

'We couldn't get in,' he said, 'it's like a battle ship. Thick steel doors. We'd need an oxyacetylene torch to cut through them.'

He looked at Matron. 'How do we get into the area at the stern of the ship?' he asked.

'We don't go there,' she said, 'it's where the brain-dead patients are landed.'

'That's not my question,' Goldfine growled, 'How do we get in?'

'Only the Senior Surgeon goes through there,' she said, 'the organs come through the service hatches when they are required; there's no need for us to go there.' Goldfine turned back to Jesse: 'You got the stern covered?'

'Yep. Our men and some marines. Nobody can get away from that end.'

Goldfine had just finished his third cigarette when a nurse came out of the theatre complex. He took a step towards the door.

'Stay there,' Matron ordered, holding her hand up, 'wait until I talk to the nurse.'

'All three ops are finished, Matron,' the nurse told her. 'The patients are in Recovery.'

'We're going in,' Goldfine said belligerently, pushing her aside. Blake and Wright followed with Matron running behind them. They walked along the corridor between the recovery rooms and the operating theatres until they came to the Surgeons' Room. The three surgeons, Klaus Bauer, Al Ryan and Fawcett had removed their outer garments and were drinking coffee.

'What the hell?' exclaimed Ryan. 'Who are you?'

'The FBI.'

Fawcett moved towards the door. 'Stay where you are, buddy,' said Goldfine, pointing his gun at him. 'You stay right there.' Ignoring him, Fawcett rushed into the theatres. The nurses were still cleaning up. 'Get out of the bloody way,' he shouted, colliding with one of them carrying a tray of instruments and sending it crashing to the floor. Goldfine followed him into the operating theatre. 'John,' he said, 'try and talk some sense into him.'

'Fawcett,' said Wright, 'you might as well co-operate. You can't get away. The ship's swarming with Marines and FBI agents.'

Fawcett grabbed a scalpel from a tray and moved towards Wright.

'You East End yob,' he snarled, 'I'll fix you if it's the last thing I do! Come on.' He beckoned with the scalpel as he moved closer. 'Come on, see how you like this.'

Wright moved back slowly until he was stopped by the operating table.

'You can't back off any more,' Fawcett yelled, flashing the scalpel from side to side.

'Get out of the way, John,' Goldfine shouted, 'let us handle him.'

Wright noticed a pair of heavy forceps lying on a trolley on his left. He suddenly picked them up. As Fawcett moved closer, he swung the forceps as hard as he could at Fawcett's face. He felt the crunch as they made contact and Fawcett screamed, putting his left hand to his face and seeing blood. 'That's the second time you've cut me, you bastard.'

Blake raised his eyebrows quizzically and thought: 'So they've crossed swords before.'

'Drop that, you stupid arsehole,' Goldfine shouted, taking advantage of the distraction and crashing his gun on to Fawcett's hand. As the scalpel dropped to the floor, two FBI agents grabbed him.

They took the computer card key from his pockets and went through into the organ-harvesting section at the stern of the ship.

'Christ!' exclaimed Wright when he saw the body on the operating table still connected to a ventilator. 'He's alive – just heavily sedated.'

'We've saved one then,' said Goldfine laconically.

'How long has this patient been here?' Wright asked the mortuary technician.

'He arrived just before your helicopter landed outside. I would have removed the organs but for that. I need them for the next patients.'

'How many of these have you done?'

'Must be hundreds – all brain-dead. I don't know where they come from.'

'This one's alive,' said Wright, 'and so were the others.'

The technician turned a deathly white and collapsed on the floor, his limbs jerking convulsively.

'Leave him,' said Wright, as one of Goldfine's men moved towards him, 'he'll come round eventually unless he's lucky. I should think he'd rather die!'

'You'd better come in here,' Goldfine said, leading him into Annette Marshall's cabin.

'She's still alive,' he said, removing the hypodermic embedded in her thigh. 'Drugged up to the eyeballs. She must have known they weren't brain-dead.'

'She'll probably fry as well,' said Goldfine.

They had no difficulty in getting Fawcett to talk. He wanted to tell them the whole story. It wasn't his fault. What else could he do? Any other surgeon would have done the same in his position.

'You can tell that to the Marines,' said Wright. 'You're the biggest shit that's ever disgraced medicine. I hope you burn slowly.'

'You've crossed swords before?' asked Blake.

'It started during our medical student days.'

'It's over now,' replied Blake, 'that's for sure. He won't be in a position to harm you again. Or anyone else for that matter.'

He sucked in the smoke from his cigarette, trying to fill every little crevice in his lungs. 'You know,' he said, 'I've never been much interested in what happened to the villains once I'd caught them; that was up to the courts. But with this lot, I'd be happy to pull the switch myself – on all of them. And that would be too quick an end for them.'

## Chapter Ten

Wright flew back to England with Blake. They parted in London, Blake to the Yard and Wright to Melanie.

They had a quiet dinner at his club in St James'.

'Darling,' she said, 'I've missed you so much.'

'How could I have lived with such a monster?' she went on, 'for all those years, as well.'

'He'll certainly go down in medical and criminal history,' said Wright, 'the medical historians and the psychiatrists will have a field day trying to analyse his mind, trying to explain it all away.'

'They'll probably blame me – say it was his unhappy marriage.'

'Darling, you mustn't think that,' he said, holding her hand on the table. 'He was just a freak. Nature throws up someone like him every now and again.'

'I wish he hadn't been thrown my way,' she said, wiping the tears from her eyes. 'All he wanted was fame and glory. He wanted to be the greatest Fawcett of them all. His parents and ancestors had all been general practitioners; he was the great surgeon, President of the Royal College. He hated to lose. That's why he hated you.'

'I'm glad he did,' he laughed, 'I wouldn't want to be liked by him.'

'Beast!' she said. 'It was your unfaithfulness which led me back to him. Once he had taken the first step, he didn't seem able to stop; he just spiralled downwards.'

'As far as I'm concerned, he's just an evil bastard, and the sooner he fries the better.'

'It could have been so different,' continued Melanie, 'if only he'd come to me with the Lloyds problem. I'm sure we could have sorted it out. My parents would have helped. They were clobbered by the same Lloyds syndicate but they still had money.' She paused whilst the wine waiter refilled their glasses. 'If he had stopped there, none of this would have happened. He was too proud to ask me,' she said. 'That's what families are for, aren't they?'

'Don't know,' he replied. 'I wouldn't have gone to mine.'

'Just think,' she said. 'If my father had baled him out, our lives would all have been so different. I'd still have been living with him, the GMC probably wouldn't have been involved, the Research Trust might have been set up with Connor's money.'

'And I would have had to go to the annual Fawcett lecture,' Wright added, 'to honour the great man.' He held her hand across the table. 'I could have put up with all that, except him still being married to you.'

'He still is,' she said, 'it's scarcely worth divorcing him now.'

'I think you should,' said Wright, 'I hate to think of you still being legally tied to him.'

'If you want me to,' she said quietly, 'I will,' and then tears welled up in her eyes again and started rolling down her cheeks. 'I'm sorry,' she said, sniffing and trying to force the tears back. 'I was just thinking how I would have coped if I had had any of his children. I would have spent the rest of my life examining them to see whether they had inherited his evil genes.'

'There certainly seemed to be an inevitability about his life,' Wright said thoughtfully, 'it wasn't just the Lloyds collapse. He could still have got back into surgery or some other career if he hadn't tried to rape Carla Narcissi and finished up in prison.'

'Let's talk about something else,' she said, 'I feel so ashamed to have been a part of him.' She put the powerfully scented Sauterne to her nose and then drank some and brightened up. 'You liked working with the police, didn't you?'

'Yes, I did. Perhaps I should have been a policeman,' he laughed. 'It would have been more in keeping with my background.'

'Nonsense,' she said, 'it was your destiny to be a surgeon; it was in your genes.'

'I don't know where they came from.'

'Permutations,' she laughed, 'just like winning the football pools.'

'How I hated it,' he said, 'when you married him.'

'So do I now. But you'd got me used to marriage; it suited my life-style to be married to another doctor. And, I suppose, it was partly on the rebound.'

They still kept very busy with their careers. Wright was teaching and operating all the time. They attended a lot of medical conferences, often at different venues.

'I've got to go to this Anaesthesia Conference in Manchester,' said Melanie on one occasion.

'Must you? Give it a miss. You know it all by now. Let's go down to the cottage for the weekend.'

'No, I've got to go. I said I would. I can't let them down.'

'I'll spend the time on my research,' he said.

'I've heard that before,' she laughed. 'I believed it then. Can I trust you?'

'I love you,' he said, kissing her tenderly.

'You couldn't say that to me,' she said gently, 'when you were young.'

'You've been a good teacher,' he said, 'you unlocked my emotions.'

'Are you sure it was me?' she said smiling, 'not Pauline?'

Melanie travelled by car and when the conference ended on Sunday evening, she stayed for dinner, intending to travel back the next day.

'I don't feel tired,' she said to a colleague at 11 o'clock, 'I think I'll drive back tonight and miss all the traffic.' She left a wet and misty Manchester at about half-past eleven and drove steadily along the motorway, which became more and more deserted as it got later. At about 1.30 a.m. she felt a severe pain in her chest. 'Sod,' she said to herself, 'cardiac. So this is what it feels like.' She drove on slowly looking for an emergency telephone, holding her chest with one hand.

'Christ,' she said, as the pain became more intense. She took the next filter and pulled off the road on to the grass verge. Fifteen minutes later she had a massive heart attack. An hour and a half later a police patrol car pulled up behind her on the deserted road. She was taken to hospital. John Wright had just got up when the front door bell rang. 'Who the hell's that?' he muttered. When he opened the door, there were two policemen standing there.

'Are you Sir John Wright?' asked one.

'Yes,' he said impatiently, 'what is it?'

'I'm afraid we have some bad news, sir.'

John Wright almost collapsed. He couldn't believe it. The thought of Melanie being dead! And dying all alone on the motorway! If only I'd gone with her! If only I'd been there I might have saved her! Why did this have to happen to her? Why couldn't it have been me? After Melanie's death he lived a lonely life, immersing himself in his work. His hair almost went white overnight and he looked ten years older.

Six months later he received a letter from Pauline in Africa.

'Dear John,

Are you still in this world?' she started. He remembered her last letter had arrived just after Melanie's death. She went on to say: 'I'm coming home soon on leave. Could we meet? I'd so like to meet Melanie. You've told me so much about her over the years.' He wiped the tears from his eyes and went to St Luke's.

'I'm terribly sorry,' she said, when they met in London, 'I know how much she meant to you.' She could see that he was blinking to hold back the tears. 'She must have been such a lovely person.' One or two tears escaped and rolled down his cheeks. 'She'll be in heaven now,' said Pauline, squeezing his hand gently.

They met on most days during her stay. 'This'll probably be my last trip to the UK,' she said, 'my parents have gone and Africa has become my home; I'm comfortable there.'

'I'd like to visit you,' he said, 'I've always wanted to see what kept you away from England.'

'I'd love that.'

A month later he was in Africa at the small general hospital with Pauline. He was accepted by the hospital community without question, and always greeted by happy smiling faces.

'Why don't you stay with us?' some of the nurses asked him. 'We need another doctor.'

He dined with Pauline every evening, and then they would sit on the verandah drinking whisky, sometimes holding hands like young lovers.

'D'you like it here?' asked Pauline.

'It's great. It's how I thought medicine was going to be when I first met you. Just treating patients,' he replied, 'not having to bother about whether they are NHS or private, no committees – it's a different world.'

'Why don't you stay then?' she asked, 'at least for a while?'

John Wright did stay in Africa and loved it.

'I've never seen such happy patients,' he said, 'they've such faith in the hospital.'

'That's psychosomatic medicine for you,' said Pauline laughing, 'I treat the body; the Church treats the spirit. Together we treat the whole patient.'

They had long discussions in the evenings about medicine, religion and the meaning of life.

'You've just lived for your Church and patients,' John said. 'I've been driven by a burning ambition to succeed.'

'You'd never have got into medicine without it,' answered Pauline, 'it was easier for me.'

They were quite affectionate towards each other, and it was not unusual for them to greet each other with a kiss in a roomful of nurses and patients.

'What d'you want out of our relationship?' John asked her gently one evening when she was in his arms and he was kissing her passionately. 'Nothing physical?'

'This seems pretty physical,' she said, squeezing closer to him.

'You know what I mean.'

'It's a bit late for that,' said Pauline kissing him, 'I guess I've missed out on it.'

She seemed to want the relationship to continue on the same platonic level as it was when they first met.

'I'll always love you,' she said, 'with or without sex.

'Is that possible between a man and a woman?'

'Of course it is.'

'Doesn't the sex make the relationship special – different from the love between two other people?'

'I'm sorry,' she said quietly, clinging to him and not knowing how to reply. They didn't talk about it again until Pauline arranged a private dinner party for the two of them to celebrate his first six months in Africa.

'Could you deal with this?' she asked, handing him a bottle of fine claret, 'I've been saving it for a special occasion.' He took the cork out carefully and decanted it. 'I haven't had so much to drink for a long time,' she said at the end of the evening, 'you're getting me drunk.'

'You've only had a dry sherry, a half bottle of wine, and two brandies,' he laughed. 'You used to be able to cope with that.' They both felt relaxed and mellow as they sat holding hands on the verandah.

'Didn't you ever want to take me to bed?' Pauline asked.

'Of course I did,' he said, taken by surprise at her question, 'I proposed to you; you turned me down.'

'If only I'd said "yes," she said, 'but, the future seemed so uncertain at the time. You were just starting medicine.' She drank her brandy rather quickly and felt it go to her head. 'I'd always hoped you would ask me when you qualified.'

'Would you have married me then?'

'Yes, I would,' she said, 'without any hesitation.'

'Are you sure? Wouldn't the pull of Africa have been too great?'

She was silent for a few moments. 'Africa has meant so much to me. But when I was younger . . .' she trailed off.

'When you were younger?' he said gently.

'If you knew how much I wanted you,' she said hesitating, 'to take me to bed. I didn't seem to know how to make it happen. It was the way I was brought up, I suppose. I was never supposed to think about sex before marriage.'

He took her in his arms. 'I used to dream of being in bed with you,' he said, kissing her, 'of holding you in my arms, making love to you.'

'I suppose all those girls at the hospital were different from me?'

'You told me to go off; and then you went to Africa.'

236

'I wasn't very clever with men, was I?' she said laughing, 'I should have committed you somehow.'

'Now you tell me,' he said, standing up and refilling the brandy glasses. She joined him, leaning on the verandah and looking out into the dark African night.

'Am I shocking you tonight?' she asked, 'It was a long time ago. We can't go back and start again.'

'I love you,' he said, pulling her close and kissing her passionately. As he gently caressed her breasts she pushed her body towards him so that she could feel him.

'Darling,' she said. They stayed together for some time and then she gently moved away. 'Stay there,' she said as he started to follow her, 'I'll get some coffee.' When she returned, they drank the coffee in silence for some minutes.

'I'm sorry, I shouldn't have said what I did,' she said, 'I don't know what came over me.'

'Too much brandy,' he laughed, 'or not enough.' Pauline stood up and walked towards him. 'I've got a long day tomorrow,' she said, kissing him lightly on the lips, 'I'd better go to bed.'

They went to their separate rooms. When she was alone, Pauline thought, 'Why can't I let myself go? Why do I always hold back? I could so easily have led him to my bedroom. Perhaps I'll go to him; that would surprise him.' She stood by her bedroom door for some minutes, trying to find the courage to open the door and go to John's room. She held the door knob and turned it, but didn't pull the door open. Then she slowly turned and went back to her bed. 'No, I'm too old. It would be a disaster; I couldn't cope, I would disappoint him.' And with a slight shrug, 'What you never have you never miss,' she tried to go to sleep.

John Wright did stay in Africa with Pauline Browne and their love affair continued, but that night on the verandah was the nearest they ever got to consummating it. Nevertheless they were very happy and devoted to each other and never returned to England.